Praise for the work of Stacy Lynn Miller

Out of the Flames

This is the debut novel of Stacy Lynn Miller and it's very, very good. The book is a roller coaster of emotion as you ride the highs and lows with Sloane as she navigates her way through her life which is riddled with guilt, self blame, and eventually love. It's easy to connect with all the main characters and sub-characters, most of them are all successful strong women so what's not to love? The story line is really solid.

-Lissa G., *NetGalley*

If you are looking for a book that is emotional, exciting, hopeful, and entertaining, you came to the right place. There are characters you will love, and characters you will love to hate. And the important thing is that Miller makes you care about them so, yes, you might need the tissues just like I did. I see a lot of potential in Miller and I can't wait to read book two.

-Lex Kent's 2020 Favorites List.
Lex Kent's Reviews, *goodreads*

If you are looking for an adventure novel with mystery, intrigue, romance, and a lot of angst, then look no further. ...I'm really impressed with how well this tale is written. The story itself is excellent, and the characters are well-developed and easy to connect with.

-Betty H., *NetGalley*

FROM THE ASHES

Other Bella Books by Stacy Lynn Miller

The Manhattan Sloane Thriller Series
Out of the Flames

About the Author

A late bloomer, Stacy Lynn Miller took up writing after retiring from the Air Force. Her twenty years of toting a gun and police badge, tinkering with computers, and sleuthing for clues as an investigator form the foundation of her Manhattan Sloane romantic thriller series. Visually impaired, she is a proud stroke survivor, mother of two, tech nerd, chocolate lover, and terrible golfer with a hole-in-one. When you can't find her writing, she'll be golfing or drinking wine (sometimes both) with friends and family in Northern California.

You can connect with Stacy on Instagram @stacylynnmiller, Twitter @stacylynnmiller, or Facebook @stacylynnmillerauthor. You can also visit her website at stacylynnmiller.com.

FROM THE ASHES

STACY LYNN MILLER

Bella Books, Inc.
P.O. Box 10543
Tallahassee, FL 32302

This is a work of fiction. Names, characters, businesses, places, events and incidents are either the products of the author's imagination or used in a fictitious manner. Any resemblance to actual persons, living or dead, or actual events is purely coincidental. The publisher does not have any control over and does not assume any responsibility for author or third-party websites or their content.

Printed in the United States of America on acid-free paper.

First Bella Books Edition 2020

Editor: Medora MacDougall
Cover Designer: Judith Fellows

ISBN: 978-1-64247-173-1

Acknowledgments

I pinch myself every day as a reminder that this thing of being a published author isn't some crazy story I dreamed up in my shower. Well, it's real, and I have many people to thank for the second leg of this incredible journey.

I'm so happy this story has found a home at Bella Books and can't thank Linda and Jessica Hill enough for their steadfast support.

Many thanks to Barbara Gould, my best friend and plotting partner in crime. Every word past "Prologue" exists because of her countless and often bizarre plot twist suggestions. Many of her strange kernels sprouted into the heart-pounding story you're about to read.

Thanks to fellow Bella Books author Louise McBain. *From the Ashes* is so much better because of her ability to sift through a rough-as-sandpaper first draft and smooth out the bumps. Plus, her pep talks are the best.

A special thanks to Medora MacDougall, my editor and huntress of the dangling modifier. Her ability to take my words and reorder them into a shiny object is simply magical. She brought out the best in me.

Finally, I owe an enduring thank you to my family. Without their unconditional love, *From the Ashes* would still be a fleeting thought.

Dedication

To JoAnne Waren.
My mom and shining example of kindness and compassion.
She taught me that love is unconditional and enduring.

PROLOGUE

Mazatlán, Mexico, 1987

At twelve years old, Vasco Sánchez had the survival skills of Rambo—his hero since he was eight. Orphaned two years earlier during a massive earthquake, he became a street urchin out of necessity. When the fat wallets of unsuspecting tourists couldn't fill his belly he relied on table scraps. He'd rummage through the garbage bins of resorts north of the city in an area known as La Zona Dorada. He became so adept that at any time of day he could tell you what leftover delicacy lined which trash bin.

Partial omelets and mango from Laguna Resort trash had tasted good this morning. Still, an angry stomach growl reminded him breakfast was hours ago. He searched the pockets of his frayed khaki shorts and found only two sticks of chewing gum and thirty-five American cents. That meant he'd have to get creative for lunch. He tapped his fingertip against his chin in the midday spring heat and then snapped his fingers as if he'd solved a puzzle. "It's Saturday." That meant two things: pepperoni pizza and a fresh crop of tourists at Las Flores Hotel.

Checking the diver's watch he'd palmed off a drunk American tourist last month during a scuffle at the open market, he realized he needed to hurry. The street children favored American pizza, and it disappeared fast.

Once he tightened his tattered backpack containing his "work" clothes over his shoulder, he dashed through service alleys like a gazelle to shave time off his route. When he turned the corner, he came to an abrupt stop, his shaggy black hair flying in his face. Someone had beaten him to lunch. A younger boy not more than ten had stooped over the plastic garbage bag and pawed at the contents Vasco had his sights on. Hungry and broke, he didn't have time to negotiate a share of the find. If he hurried, he could make enough money for a week of meals at his favorite taqueria.

Towering over the kneeling boy like a giant, Vasco recognized him. He'd dealt with this waif before. "Ese es mi almuerzo." *That is my lunch*.

When the boy turned his head, Vasco clenched his fists, his stare boring a hole through the boy's skull. The boy gulped. Then, in a blink of an eye, dirty napkins and empty potato chip bags blew up in a dust cloud when he ran down the alley and out of sight.

Vasco chuckled. The runt should've known better than stand toe-to-toe with the king of La Zona Dorada's orphans. Vasco had made only one mistake as he worked his way up the pecking order of the streets. He'd picked the pocket of a north-of-the-border drug mule for Los Ochos, a smaller gang and direct competitor of the Sinaloa Cartel. The gang leader usually meted out death as his brand of punishment, but children were off-limits. Vasco had ended up paying what he considered a small price—half of his left pinky. He took it without as much as a whimper, which earned him points from the leader of Los Ochos.

As on most days since his parents died in the earthquake, wasteful Americans provided lunch today. Sifting through the garbage bag, Vasco found four half-eaten pizza slices. Once he filled his belly, he rechecked his watch and determined he had only five minutes. He needed to make money off the dozens of new naïve hotel guests or *bobos* as he liked to call them.

He changed into the only items he kept clean, black pants and a white long-sleeved shirt that matched the primary uniform of the resorts. Using some rainwater he found in the alley, he slicked back his hair and made his way to the hotel entrance. There, the bobos waited for the three o'clock bus to take them on a guided tour of old town. He took a position behind an untended table filled with complimentary fruit and "safe" water suitable for the tourists' delicate digestive systems and handed them out.

A keen smile and cheerful manner earned him a pass from the staff even though they'd seen his game before. He'd discovered early on he could better attract unsuspecting prey if he looked and acted the part. His only tell was his white sneakers instead of the black dress shoes worn by the real employees.

"Thank you, young man," a plump bobo said when she handed him a dollar tip. "You're about my grandson's age."

"Gracias, Señora." Vasco's wide grin distracted her and other women when he helped them onto the tour bus and helped himself to the contents of their bags. When he offered his arm to the last woman, she clutched her bag extra tightly and the hand of the toddler following behind her.

"I have them." A gringo eased Vasco to the side. "Here, Cathryn, let me."

"Thank you, Daryl." Her smile beamed when he helped the young girl aboard.

"I got you, Manny," the overly protective father said.

Only one missed opportunity. Proud of his effort, Vasco waved at the bus as it rumbled down the road. "So gullible."

As Vasco counted his take after the bus pulled out of sight, laughter from a nearby restaurant patio table caught his attention. He'd seen this dark-skinned, mustached-man before, dressed to stand out in his three-piece white suit. When their gazes met, the man snapped his fingers, prompting an enormous bodyguard standing a few feet away to pop to attention. He whispered something into the guard's ear, and the guard motioned with his hands.

Vasco sensed someone closing in and the instinct to run kicked in strong. He tightened the grip on his cash, but before he could make a quick getaway, someone grabbed him by the collar.

"Alguien quiere hablar contigo, pequeño ladrón," an even bigger muscleman said, twisting the white fabric extra tight. *Someone wants to speak with you, little thief.*

Vasco struggled to break free. "I found it. I swear. I found it," he repeated several times while Goliath pulled him toward the dining patio.

The mustached-man inspected him from head to toe. "You speak perfect English, little man, yet you let your marks believe you don't."

Caught at his own game, Vasco froze. On instinct, he flexed his left hand before recoiling. Only two types of people would have used the word "mark," and he suspected which one he was facing. Vasco wished the mustached-man was a police officer and not a fellow criminal. He could better deal with the law's wrath than this man.

"It's all right, little man. You are quite the *caco*."

The corner of Vasco's mouth turned upward. The man had called him caco, a term used in Mexico's criminal community to describe a tricky thief—a pickpocket. He pounded his chest with a fist. "The best in all of La Zona Dorada."

The mustached-man pointed to Vasco's left hand. "Maybe not as good as you think."

Vasco whipped his hand behind his back to hide his constant reminder that he still had a lot to learn about being a thief.

"You're the one Los Ochos made an example of last year." The man received a tentative nod from the boy. "Word has it you took your punishment like a man. You have my respect, El Caco."

Vasco beamed with pride. The man didn't consider him any caco, but "the" caco, a title he'd worked hard at earning. He then studied the man's familiar face to confirm his earlier suspicion. "You are El Padrino, aren't you?" The man nodded. "Word has it you are a fair and forgiving man. You have my respect." Vasco bowed his head to emphasize his point.

El Padrino gave a hearty laugh. "You are a clever one. I'll give you that. But you know we've set the resorts off limits. We need the gringos to feel they are safe in Mexico. The safer they feel, the more they spend and the more often they will come back. Understand?"

"I only take what I need to stay warm at night, put clothes on my back, and food in my belly." Vasco's stomach knotted tight, hoping he'd given an acceptable reply. El Padrino, the legendary head of the Sinaloa Cartel, ran a tight ship. While he had a reputation for honoring loyalty and respect, he meted out swift and severe punishment when it was deserved. The last thing Vasco wanted was to be in this leader's crosshairs.

"I'm sure you do, Caco. How old are you, young man?"

"Twelve, but I'll be thirteen next month."

"You're not much older than my son"—El Padrino nodded—"but you seem much more mature, self-assured."

"You need to be on the streets of Mazatlán," Vasco replied, shrugging off the compliment. The first weeks following the earthquake seemed plush now compared to the months that had followed after the Red Cross pulled out of town and took their shelters and soup kitchens with them. To fill the void, he used old ponchos to protect himself from the rain at night and scoured trash cans for food when the stronger, older boys didn't beat him.

"Or the streets of Culiacán, where I toughened my skin." El Padrino considered the boy again. "How would you like a job, Caco?"

As a child of the streets, Vasco had resigned himself to a life of crime. The offer of a job intrigued him. "What kind of job? What would I have to do?"

"I need a runner and a lookout. Someone I can trust. You'd have to be here every afternoon, run errands for me, and warn my men when the police are around."

Vasco considered El Padrino's offer. He knew the streets like the back of his hand, could spot a police officer, even undercover, and could outrun anyone. "Hmm. What would I get?"

"A warm bed, clothes on your back, and all the food you can eat. And if you prove yourself worthy, money."

Vasco squinted to tally the benefits. The pros outweighed the cons. A year had passed since he'd slept off the ground. The last time was on a cot the church had put up in the chapel during a hurricane, and staying warm and dry appealed to him.

Following a long pause, he extended his hand. "Okay, I'll do it."

"There's only one catch."

"There's always a catch." He withdrew his hand, skepticism growing inside him.

"You must do well in school to keep your job."

Vasco dipped his head and frowned. Not since the earthquake had he seen the inside of a classroom. A mediocre student then, though he liked to read and write, he feared he'd be years behind other kids his own age now. "I don't have a school."

"I gathered as much. You can go to school with my son. He's a year younger, but if you can keep up with him, you can keep your job."

Food, clothes, a real bed, and money posed a fair tradeoff. Vasco extended his hand once more and shook El Padrino's. "You have a deal."

Those four words would forever change his life.

* * *

Mazatlán, Mexico, 1998

Dozens of guests had flowed into El Padrino's sprawling compound, congregating on the back patio to celebrate the college graduation of his younger son. Outdoor ceiling fans stirred the balmy ocean air to dry the beading sweat from their brows. The festive beat of mariachi music bounced through the air and past the open windows of El Padrino's personal study. There, the graduate waited for his father along with his sister and Caco, his adoptive brother.

With envy, he eyed Melina. She could dress any way she pleased and still be Daddy's little girl at seventeen. Cut too high above the knee and too low at the bustline, her little black floral number was inappropriate for the party but was probably the closest thing to traditional in her massive walk-in closet. While she could do no wrong and would get a pass on her outfit today, their father demanded much more of his sons. If either of them showed up for family dinner without a tie, he would refuse to say grace until they put one on.

With a critical eye, he scrutinized Caco, who was preparing drinks at the built-in bar nestled in one corner of the room. He wanted to throw those drinks in his face. The once dirty little urchin now loved fine suits and overpaying for haircuts that accentuated his chiseled features and made the women swoon. The fact Caco had four inches on him and twice the muscle mass made matters worse. The girls paid more attention to Caco, relegating him to sloppy seconds.

The only advantage he had over Caco was his stellar grades. An average student at best, Caco had never shed the brutish edge from his boyhood. Their father had rewarded that at every turn, teaching Caco the family business while he sent his other son to college.

Despite the fact that today's celebration was intended to mark his personal milestone, he predicted that Caco would share in the spotlight somehow. From the day that ruffian had come to live with them, whether his father knew it or not, they had been competing for his love and attention.

"Brandy, mano? Melina?" Caco poured himself a glass of their father's favorite imported brandy and then waited for a response.

He nodded, as did their sister. After accepting the drink, he seated himself beside her while Caco sat on the opposite couch.

"You should be proud, mano. Second in your class is quite the accomplishment." Caco raised his glass, which he met in kind despite his internal seething. If Melina had said those words, he would've considered them a compliment. But the brothers' competition had reached an epic level, and he'd come to expect digs of this sort.

"First would be more to Father's liking, but I'll have another chance to get it right in law school."

Caco nodded his head as if he and their father expected nothing less.

"I'm sure Rosa is looking forward to three more years with you in Mexico City." Melina patted her brother on his thigh. "You two have become serious, no?"

"She's more serious than I, and yes, she would like more time with me."

"Have you told Father about her yet?"

"Of course not." Like Caco, he never made a habit of sharing details of his love life or sexual conquests with their father. The siblings understood the dangers and allure of the family business, and they went to great lengths to keep their relationships casual. Most local women knew about El Padrino's sons. The good ones steered clear. The bad ones threw themselves at Caco, who used them for a night or two before tossing them aside like the trash he had rummaged through as a young boy.

Rosa provided a refreshing exception. Once out of their father's reach at the university, he had connected with a new group of women who didn't recognize him. Rosa, smart, beautiful, thoughtful, and kind, was the best of the lot. Even Caco, who met her in Mexico City one weekend, mentioned she would make the ideal wife—if not for her Yucatan roots. Padrino would never approve of anyone from that region.

"If we're still together after law school, that might be the time. Rosa thinks I'm the son of a rich businessman. I'd like to keep it that way for the time being."

"I get that, mano. Our line of work is never easy on relationships." Caco tipped his glass again, punctuating the gesture with a smug grin that grated on his nerves.

The siblings sipped on their brandy, falling into a comfortable silence as they waited for their father. Minutes later, El Padrino entered the room, dressed in his signature white suit and accompanied by his younger brother, a trusted deputy.

"Ah, mijos, I see you've already helped yourself to my Osocalis."

The two young men bounced to their feet while Melina remained seated, smoothing the hem of her dress. Caco walked toward the bar. "Would you care for a glass, too, Tio?"

"When have I ever turned down brandy?" The uncle laughed.

El Padrino sat in his favorite chair, a leather one that matched the couches, after accepting a glass of brandy from Caco. "You look beautiful, mija."

"Thank you, Father." Melina produced her most innocent smile, the one that her sibling found laughable. Though he would never utter the word, he considered her slutty. Her dress matched her lifestyle—sex on the menu for anyone desiring a sample. "I got it especially for today's party."

"Enjoy your youth while you can, mija, because I have plans for you when you turn eighteen next year." He patted her on the knee. "Now, you should return to your friends. I have business to discuss with your brothers."

"Of course, Father." She kissed him on the cheek.

He and Caco smirked at this equally laughable gesture of obedience. He hoped their father's plans included her losing her daring wardrobe and saddling her with a fat American husband and a brood of snotty kids to mother. She desperately needed to be taught a lesson.

Melina left, leaving talk of the family business to the men. His father turned soft eyes on him. He welcomed the rare, warm look.

"Mijo, you have done well. You are the first in our family to graduate university, and like your sister, I have great plans for you and your brother."

And there it is. Sharing the spotlight with Caco today made him wish he could join his flighty sister, drink endless amounts of his father's beer, and for once, forget he had a brother. But that was out of the question. When his father had plans, no one had a choice but to agree, a lesson learned through his mother, who had paid in bruises for questioning once how El Padrino ran his family.

"Thank you, Father."

"You were always one for the books, mano." Caco tipped his glass once more toward his brother. "Father was wise to set you on this path."

"Thank you." His smug grin was well earned—he had always outmatched Caco in that arena. He raised his glass and offered Caco a polite but insincere nod.

When his father turned to Caco, there was a glint in his eyes, something which never failed to irritate the younger son. "My plans include you as well." He nodded at both sons. "It will take a tremendous amount of sacrifice from you both. Are you two up to the task?"

"Of course, Father," Caco said with unmistakable eagerness, proof that his hunger for more responsibility and riches had yet to wane. The younger son wanted none of it, preferring a small law practice in Mexico City and a young wife waiting at home—Rosa, perhaps.

El Padrino turned his attention to the boys' uncle, who sat on a barstool, sipping his brandy. "Care to tell them what you told me last month?"

The uncle sipped again before rising from the stool. "Los Ochos has grown in both size and influence in the last six months and has aligned with Juarez. Word has it they're expanding their operations north of the border."

"They're taking quite the liberty, aligning themselves with your greatest rival," Caco said. "What do you plan to take from them in return?"

What a hypocrite. Caco has taken liberties all his life, he thought, first on the streets and then insinuating himself into this family.

"True, Father. After all, when Caco took liberties with Los Ochos years ago, they took his pinky. Surely they deserve punishment for that as well." He smiled inwardly as Caco reflexively rubbed the stub that was a reminder of his childhood misstep. His missile had hit its mark.

"I will not start a war over this." El Padrino tugged on his crisp white vest and straightened his shoulders, a signal his mind was made up. "But I will beat them at their own game. Los Ochos wants to smuggle product across the border. That is short-term thinking. I intend to set up operations for the long-term. We'll place a trusted man inside the American government, someone who can misdirect the authorities on the other side of the border toward our competitors."

El Padrino turned to his newly graduated son. "That is where you come in, mijo. You will be my trusted inside man. I have arranged for you a new identity and have secured your entry into Stanford. When you complete law school, you will work your way into the American government, where you will lead them away from us and toward our competitors. Once you're in place, Caco will head up northern operations in California. When the time is right I hope your sister will also play a role. Together, we will crush Los Ochos and Juarez."

Caco jumped to his feet and extended a hand. "I shall serve you well, Father. I won't let you down."

"I won't let you down either, Father." He rose and also shook his father's hand, hoping his voice didn't reveal the reluctance in his gut. Once again, his life and his future were in the grip of El Padrino.

CHAPTER ONE

San Francisco, California, present day

Whether she knew it or not, Manhattan Sloane had hooked Finn Harper like a fish and had her hoping for the day she would reel her in. Three days ago, when they were in that pool and surrounded by fire at Three Owls Vineyard, Finn had realized that Sloane, the first girl to make her steal glances, had been *the one* since they were thirteen. Looking back, she realized that she had always measured every love interest against her. Even Isabell, her first love, had met the teenage Sloane standard of looks, intelligence, and kindness. With Sloane back in her life, everything they shared—from mint water to taking in the view from the window of her chic Market Street condo—had a sweeter taste or more profound meaning.

But on this Sunday morning, Finn was alone, counting cars as they emerged from the fog atop the Bay Bridge on their way into the city. It wasn't the same without Sloane. After escaping the Santa Rosa wildfire, they each had set aside today for family— she with her father and Sloane with Reagan, her stepdaughter.

Three days had also passed since she and Sloane had shared their first kiss, and her lips still tingled at the echo of their last one in the smoke-filled garage. Finn chased that feeling, running two fingers across her bottom lip and wishing they were Sloane's lips. The memory of those few kisses would have to sustain her until Sloane continued to work through her grief over the death of her wife months earlier and wanted more.

When she focused on the image reflected in the glass of her dining room window, she realized she looked as tired as she felt. If not for her father picking her up for breakfast soon, she'd dump her coffee and go back to bed. But sleep hadn't come easily since her return. Sensitive facial burns kept her awake, but not as much as the nightmares. Each time she closed her eyes, images of Caco's charred body and the flames that had threatened her and Sloane from every direction replayed in her head.

Glancing at the clock, she calculated her father should be minutes away from her building. She ran her free hand through her shoulder-length dark blond hair to smooth several errant strands, inadvertently grazing the worst of her burns along her left cheek. It reminded her of her father's reaction years ago when she announced her plan to join the Drug Enforcement Agency following graduation from Stanford Law School. "Can't you find something less dangerous?"

"Maybe you were right, Daddy." Finn never thought she would entertain those words, but after her and Sloane's brush with death, she regretted quarrelling over something he may have been right about all along. Their arguing had led to a routine wherein their paths crossed but once a month for dinner. She missed him, especially the Sunday cookouts they had shared during her college days.

The buzz of the doorbell ripped her gaze from the foggy cityscape. Forcing a warm smile, she opened the door. "Daddy, come in. I'm almost ready. Give me five minutes, and then we can take off."

Dressed as if ready for a chilly round of golf at Pebble Beach, Chandler Harper smiled. Sporting a fresh business cut for his salt-and-pepper hair, he raised a large takeout bag from Finn's favorite neighborhood diner. "I thought you might be too tired to go out, pumpkin, so I picked up breakfast."

She inhaled deeply as the tempting scent of bacon seeped out of the bag and over the threshold, grateful for his soft spot. Despite their never-ending disagreement over her career choice, her father showed her love at every turn.

"You read my mind." Changing out of her lounge clothes in her current condition would have equated to scaling Mount Everest, a challenge she preferred not to accept. Her leggings and light, pullover sweater could now suffice for dining wear.

"I'll reheat while you get the drinks." Chandler scooted past her toward the kitchen, the musky scent of his aftershave tickling Finn's nose.

They worked and chatted about unimportant things until they sat at the dining table overlooking the Bay Bridge. She suspected he was holding back, just as she was. When he had answered Finn's phone call from the Santa Rosa hospital days ago, he'd told her, his heart had almost stopped. She had done her best to play down the harrowing time she spent huddled in the pool with Sloane as flames swept over them, joking, "We were perfectly safe, but I don't want to see the inside of an oven anytime soon." He hadn't let on in the following days, but she suspected his vying for more time with her this weekend meant the news reports that she and Sloane had barely escaped with their lives rattled him.

Finn pushed the food back and forth on the plate with her fork and stared at it as if trying to solve a kid's puzzle, a nervous habit she picked up from her father in her youth. Whenever he'd been worried about his fledgling law firm, he'd done the same thing at the dinner table.

"How are your burns coming along?" he asked finally. "The redness seems to be fading."

"Getting better."

She debated bringing up Sloane. Not since losing Isabell in a car accident years ago had they talked about her love life, never discussing Kadin Hall, her latest ex, for instance, unless they couched the topic in vague terms. A geometric pattern of fruit formed on her plate while the debate raged in her head.

"Something is bothering you. Is it the fire?" Chandler sprinkled enough concern into his question that Finn realized her suspicion was correct. He *was* rattled.

"No. Well, yes, but that's not what I was thinking about."

"Then what is it?"

A sheepish feeling that harked back to when she first embraced her sexuality during her high school years swept over her, but she finally raised her gaze to meet his. "You remember Sloane from the hospital? The one from the fire?"

He studied her expression. "You like her, don't you?"

"I do, Daddy. You probably don't remember, but Sloane and I went to junior high together. Her parents were killed in that car accident."

Chandler rubbed his clean-shaven chin. "Wasn't she in choir with you?"

Finn nodded. "We reconnected, and…she's *the one*, Daddy. I know it. She's *the one*." She expected a surprised look, but he grinned. Following a lengthy pause, she said, "Well, say something, will you?"

A twinkle appeared in Chandler's hazel eyes, eyes that looked so much like her own, signaling a level of delight that had been absent for years. "Refreshing." Her father had never used that adjective to describe her attractions. Considering how she felt about Sloane compared to her exes, though, she liked it. "From the way you two looked at each other, I gathered it was much more than a case of professional admiration."

"Were we that obvious?" She forked a piece of fruit and popped it in her mouth to combat the growing tightness in her lungs. *I feel like a teenager again.*

"Only to someone who knows you, pumpkin. We may only see one another once a month, but you never looked at Kadin the way you looked at Sloane. And she looked at you the same way." He paused when Finn's cheeks heated to what must have been the shade of the strawberries on her plate. "So, when can I officially meet her as your girlfriend?"

"Sloane's recently widowed, so we're taking it slow."

Her father's eyes grew distant as she pondered the term "girlfriend." Dare she consider that yet? She braced herself for having to wait a considerable amount of time before Sloane would entertain a relationship, but she hoped it wouldn't take too long. Finn had lost a woman she loved, but she'd never lost a wife. Her father had, though, to breast cancer—an ugly disease by any measure. He, of all people, would know what hurdles might be in store for Sloane. She met his gaze.

"Daddy, do you have any advice in that department?"

Chandler shook off whatever memory had distracted him. "Patience is the key, because it's all about the mindset. It may take time before she stops thinking of herself as married."

"I was there when her wife died in that explosion." Finn's voice cracked as horrible memories flooded back. "We pulled Sloane to safety, but…" She lowered her eyes in painful regret, unable to forget the images of Sloane's frantic efforts to save Avery, trapped beneath the rubble, nor the agony in Sloane's screams when the building exploded. "…we couldn't save Avery."

Her father's hand fell atop hers. The gentle squeeze that followed was a welcome gesture, the kind that meant he understood her pain.

"I can say from experience losing a spouse is one of life's most painful moments. You and Sloane will be connected forever."

"I hope in a good way." Finn squeezed his hand in kind.

Before he withdrew it, he gave her a gentle pat. His voice took on a wistful tone. "Now, if only I could convince you to find a safer career, I wouldn't worry about you day and night."

"I know, Daddy." Any other day, the comment would've been annoying, but today she agreed with him. The burns on her face would heal, but for now they served as a constant reminder that she'd come close to again losing a woman she loved. She never again wanted to feel the pain she'd felt when Isabell died.

He jerked his head back comically. "What? No argument?"

"Not this time. After last week, I'm thinking a change of pace might be good." Once she said it out loud, she oddly felt relieved, but that feeling was quickly tempered by questions.

Would Sloane like it if she quit her job? Would they have a future together if she wasn't in law enforcement?

Her father's charming smile returned. "I'm thrilled you're considering the idea. I don't want to seem pushy, but I'd love to have you in the firm. I could—"

Finn put up her hands in a stopping motion. "Let's not get ahead of ourselves, Daddy. I'm only considering leaving the DEA. I'm not sure if practicing law would be a good fit."

She braced herself for another sweet-talking session when, thankfully, her cell rang from across the room. "Saved by the bell." Glancing at the phone after retrieving it from the entry table, she didn't recognize the caller ID.

"Finn Harper."

"Agent Harper, this is Deputy Foster from the Sonoma County Sheriff's Department." The deep male voice had a distinct drawl, reminiscent of a young Sam Elliot. "You asked us to notify you if any unidentified survivors from the wildfire popped up."

"You have something?"

"Yes, ma'am. An out-of-town firefighting unit found him near the Three Owls Vineyard you mentioned in your report. No one has claimed him since, so the hospital called us."

Finn had expected the fourth person from that hellish night to show up dead, but this presented a much better scenario. A survivor meant she and Sloane had another lead to finally determine who supplied Los Dorados in their drug operation and who in the government was helping them.

"Where is he? Can you send me a picture?"

"Valley Hospital, but the vic has bad burns. A picture won't do you any good."

"Thank you, Deputy Foster. I'll get there as soon as I can."

She ended the call, a pit forming in her stomach as she hit speed dial. *This isn't over.* The call connected, and following the exchange of a few pleasantries, she said, "You're going to have to cancel. They found a survivor."

* * *

Sloane rested her elbows on the thin metal railing of the back deck at her Hunter's Point townhouse. She trained her gaze on a lone tanker in the distance as it cut through San Francisco Bay at a snail's pace. Before it disappeared behind an outcropping a mile down the shore, an airplane climbed off the Oakland tarmac across the bay and then vanished into stubborn low-hanging clouds.

It's going to be a cold morning for a hike, she thought as a brisk breeze ruffled her hair, brushing shoulder-length strands of brown hair against the collar of Avery's wool sweater. Absentmindedly she tucked the strands behind an ear.

The low sound of rustling leaves and chirping birds in the nearby trees merged into a soothing near-quiet. She'd come to this private oasis a hundred times over the years, seeking it whenever she felt troubled. Each time its quiet and calming effects had left her closer to a solution to her worries and ready to face the world. Today, though, she was still at a loss.

Clothes drying on the next-door neighbor's line caught her eye, bobbing up and down in the wind, shirtsleeves and pant legs waving frantically. As she unpacked what her sixteen-year-old stepdaughter had dumped on her over Sunday breakfast minutes earlier Sloane felt equally helpless. She had expected Reagan to be moody and emotional since losing her mother, just as she had been. She hadn't expected the calm and measured plea she'd just received. Reagan, however, was not only the mirror image of her mother with her dark blond hair and athletic body, she also had Avery's strength and the courage to speak her mind. To look her in the eye and say, "I can't bear losing you both. Every day I hold my breath until you walk through the door and I know you're safe."

Struggling with this revelation, Sloane squeezed her coffee mug tighter, trying to transfer its warmth into fingers numbed by the saltwater air. How should she respond to Reagan's concern? At thirty-four, she had never considered doing anything other than police work. How could she make Reagan understand that her job defined her? Should she even try? She was a single parent now, and that had to take precedence.

She needed to decide if she was a mother or a cop first. The answer to that should've come easy, but as hard as she tried, she couldn't see herself being happy as anything but a detective working the streets. Her grandmother had understood. She remembered Nana's words after she announced her acceptance to the police academy. "If you're happy, I am too." Pride had oozed from her the morning she first saw Sloane in uniform. She had fussed over her seven-point sterling silver badge and matching shiny buttons as if they were priceless jewels. Other than in the days following the car accident that had taken her son and daughter-in-law, that proud day marked the only time Sloane witnessed that strong woman shed tears. How could she give that up?

But what kind of mother would she be if she considered a career more important than her daughter's peace of mind? Reagan had put her grief and fears on hold following Avery's death in order to keep their fragile family from crumbling. She'd put Sloane first, and now Sloane had to reciprocate.

Deep down, though, she hoped to find a way to balance the two. While investigations required hours of research and paperwork, Sloane didn't consider working as a desk jockey to be real police work. She couldn't shake the idea that real crime happened on the streets, and real cops stayed there.

The creak of a wooden plank was followed by Reagan sidling up to the railing next to her. A quick glance confirmed she was mirroring Sloane's gaze as it trailed another tanker.

"I didn't mean to upset you, Mom, but Eric said I should talk to you."

Of course, she talked to him. Beyond being Sloane's partner and friend, Eric Decker had acted like an uncle to Reagan after Avery died, serving as her rock when Sloane couldn't.

"I understand you're scared, but I've never done anything else."

"Can't you do it sitting behind a desk like you did when you broke your ankle?"

"I spend half my day chained to that desk as is." Sloane faced Reagan, trying to gauge her response. In her eyes she saw genuine fear. In that instant, Sloane became first and foremost a mother, a shift she doubted would've happened if Avery were still alive.

From the first day she pinned on the badge, Sloane had accepted the idea one day she might make the ultimate sacrifice. Today, though, she worried what would happen to Reagan if she did. Which set of grandparents would take her? The Tenneys? She hoped. The Santoses? She feared. Her pride wasn't worth the risk.

With that realization came another jarring doubt. Feeling as she did, would she still put her life on the line for Eric? Sloane returned her gaze to the water that had centered her for two decades. She searched inside for that sense of unwavering commitment, but it never came. That shook her to her core.

She swallowed the growing lump in her throat and turned her gaze back to Reagan. "I've never done anything else," she repeated. "But I'm willing to discuss possibilities as a family."

"Thank you, Mom." Reagan's deep sigh suggested Sloane had just lifted the weight of the world from her. The crack in her voice, however, signaled they'd better work through those possibilities sooner than later. Sloane had to consider practical things like paying bills and funding college, but this wasn't the end of the conversation.

"We're family, Reagan. No matter what we decide, I want you to promise me you'll never stop talking to me, especially about things that upset you." Sloane lowered her eyes at a stinging memory. "I never got that chance after my mother died, but I want that for you."

"You never talk about your mother." Reagan cocked her head as if trying to recall the details. "It was a car accident, right?"

"A horrible accident." Sloane hesitated as the image of the fireball that marked her parents' death flashed once more through her mind. "But I survived."

"Were you hurt?"

"A few scrapes, but losing my parents hurt me in a way that took a long time to understand. I want you to know I get what you're going through. I was just thirteen when I moved here with my nana after the accident. She was old, and it scared me to think she'd die and leave me all alone."

Reagan's lips trembled when they parted. She dipped her head. "Then you understand why I can't lose you."

Sloane rubbed Reagan's arms, reassuring herself as much as her daughter. "I do understand. Let me think about this for a few days, and then we can talk some more." The thought of losing her again, especially her last link to Avery, terrified her. She never again wanted to feel the paralyzing fear she felt when she thought she might lose custody to her former in-laws. She needed to get her adoption of Reagan on the fast track.

"Okay." Reluctance laced Reagan's voice when she accepted Sloane's embrace.

The cold air nipped at Sloane's ears. It reminded her they needed to get ready for their newly dubbed Sunday "family day"—a leisurely breakfast before an activity of their alternating choosing. Reagan's choice of a water's edge walk underneath the first span of the Golden Gate Bridge seemed like the perfect start. "We should head out to Fort Point before it gets too crowded." She considered her garb. Avery's sweater was too precious to chance ruining, so she returned it to its home in the deck storage.

Once in her room, Sloane picked out heavy jeans to protect her legs from the cold ocean spray and then slipped on a T-shirt and a different sweater to layer under a Windbreaker. The paved trail at Fort Point wasn't steep, but thanks to her reinjuring it during their escape from the wildfire her left foot was still in a walking boot. She chose a sturdy hiking sneaker for the right one to compensate.

When she finished dressing, she sat at the end of the bed and replayed the conversation with Reagan. The idea of leaving the place where she met and fell in love with Avery seemed too much to fathom. Could she leave the department? Was she ready to cut those ties?

Before she could answer that question, a unique ringtone from her cell phone made her heart flutter. She hadn't seen Finn for three days, not since the fire, the guardianship hearing, and the celebratory dinner afterward. She missed her.

I think I'm letting go, Avery.

She swiped the phone's touchscreen. "Finn, I'm so glad you called. Would you like to join Reagan and me on a hike?"

"You're going to have to cancel. They found a survivor at the vineyard."

* * *

Santa Rosa's Valley Hospital was overflowing with wildfire victims, filling several wards and requiring all hands on deck. Doctors had sent the worst of the worst survivors, those whose wounds were beyond the expertise of the emergency room, to the surgical intensive care unit. Sloane and Finn headed there to find out more about the Three Owls burn victim. Interns, nurses, and attendants all buzzed around, tending to their new patients and trying to comfort the many loved ones vying for information on their prognosis.

The last time Sloane and Finn were in this hospital they were patients themselves, being treated for the burns and the smoke inhalation they suffered during their escape from the wildfire. That night had marked a turning point for Sloane. When she had confronted Caco, the man she held responsible for Avery's death, she'd been forced to choose between her thirst for vengeance and the oath she'd taken.

As a rookie, she'd been instructed by the law and procedures manual about what was right and what was wrong. But years as a street cop and as a detective with Eric as her guide had taught her that strict adherence to the rules seldom yielded justice. When she was faced with the possibility of becoming as evil as the man she'd been chasing, Eric's words on her first day as a detective had taken on new meaning. *"You know the difference between the law and justice, and that the two don't always mean the same thing."* In the end she'd decided that without the law there was no justice. Her instincts told her it was her new understanding of justice that brought them to the hospital today.

While they waited until a doctor was available to talk to them, Sloane used the time to observe visitors in the crowded, tiled corridors, looking for anything suspicious or out of place. The only thing that stood out, though, was the antiseptic smell, a reminder of why she hated hospitals—germs.

Within an hour, a young redhead with eye-catching high cheekbones and a trim body clad in blue scrubs approached, rubbing the back of her neck. Following customary greetings and the explanation she was winding down from a grueling double shift, Doctor Sarah Freeman said, "I understand you're interested in our John Doe."

"We are. What can you tell us?" Sloane asked.

"He has burns over eighty percent of his body, and I'm afraid his facial burns make it impossible to identify him. No one has claimed him yet, so we think he might be a migrant worker who couldn't make it out of the vineyards."

"Is he awake?" Finn asked.

"We placed him in an induced coma." Doctor Freeman shook her head without a hint of emotion on her face, a sign of a well-trained doctor. "He's touch and go. Most patients with burns this extensive rarely recover."

After thanking her, Sloane and Finn entered John Doe's room. They studied him from the foot of his bed, the numbers and lines on the nearby beeping machines telling the story that he barely clung to life. He appeared to be tall with a medium, muscular build, but nothing too distinguishing. The small patches of his skin left untouched by the flames seemed to be light brown, which meant he could be of Hispanic origin. He could be a man from Three Owls or, as the doctor suggested, he might be a migrant worker who couldn't escape the fire.

Sloane cocked her head, trying to recall the faces of Caco and his men. "What do you think?"

"Couldn't be the guy we dragged to the bushes," Finn said. "He was bigger. Could be the one we tossed in the SUV."

Finn stepped along the left side of the bed, where multiple bags of fluids on an IV stand connected to a line that ended on the man's left hand. She stared at it for several beats before her mouth dropped open to emit a short gasp.

"What is it?" Sloane asked.

"Half his pinky is missing. This has to be Caco."

"Are you sure?" Sloane stepped closer to examine the man's hand.

"I noticed it the night of the fire." Finn nodded with a certainty that sent a coldness coursing through Sloane.

"Why couldn't you stay dead, you son of a bitch?" Sloane's chest tightened. Somehow, this bastard had crawled from the ashes, escaping the fate he deserved.

She focused on the oxygen tube inserted in his mouth, the only thing keeping him alive. The coldness in her spread as she eyed the man responsible for killing her wife. How long would she have to crimp that thin plastic hose before the lack of oxygen choked the life out of him?

"Whatever you're thinking, it's not worth it." Finn placed a hand on Sloane's shoulder as she eyed Caco's charred body. Its warmth barely registered.

"He needs to die." Sloane grabbed Finn's warm hand and squeezed it, hoping to thaw the iciness that was threatening to overwhelm her. The grief caused by this wretched man had all but consumed her at one point, and now, just when she thought she'd finally fought her way through it, he was choking her with it again.

"He deserves to die, but if he doesn't, he'll be in agony the rest of his life." Finn returned the squeeze, sending more warmth and strength her way. "What do you want to do about him?"

Resisting the urge to end him didn't come easy, but… "I'm not ready to turn him over to the Feds."

"Neither am I."

"Maybe we can use him to flush out the leak. We know it's likely Quintrell or your boss's secretary."

Finn offered an affirmative nod. "We're down to an Assistant United States Attorney or a mother of four."

"Odds are, the leak may know Caco and," Sloane raised her left hand and wiggled her pinky, "know about little piggy." She sorted through the factors. If he died, they would lose any chance of using him. If he survived, which she hoped he wouldn't, they would have to officially notify the DEA since he was their suspect. She focused on what kind of trap could flush out the rat.

"I'm betting he'll die, so we have to act fast."

"We'll get only one chance to do the right thing," Finn said.

What was the right thing? Sloane studied Finn's face for guidance. Noticing the mild burns on her cheeks had almost healed, she traced one with an index finger. If not for her ill-advised quest for revenge, those burns wouldn't exist, and that bothered her. As soft as her touch, she said, "I'm sorry you got hurt."

Finn's eyes told her she'd already been forgiven. "I'm fine."

Sloane dropped her hand. "I have a plan in mind."

"Whatever it is, we're in this together."

"I wouldn't have it any other way. The tricky part will be getting both suspects in the same room at the same time." Sloane used her phone to snap several pictures of Caco, including a close-up of his left hand.

CHAPTER TWO

Bay area traffic was a unique animal. No matter the day of the week, it snarled all day, switching to a light growl after midnight but roaring again by four. Today, a jackknifed big rig near the Golden Gate Bridge toll plaza had brought traffic heading into the city to a standstill. Going around the mess posed the only option for Sloane and Finn to get home at a decent hour.

The detour routed them through the East Bay and their hometown of El Sobrante. Sloane didn't consciously avoid it, but it had been years since she came this way outside of a case. Whenever she drove past, it brought up painful memories that she preferred remain buried deep in the past. Today, though, as they neared the freeway exit that she'd taken countless times in the backseat of the family car, the past pulled at her like a magnet.

"Would you mind taking another detour?"

"I was thinking the same thing." Finn glanced at her with a smile that conjured up memories of childhood innocence. "To the junior high school?"

Sloane offered a slow, tentative nod.

When Finn took the off-ramp and made the turn toward the school, Sloane's breathing grew labored. The closer they got, the harder her heart thudded. She reached for Finn's hand. "I haven't been back here since that night."

"We don't have to do this." Finn's soft squeeze matched the tenderness in her voice. She appeared ready to merge into a different lane in the event Sloane changed her mind.

"It's time." She was unsure if she would have been up to doing this with Avery, but with Finn… Finn connected her to the past. That last day at school had been both exhilarating and horrifying. When Finn had thrown on her leather jacket and tossed her a smile meant only for her, Sloane's heart had pounded so hard she thought it would burst. Then Finn had grabbed her hand and she tasted the chicken nuggets and fries bubbling up in her throat. She didn't have a label for it back then, but that was the moment she realized she was gay. Different from the other girls. But that didn't matter as much as the way she felt. She had a dizzying, can't-wait-to-see her crush. That high, though, was short-lived. Within the next hour, she became an orphan.

Several turns later, Finn pulled into the teachers' parking lot, empty on a Sunday, that guarded the front of Juan Crespi Junior High School. Stepping out of the car into the warm early fall air, they shed their jackets.

"It seemed a lot bigger back then." Finn surveyed the vacant campus from one end to the other.

"I think everything seemed big when we were kids." Missing were the teenagers who had swarmed the passageways between the rectangular, single-story buildings and the deafening hum generated by their chatter when they lined up outside the snack bar window for lunch. Now only the clanking of tetherball chains bouncing off the playground poles in the breeze broke the silence. Each building had a fresh coat of paint, and the grounds had new landscaping. However, the campus still had the strong, familiar smell of eucalyptus from the trees outlining the PE fields.

They meandered through the grounds, peering through dirt-streaked windows to glimpse at their past. "Wasn't this Mrs. Teel's room?" Finn asked when she peeked into a particular classroom. "I had her for third-period seventh-grade history."

"I had her for fifth."

A smile grew on Finn's face. "Now that I think of it, she was my first crush."

"I thought I was your first." Sloane pouted. Though, looking back, she had to admit having a particular attraction to Miss Sanders, their blond P.E. teacher.

"She was definitely my type—tall, athletic, brunette." Finn winked. "And the way you turned out, my instincts were right about you. That's why I crushed on you the first day in choir."

What I wouldn't have given back then to know I was your crush. Sloane turned her face down to hide an insistent grin after Finn inspected her from toe to head, the same way Avery had when they first met for "just drinks." Months after that first date, Avery had admitted Sloane had her hooked that day. *Have I hooked you, Finn?*

"Come with me." Finn grabbed Sloane's hand and led her to another part of the school. Stopping at the bottom of the stairs leading to the auditorium door where they attended choir practice, she adjusted her feet to a precise spot and straightened her back. "This is where I saw you for the first time." She looked up the stairs. "I remember how anxious I was when I grabbed your hand that last day, but I had the feeling you liked it. Then you looked me in the eye, and butterflies fluttered in my stomach."

"I did and had the same butterflies." Sloane had chased that incredible feeling for years, re-creating it only twice—when meeting Avery and reconnecting with Finn.

"I couldn't wait to see you the next day, but I never got the chance." Finn's gaze lowered, and her voice turned softer. "Days later, I learned what happened."

In her nightmares, Sloane regularly relived what happened after they said goodbye. Haunted for years by the images, sounds, and smells of that night, she had never wanted to return to the place where her parents took their last breaths, but a tingle of courage now shot up her spine.

"Take me there."

"Are you sure?"

"With you, yes." She squeezed Finn's hand, ready to face her painful past.

Minutes later, they were back in Finn's car, approaching the curve in the road where Sloane's father had lost control.

"Pull over here." Sloane pointed to the soft gravel shoulder at the apex of a curve.

Finn parked and checked her rearview mirror for approaching traffic. Exiting the car, she crossed to the passenger side, stepping over the crumbling edges of the asphalt.

Sloane remained in the car, her gaze fixed at the side of the road several yards ahead, beyond the section of shrubs where Bernie had found her that night. Her body numbed. Nothing had prepared her for this moment. No one had told her what to expect, but if she were ever to heal, she felt she had to face all of it.

Like a teakettle screaming it had come to a boil, courage came to her. Opening the car door, she stepped onto the uneven pavement. The area appeared different in the daylight. She could see now the tight curves that made the road treacherous and how steeply the embankment fell off at the shoulder.

She focused on the shrubs and tree branches at the curve as they swayed in the breeze and blocked the view of oncoming traffic. Cocking her head, she imagined them as they would have appeared twenty-one years ago. Despite periodic maintenance, they were not much different, she surmised. *No wonder we didn't see the other car until it was too late.*

Finn followed close behind when she got out of the car and stepped toward the shrubs.

"This is where Bernie found me. The fog made the ground damp that night. When I clawed my way up that embankment I got so much mud under my nails that I thought I'd never get them clean again." The memory prompted her to curl her fingers and inspect them. She realized now why she couldn't stand it when her nails were dirty and why she always kept them ultra-short.

Lowering her hands, she raised her chin to scan the area. Images of that night rolled in her head like a movie in slow motion. There were sights and sounds, but no smells. Without them, the sense of horror was dulled.

"I don't think I was there long before he came along, because it still felt hot like an oven. He carried me to his police car and placed me in the backseat." She took a few confident steps toward the end of the curve.

"This is where Dad swerved off the road to avoid the other car. I think we flipped once or twice because I remember things being upside down." An image of her mother's long brown locks and necklace mixing with chunks of glass and other things in a midair dance made her shudder. "Yes, we flipped over."

A few steps further on, she peered down the embankment where the shoulder dropped off into a trench. Shrubs and weeds had overtaken the area, but she could make out the approximate spot where their car had ended up.

"This is where we went off the road and landed nose-first. The jolt hurt when the seat belt grabbed." Sloane clutched the front of her shirt as an echo of the sharp pain she'd felt in her chest that night threatened to bend her in half now. "I had bruises for weeks."

"It saved your life." Finn moved to her side and interlaced their fingers. Her soft, steady voice gave Sloane strength to go on.

"The wreckage had pinned my parents' legs." Sloane heard her voice take on a more monotone cadence as she tamped down the emotion threatening to burst the dam. She swallowed hard to shore up her resolve. "I couldn't free them. Then the engine caught fire. I pushed and pulled on everything, but nothing worked. When the flames got bigger, they begged me to save myself." She finally looked Finn in the eyes. Moisture had pooled in their lower rims, as it was doing in hers. "Just like Avery did."

Finn gasped and squeezed Sloane's hand tight.

"I kissed them both, said goodbye, and crawled out." Turning and pulling Finn with her, she retraced her steps toward their car. "I was clawing my way up that muddy embankment when I heard the most horrible screams. They sounded like Caco's the night of the wildfire. I turned around and saw my mother engulfed in flames."

With her free hand Finn covered another gasp.

"Then the car exploded."

Sloane sagged slightly. Having finally brought to the surface the full depth of her horror, she no longer had to carry the burden from that night alone. She had Finn to share the load.

Finn pulled Sloane in close and wrapped her arms around her.

"I'm so sorry." Finn squeezed harder. "I love you," she whispered.

Sloane froze. She'd feared she'd never hear those three words from a woman again, but now that she had…

"I…" Sloane pulled at the fabric on the back of Finn's shirt, trembling, unable to return the words though she knew they were true. How could she love someone so soon? The idea scared her, and then her quaking turned into uncontrollable sobs. "I couldn't save any of them," she repeated over and over, every ounce of energy draining from her body.

Finn tightened her embrace until she quieted. By the time she did, Sloane was sure visiting this site wasn't a mistake, nor was loving Finn.

"Let's get you home," Finn said softly.

Back in the car, Finn grabbed the shifter to put the car in drive, but Sloane placed a hand atop hers. "Not yet."

Not since Avery died had Sloane felt this emotionally raw, but Finn had made it bearable. The woman she'd always loved, loved her too. Yet returning her admission now was impossible. The ring on her left hand made it so. Whether she would ever be ready to tell her she didn't know. In the meantime, though, Finn's words deserved a response.

She caressed the back of Finn's hand, a measured, exploratory touch. A lazy trace trailed the tender skin of Finn's slender, yet sturdy hand and outlined each bone and tendon. She'd never admit it, but before the wildfire at Three Owls, she'd fantasized about those fingers and what they'd feel like against her skin in places where she shouldn't have considered while grieving her wife. She watched goose bumps form on Finn's arm in her fingers' wake. If not for the damnable circumstances they were in, that was the result she would've craved.

Finn's breathing deepened, and Sloane raised her head. A searing desire met her gaze—a feeling she couldn't reciprocate. At least not yet.

"Don't stop," Finn whispered.

"I wish…" Sloane searched for the right thing to say or do. She wanted this as much as Finn but didn't yet have the strength to let go of Avery.

Sloane returned her gaze to the hand on the shifter. That hand had pulled her to safety at the drug lab explosion where Avery died and later at Three Owls, where she almost drowned, demonstrating tremendous strength. And when her heart broke after Avery's death and here at the site of her parents' accident, it had tendered overwhelming comfort.

Sloane brushed the length of Finn's forearm before settling at her hand again, cupping and squeezing it. Finn's hand searched out its mate, interlacing its fingers with hers, and they clung to each other, palm to palm. Sloane released her grip and started a slow, deliberate exploration of Finn's palm, tracing each crease with the curiosity of a palm reader. One by one, she outlined each finger, eliciting a reaction that she would have welcomed under any other circumstances. Judging from Finn's irregular body shifts, Finn needed to be touched, but that was an intimacy she couldn't bring herself to embrace. The most she could do was to entangle their hands in a slow, erotic dance.

Torn between desire and grief, Sloane was stopped by a sudden realization. She had been chasing the memory of Finn all along, even when she fell in love with Avery. Tears filled her eyes. "I loved her."

"I know you did." Finn lowered her head. Her voice cracked, not much above a whisper.

Sloane lifted Finn's chin and turned her face toward hers. "But she wasn't you."

She kissed Finn on the lips with a hunger that was met in kind, the contact igniting a depth of desire she previously had thought unobtainable. Parting her lips, she sent her tongue searching, and when it reached its counterpart, the smoldering caught fire. She wrapped a hand around Finn's head, pulling her in hard, the sudden pressure eliciting moans from them both. Their tongues went deeper, as did Sloane's craving.

An image of Finn easing her naked legs apart, allowing Sloane to slide between them, sent her pulse into overdrive. The fantasy built, and the thought of inhaling her musky scent for the first time woke Sloane's core with a shout. She shuddered at the notion of feeding on Finn's center and groaned at the prospect of Finn doing the same to her. Her racing heart reached a crescendo, making her feel more alive than she had in months.

In a tentative first brushing, her hand drifted to Finn's breast. The fabric of her shirt and bra did nothing to mask the hardness of the nipple encased beneath. The touch had its intended effect, exciting her as much as it did Finn. A pulse traveled through her core, the first she'd experienced since the morning Avery died.

This is wrong. Sloane ripped her lips away as if something had stung her.

"Are you okay?" Finn asked in a soft, curious tone.

"I'm sorry, I shouldn't have…" The conflict brewing inside her became clear when her voice trailed off.

"Shhhh." Finn rested an index finger on Sloane's lips. "I'll wait as long as it takes."

She took a deep breath and then, after putting the car in drive, resumed their route—with Sloane's hand atop hers the rest of the way home.

CHAPTER THREE

Sloane's kitchen was filled with the sounds of running water and clanking dinner dishes. Missing was the chatter between Sloane and Reagan about school or her boyfriend, Emeryn, that accompanied their cleanup routine the last few nights. The events of the day—discovering that Caco had survived, facing her past at the accident site, and sharing a prelude to intimacy with Finn when she wasn't ready for it—had Sloane distracted. While she loaded the dishwasher, Reagan dished up their favorite comfort food. Finished, Sloane turned around, wiping her hands on the dishtowel.

"Ice cream?" Reagan had a bowl in each hand and extended one toward Sloane with the same smile Avery used to give her when they strayed from their healthy diets.

"Ooh, Oreo Cookie. My favorite." Sloane's mouth watered. She always had room for the sugary treat, especially when she was troubled.

Reagan led the way to the couch. When she sat, she tucked a foot under her bottom, another habit she shared with her mother. Sloane did the same at the other end and went to work on her sweet and crunchy dessert. This proved a much better distraction. Instead of debating what to do about Caco, she swirled a bite around her tongue and concentrated on the melting coldness. Instead of torturing herself with images of Finn's lips against hers, she bit into the cookie chunks and focused on the chocolate as it tickled her taste buds. She came shy of releasing a satisfied moan.

"Mom, can I ask you something?" Reagan asked.

"Sure, hit me." Sloane pulled her focus from the spoon, bowl, and its contents.

"You told me this morning to never stop talking to you, especially about things that upset me."

"And I meant it."

"I think that should work both ways." Reagan's tone sounded more serious than a sixteen-year-old's should.

Sloane raised a curious eyebrow. "Where's this coming from?"

"I can tell something is bothering you. I want you to feel you can talk to me too."

Wow! You'd be proud, Avery. Sloane wished Avery were here to see how much Reagan had grown up in the last few months. She debated how much to tell her about Finn. But they had promised to be honest with each other. *Maybe just the basics.*

"Something did happen on the way back from Santa Rosa today."

"I thought something was up."

"I said I was late tonight because we had to detour around bad traffic. That part was true, but we also made another stop." Sloane shifted uneasily on the couch. "Do you remember me telling you that Finn and I went to junior high school together?"

"Sure, you knew her before you moved to San Francisco." Reagan nodded.

"What I didn't tell you was that she was my first crush, and I was hers, so we stopped at our old school. Kind of a stroll down memory lane."

"That's sweet."

"We looked around and went to the spot where we first met." Sloane placed her bowl down. Ice cream couldn't cool the sting of what she had to say next. "That was also the place where I last saw her. She was the last person I saw before the accident."

"No wonder you two are close."

"She took me to the accident site today."

Reagan's brow knitted tightly, her curiosity morphing into concern. "How did that go?"

"It was rough. I hadn't been back there since that night and never wanted to until today. Somehow with Finn, I knew it was time."

"Are you glad you went?"

"I am. I'd never shared details of the accident with anyone, and once I did, it was like a dark cloud had lifted."

"You never told Mom?" The uptick in Reagan's tone hinted at disappointment, which Sloane understood. She was struggling with it too.

"No, honey. I wasn't ready. I don't know how to explain it other than Finn was part of it, so it felt natural to share it with her."

Reagan's lips quivered. "She was there when Mom was killed, right?"

"Yes, she was." Sloane's lips trembled too. "If not for her, I would've died too."

Reagan cleared her throat and patted Sloane on the hand with what seemed like forced sincerity. "Then I'm glad you two are friends."

They *were* friends, but after today, Sloane considered Finn as much more. Though uncertain whether Reagan would accept that, she decided she deserved the truth, not just the basics. "What if we became more than friends?"

Reagan slid her hand away. She said nothing, yet the distance in her eyes sent a loud and clear message. Just like her mother's had. Reagan's silence meant Sloane had upset her.

"You know I loved your mother very much, and I always will. It's just—" She paused when tears welled up in Reagan's eyes. *This is too much for her*. "Honey, I don't mean to upset you, but good or bad, I promised to be honest with you."

"It's just"—Reagan's voice thickened again—"I didn't expect you to move on so soon."

"But I haven't. Sometimes I feel like I never will. Other times, I think it's possible. I loved your mother so much. After my parents died, I walled myself off and avoided commitment, but your mother changed all of that. She made me happy when I had all but given up on the idea. For the first time, she made me want to build a life with someone. With her, I learned how to love." The tears rolling down Reagan's cheeks released those in Sloane's eyes. "If I ever move on with someone else, it will be because of your mother. She taught me I wasn't meant to be alone. That I'm supposed to share my life with someone I love."

"And you think that might be Finn."

Sloane let out a long, halting breath. Deep down, she already knew the answer. But moving on was a long way off. "I don't know where things are going with Finn, but I feel a connection with her. Before I open myself to possibilities, I need to know you're okay with it."

"To be honest, I don't know what to think."

"All I want from you is honesty and to get to know her."

"I don't know."

Reagan's skeptical, hurt look made Sloane imagine the conversation Avery must have had with her two years earlier when they first dated. "*I know this is different, but she makes me happy. If you get to know her, I know you'll like her,*" Avery likely said. However it went, it worked—eventually. Sloane hoped she had handled today with Avery's finesse.

"All I can ask is for you to think about it. In the meantime, how about we get the ball rolling on the adoption?"

"The sooner, the better."

"I'll call Kadin Hall tomorrow." However things progressed with Finn, Sloane was sure she and Reagan were on the right track. She picked up her dish. Planning how to smoke out the government leak who helped Caco would have to wait until morning. No sense in wasting a bowl of the good stuff.

* * *

Months had passed since Finn last visited her father's house. Other than him, nothing about the place stirred up feelings of home. The streets of suburban, middle-class El Sobrante, where she had done most of her growing up, were lined with trees and grass. Here, in the sprawling upscale Atherton neighborhood, the scattered houses hid behind stone or metal tall walls and gated entrances. Within a week of moving in when she was a high school sophomore, she rode her ten-speed bicycle from one end of the community to the other. Not once did she come across another kid, except those riding in the backseat of a Mercedes. Piano and ballet lessons were the afterschool activities of choice, not bike riding. Within a month, she longed for her old neighborhood and playing evening kickball games in the street while dodging old station wagons.

Despite having lived in Atherton for three years until she left for college, letting herself into the house now for an impromptu visit had her feeling like an interloper. Taking a deep breath, she opened the French doors leading to the covered back patio. Seated in a wicker lounger, Chandler turned his gaze toward the motion. His voice was laced with pleasant surprise as he leaped to his feet. "Pumpkin? Twice in one day?"

"Sorry to stop by unannounced."

"No need to apologize." He gave her a hearty hug, one that made Finn feel guilty for not stopping by more often. "I'm always happy to see you. Can I get you something to drink?"

"Just water, please."

"Coming right up." Chandler retrieved a pitcher of mint water from the built-in stainless steel mini-refrigerator on the left end of the outdoor patio kitchen.

"I see Carmen is on her game."

"What can I say? The first maid spoiled me. Carmen's keeping up the tradition." He handed her the glass. "Not that I'm complaining, but what brings you out here?"

"I want to talk to you about Sloane." She slumped, confusion beating her up.

"Sure, pumpkin." He suggested they sit on the wicker chairs overlooking the pool. "Has something changed?"

"No. Well, yes." She shifted in her chair, eyeing sparkling clear water that reflected a darkening blue sky. The prospect of a frank discussion about relationships with her father always made her uncomfortable, and this one did doubly—because she wanted to be reeled in. "Something happened today that has me wondering if we're moving too fast."

"Did you sleep with her?"

"Daddy!" It didn't help that their blood-pumping make-out session had her thinking of nothing but having sex with Sloane. "I didn't sleep with her."

"Then what is it?"

"Today we went to the site where her parents were killed, and she recounted the horrible details."

"That must've been very emotional."

"It was for both of us. Did you know they survived at first, and she tried to free them? Then the car caught on fire." Finn couldn't hold back the single tear that fell from each eye. "They told her to save herself." She rubbed her forehead to erase the image from her mind. "God, Daddy. She watched them burn and die in the explosion."

Chandler leaned back. He gazed at the pool too as if searching for the words. "That poor child."

The image of Avery lying trapped beneath the rubble, pleading for Eric to save Sloane, popped into Finn's head, cutting her to the quick. She could only imagine Sloane's horror, knowing her wife would soon meet the same fate as her parents. Sorrow constricted her throat, prompting her to sip her water again.

"Her wife died in almost the same way. No wonder she wanted to die with her."

"Dear God." Chandler's Adam's apple bobbed after what must have been a hard, lumpy swallow. "And she almost lost you in the wildfire."

"I get it now, Daddy." Sloane's words as they escaped the flames all made sense. "That night, when we thought we might not make it out alive, she told me, 'I won't let it take you, too.' I didn't understand it then, but I do now. She was talking about the fire."

"She's been through too much."

"And I made things more confusing today." Her head tilted down as she regarded what she was sure was a misstep. She had tried to hold back, but she'd never felt closer to a woman and the words had just spilled out. "I told Sloane I loved her."

"You think it's too soon?"

"Isn't it?"

"Not necessarily. Everyone grieves on his or her timetable."

"How will I know when she's ready to move on and we're not rushing things?"

"There's no telling. My advice is to let her set the pace."

"This might be a little too personal." Finn bit her lower lip at the prospect of entering the "forbidden zone" they'd established with each other about their dating. "But Sloane did this start-stop thing today. How did you know when you were ready for intimacy again?"

His eyes scanned the grounds again as he searched for the answer. "I'd have to say when I wasn't afraid to be happy again. I feared if I let myself enjoy happiness, it meant I'd forgotten your mother. Then one day, I accepted the notion she wouldn't want me endlessly roaming the house reliving some memory of her. She would've wanted me to enjoy whatever life I had left and if that was with someone else, so be it. Sloane just needs more time. Let her take the lead."

So, his experience was much like hers after her first love, Isabell, died. But this thing with Sloane seemed different. How could she tell if Sloane had only been chasing an echo of Avery in the car today? Her saying "She wasn't you" had her hoping and wishing but didn't prove a thing. Finn leaned back in her chair and hoped she hadn't torpedoed their relationship before it got off the ground. *Let Sloane make the next move. Just focus on finding the government leak.*

CHAPTER FOUR

Arriving with Eric at the bank of elevators in the lobby of San Francisco's Federal Building, Sloane repositioned her cell phone on her ear to hear better. "How soon can Social Services conduct the home study, Kadin?"

"If we pay for a private contractor, we can have it done this week." The chatter of a group of men near the elevator made it hard to hear her reply.

"Do it." Sloane pressed a finger against her other ear to drown out the background noise. "I want the adoption done as quickly as possible."

While bureaucratic red tape had its purpose, it made no sense in this case. Both Reagan's biological parents were dead, and days ago, Judge Gonzalez had confirmed Sloane as her legal guardian. In any reasonable system, a single stroke of the pen by the same judge should declare Sloane as Reagan's legal parent. But as Sloane had often encountered in her job, reasonable outcomes seldom materialized without considerable intervention. They required jumping through too many frustrating government hoops.

"Consider it done, but I have to warn you. Once I file, the court will notify both sets of grandparents of your petition. We may have a fight on our hands with the Santoses."

"I have two words for them: Bring it." Sloane was stronger and more determined than ever after her brush with death. Despite her homophobic in-laws, she would do everything to become Reagan's legal parent.

"All right then. I'll let you know when I line it up."

Sloane ended the call and slid her iPhone in her coat pocket. Boarding the elevator with her, Eric ran a hand through his trimmed light brown hair before brushing back the flaps of his tailored dark blue suit coat. He locked both hands on his trim waist, a move that accentuated his brawny shoulders. "You seem different."

"Good or bad?" Sloane asked, tilting her head.

"Good. But distracted."

She felt different. The Sloane who had existed before the wildfire had been fixated on the past and what she had lost. The new Sloane, unburdened by guilt, was considering the future and options she previously labeled inconceivable, like single parenting and turning in her badge. While putting bad guys away still called to her, the long, irregular hours and dangerous situations she sometimes found herself in didn't have the same appeal anymore. Reagan came first, with Finn a close second.

"It's been an emotional couple of days."

"I know it has." His eyes softened when he lowered his arms to his sides. "I have a feeling that Finn has something to do with it."

"She's part of it."

"She's good for you, Sloane." Eric was more than a partner. He was her best friend. Having his stamp of approval made her think that, given time, moving on was within reach.

The elevator door slid open, and Sloane came face-to-face with Finn. She barely noticed the others waiting to board. Something about Finn appeared different. Sloane paused to drink its spellbinding property. *Her hair*. It had a new wave to it that mirrored the curves of her body. *I like it.* She let a smile build until her cheeks hurt. "I think you're right."

"Right about what?" Finn asked, her eyes arched with curiosity.

Eric stepped around a motionless, smitten-like-a-teenager Sloane. "That this plan of hers to smoke out the leak might have a chance of working." He slid past both women and glanced over his shoulder. "Are you two coming?"

The strong pull between them made it impossible for Sloane to focus on anything but Finn. When the door started to slide shut, Finn slammed a hand holding a manila folder against its leading edge. "Shall we?"

As Sloane and Finn walked side by side down the crowded corridor, their hands brushed several times. The contact reminded Sloane that working together was like a stout tonic. Every dose healed and strengthened her a little bit each day.

They arrived at the conference room early enough to go over last-minute details. Sloane hadn't ironed out all the minutiae of her little ruse before scheduling this meeting, so she and Finn were completing it on the fly.

As Finn circled the large conference table, moving toward a credenza to reach a desk phone sitting on its top, her boss walked in. Special Agent in Charge Nate Prichard, a paunchy fifty-something bureaucrat, wore a white long-sleeved button-down dress shirt that matched his pasty white skin. The last time Sloane had seen him was in the hospital waiting room following the Santa Rosa wildfire. Sloane swallowed hard, recalling his stiff reaction when Finn explained why they'd left him out of the loop on the Los Dorados investigation that night.

"You suspected me?" Prichard whipped his head toward Finn.

"We knew the leak was someone in our building with access to the Rojas file." Finn didn't grovel, resolute with her tone and stance. "I followed protocol and left all suspects out of the loop."

Prichard harrumphed.

Sloane's boss, Lieutenant Morgan West, came to Finn's defense. "We kept you in the dark until now for good reason."

Prichard's right eyebrow arched. "We? So, you were part of this too?"

"Only after they cleared me too. So, I know how much being under suspicion gets under your skin." West had glanced coldly at Sloane, eliciting a regret-filled sigh from her. She had a lot of repair work to do.

"Sloane, Decker, and Harper knew someone in the government had leaked information to Caco about Diego Rojas. The raid in the Lower Bottoms was a ruse to locate Caco. It worked because someone near the Bay Bridge called his burner. You were with Sloane and me when that call was made, so we ruled you out. That narrowed the suspect pool to two—your secretary and Quintrell."

Prichard's tense posture relaxed, the redness in his face fading. He turned his attention to Finn. "I was wondering if I had made a mistake bringing you up, Harper. I'm still pissed, but I can see you were the right choice. You've done good work."

"Thank you, sir." Finn gave him a tentative nod, a sign of relief and respect.

Sloane furtively grazed a hand against Finn's pant leg and blew out a cleansing breath. Finn's job was safe.

Sloane shook off the memory of that night and decided to hip-pocket her descriptive nickname for him for Finn's sake.

"Thank you for coming, Agent Prichard." Her polite greeting marked the first time she paid him any amount of respect. She expected, though, that he'd eventually show his bureaucratic side again and earn the barb of "Prickhead" in full measure. "We only have a few minutes. Finn, you know Carol the best, so you and Eric should watch her reaction. Agent Prichard, since you know Quintrell, you and I will watch him."

Prichard nodded before he turned to Finn. "How are you getting Carol up here?"

"I left my cell phone in the office." Finn picked up the phone handset and winked as she dialed. "Oh good, you answered. I left my phone at my desk, and I need some information from it. Prichard and Quintrell are already on their way. Can you run it down right now?" She paused for some response. "Thank you, Carol. You're a lifesaver."

Finn hung up the phone. "We're all set."

Minutes later, a deep male voice boomed from the open door. "This possible Los Dorados survivor had better not be a waste of my time."

All eyes turned to Quintrell. The pompous, dark-haired, well-tanned Assistant US Attorney was dressed in his signature tailored dark Brioni suit. He took a seat at the head of the table, earning Sloane's disdain. Finn was right. He had to appear in charge. Based on Finn's description of his personality, the fact that he was on time surprised Sloane, but this played well into her plan. It could be that as a man in his late forties he had finally learned politeness, but she doubted it. Her antenna remained up.

A moment later, Carol appeared in the doorway, holding Finn's cell phone. Perfect timing.

"Let's get right to it." Finn waved a hand, beckoning Carol to come in and wait. "Yesterday, I received a call from the Sonoma County Sheriff's office informing me that firefighters found a severely burned survivor near our crime scene at the Santa Rosa vineyard. Suspecting the John Doe was connected to our case, they asked me to make an identification. I took Sergeant Sloane with me since she was there the night of the fire and got a good look at the suspects. When we arrived at the hospital, we determined that facial recognition was impossible."

Finn pulled a small stack of color photographs from a folder and laid them on the table. "However, closer inspection revealed a partially severed small finger on the left hand."

Finn had reached a critical point in Sloane's plan: observing the reactions of both suspects. Now, they had to wrap this up and compare notes.

"We recalled one suspect having a similar deformity and believe the survivor could be Caco." Finn pointed to the close-up of Caco's hand, keeping an eye on Carol as she did so.

"Is he conscious?" Prichard asked, following Sloane's script. "Can we interrogate him?"

"I'm afraid not." Finn shook her head. "He's in bad shape, so the doctors placed him in an induced coma. The prognosis isn't good."

"Then, unless he wakes up, it appears this has been another waste of time, Agent Harper. I suggest you close the book on this one." Quintrell buttoned his pricy suit coat and left without another word.

Waste of time? Anything but, Sloane thought.

Carol appeared impatient and motioned to Finn, who nodded and thanked her for retrieving her phone before she left. Finn closed the conference room door behind her and then turned to the group. "I got nothing. Carol was grossed out by the photos."

"I agree," Eric said.

"Quintrell's our guy." Every twist in Sloane's gut told her she was right. "He tried to hide it, but the eyes don't lie. When he saw the missing pinky, I could tell he knew it was Caco before you said his name. I'm sure of it."

"I knew something was off when he arrived on time." Prichard nodded in agreement. "Quintrell operates on his own clock and usually makes everyone wait for him."

"The question is: Why was he all hot to get to this meeting but couldn't get out of here fast enough," Eric said, rubbing his stubbled chin.

"Because he's our guy," Sloane insisted.

"This is a mess." Prichard shook his head. "Going after an Assistant US Attorney means stirring up a hornet's nest."

"For this, I'm willing to get stung," Sloane said. Quintrell may have been too arrogant for her taste and perhaps bias clouded her judgment, but instinct told her everything added up. Wiping that smug grin off his face would be a bonus.

* * *

An hour later, Finn and Prichard walked through the Vice/Narcotics squad room doors at 850 Bryant to plan their next step. Her boss was right, Finn thought. Snaring an Assistant US Attorney would be messy. Her primary concern surrounded secrecy. The more people who knew about their suspicions, the greater the chance of another leak. Relocating operations to outside the Federal Building was the most prudent suggestion Prichard had ever made to her.

She zigzagged through clusters of 1960s industrial-style metal desks and a dozen detectives before stopping dead in her tracks. The chatter faded into white noise, and all other activity blurred when Sloane stood from her desk chair and arched her back to slip a jacket off her shoulders. The contrast of Sloane's brown leather shoulder holster against the pale blue cotton of her button-down blouse highlighted the swell of a breast. Perfection came to mind. Every tantalizing curve teased Finn.

When Sloane caught sight of Finn, her smile brightened their dark day. She waved and mouthed, "*Over here*." The motion of her hand brought the activity in the room back into focus.

"We're early, sir," Finn said over her shoulder. "I'm gonna catch up with Sloane."

"All right," Prichard said. "Meet you in West's office."

Finn navigated her way through the remaining maze of desks, her grin matching Sloane's reticent one. "Hey. Where's Eric?"

"Bathroom. But don't worry, we have plenty of time." Sloane's gaze focused on Finn's lips before returning to her eyes, fanning the heat simmering inside Finn. She was sure her cheeks were broadcasting her arousal like a flashing neon sign.

Sloane broke the trance. "You look nice today. I like what you did with your hair."

"Thank you." Finn tugged on a few strands. She *had* done a little something extra, giving a slight wave to her straight dark blond hair. Apparently, the last-minute style choice she usually reserved for special occasions worked to get Sloane's attention. She leaned in and whispered, "We should talk about yesterday."

Sloane scanned the squad room abuzz with detectives talking with each other, speaking with witnesses, or engrossed in what was on their glowing computer screens. "Not here. Follow me."

Sloane was right. No matter how softly they spoke, the squad room wasn't the place to talk about the events of yesterday. Whether it was about Quintrell, the accident, or their intimate encounter, their talk required privacy.

Sloane led the way to the interview rooms. She was lumbering a little less today in her walking boot. Finn hoped her physical healing was an indicator of her emotional healing as well. Sloane steered her into the observation chamber of an empty room and then stepped closer. Finn shifted her focus to Sloane's lips. At the prospect of kissing them again, the saliva in her mouth built to a level she couldn't ignore. *Let her make the next move*, Finn chanted in her head.

"Yesterday was very important to me. I hope you don't have regrets," Sloane said with a sense of certitude that turned the heat up even more.

"Not at all." Finn licked her lips at the memory of bringing herself to climax last night by conjuring up images that went well beyond the scope of their roadside encounter.

"Good, because I don't either." Sloane leaned in closer, her mouth inches from Finn's. "I dreamed about you last night."

"I did the same."

"Tell me about your dream." The rasp of seduction in Sloane's voice was an octave lower than her usual tone.

Finn's arousal settled in her throat, forcing a hard swallow. When more images from her fantasy reappeared, her skin tingled, driving her to close her eyes. "You were between my legs." Her breath hitched on the vision. "Your mouth was hungry to taste me."

"I had the same fantasy." Sloane's breath quickened into steam, mixing with hers.

The heat of Sloane's words fanned Finn's embers. Their lips inched so close to each other that a wisp of Finn's wavy hair couldn't have passed between them. *Let her make the next move*, Finn chanted again in her head, but those thin, cherry-red lips taunted her. A millimeter lean forward, and she would taste whatever sweet or salty delight Sloane had snacked on after lunch. She dug deep, pulled back, and focused again on Sloane's mouth. Sloane would have to initiate this.

Right on cue, Sloane captured her lips in a fiery kiss, darting her tongue in with the force of a serpent. The taste of chocolate—and pretzel?—invaded her mouth and teased Finn's hunger. Every inch of her ignited when a hand pressed against the swell of her back, forcing their hips together. Then the other clamped onto her breast. Damn her shirt and bra. If only she could make them disappear. She wanted Sloane's touch to burn her skin like it did in her fantasy.

As if reading her mind, Sloane tugged at the lower part of Finn's shirt and yanked it past her navel, turning her fantasies into reality when their bellies touched skin to skin. When had Sloane untucked her own shirt? Finn had no time to figure that out before melting into the sensation.

The tingling where their skin collided radiated and spread like ripples in a pond. Finn had wanted this since the moment she turned around in the lieutenant's office months ago and saw the girl of her childhood dreams.

A chill traveled up her spine when she remembered why she'd lost track of Sloane in the first place and why she was so available and in her arms today. Sloane had lost so much. She deserved better than a hot, sweaty office romp where the goal was to climax before someone even noticed they were gone. This would never do. She deserved silky sheets, soft music, and an opulent Bordeaux, not a hookup in a room that reeked of urine.

Finn ripped her lips away and pushed Sloane back with the pads of her palms. "Not here."

But Sloane didn't stop. She pushed her backward until Finn's bottom slammed the wall. In a frenzy, she fumbled with the buttons of Finn's shirt, exposing more of her skin, and devoured Finn's long, smooth neck. One moan after another escaped her lips as their bodies rocked in a perfect rhythm.

If they were alone in the darkness of her condo, this would be sexy as hell. But desperation had tinged this encounter, and common sense told Finn it needed to stop. Before she could act on that thought, though, their tongues rejoined the fray and all caution evaporated. She threw her arms around Sloane's neck and a leg around her hip. She rocked her center against Sloane's thigh, the friction raising the heat in her core to a searing level.

With a loud whoosh, flushing water rushed above her head, and the scent of sewer floated past her nose, breaking through the sensual tsunami. *This has to stop*. Finn placed her hands on

Sloane's cheeks and forced their lips apart again. "Sloane." Finn pleaded with her eyes as much as with her voice. "Please, not like this."

Confusion swirled in Sloane's eyes as she slowed her thrusts.

"Not like this," Finn repeated.

Sloane stilled her hips and lowered her hands but kept them against Finn's belly skin as if clinging to a life vest in the middle of the ocean. "I need this." Her words came out in a pained whisper.

"I know you do." Finn grazed Sloane's cheeks with her thumbs. The totality of yesterday had them both on edge, and it would've been too easy to let Sloane take what she wanted. They would both, however, regret not waiting until Sloane was ready. "When we do this—and trust me, we *will*—I want it to be about us and not your grief."

Sloane took a step back, breaking their contact. "You're right." She averted her eyes, underscoring her point with a deep sigh. "I never thanked you for saving my life that day in Diego's lab. If it weren't for you and Eric pulling me out, I wouldn't be alive." She raised her stare to meet Finn's. "Thank you."

Those words communicated more than gratitude. To Finn, they meant Sloane was healing.

"You're welcome, and thank you for doing the same for me in the fire."

"We saved each other that night." A faint smile appeared—the exact thing Finn wanted to see.

"Yes, we did. I don't expect you to respond, but I'm sure of what I said yesterday. I love you. And I'll repeat it. I'll wait as long as it takes." Those words rolled off Finn's tongue as if they formed the most straightforward truth in the world. And in her bones, she was sure Sloane felt the same.

When Sloane parted her lips to say something, Finn placed an index finger over them. "No. Don't force it and no explanations. You'll say it when you're ready. Now, let's go find your partner."

As Sloane and Finn approached Lieutenant West's office, Eric raised an eyebrow and checked his watch. "Cutting it a little close. I was about to send out a search party."

"We needed to discuss a few things." Sloane's flushed skin had thankfully returned to its normal color.

Eric scanned both ladies and pointed at a single tip of Finn's shirt overhanging her waistband. "Uh-huh. After all that talking, you may want to tuck that in."

Finn felt like she and Sloane had just been busted by the vice principal. Thankfully, ADA Kyler Harris appeared through the doors just then, providing a timely distraction as Finn tidied her clothes.

"Hope I didn't keep you waiting." Kyler pulled up to the group in her sensible mix-and-match department store business suit. Middle-aged and not to mention cute with her bobbed black hair, she was professional to a fault and always arrived on time.

"Not at all." Sloane shot Eric a look that told him to mind his own business. "Shall we?" She led the group into Lieutenant West's office.

"I hate this damn thing." West tinkered with her computer mouse from behind her old, neatly organized metal desk as everyone entered. The poster image of a professional woman, she tapped the ancient mouse several times against the edge of her desk to get it to come to life like magic but had no luck.

As if she felt as comfortable in this office as West was, Kyler retrieved a can of compressed air nestled on a bookshelf over West's right shoulder. "Let me. Sometimes these old things get a lot of dust buildup." Kyler shot the compressed air into every hole of the device and gave it a test run. It worked flawlessly. "See? Like new." She handed it back with a wink.

"Thank you. You've saved me another headache." West's hand lingered when Kyler slowly brushed her fingertips against it while returning the mouse, the furtive movement catching Finn's eye. Close in age and in careers that often crossed paths, they would make a good couple, she thought.

West motioned for everyone to take a seat at her small conference table. "Nate, I understand you may have narrowed down the mole."

"This is Sergeant Sloane's case. She deserves the credit." Prichard glanced toward Sloane, offering her a kind nod. This first show of respect gave Finn hope they hadn't burned all their bridges with this investigation.

West turned her attention and stiffened her neck. "All right, Sergeant Sloane. Let's hear it." The lingering chill in her voice signaled Sloane had a little extra repair work in her future.

Sloane shifted in her chair, a concerned expression developing on her face. "I'm not sure how much you briefed ADA Harris—"

"She's up to speed." West's crossed arms in front of her chest reinforced the bitterness in her tone. The chilly "up to speed" meant that West and Kyler were still reeling a bit from Sloane, Eric, and Finn having once suspected them of leaking intelligence to Los Dorados. And that Kyler had been informed that Sloane and Finn went rogue to pursue Caco in Santa Rosa without West and Eric.

Sloane offered West and Kyler each a respectful nod. "We've figured out who's been tipping off Los Dorados."

"I'm listening." West's tenor thawed a degree, a sign the rift between her and Sloane might be repairable.

"When we briefed AUSA Quintrell and Prichard's secretary about Caco and showed them the pictures of his hand, Quintrell was the only one who showed any sign of recognition. My gut tells me he's our leak."

Kyler rubbed a worried hand across her lips. "We'll need a lot more than a gut feeling to take down an Assistant US Attorney."

"I have the same concern," Prichard said. "We'll need rock-solid proof before we kick it up to DC."

Finn and Sloane hadn't put everything on the line and come close to death to turn this case over to someone who wasn't vested in the outcome. She glanced at Sloane's face and recognized the anger and disappointment brewing there because she felt it too. She knew her boss. If she didn't offer an alternative solution immediately, Prichard would turn over Avery's murder case to some bureaucratic federal attorney.

"This is about the murder of an SFPD CSI. The case belongs here."

"I have to agree with Agent Harper," Kyler said. "Avery Santos was one of our own. We need to bring everyone responsible for her death to justice in a San Francisco courtroom."

Prichard squirmed in his chair. He was a bureaucrat through and through, and Finn rightly feared this would take some convincing. She looked at Morgan West for support.

"Let's think about this, Nate." West shook her hand up and down to cajole him into hearing her out. "First, we don't know how far this goes. We still don't know who made the phone call that tipped off Caco the night of the fake raid. It could be Quintrell or someone else we haven't considered yet. If we bring in outsiders, we lose control and the element of surprise."

"I'm listening." Prichard relaxed his posture, a sign she held his interest. The way he eyed West, Finn got the impression his interest was more than professional. She smirked. He was sniffing up the wrong tree.

"Second, everything we have on Quintrell is circumstantial. Harper, Sloane, and Decker have been a well-oiled machine. They know the players and the turf. Let's not bring in any outsiders until we have to. They can continue investigating and bring Quintrell in for questioning when the time is right."

"My office," Kyler said, "will give them all the support they might need."

"All right," Prichard said, "but if this starts going sideways, I'm up-channeling it."

Finn turned her gaze back to Sloane. The grin on her face matched her confidence that everything they went through at the vineyard would soon pay off.

"What's the next step, Sloane?" West's less formal voice gave Finn a little more hope they were on the right track.

"I have a feeling he'll make a move soon," Sloane said. "I want to tail him twenty-four-seven."

"How many teams? I can't spare many."

"Considering the situation, the fewer people in the know, the better. There's no telling where loyalties lie. It should be just the three of us."

CHAPTER FIVE

There were two problems, at least, with sitting stakeout alone in an unmarked sedan, Sloane discovered—too much time to think and bathroom breaks that were infrequent and required considerable logistical coordination. The sun radiating through the windshield compounded the problem of the increasing pressure in her bladder, pushing her past uncomfortable to nearly unbearable.

I shouldn't have had that extra cup of water after lunch.

Sloane's shift was almost over, but this couldn't wait. Her urgent call of nature had necessitated an early request for relief. Until it showed up, she did her job, keeping her eyes pinned on the only exit from the Federal Building's underground parking garage, where Quintrell had left his Mercedes this morning.

She said five minutes. It's been six. Sloane leaned back in her seat to relieve the painful pressure before rechecking her watch. *Seven minutes.* She turned toward a rap on her side window. The contrite face staring at her meant relief had arrived. She clicked the lock.

Finn swung the door open. "I'm so sorry. I had to take a call."

Sloane slid out of her seat, brushing up against Finn as she did. A day had passed since their blood-pumping interrogation room encounter, along with one and a half stakeout shifts in which to fantasize about taking that entanglement to its natural conclusion. Their kiss that day had sparked a visceral response she didn't expect, more even than the one at the accident site, and that level of arousal overpowered her. When they were skin to skin, Avery had become a distant past, and satisfying her physical ache had become the sole focus.

Maneuvering past Finn, she ignored her pained bladder long enough to register the citrus aroma of her blond hair. Images of orange trees popped into her head, just like the ones she'd conjured up that last day she'd held Finn's hand when they were kids. "Oranges? Your hair used to smell like this."

Finn's smirk gave the impression her choice of fragrance was deliberate. "I've always liked citrus shampoo and thought I'd try it again."

"I'm glad you did." An urgent ache reminded Sloane she needed to go. "I'll be right back."

Once Sloane emptied her bladder, her pace from the Federal Building was unhurried, unlike her fast clip going in. Her thoughts bounced between the surveillance and Finn, hoping she'd stay until her shift was over. She stepped onto the sidewalk, slowing as Finn's silhouette in the car came into view. Finn had twice said she loved her, and despite knowing it to be true for herself as well, Sloane couldn't bring herself to return the words. Saying them meant letting go of her wife.

A chirping sound in her pocket prompted her to fish out her cell phone. She glanced at the caller ID before swiping the screen. "Hey, Kadin. Tell me you have good news."

"Some good. Some not so good."

Sloane stopped, unable to take her gaze from Finn in the front seat. "What now?"

"The Santoses are contesting."

"I expected as much." Expecting a pain in the ass never made putting up with one easy. Though the fact she'd battled her homophobic in-laws once already and won made the Santoses' meddling less worrying this time. "What does this mean for the adoption?"

"Besides taking more time, it means they can testify at the hearing."

"How much more time?"

"Could be months."

"Fucking great."

"The good news is that Social Services is processing our request for a private contractor. I called in a favor, and we could have the home study scheduled within a week."

"Thank you, Kadin. You've been going above and beyond."

"Anything for one of the city's finest…and for a friend of Finn."

A flag went up at the way she said Finn's name. Kadin's slight pause and faint, breathy sigh hinted at their having a history between them. Sloane strained to take in Finn's features. She imagined the two of them together and came to the disturbing conclusion that she and Kadin would make an attractive couple.

"I'm working, Kadin, so I gotta go. Keep me posted." She hung up and couldn't tuck away the phone nor her misgivings fast enough. With each step she took toward the car, the thought of Kadin and Finn together grew in her head until it drowned out every street noise. Had they been lovers or a serious couple? Were they still a thing? Should she even ask at this point?

A voice in her head told her, *don't force it*, but her gut told her she was on the right track. She shook off the awkward feeling and knocked on the driver's window. Finn lowered it.

"I wrapped things up for the day." Finn added a smile. "Why don't you hop in the other seat?"

That was precisely what Sloane wanted to hear. She swooped around to the passenger side and joined Finn. "Prickhead won't ding you for leaving work early, will he?"

Finn snickered but kept her stare on the garage exit. "I thought you weren't calling him that anymore."

"It's a hard habit to break." Sloane shrugged, settling into a half grin. She still had a bit of a filter problem.

"You know, if I'm not careful, I might call him that."

"We can't have that." Sloane squeezed Finn's hand before absentmindedly running a finger up her bare arm. "The last thing I want is to give him one more excuse to fire you."

"I'm federal." Finn drew her stare from her target to the goose bumps emerging in the wake of Sloane's touch. "It's hard to fire me. I'm more worried about a transfer to Bakersfield."

"Bakersfield?" Sloane stopped. She and Finn were just beginning to connect, and the idea of her moving three hundred miles away made her uneasy. More than that, it made her sad. She privately vowed to never call him Prickhead again. "He's still that frosty?"

"Hard to tell, but that's where he threatens to send everyone who pisses him off." Finn followed with a breathy sigh. "Ordinarily, I wouldn't care, but a transfer would take me away from you and Daddy."

"And Kadin?" Sloane pulled her hand back, regretting the question the moment she asked it. Finn's closed eyes and second deep sigh confirmed her hunch, the sting of it turning Sloane's uneasiness into embarrassment. "So, you two had a thing?"

"Yes, we did, but that ended months ago." Finn shifted in her seat, her face plastered with a devilish grin. "Are you jealous?"

The awkwardness of the situation had peaked and required an ambiguous yet playful response. "Should I be worried?"

"You *are* jealous." Finn's grin transformed into a broad smile.

Am I? Had she already let go of Avery? Was it time? With every passing day, with each touch and kiss, she and Finn inched closer, but she worried still that she might be rushing. "Can we change the subject?" Sloane said good-humoredly, warming cheeks betraying an underlying truth she wasn't ready to share. *I am jealous, and I am rushing*.

"Sure. And no, you have nothing to worry about." Finn's grin faded. "What kind of day did Quintrell have?"

"Exciting. He had lunch on Sutter Street. Then he picked up a bottle of wine before returning to the office."

"Sounds like he's not interested in taking the bait."

"Not yet, but I'm betting he will." A unique chime alerted Sloane to an incoming message from her daughter. She fished the phone from her jacket pocket and scanned the text. "Reagan's making spaghetti tonight. I better head home."

Finn turned toward Sloane. "Tomorrow then?" In her eyes she could see reflected the disappointment she also felt. These back-to-back shifts meant sharing scant minutes inside a hot, smelly car, leaving her wanting more than the quick peck on the lips they had shared each of the last few days.

She leaned in until their warm, moist breaths mixed in the stale air, raising the temperature between them. She pressed their lips together, holding for a few extra beats. How long would it take until she invited those lips elsewhere on her body? Soon, she hoped, but before either could deepen the kiss, she inched back. In a voice as soft as Finn's lips, she replied, "Tomorrow."

* * *

Tomorrow had come, and as she dried off from her morning shower, Sloane glanced at her phone on the bathroom counter and Eric's predawn text. *Fox still in the den.* He nailed it. Quintrell was sly as a fox, but her confidence remained high that she'd snare him in her trap. Patience was the key.

Half an hour later, she drank down the rest of her semisweet coffee and cleared her and Reagan's breakfast plates from the dining room table. "I'm not sure if I'll make your volleyball game today, honey. No guarantees with this stakeout."

"It's okay, Mom. I get it." The droop in Reagan's shoulders telegraphed her disappointment as she placed the leftovers in containers in the refrigerator.

"It's not okay, and I plan to make it up to you once this case is over." Besides wanting to spend more time with Reagan, she wanted to wrap things up with Los Dorados for Finn, whose reputation at work had taken a beating. Without a doubt, she owed them both a speedy conclusion.

"Well, if you're feeling that guilty, there's a nice pair of jeans I've had my eyes on," Reagan said with a cunning wink.

Teenagers. Sloane shook her head, adding a cheerful smile. "We'll see."

An hour later, Sloane parked her new SUV on a side street near the stakeout site. In a way, she was glad her old one had burned up at the vineyard. She'd gotten a good deal at the Subaru dealership on Saturday and finally had heated seats. Making the rest of her way on foot, she stuffed her hands in her coat pockets to shield them from the morning cold. Every house along the avenue, which faced the eastern perimeter of the Presidio, shouted money. With their arched windows, light-colored stucco finishing, and low-pitched, red-tiled roofs, they were more expensive than a government lawyer should be able to afford. A background check had revealed Quintrell didn't inherit his upscale Mediterranean-style home and that he carried a reasonable mortgage on it. Sloane's conclusion—he was dirty, came from a wealthy family, or both.

Approaching the other unmarked sedan that she, Finn, and Eric used for the surveillance, she knocked twice on the rear fender to alert Eric of her presence and then the same on the passenger window. Eric unlocked the door and invited her to slide into the passenger seat. "Morning."

"You're early." He rubbed his hands together to ward off the chill in the car. He had taught her early on that idling engines and fogged-up windows attracted attention during stakeouts. So, even though it meant freezing in your seat, cracking a few windows was necessary. Though the temperature today wasn't cold enough to mist her breath, she zipped her outer jacket up higher to combat the moist peninsula air.

"Finn agreed to relieve me early so I can go to Reagan's game tonight. Thought I'd do you the same favor."

Eric stretched to a muffled yawn. "An extra hour of sleep would be nice."

"Anything overnight?" she asked.

"Nothing." He placed a fist over his mouth to capture another yawn. "Finn said he came home right on time. Lights went out about midnight. Looks like another boring day."

"Something will break soon. I can feel it," she said.

Perhaps the best lesson Eric had taught her was that of patience. Ninety-nine percent of the time nothing would happen during a stakeout, but during that one percent, all hell could break loose and make the case. This investigation was personal, and that alone was enough to keep her motivated.

An hour after Eric left, an hour she spent deliberating her feelings for Finn versus her memories of Avery, Quintrell's garage door opened. *A little early*, she thought. His Mercedes rolled down the driveway with the door closing after it. Sloane picked up her binoculars and focused on the person behind the wheel. Quintrell looked smug with his black hair neatly clipped around the ears, dressed in another expensive suit. Tossing the binoculars to the passenger seat, she started the car, put it in drive, and followed.

Mimicking the same route he'd taken yesterday, Quintrell drove north. At the first stop sign, she was prepared for him to turn right and go east toward the Federal Building, but he didn't. He drove straight on, raising Sloane's senses along with her pulse. She sat straighter in her seat.

Minutes later, he pulled onto the Presidio Parkway, heading north into moderate traffic. When he moved to the left lane that meant only one thing: he planned to cross the Golden Gate. She dug her fingers into the vinyl of the steering wheel and twisted as if wringing out the tension that had built for the last two days. This was it. He'd taken the bait.

When she emerged from Battery Tunnel five or six car lengths behind Quintrell, she had no doubt about his destination. As with most things these days, her first instinct was to reach Finn. She picked up her iPhone from the center console and dialed.

"Hey, you," Finn answered with a soft, sexy lilt.

That voice usually served as a calming respite, but Sloane hadn't the time today to soak in its relaxing properties. Her mind was sharply focused like a needle on the Mercedes ahead of her. "Fox is on the run."

"Where?" Finn's tone turned serious.

"North across the Golden Gate."

"Santa Rosa." Finn's words formed more of a statement than a question.

"That's my guess."

"Do you want me to meet up with you? I can move my classified briefing."

Sloane's pulse settled once she crossed the final orange-vermillion span and was traveling against the morning rush. Traffic had thinned, easing the task of changing lanes and minimizing the chance of losing Quintrell. Focused now on Finn's question, she realized she couldn't risk tipping off the fox at this point. "No. He knows your face. He's only seen me once, and I doubt he'd recognize me from a distance. I'll let you or Eric know if I need backup."

Sloane said goodbye to Finn and called Morgan West to tell her of Quintrell's movement. She settled into a comfortable pattern of remaining several car lengths behind him and delaying lane changes to avoid detection. Their direction of travel didn't change, and the steady route convinced her he'd taken the bait.

An hour later, Quintrell took the same freeway exit she and Finn had taken days earlier. Familiar with the streets, Sloane didn't worry about losing him in Santa Rosa traffic, so she laid back a few extra cars. Minutes later, he pulled into the mostly full Valley Hospital visitor parking lot.

Sloane parked an aisle over and several cars down before following him on foot toward the lobby. Inside, he asked for directions at the information desk. Sloane busied herself at the water fountain, keeping her peripheral vision on him. When he headed toward the bank of elevators, she ducked into the stairwell, predicting his destination.

Damn boot. The cumbersome device slowed Sloane down, limiting her to taking one stair at a time. Counting on the busyness of the elevators to buy her an extra minute, she doubled her pace and hobbled up two flights to the third floor. When she reached the top stair, she darted through the door and zigzagged through congested hallways to the waiting area outside the burn ward, slowing to catch her breath before walking in. Familiar with the process of entering the secured ward, she decided to wait until Quintrell used the wall-mounted phone to alert the nurses station.

Two groups of people occupied the room. They were seated against the walls in well-worn wood-framed guest chairs upholstered in a fabric that reminded Sloane of bathtub bubbles set against a tan background. In the first group, a Caucasian male and female in their early thirties entertained two preschool-age boys. The second group had three adults. A Hispanic male, seventies, gray hair, closely shaved beard, and a flashy white suit. Seated next to him was a Hispanic female, forties, long black hair, jeans, and a dark warm-up jacket. Next to her sat a Hispanic male, twenties, short black hair, khakis, and a fully zipped tan Windbreaker.

Sloane walked past both groups, grabbed a magazine off one table, and took a seat in a corner. She pretended to read, positioning the magazine to hide her face from everyone in the room.

Less than a minute later, someone entered. She peeked around the magazine and recognized the unmistakable dark Brioni suit. The gray-haired man stood and greeted Quintrell with a warm, yet brief hug. "*Mijo*," the man said with a hint of sadness in his voice.

Quintrell nodded and after glancing at the young man still in his seat turned his attention to the woman who had also risen. His back stiffened when he spoke to her. "Rosa, you two shouldn't be here."

Sloane lowered her right hand and pulled her iPhone from her front jacket pocket. After a quick thumb swipe, the camera function activated, and she snapped several pictures. She hoped the angle would yield at least one useful image.

"It wasn't my decision." Through her thick Spanish accent, Rosa's meek voice sounded pregnant with regret. Her full black hair draped over her shoulders when she lowered her gaze to the floor. The tension between her and Quintrell spoke to a turbulent history between them.

"I see." Quintrell rolled his neck and buttoned his tailored jacket. He turned to the gray-haired man. "Let's go to his room."

Rosa stepped back to the row of chairs where the younger man, eyes focused on the floor underneath a chair along the opposite wall, was sitting on the edge of his seat, rocking back and forth. She rested her hands on his elbows, urging him to stand. "Come, Antonio. Time to see your father."

Antonio was close to Quintrell's height and thinness, Sloane noted, but he didn't have his external confidence, failing to make eye contact with anyone in the room.

"Wait here, Rosa," the gray-haired man said in a firm tone. "This is for real family."

"You know he doesn't do well in new places without me." Her voice stayed calm, but her hands trembled.

"He'll be fine with his *abuelo*," he insisted before placing a hand on the young man's arm. "We'll do fine, won't we? Come, Antonio. Be a good boy."

When the older man pulled, Antonio remained frozen. The next moment, he repeatedly twittered his hand, thumb pressed against his index and middle fingers as if he had burned it. Then, between shakes, in a predictable pattern, he tapped his thigh with the same hand.

Rosa placed a calming hand on his arm. "Be a good boy and go with *Abuelo*. I'll be right here after you see your father."

His eyes didn't meet hers, but he moved along. "I'm a good boy."

He has autism. Sloane snapped another picture.

Quintrell picked up the phone receiver near the doorway to request access inside the burn ward. He turned his back to Sloane, and his voice was muffled when he spoke, making it impossible to decipher from a distance what he said. When the three men turned to leave, Rosa returned to her seat. She rapidly tapped a foot up and down while clutching her purse against her chest. *An unwilling subservient*, Sloane thought.

She pondered several facts. *Rosa wasn't real family, so maybe Caco isn't her husband. Yet, she has a son with him. But Quintrell must be family. This just got interesting*, she thought, but she knew she needed more information to be rock-solid sure of Quintrell's connection.

Placing the magazine back on the table, she followed the men into the burn ward, scooting in before the door mechanically closed. Steps behind them, she trained her gaze on Antonio, who outpaced the others in an anxious stride. Several times, Quintrell pulled him back, trying to match the gray-haired man's slower pace. Each time Antonio slowed, hummed, and shook a fist near the corner of an eye, Quintrell chastised. This cycle continued until they disappeared into Caco's room.

Sloane settled into a position outside his door. A moment later, a hand fell to her shoulder. She recognized the redheaded doctor. "Sergeant Sloane, what brings you back?" Doctor Freeman's question was loud. Sloane could only pray that the boy's humming or the older man's impatience had drowned out her voice.

Shit. Sloane pulled Doctor Freeman several rooms down. "I don't have time to explain," she whispered. "I'm working. Pretend you don't know me."

The doctor nodded and winked her understanding before returning to the nurses station.

She retook her position outside Caco's door. The low voices inside made it difficult for her to understand what they were saying, so she inched closer to the door opening. Straining, she made out, "…brother…" "…Mexico…" "…product…" "…DEA…"

Sloane pieced together the few words she overheard along with what she learned in the waiting room. She'd already figured out the gray-haired man was Caco's father and Antonio was Caco's son. *Quintrell could be Caco's brother and the gray-haired man his father*. Her mind raced. If this were true, that meant he'd not only tipped off Los Dorados but had likely influenced other drug cases for years.

Her mind drifted back to the day Finn had reentered her life and briefed her and Eric that the DEA suspected cartel involvement in the production and distribution of Kiss, the street drug that had killed one of Reagan's best friends. Her gut twisted. *The old guy is cartel.*

"…bathroom," someone inside the room said.

"I'll take him," Quintrell said.

Her adrenaline spiked. If Quintrell saw her up close, he might recognize her. Turning on her booted heel, she walked down the hall at a relaxed pace so as not to attract attention. Footsteps at her back told her Quintrell had taken the same route. *Shit.*

The boot made her slower, and Antonio likely walked faster. *Think.* An approaching wall of windows on her left would cast her reflection. *Think.* Ducking into a patient room might cause a ruckus. Nothing else was in sight except the unoccupied nurses station. Before she passed by it, someone emerged from a room behind the counter. *The redhead.*

Sloane turned at the end of the counter and walked directly toward her in the employee-only area. When Doctor Freeman opened her mouth to say something, Sloane raised an index finger to her lips and mouthed, "*Shhhh.*"

The doctor again nodded and pointed to a chair facing away from the corridor. Sloane sat and waited for Quintrell and the younger man to pass.

"The coast is clear," Doctor Freeman said moments later.

"Thank you, Doctor." Sloane shifted to face her.

"Just Sarah, please."

"Thank you, Sarah." In her head, Sloane sifted through her options. Confirming Quintrell's relationship with Caco topped the list, but she couldn't chance him spotting her. That left only one option. "Can you help me?"

"What do you need, Sergeant Sloane?"

"Just Sloane, Sarah."

"Sloane it is," she said with a wink.

"I suspect our John Doe is a terrible guy, responsible for several deaths, and that his visitors are too." Sloane paused when

Sarah nodded. “I need to talk to a woman in the waiting room but can’t chance the others seeing me.”

“What do you need from me?”

“For you to warn me if the men leave the room.” Sloane scribbled her phone number on a piece of paper. “All you have to do is send me a text.” She begged for cooperation.

“I don’t know, Sloane.”

From the corner of her eye, Sloane watched Quintrell and Antonio begin to retrace their steps toward Caco’s room. She turned to hide her face and whispered, “Please, Sarah. It’s important.”

Sarah stared at the men walking past while Sloane snuck a peek. When Quintrell once again grabbed the younger man’s elbow roughly to get him to slow down, Sarah’s eyes narrowed. She took the piece of paper and slipped it into her lab coat pocket. “You got it.”

When Quintrell had turned into Caco’s room, Sloane rubbed Sarah’s arms. “Thank you.”

Back in the waiting room, Sloane discovered that a new group of people had arrived, which played to her advantage. She took a seat, leaving one empty chair between her and Rosa. Expecting she wouldn’t have much time, Sloane jumped right into role-playing.

She needed to gain Rosa’s attention, and then her sympathies, in order to spark a conversation. Judging by Rosa’s conservative, pedestrian attire, she didn’t buy into the trappings of untold wealth. Unlike the stereotype of a cartel wife or baby-mama, she might also be open to engaging in idle chat.

Leaning forward in her chair, Sloane rubbed her face with her hands and sighed loud enough for Rosa to hear. She then rocked back and forth on the edge of her seat, mimicking to a lesser degree some of the mannerisms Rosa’s son had exhibited. When Rosa glanced her way, Sloane suspected she hit a chord and continued to rock.

Rosa glanced again. “Are you okay, miss? Can I get you some water?” Her concern seemed genuine.

Step one complete. Next, she needed to get Rosa to talk about why she was there. She feigned disorientation and snapped back in her chair. "Thank you, but no. I'll be fine." She tapped the side of her leg with a fist.

"Hospitals can be upsetting." Rosa's tone had a practiced, calming lilt.

"Yes, they can. Waiting is the hardest part. Wait until the surgery is over. Wait until his numbers are stable." Sloane tapped her leg again. "I guess the stress is getting to me."

"I can tell." Rosa pointed to Sloane's leg. "My son does the same thing when he's stressed."

"Do you have a loved one here, too?" Sloane slowed her rocking and tapping.

"Of sorts. My son's father was burned in the wildfire. How about you?"

"A friend. Sorry about your…?"

"Husband." Rosa's sharp tone suggested underlying animosity, maybe. Tension, definitely.

"Oh, I thought the other man in the suit was your husband?"

"If only it were true." Rosa's lips turned downward. Sloane thought she detected disappointment in her tone, supporting her suspicion that she and Quintrell shared a history, possibly a romantic one. "No, he's my son's uncle."

"I'm glad you have family with you."

"Family…yes." Rosa's tone told Sloane that except for her son, she considered those in that hospital room something other than family.

Sloane's iPhone buzzed to an incoming message. Sarah's text read: *They stepped out. Good luck.*

"It was nice meeting you, but I have to go. Hope everything works out." Sloane hurried from the waiting room and walked to the stairwell as fast as she could without arousing suspicion. Minutes later, the information desk clerk in the main lobby was giving her directions to the security office.

She focused on the next step: getting proof. She flashed her badge at the black-haired twenty-something uniformed male at the security office reception desk. "Sergeant Sloane, SFPD. I need to see your security footage."

Unmoved by her urgent tone, the guard looked up and used a napkin to wipe greasy potato chip salt from his fingers. "Let me get my supervisor."

Moments later, the guard returned with a dark-skinned woman dressed in a similar uniform, only much more put together. Her crisp white buttoned-down shirt, pressed black dress pants, and spit-shined black leather shoes, not the cheating patent leather type, screamed that she was in charge. The chevron insignia on her collar signified the equivalency of a sergeant. Everything from her uniform to her hair and fit body said she took pride in herself and her work.

"May I help you?" she asked Sloane.

"Yes, ma'am. I'm Sergeant Sloane, SFPD." Sloane displayed her badge again. "I've tracked a murder suspect here. He's a patient on the third floor. I need help identifying the visitors he had today."

The supervisor rested her forearms on the gear mounted on her Sam Browne belt and looked Sloane up and down. Sloane worried she might not cooperate without a warrant, but she gestured toward a back room. "Come with me."

She guided Sloane to a video surveillance room occupied by two other guards. Eight large-screen monitors lined the far wall, each displaying twenty different video feeds. Sloane marveled at how state-of-the-art everything appeared; the room's cleanliness and organization showed a superior level of professionalism.

"Can you narrow down the time and location, Sergeant?"

"At least the last hour, third-floor waiting room outside the burn ward."

The woman in charge tapped one guard on his shoulder. "Bring up feeds three-ten through three-fourteen. Roll back to o-nine hundred." She returned her attention to Sloane. "What are we looking for?"

Definitely a pro. "An elderly man with a close-shaven beard and in a white suit, accompanied by a dark-haired woman in her forties and a younger man in his twenties."

Both women focused on the five feeds. The timestamp seconds and minutes rolled by at high speed with images of people floating in and out of view until the supervisor called out, "Stop." All five screens froze. "There on three-ten. Is that who you're looking for?"

Sloane bent closer to the monitor and squinted. "Damn, you're good. That's them."

"I assume you'll want a copy of the footage."

"That and stills of the best facial capture on each of them." Sloane handed her a business card. "Can you email me the files?"

"Sure thing, Sergeant Sloane. I hope it helps your case."

Sloane stared at the frozen image on the screen of Rosa, her son, and the gray-haired man. Her gut told her they were the key to shutting down Los Dorados and their Kiss operation. Their brand of business had come at a very high price. It took one of Reagan's friends and led to Avery's death. This time, she would turn the tables.

"I'm sure it will."

CHAPTER SIX

Following a consultation with the on-duty burn ward head nurse, Quintrell returned to Caco's bedside. The slow, rhythmic monitor beep, combined with the mechanical vibrations of the nearby ventilator, proclaimed that his brother continued to cling to life. The numbers on the screen changed often, though, and hovered well below those of someone on the mend. Quintrell interpreted each blip as a predictor that Caco would soon die—not an unwelcome fate.

He stared at Antonio, who rocked in his chair and tapped a leg to relieve the stress that often overpowered him in unfamiliar or noisy environments. Several years had passed since Quintrell last saw him, and he still acted more like a boy than a man. This was the first time he was grateful for his nephew's condition; he took comfort that Antonio didn't understand the gravity of his father's situation.

David Quintrell turned his attention back to Caco. His focus fell on the deformed hand that had taunted him from the first day his father brought that street urchin home. "I hate this hand," he said out loud for the first time in his life.

"This hand was his badge of courage." From the right side of the bed, his father's gaze drifted up from the charred, mangled flesh. "Something you know nothing about."

How could picking a man's pocket earn his father's respect so easily?

Stories of how the gangs of Mexico, including those of his father, doled out punishment hadn't escaped Quintrell growing up, but the mutilation on Caco's hand was the first time he'd seen the cartel form of retribution up close. Children, he'd learned, were never to be killed. But they were to be punished. He knew most men feared his father more than Los Ochos. The gruesomeness of young Caco's severed pinky made him understand how brutal his father truly must be.

It didn't take long after Caco moved into his childhood home for Quintrell to resent everything that hand represented. It had forced him to compete for his father's affection against a boy who had stood toe-to-toe with Los Ochos—an improbable feat. And when as a young man he had not shared his father's thirst for power and money, Caco had. That hand served as a sharp reminder he never would measure up.

"After he moved in, I was never good enough in your eyes." Quintrell smoothed an imaginary crease on the material of his suit jacket. "That hand was a curse."

"You speak as if he is already dead."

"He's as good as."

"He's your brother. You should be ashamed of yourself."

Since childhood, he halfheartedly had wished his adopted brother dead for many reasons, something about which he felt guilty for many years. But it was Caco's betrayal during law school that had erased all civility.

"The day he married Rosa"—he rolled his neck to relieve the tension in his muscles—"he stopped being my brother."

"You have no idea how wrong you are." His father's voice sharpened like a knife.

The next instant the slow beep of the monitor sped to a jarring, steady, piercing sound. The blips on the screen faded into a single flat line. Antonio hummed and rocked hard in his chair, increasing his tapping twofold. Then two people dressed in medical scrubs flew into the room. Their gazes shot to the monitor. One twisted his neck toward Quintrell. "I need everyone to step outside."

Quintrell grasped Antonio by the elbow and, with some doing, guided him into the corridor. A redheaded doctor ran past him into the room. Through the open door, Quintrell and his father watched as she and the others worked at a feverish pace, administering medication and readying the defibrillator. Over twenty minutes passed. The ventilator continued to operate, but after multiple shocks and nonstop chest compressions, the monitor never registered a heartbeat. The doctor stopped. She removed her latex gloves before wiping the sweat off her brow and glancing at the clock on the far wall. "Time of death, eleven seventeen."

In the hallway, Quintrell's father clenched his fists. He glared at his son's body, the muscles surrounding his jaw straining to their maximum. "Who is responsible for this?"

"DEA Agent Finn Harper and San Francisco Detective Manhattan Sloane." Quintrell swallowed hard. Saying their names sealed their fate.

"You're the second one to tell me Detective Sloane's name. I want them both dead."

"This isn't Mazatlán, Father. It's too risky to go after law enforcement. They will bring every resource to bear."

"If you won't do it, I'll find someone else who will."

* * *

"Son of a bitch," Sloane muttered to herself as she weaved her way to her car through the hospital parking lot. If anyone had told her that an Assistant United States Attorney was the brother and son of a cartel drug lord, she'd have thought they were nuts. With every step she took toward the car, though, she became more convinced the gray-haired man was the kingpin. If that were true, she'd stumbled across the largest corruption scandal in her memory. She didn't know much of Quintrell's job history, but she had no doubt his deception spanned many years and several states.

The moment she escaped the earshot of passersby, she dialed Finn. "Pick up, pick up, pick up." The call went to voice mail. "Damn it, Finn. Call me." Her mind raced after hanging up; she needed to up-channel this. She dialed her boss. "L-T, I tailed Quintrell to Valley Hospital in Santa Rosa."

"So he took the bait," Morgan West said.

"Get this. Quintrell is Caco's brother."

"He's what?" West's voice ended in a sharp uptick. If her reaction was anything like Sloane's, she needed a moment to process the news.

"Caco and Quintrell are brothers, I tell you. Quintrell met Caco's father, wife, and son here. I overheard them say 'brother,' so I struck up a conversation with the wife, and she all but confirmed it."

"This just got huge," West said. "Where's Quintrell now?"

"He's still in the hospital." Sloane unlocked the unmarked sedan, slid into the driver's seat, and shut the door. "I got the impression Caco's-slash-Quintrell's father is key to all of this."

"Did you get any pictures of this man?"

"Security has him on video. They're sending me the files."

"This is good work, Sloane. We should have enough to get an arrest warrant on Quintrell."

"What about the old man?"

"Quintrell is the one we want. He's the leak. If he wants a deal, he'll give us the man he works for."

Sloane finished the call, unhappy with West's orders. She waited in her car, watching the hospital entrance and tapping her phone on the steering wheel. She wanted Finn's take and willed her to return her messages. As curiosity turned into concern, she received a text from Doctor Freeman. It read: *FYI, John Doe died at 11:17.*

"Damn it, Finn. Where are you?" Her mind focused, and she remembered Finn saying something about a classified briefing today. She might not even have her phone with her.

On her own and with circumstances changing fast, she needed to decide who to follow if Quintrell and the others separated. Even if she woke Eric, he was an hour away, which wasn't much help. *Think, think, think.* Lieutenant West was electing to take a conservative, by-the-book approach, but her instincts told her the old man was who she wanted.

Within minutes, she saw Quintrell, the gray-haired man, Rosa, and Antonio emerging from the main entrance. She only had moments to decide who to follow. When Quintrell split off, she kept her eye on the rest of the group. Moments later, a Lincoln Town Car pulled up to the entrance, and Rosa, Antonio, and the gray-haired man hopped in.

"Screw orders."

Training be damned. Sloane didn't suspect Quintrell had made her, and she had no reason to think he would run. He would have to wait. She followed the Town Car. As they were pulling onto the freeway, she spotted Quintrell's Mercedes coming up from behind and fell back, allowing Quintrell to settle into a position right behind the Town Car.

She eased back in her seat with a smirk on her face. "Nothing like making my job easy."

With thick midday traffic, it took every ounce of skill for Sloane not to lose the cars and yet remain a reasonable distance back to avoid detection. Once they crossed the Golden Gate, she had the advantage. They were on her turf. She anticipated traffic patterns, even lane changes, and remained confident they wouldn't spot her.

When their informal caravan turned onto Polk Street, her senses perked up. This was the route on which she'd previously followed Quintrell as he headed to his office in the Federal Building. She began to doubt her theory. If the Town Car stopped there, that meant the gray-haired man didn't fear law enforcement. Maybe Quintrell hadn't worked with them.

At the next corner, the Town Car turned left while Quintrell's Mercedes continued toward the Federal Building, dispelling her doubt. Sloane pounded the steering wheel with a fist. "I knew it."

She followed her instincts, leaving Quintrell on his own. Two miles and several turns later, the Town Car stopped at the street entrance of a luxury hotel. With no place to pull in behind it, Sloane drove forward, parked in front of a pharmacy two shops down, and adjusted her rearview mirror. When a backseat door of the Town Car opened curbside, Rosa exited, followed by Antonio. Seconds later, the car merged back into traffic. Sloane followed it. Minutes later, they were eastbound on the Bay Bridge. Shifting taller in her seat, she tightened her grip on the wheel to ready herself for unexpected moves.

"All right, show me who you are."

Half an hour later, the car turned onto Peralta Street. Deep in the Lower Bottoms of Oakland, this was the same street where Miguel Rojas said he had introduced Caco to his brother Diego, the now-dead drug dealer who had put all of this in motion. When the Town Car parked, she pulled to the curb several houses short and checked the house numbers. They were where Los Dorados managed their operations.

"Son of a bitch. I knew it."

Her pulse quickened. When a tattoo-laden guard held the front door open for the gray-haired man, she clenched a fist so hard she dug her nails into her palm. Caco and Los Dorados reported to this man. He, in his flashy, white suit, had made her a widow.

"I'm taking down your whole damn operation."

Inside

For the first time, El Padrino stepped into the filthy, unfurnished headquarters where his beloved son had run the northern operations of the family business for the last two years. Scant light filtered through the wooden slats covering the windows, and dust covered everything in sight, even streaking the linoleum floor. This wasn't how he liked to maintain any of his bases of operations, but his son was right. To avoid the interest of law enforcement, it needed to blend into the rest of the neighborhood, inside and out.

His guard led the way to the back where every Los Dorados lieutenant stood gathered to hear their feared cartel leader's orders. No one moved a muscle. Word had already spread that Caco had died, and the dread in the room was palpable, with heavy breathing and sweat making the air rank. Each man lining the walls dared not look Padrino in the eye and turned his gaze to his feet, including the one in khakis and a nylon bomber jacket. His clean-shaven face and attire stood out in the sea of tattoos, three-day beards, jeans, and leather. *That must be Gringo, as Caco called him*, thought Padrino. His unique knowledge would be essential by the end of the day.

The bodyguard motioned for Caco's second-in-command to take a position in the center of the room. The younger man stepped forward, his eyes still focused on the floor. Padrino considered up and down the man who Caco had said was indispensable. Who he said he trusted with his life. That assessment would soon be tested.

"Look at me, Rafael." Padrino waited for their eyes to meet. "You are now in charge."

"El Padrino, we are saddened by Caco's passing."

Padrino offered him a slow nod, the sting of losing his son guiding his every action. "Report on production."

"Caco was waiting for heat from the DEA to cool down before replacing the lab in San Francisco. The four remaining labs have upped production by twenty-five percent to compensate."

"And what of sales?"

"Unchanged."

Another nod from El Padrino. He motioned for his bodyguard and whispered something in his ear. The guard announced, "Except for Rafael and Gringo, clear the room."

The others filed out. Once the last man closed the door, El Padrino steeled his eyes. "My brother tells me Los Ochos are watching closely. They must be shown that if they dare to strike at my business or family during my time of mourning, they will pay a steep price."

"What are your orders, El Padrino?" Rafael asked.

"We strike at the ones responsible for my son's death. DEA Agent Finn Harper and San Francisco Detective Manhattan

Sloane will feel my pain." He turned to Gringo. "Find out all you can. You have one day."

Outside

Sloane couldn't risk losing track of the gray-haired man in the rundown neighborhood of the Lower Bottoms. Idling at the curb between two decades-old cars whose faded paint and body dings told their ages, she wasn't well camouflaged, but she had no other choice.

One guard maintained watch on the front porch of the house the old man had entered, while a second had a prime perch on the nearest street corner. There were likely more, but her attention was already divided. Last month, gangs had targeted cops in this neighborhood, so she remained vigilant, checking her mirror every few seconds. She cracked a window open a few inches not only to ventilate but to alert her to any sounds or movement outside her door.

A number of men filed out of the house, a few chattering but most walking in silence. Once off the porch, they spread out in different directions like locusts. Soon, the gray-haired man reappeared. Behind him were two men, one dressed differently from the other two and carrying himself with an air of middle-class suburbia, not street toughness. Her eyes followed him until the gray-haired man entered the waiting Town Car.

When the car pulled away from the curb, Sloane did the same, following several car lengths behind. She'd already confirmed a connection to Los Dorados, and she wasn't about to lose him. At the next block, the sedan turned right. Moments later, another vehicle whipped into the traffic lane at an angle between her and the Town Car, cutting her off.

Damn it!

She maneuvered to go around, but a second car, coming from the opposite direction, stopped next to the first, blocking her route. She eyed the men driving both vehicles and suspected they were from the headquarters.

They made me.

She breathed so fast, she thought she might pass out. Alone, outnumbered, she had only her sedan, her Sig Sauer, and two extra loaded magazines.

No way forward.

She checked her rearview mirror. A third car was roaring up the middle of the street. If it stopped, it would box her in, leaving no avenue of escape. In front of her, male passengers in each of the cars blocking her leaned out of their windows. They aimed pistols in her direction. She had no time to weigh options.

She slammed the car into reverse. Then flinging her right arm over the back of her seat, craned her neck to look out the back window and floored the gas pedal. The tires squealed, the smell of burning rubber wafting through the cracked window and accenting the gravity of the trap she was in.

Gripping the steering wheel like a vise, she jigged her car toward the side of the approaching vehicle, where she assessed she had a higher chance of getting by. With only inches to spare, she wedged the tail of her sedan between a parked car and the one barreling toward her. A bang and jolt signaled she'd collided with both vehicles, the impact forcing her jaw to clench hard.

The grating screech of metal scraping on metal at an increasing speed sounded like nails on a chalkboard. She gasped, unable to take another breath, as a passenger in the other car pointed a gun past its driver and toward her. She ducked and the shot whizzed past her head, sending her heart into overdrive.

Sloane continued to gun the engine in reverse. The sound of scraping metal grew louder until she pushed the back half of the other car out of her path. The only sound then was the squeal of skidding tires and the roar of the engine. She'd beaten back the immediate threat but wasn't out of danger yet.

At the next corner, she turned right, slammed on the brakes, threw the shifter into drive, and sped off. A quick check of her rearview confirmed no one followed. Hands shaking and damp from nervous perspiration, she continued to speed. Thoughts flew through her mind at lightning speed.

Get to Finn.

Caco died.

Quintrell and the old man are cartel.

Finn didn't answer her phone.

It all added up: Finn could be in danger.

Regulations required her to stay in Oakland and report the shooting and accident, but she had to get to Finn. Continuing toward the Bay Bridge at high speed, she dialed Finn's number. Still no answer. "Damn it, Finn!" She dialed Eric. No answer. "Where the fuck is everybody?" She threw her phone on the passenger seat.

When she pulled onto the freeway, a virtual wall of cars blocked her path. "Fuck!" She pounded her hand on the steering wheel. There was only one way to get through it. She hit her siren and flipped on the emergency lights camouflaged inside the windshield between the visors. The red and blue flashing glare along with the long, wailing scream of the siren parted the cars in front of her like she was unzipping a jacket, though it still took repeated nudgings of the siren to make her way through.

With each passing minute, her mind conjured up one nightmarish fate after another for Finn. Was she shot? Was she lying in a hospital? A morgue? Each gruesome image had her heart racing as fast as her battered sedan. Minutes later, she parked in the underground lot at the Federal Building. She hobbled at a fast clip to the building entrance, ignoring the painful throbs in her left foot.

At the elevators, she tapped a fist against her thigh, hoping to take the edge off the wait and the pain in her foot. On the way up, she continued to pound on her leg. She was sure she'd have a bruise for days. The lit numbers on the control panel couldn't count up quickly enough. When the doors slid open, she flew down the hallway as fast as her boot allowed. Inside the DEA office suite, she rushed to Carol, who was seated at her secretary's desk.

"Agent Harper? Have you seen her?" Sweat dripped from her forehead. Panic had set in her voice.

"Sergeant Sloane, right?" Carol's eyes narrowed with curiosity. "She's—"

Movement over Carol's right shoulder caught Sloane's attention. Her breath caught when Finn appeared at the threshold of her office door. "Thank God." Sloane moved in and swept Finn into her arms. Her body trembled as she buried her face in the crook of Finn's neck. She couldn't reciprocate yet, but the words Finn had whispered in her ear at the site of her parents' death replayed in her head. *I love you too*, she wanted to say.

"I thought I lost you."

"Lost me?" Finn relaxed her embrace. She scanned the room left and right as if checking to assess who might have seen them. "You're not making sense."

Prichard poked his head out of his adjoining office. His expression and gesture hinted a concern that Sloane's presence might jeopardize their investigation. "What's going on, Harper?"

"I'll handle it, sir." Finn respectfully waved him off before redirecting her attention to Sloane. "Come into my office."

The door closed. Sloane spun Finn around and took her into her arms again. The warmth of Finn's body reassured her she was safe. *I love you. I love you*, her heart thudded. Her nerves settled a little, but she couldn't break their embrace. When Finn dropped her arms, Sloane grasped her hand and focused on it.

"You didn't answer your phone. I thought they got to you."

"Who?" Finn tipped her head to look Sloane in the eyes.

"Los Dorados. They made me. I barely escaped."

"They came after you?"

Sloane nodded with the vigor of unfolding relief. "Caco died. I followed his father to the Oakland house. When he left, Los Dorados ambushed me. Then you didn't answer your phone. I thought…" A horrifying image of Finn lying in a pool of blood forced her to cover her mouth with her other hand.

Finn pulled Sloane into another embrace. "I'm so sorry I worried you. I was in the SCIF most of the day. When I got out, my phone was dead." She pulled back and moved them toward the chair in front of her desk. "Last I knew you were following Quintrell toward Santa Rosa. What happened?"

Sloane overfilled her lungs, taking in a calming breath. On the exhale, her hands stopped shaking. "Quintrell went to the hospital. Caco's father, wife, and son were there. The way I piece it together Quintrell is Caco's brother."

"What?" Finn's eyes rounded like hockey pucks. "How?"

"I overheard Quintrell and the old man mention 'brother.' Then I chatted with Caco's wife, and she said Quintrell was her son's uncle."

"Holy shit. He has access to everything. Every case. Every piece of intel." Finn collapsed in the chair.

"It floored me, too. When Caco died, I followed his father to the house Diego's brother mentioned. I staked it out and tried to follow him when he left, but Los Dorados boxed me in and started shooting."

"I almost lost you?" Finn's eyes welled with the same tears Sloane had struggled to hold back since she realized Finn could be in trouble.

"You didn't lose me." Sloane pulled her up into her arms again, thankful that bullet hadn't found its target. "My only thought was to get to you."

CHAPTER SEVEN

The entire Vice/Narcotics Division floor had gone quiet. Despite the time, late in the workday, there was not a single sound. Everyone, from rookies to bombastic old-timers with loose ties and rolled-up sleeves, stood stunned in the wake of the public dressing-down that had just been doled out to Sloane. Eventually, the sound of the men's room toilet flushing on the floor above broke the silence.

Over the years, Sloane had committed her fair share of minor infractions, both as a street cop and a detective, one or two of them earning her a verbal reprimand. Today, thanks to her blatant disregard of proper procedure, it was fully deserved. The bureau captain's tongue-lashing had not only embarrassed Sloane, however. If the faces of the others were any measure, it had also mortified everyone who witnessed it.

Sloane had to admit that leaving Oakland after the ambush was stupid. She hadn't, however, expected Captain Nash to deliver the reprimand in the department's version of the public square.

The glass doors of the division flapped shut behind the captain like saloon doors after a big Wild West shootout. When the dust cleared, one of the old-timers sought to break the tension that had settled like stale air. "Captain sure has his panties in a wad today. Pay him no attention, Sloane. You did good out there today."

That affirmation from the old male guard, followed by the collective grumbling in agreement, didn't escape Sloane. In their eyes, she'd earned her chops as "one of them" and confirmed she was their equal. That meant more to her than any of the medals the brass had pinned on her chest over the years.

"Let's get back to work, everybody," Lieutenant West said in a reassuring voice. "Sloane. Decker. My office."

Once inside, West settled into her well-worn desk chair. "First, I covered for you with Nash and the others. I told them you were there on my orders following up on a tip related to Los Dorados. Second, I don't agree with the captain's tactics, but we both know you should've reported the ambush the minute you were in the clear."

Sloane kept her contrite gaze on West, bracing herself for a second ass-chewing. When Eric opened his mouth, likely to defend her, West raised an index finger to shush him. "Having said that, I would've done the same thing. Agent Harper is your partner in this case, and my primary concern would've been for her safety."

The tension in Sloane's neck eased.

"Now, I expect you to accept punishment as a professional." West paused at Sloane's respectful nod. "Good. A one-day suspension without pay after we close this case should do it. Consider yourself reprimanded." West winked. "You concentrate on the case, and I'll clear up this mess with the Oakland PD."

A knock on the closed door paused their one-sided conversation.

"Come in." West stood to change seats to her conference table. When the door opened, she smiled, her demeanor instantly brightening. "Kyler, right on time."

"This is the biggest case of my career." Kyler Harris returned the smile, one that hinted at attraction, Sloane thought, as well as a professional eagerness. "Wouldn't miss this for anything."

Once seated, West said, "Today, Sloane not only confirmed Quintrell is the leak but that he's Caco's brother."

"You're kidding." Kyler's jaw slackened. She turned to Sloane, eyes wide in a stunned expression. "What evidence do you have?"

"He took the bait today and went to Caco's hospital room where he met Caco's family. I engaged one of them in conversation and determined Quintrell was Caco's brother."

"You're sure?" Kyler's eyes widened even more.

"Positive," Sloane said. "The wife confirmed it. She said the older man with her was her husband's father, and Quintrell was her son's uncle. I have no doubt the old man is the head of a cartel."

"What makes you think that?" Kyler asked.

"I followed him to that house in Oakland we told you about, and when he left, Los Dorados ambushed me."

Eric briefly placed a comforting hand on Sloane's shoulder. Hours had passed, but her close call still had her on edge. His reassuring touch helped ease the tension.

"Glad you made it out." Kyler offered Sloane an appreciative nod. "So, why am I here?"

"Since the ambush, Prichard has been antsy," West said. "I'm not sure how much longer I can hold him off from bringing in DC."

"Damn it." Kyler shook her head. "I was afraid of this. What can I do to help?"

"I thought your boss might have some pull with him," West said. "Maybe hold him off for a few days while we follow up on the father."

"I'll set it up," Kyler said. "With DA Cole making a run for mayor, she has every reason to keep this case local."

"In the meantime, we find out what we can about these new players." Sloane mentally kicked herself. She didn't regret her concern for Finn but realized her overreaction might cost her control of this case. She recalled Finn's words to Prichard when she reassured him that they were on the right track: "We can still leverage Quintrell. His father is the key. We learn all we can about him, and we'll have Quintrell."

* * *

The moment Sloane entered the DEA technical operations center steps behind Finn, she regretted ditching her outer jacket. Air-conditioning in the high-tech room was on high to counter heat produced by multiple computer servers and half a dozen large, mounted monitors. Seeing that the four technicians in the center of the room were wearing jackets and bulky sweaters at their workstations confirmed it—she was woefully underdressed.

"Hi, everyone. We need the room." Finn's directive contained the right amounts of authority and politeness. Each tech saved their work, gathered up their belongings, and filed out. Their grumble-free compliance gave Sloane the impression that Finn was well respected and her orders were commonplace. Once the door shut and Sloane handed her a flash drive, Finn took her position at a workstation. "Let's see if we can get a hit on this mysterious gray-haired man."

While Finn worked the keyboard, Sloane moved a second chair to sit next to her. She focused on her hands as they glided across the keys, the same hands that only days earlier she'd been caressing as if they were already lovers. But on that roadside, their connection had gone beyond the physical. They had shared something so powerful that they'd become closer than she'd ever been with Avery. The panic she flew into earlier when she feared Finn might be in danger proved it.

I should tell her.

Finn concentrated on the images flashing on the monitor as the facial recognition program compared still images from Valley Hospital against national and international databases. Sloane shifted her gaze to the angles of Finn's jawline up to her eye. Her skin showed the lines of maturity, but lying beneath it was the same youthful face she fell in love with decades earlier. Sloane parted her lips to tell her as much.

"Finn..." Maybe Sloane's wistful tone caught Finn's attention, because when she turned, her eyes seemed to expect something tender.

"Yeah?" A loud beep came from the computer running the facial scan. Finn returned her stare to the monitor. "We got a hit."

Sloane spun toward the screen, and the tender moment evaporated. "That's him." She read the words on the monitor aloud, the rage that had subsided after the wildfire working its way to the surface again.

"Arturo Campos, a.k.a. El Padrino, suspected head of the Sinaloa Cartel headquartered in Mazatlán." Her blood boiled at the smugness on the face of the man who set her wife's death in motion. "You were right all along, Finn. Los Dorados is part of the cartel."

"But you made the connection, Sloane. He's the big fish we've been looking for."

Sloane didn't expect Finn to pull her close by the cheeks and press their lips together in celebration. She didn't expect her mind to go blank and the seething in her blood to recede. Only one other woman had been able to calm her with a touch of a hand or a caress from her lips, and she had married her.

The moment Finn pulled away, Sloane was sure it was only a matter of time before they were lovers. For now, though, she had to focus on doing what she did best—investigating.

"He *is* the big fish," she said. "But we need Quintrell first, and I know how we can get him."

"And how do we do that, beautiful?"

The pull between the would-be-lovers was more palpable than ever. Sloane took in a deep breath, fighting to concentrate as Finn grazed a finger down her cheek.

"The sister-in-law." Sloane nodded confidently, her skin still tingling where Finn had touched her.

"She didn't pop on any intelligence agency system," Finn noted. "That tells me the cartel went to great lengths to keep her low profile."

"The question is why. They're hiding something," Sloane said. "The way Rosa talked about Quintrell, I get the feeling they used to be lovers and that she'd rather be anything other than a cartel wife. Rosa's our angle."

"What do you propose?"

"We offer her an out."

* * *

In the elevator from the luxury hotel's parking garage to the lobby, Sloane forced herself to focus on details of the investigation. Finn's citrus scent, however, made it difficult. She didn't have much time to sift through options on how to leverage the tension she sensed between Rosa and El Padrino. Whatever plan she came up with, Padrino needed to be nowhere in sight.

Concentrate, she reminded herself. *Stop thinking of orange trees.*

Finn placed a hand on Sloane's arm. "Sloane?

"Huh?" Sloane pulled her mind back to the moment.

"I asked about your call with Reagan? Was she disappointed you missed her game?"

"Sorry. She said it was all right, but I could hear it in her voice. She worries when I'm not home. That's why I haven't told her about the ambush yet."

"Do you plan to tell her?"

"I have to. After the fire, she asked me to consider a new career, and we promised to be honest with each other."

"Are you thinking about quitting?"

"I'm weighing my options." Sloane wrapped a hand around Finn's. "And that terrifies me. A cop is the only thing I ever wanted to be and now—"

The elevator door swooshed open, revealing Eric, who had been waiting for them. Heat rushed to her face. More than a partner and more than a friend, he was family. He unconditionally had her back even when she didn't deserve it. Before this case ended, she owed him the truth. The moment she began to question if she still could take a bullet for him, she should've told him.

Eric tossed his chin toward a secluded area off the lobby. Sloane and Finn followed.

"I checked the hotel security video and tracked Rosa to a suite on the twenty-third floor. Room service said she and a younger man were in there an hour ago."

"Good." Sloane could rely on Eric to have all this worked out by the time she arrived. He was always quick to take action. That made the uncertainties she had about the job ten times worse. He deserved a partner who wouldn't flinch when he needed them the most. She swallowed her doubts long enough to focus on the present. "Does that mean the old man isn't there?"

"Video doesn't show him coming back yet." Eric shook his head. "He's staying in the suite right across the hall, so security will call me if he rolls up."

This boded well, but if the delicate chat Sloane planned to have with Rosa had any chance of working, she needed to play it out fast and with tact. "I think Rosa might react better if it's only Finn and me. Eric, you should stay down here and warn us if Padrino returns."

It took some convincing, but he agreed.

On the twenty-third floor, Sloane knocked and a voice called through the suite door. "Who is it?"

Sloane raised her badge to the level of the brass peephole and spoke quietly. "San Francisco Police. We need a word with you."

Rosa opened the door a foot and gave a sign of recognition. "You? I saw you in the hospital."

"Yes, Rosa." Scanning over Rosa's shoulder, Sloane didn't spot anyone else in view. "I apologize for the ruse. Is Antonio asleep?"

Rosa appeared unnerved at Sloane's intimate knowledge of her life details, the response she needed in order to keep Rosa thinking she knew more than she did.

"May we come in?" Frustration grew in Sloane when Rosa stood her ground. "Look, Rosa, we know Arturo isn't here. We have another team watching for him. If you're concerned about your son's safety, you'll want to listen to what we have to say."

Rosa reluctantly swung the door open to allow Sloane and Finn inside the sitting area of the posh two-bedroom suite.

After inviting them to sit on the dark blue cloth couch, Rosa sat on the matching armchair to its side. "What is this about?" Uncertainty laced her tone.

Sloane decided her first assessment of an unwilling cartel wife was accurate. She stuck with her initial plan. "I know your husband passed away today, and for that I'm sorry. Though, in the waiting room, I got the impression your loss might be welcomed. Am I wrong?"

Rosa gave a tentative headshake.

"We're here to offer you and your son a way out. We know it hasn't been easy for you, raising a son with special needs under El Padrino's reach." Sloane had Rosa's attention. Now, she had to choose her words wisely to not tip her to the fact that she'd reached the end of her intel. "We know it's difficult having the man you once loved so far away. Living under a different name. Doing El Padrino's bidding to further their drug operation. I'm sure you had other hopes for him."

When Rosa's bottom lip quivered, Sloane knew she'd hit the mark. She glanced at Finn and gave her a nod.

"I'm with the DEA. We can offer you and your son US citizenship and federal witness protection if you help us," Finn said. "We can make it so El Padrino will never find you."

Rosa raised her head, the rims of her eyes red and swollen. "How can I help you? I know nothing about the business."

"But David does," Sloane said, hoping Quintrell hadn't changed his first name. "We know he's been using his position to pass along information to your husband and El Padrino's organization. We need you to get him to tell us the truth so we can shut it all down."

"I can't." Rosa shook her head. "David is a good man. If he goes to prison, his father will kill him. He's the *real* monster."

Sloane reached for Rosa's hand, begging her with her eyes for her cooperation. "Rosa, my wife was killed because your husband rigged one of his drug labs with a bomb. She left behind a daughter not much younger than Antonio. I'm asking you as a parent to help us stop this. If David is the good man you say he is, given a way out, he'd want to stop the killing."

"Are you saying he won't go to prison if he helps you?"

"We can't promise that," Finn said. "But we can promise a deal that will keep him safe and get him back to you sooner."

Sloane's phone buzzed, alerting her to an incoming text message: *Padrino in lobby.*

"Your father-in-law is on his way. We have to go." Sloane stood and handed Rosa one of her business cards. "Think about it overnight. If you're willing to help, call me, and we'll get you and Antonio out within the hour."

After a quick exit, Sloane and Finn proceeded to the lobby, where they found Eric with another narcotics detective team huddled in a secluded corner.

"Hey, Jim. Art." Sloane shook their hands. "West send you?"

"Yeah, she figured your team would need a break tonight. Eric filled us in. We'll tail this Padrino guy overnight."

Sloane pulled out her iPhone and texted a picture to Jim. "Keep an eye on this woman too. She's in the suite across from him. Call me if she tries to leave."

"You got it, Sloane." Jim took up position in the lobby while Art returned outside to surveil the hotel exit.

Sloane turned her attention to Eric. "I think we might have her. I'm guessing if she wants to run, we'll hear from her in the morning after her son wakes up."

Eric pressed his hands on her sagging shoulders. "All right. You've had a long, rough day. Go home, get some sleep, and let's regroup here around seven."

The excitement and weight of the day had hit Sloane and drained her of energy. She needed food and sleep in that order. "You're right. I'm running on fumes."

"We all are." Finn stroked Sloane's back, the touch relaxing her like a smooth cocktail.

"You hungry?" she asked Finn, hoping she'd say yes.

* * *

At the Shaker-style coffee table in Sloane's townhouse, Finn set up the Chinese takeout she and Sloane had picked up on the way there. When she finished organizing each selection along with plastic utensils and napkins, her gaze tracked to Sloane in the kitchen. Pouring water for each of them, Sloane turned with full glasses in hand. Their eyes met.

Are you ready? Finn thought before saying, "You look tired."

"I'm exhausted." Before sitting, Sloane placed a water glass next to each place setting.

"How was Reagan?" Finn asked her question with enough concern, she hoped, that Sloane wouldn't mistake it as idle chitchat.

"Sleeping. I left a note on her dresser mirror so she'll see it when she wakes up."

"You're a great mom."

"I'm working on it." Sloane's smile seemed reluctant, but even Finn could tell she was easing into her new role as a single parent. And the best part—it appeared natural.

"Mmm, mint water?" Finn savored the familiar taste. She'd forgotten Sloane had served it the last time she was here—when they were planning how to track down Caco.

"You've spoiled me," Sloane said. "It helps me drink my eight cups a day."

Finn didn't realize how hungry she was until she took her first bite. Words about the case and Reagan passed between them until they finished their food. When their plates were empty, Sloane leaned back on the couch and yawned, Finn's signal it was time to call it a night.

"I should get going," Finn said, wishing she didn't have to. She bent over the coffee table to gather the containers and used utensils, but Sloane wrapped a hand around her wrist and pulled her back.

"Please, don't go," Sloane whispered into her ear. "I don't want to be alone tonight."

Finn had wanted to hear those words since the day she walked back into Sloane's life. Their intimate encounters had left her hoping she'd hear them soon. Now that she had, though, she couldn't tell what Sloane had in mind. Was her request an overture for another physical encounter or merely a desperate plea for companionship? She welcomed either but didn't want to take advantage of Sloane's raw emotional state.

Sloane leaned in, nuzzling Finn, her warm breath leaving a moist trail from the soft patch of skin below Finn's ear to the crook of her neck. That made what she wanted pretty clear. Letting Sloane push her back against the couch cushions, Finn melted into the lips that were still exploring the soft skin along her clavicle. What thoughts were going through Sloane's mind when she positioned her body atop hers? Did she want Finn's legs wrapped around the backs of her knees? Did she want Finn's hands to slip beneath her dress shirt and up the smooth skin of her back? Finn gave her both, and Sloane rewarded her with a hard thrust into her hips. To hell with companionship. Sloane wanted sex, and so did Finn. Mind and body in sync about the matter, she wanted Sloane's lips and hands to explore every inch of her.

Sloane untucked Finn's shirt between powerful thrusts. Her hand crept to a patch of exposed belly skin and slid under her waistband, the sensation curling Finn's toes. Sloane's fingers inched down Finn's skin like a lion sneaking up on its prey, her abdomen shuddered, craving for those fingers to be inside, pumping her toward orgasm.

The point of no return had arrived. She pressed Sloane's face into her neck. Seconds away from being touched, her core clenched in anticipation. "Please, Sloane."

But then Sloane's movements inexplicably slowed. Seconds later, they stopped altogether. When Sloane withdrew her hand and rubbed her face along the top of a breast, Finn knew she wasn't ready, even though the full weight of her body was pressed against Finn. She ran her fingers through her hair, soothing her. Within moments, Sloane's ragged breaths settled into a predictable rhythm and then turned into a gentle snore. Exhaustion had overtaken her.

Without hope for more intimacy, Finn cradled her in her arms. Would Sloane dream tonight? Would her dreams bring her peace?

She brushed through Sloane's silky hair again, hoping both for her, and whispered, "Sleep well, babe. I love you."

CHAPTER EIGHT

Lower back muscles strained when Sloane shifted her half-asleep, facedown body. Movement beneath her caused her to stiffen. *Oh, God.* Her eyes sprung open to conduct a quick inventory of her surroundings. She was lying half-atop Finn, a position she assumed she'd stayed since falling asleep last night.

As the fog of sleep slowly receded and pale light brought things into focus, she struggled to recall what had happened after she begged Finn not to leave. Flashes of their bodies pressed together and the need to touch, skin to skin, flooded back, but things blurred after that. She took a sharp breath. *Did I? Did we?*

Managing to sit up without waking the woman beneath her, Sloane studied her relaxed face and outstretched, alluring body. Both fascinated her. Was it too soon to have sex? She'd always loved Finn and had made peace with that. Hadn't she? But last night something had held her back. She needed answers. More importantly, she needed coffee to clear away some of this mental haze.

The moment she lifted Finn's legs to escape from the couch, Finn stirred and said without opening her eyes, "Good morning, beautiful."

"Good morning, you."

Sloane cringed. Her impersonal reply was out of character, proof she needed time to process what was going on. Last night became clearer, starting with the uncontrollable desire to have Finn beneath her and ignite the heat that had been simmering inside. When Finn had wrapped her legs around her for the first time, the craving to touch her had exploded. But the moment she swept a fingertip across the first line of Finn's short, coarse hairs, she froze. She couldn't be sure whether fear or exhaustion stopped her, but the last thing she recalled was collapsing into Finn's arms.

She grabbed the hand Finn held out, blindly searching for her. "I'm sorry about falling asleep like I did."

"You were wiped out." Finn pried her eyes open and propped herself up by the elbows. "Though I must admit you left me in an uncomfortable state."

"I don't mean to tease you endlessly, but—"

Finn placed an index finger over Sloane's lips. "You have nothing to explain. We'll know when the time is right."

Finn was right. When she was ready, she wouldn't pull back, and Finn would already know that she loved her. A grin snuck up on Sloane as she conjured up a time when nothing would hold her back, a time marked by romantic, dim lighting and soft sheets. She kissed Finn's hand before standing. "Coffee?"

"Yes, please." Finn stretched her arms above her head and rolled her neck, working out the knots from a night on the couch. "If Rosa takes our offer, this could be a long day."

Once in the kitchen, Sloane prepared the coffeemaker, hoping it would cooperate this time. She made a mental note to buy a new one before it crapped out for good. When she turned toward the refrigerator to retrieve the creamer, a handwritten note tacked to its door by a magnet caught her attention. She read the first line, her legs weakening at the knees. "Shit."

"What's wrong, babe?" Finn came up behind her, placing her chin atop Sloane's shoulder and a hand along her hip.

"Reagan saw us on the couch last night." She scanned the rest of the message and read it aloud. "'Saw your note and came up to check on you. Found you and Finn asleep. This is hard, Mom. I went to Deni's house to think. I'll see you after school today.'"

Sloane crumpled the note in one hand and leaned against the edge of the counter with the other. "I knew something felt wrong. We shouldn't have fallen asleep together. She didn't react well when I broached the subject of you. This is all too fast."

"Go. Find her." Finn rubbed her back, but it did little to ease the sting of regret Sloane was feeling. "I'll go home to shower and meet you at Rosa's hotel later."

Sloane pulled Finn close, savoring every inch where their bodies touched while she could. If Reagan was unprepared to see her with another woman, she'd do whatever was necessary to put her first. She didn't want this to be the last time she'd hold Finn in her arms, but she'd do what she had to, even if it meant breaking her and Finn's hearts. She inhaled Finn's scent one last time. "Thank you for everything."

* * *

Fog and damp ocean air coated the Scotts' plastic front porch chairs with moisture, leaving Sloane no choice but to stand. With so much on her mind, she couldn't stand still though. She paced the slick wooden porch slats in her fresh clothes and walking boot, gripping her cell phone and hoping she hadn't completely messed things up. Checking her watch, she figured she'd wait two or three more minutes for a return text before calling Reagan.

The front door cracked open. Reagan took one step out, shivering and clutching the midsection of her light sweater. Her thin pajama bottoms appeared inadequate against the chilly morning air. "It's too cold, Mom. Come inside."

Once they were inside the entry hall, the warm air loosened Sloane's tense muscles but couldn't steel her sheepish voice. "I wanted to make sure you were okay."

"I'm fine." Reagan kept her head down, her gaze trained on the worn carpet.

Sloane lifted Reagan's chin with a fingertip. "You don't seem fine. I'm sorry about last night. I shouldn't have let Finn stay."

"I understand you two are getting closer." Reagan's lips quivered. "But it was hard seeing you together." The tears threatening to fall from her eyes tugged at Sloane. "You and Mom used to fall asleep like that."

Those words and the pain in Reagan's eyes broke Sloane's heart in two. *What have I done?* She pulled Reagan into an embrace, ashamed of her selfishness. Ashamed that she'd put her needs above her daughter's. She questioned everything she did last night. *Why did I ask Finn to stay? Why did I allow myself to fall asleep in her arms with Reagan downstairs?*

"I'm so sorry, honey." For several minutes, they held each other, crying. When Reagan quieted, Sloane pulled back and braced herself, issuing a cleansing breath. "Finn is important to me, but you're my priority. If you're not comfortable with her, I'll stop seeing her outside of work."

"No, Mom." Reagan shook her head. With certainty? Sloane couldn't be sure. "Whatever happened to you two during the fire, I can tell you're less sad now. Maybe you were right. I should try to get to know her."

Those words partially doused Sloane's doubt, making her think that moving forward was possible. "How about we invite her over for dinner?"

"I'd like that."

"Thank you, honey. It means a lot to me that you're trying. I'll set it up as soon as we're free." Sloane handed her some money from her wallet. "Here's something for lunch and extra if you want to order pizza tonight. I have a complicated case and might not be home for dinner." Guilt worked its way back into Sloane's throat. She'd missed too many dinners for her liking this week.

Reagan smiled as she folded the bills into her bra. "Maybe you should feel sorry more often."

"That's the Reagan I know and love." Satisfied they were back on the right track, Sloane let a lopsided grin form on her lips. "Invite Emeryn over if you'd like, but no going into your room with him, all right?" When Reagan rolled her eyes, Sloane sensed her uneasiness had passed—at least for now.

CHAPTER NINE

When the buzzer sounded, Sloane pushed the heavy door open with a shoulder. She stepped inside the hotel's dimly lit security room, balancing a bag of breakfast wraps and three coffees wedged into a cardboard to-go tray. She needed a moment for her eyes to adjust to the darkness, the primary illumination coming only from a dozen large-screen monitors tiered along two walls.

Though she only caught a glimpse of her back and at a slight angle, Sloane spotted Finn's unmistakable shoulder-length hair pulled back around an ear. The sight of her smooth, white neck made her hungry again for that patch of exposed skin. Her memory flashed to the way Finn's breathing had become ragged with arousal last night and spurred her to touch more skin. Before, in the interview room, she'd entertained the idea of sex for its physical properties. But last night, when she covered Finn's body with her own and pushed their hips together, she had wanted it for how it brought her closer to Finn. She was letting go of Avery a little more every day.

Before Sloane took another step deeper into the dark room, she realized that Avery didn't cross her mind once last night. *Letting go shouldn't be this easy*, she worried. Thumbing the gold band around her left ring finger, she admitted she wasn't ready—not yet—to relegate the woman she had woken up next to for over a year to a distant memory. *Time*, she thought. She just needed more time.

She squared her shoulders and her emotions before walking past the on-duty, twenty-something, athletic, male guard scanning the various monitors. She placed the food and drinks on the console in front of Finn. "I wasn't sure if you took time for breakfast."

"Just a banana." Finn's stomach rumbled like the sound of distant thunder when she peeked inside the white paper bag. "Ooohh, this smells good."

While Finn distributed the sandwiches, Sloane handed one of the coffees to the guard. His simple head nod, absent a thank you, hinted at annoyance about police oversight. *Too freaking bad.* Once seated in a chair next to Finn, Sloane angled her chin toward him. "A little testy," she whispered.

Finn whispered back, "Which is why I'm here. Eric got a bad vibe."

Sloane glanced over her shoulder at the guard. Did Eric sense shadiness or incompetence? Based on his wrinkled uniform and fascination with his cell phone, she guessed the latter and nodded.

"How did it go with Reagan?" Finn dug into her sandwich.

"She's having a hard time."

Finn's chewing slowed to an almost nonexistent pace. "I understand."

Sloane checked to make sure the guard still had his head buried in his phone before grazing Finn's hand. "She wants to get to know you. We want to make you dinner."

"Really?" Finn half-smiled. Her chewing picked up again, a sign she was as relieved as Sloane.

"Yes, really." Sloane tempered her good feeling. If she had misgivings about moving too quickly, Reagan would too. *Take it slow. Don't force it. Dinner would test the waters well enough.*

Sloane and Finn finished breakfast and provided a restroom break to Eric, who was sitting stakeout in front of the hotel. When the clock neared ten, Sloane grew concerned Rosa wouldn't take their offer of witness protection. Her phone alerted her to an incoming text message from Kadin: *Arranged home study. Call me.*

"Damn, she's fast," Sloane mumbled.

Finn glanced over, but Sloane yanked her phone from her view. She immediately regretted her kneejerk reaction. Being jealous felt foreign and didn't suit her. No wonder the insecure types never lasted long with her. Jealousy, she was learning, was toxic.

"I gotta make a phone call about the adoption. I'll be right back."

Finn stopped Sloane with a hand on her forearm. She glanced at the security guard as Sloane had before and lowered her voice. "I don't want this thing about Kadin to be weird between us."

"It's not." Sloane gave her a reassuring smile that did little to assure herself it wasn't true.

She stepped into the hallway and leaned against the wall to think. Her eyes focused on the ceiling, searching for an answer to this foreign, disconcerting feeling. Avery never gave her cause to worry, and before that, her string of fuck buddies and one-night stands never called for it. Finn was a different story. Her history with women differed from her own. Finn only did relationships, and having an ex woven so tightly into her life picked at Sloane's patience.

"Kadin's just doing me a huge favor," she told herself. Blowing out a long breath to recapture her composure, she swiped her phone and dialed.

"Hello, Kadin. You work fast."

"Glad you reached me, Sloane. I called in a favor from a contractor for whom I did pro bono work. He cuts no corners and says he'll play this one by the book, but he's willing to move you up in the queue. Can you meet him at your house tomorrow after Reagan's school lets out?"

"I'm not sure. I'm working on an intense case right now."

"I remember with Finn how investigations can be unpredictable."

Kadin's not-so-subtle reminder of their intimate past prompted Sloane to slide the phone away from her mouth to stifle a sigh. *Focus*. Moving it back, she replied, "I can try to be there, but no guarantees."

"I get you're busy. He just has to run through the house and interview you and Reagan. Since Reagan is almost seventeen, he can conduct the interviews separately if he has your permission."

"That could work out."

Sloane wrapped up her call and returned to the security office, pausing inside the door. Her gaze fell upon Finn as she studied the monitors and watched for any sign of Rosa or Padrino. She was lucky. Finn had come back into her life, and the last thing she wanted was for jealousy to screw up what they were moving toward.

Sloane retook her seat, and Finn met her with a concerned expression. "Everything okay with the adoption?"

"It's going well. Kadin's pulling strings to speed up the process."

"She's great like that. Kadin always gets what she wants." Finn turned her attention back to the monitors.

Then again…maybe I should be worried.

Moments later, Finn tapped her on the arm. "We have movement."

Sloane focused on the action on the monitor—a suite door opened. When Rosa stepped out, Sloane hoped she'd have a suitcase in hand and Antonio on her heels. Alone instead and dressed in sunglasses and athletic wear, Rosa carried only a smartphone and a set of earbuds, dashing hopes of her cooperation. Within seconds, a large, business-suited Hispanic man stepped out of the suite across the hall. Without so much as a nod of recognition, Rosa placed a bud in each ear and strolled down the hallway while he trailed behind her.

"She's being followed." Sloane gritted her teeth at the realization their visit last night may have endangered Rosa.

She'd assumed Padrino would have bodyguards around him but with no one obviously standing watch the previous night had dismissed the idea for Rosa.

"We need to get to her and offer an immediate out." The urgency in Finn's voice matched Sloane's.

When Rosa and the man boarded the elevator, Sloane turned to the guard whose phone still had him mesmerized. "Hey, you. Tell me what floor the elevator stops on."

Rolling his eyes, the guard leaned forward in his chair and placed his phone on the desktop. He turned his attention to a computer screen and typed a few things on the keyboard. "Twelve."

"What's on twelve?" Sloane's clipped words and narrowed eyes telegraphed no patience for his lackadaisical work performance.

"Conference rooms and the sports club."

Sloane turned to Finn. "Do you have any workout gear in your car?"

"Yeah, why?"

"I have an idea, but with my boot, you'll have to make initial contact."

* * *

A rhythmic thudding flooded the reception area when the glass door leading into the hotel gym swung open. After flashing her badge at the young pimple-faced brunette at the welcome desk, Finn clipped it underneath her waistband and covered it with her flowing tank top. "Official business. I won't be long."

She grabbed a towel and a complimentary bottle of water to blend in with the rest of the guests. Once she entered the main exercise room, a cacophony of running treadmills, cross-trainers, and piped-in rock music hit her like a gust of hot air. It all blended to create a hypnotic hum. The smell of sweat grew stronger the further in she went. A mix of hotel guests and business types had filled the room to about half its capacity and were working to fit in their cardio following the early morning rush.

She spotted her target. Rosa had worked up a mild sweat in her form-fitting leggings and long-sleeved warm-up jacket, maintaining a leisurely pace on an elliptical machine. Finn continued to scan the room and found the man who had followed Rosa, likely one of Padrino's bodyguards. He was watching her from across the room, along the wall farthest from the reception area, a vantage point that provided a good view of everyone on the floor. A bulge near the inside left flap of his suit coat hinted he carried a weapon.

Finn approached the elliptical machine next to Rosa's, crossing her path. Rosa's pace slowed, a sign she'd recognized her. Without looking up, Finn turned at an angle to shield her face from the goon. "Keep going. Don't look at me."

Finn flung her towel over the front console and placed her bottle in the cup holder, keeping her back to the guard. "In five minutes, go to the women's locker room. He can't follow you there. My partner will meet you."

Finn mounted the machine, set a timer for five minutes, and began a slow-paced workout. Rosa kept her mouth shut and her focus on the television screen mounted on the far wall. The passing minutes bordered on excruciating. Nailing Quintrell and shuttering Los Dorados' drug operation rested on what this scared cartel wife did in the next few minutes.

When the timer on Finn's machine counted down, Rosa didn't alter her gait. Finn debated how much longer she should wait until she should pack it in. Another minute passed. Then another. *Damn it. We've lost her.*

The next minute, Rosa stopped her workout and dabbed the sweat from her face and neck with a white cotton towel. Without as much as a glance toward Finn or the guard, she walked toward the locker room.

Thank goodness. Finn continued her workout without altering her pace, her gaze on the bodyguard as he took up a position right outside the door after Rosa entered. Given his evident impatience, she hoped Rosa wouldn't take long to convince.

Inside the locker room, Sloane cracked open the door from the accessible stall and leaned around the doorframe for the sixth time. One woman washed her hands at the sinks. Another changed clothes on the bench anchored to the floor in front of a short row of wall-mounted lockers. There was no sign of Rosa. *Patience*, she reminded herself. Rosa was scared and simply needed more time to build up the courage.

Within moments, Rosa was nearing the toilet stalls, her gaze searching. Sloane waved her over. Closing the stall door behind Rosa, Sloane said in a low, reassuring voice, "We know Padrino's man is following you. Did he find out we were there last night?"

Rosa offered a shaky nod, one that confirmed Sloane's suspicion—she was terrified. "His man told him I had visitors. I told Arturo you were hotel management, addressing a complaint I had about housekeeping."

"Did he believe you?" Sloane ran her hands up and down Rosa's arms, eliciting a wince. She instantly regretted not being more careful last night. "Did he hurt you?"

Rosa said nothing, but her expression was that of a scared and desperate trapped animal. Sloane sensed that she wanted to reach out for help.

"I know leaving is scary, but you and I both know staying is worse. We can protect you and Antonio." Sloane realized she struck a nerve when tears dropped from the corners of Rosa's eyes. "Do you want to come with us?"

"I don't know."

"We don't have much time before your bodyguard comes in here. Decide. Yes or no."

Rosa's eyes darted back and forth. She bit her lower lip. "Yes, but I need to get Antonio."

Sloane took in a deep, relieving breath. "Go back to your suite. Don't pack your bags. Only take what you can fit in your purse or a backpack. If you take more than that, Padrino's man will get suspicious. Say you're going sightseeing. Go down to the ground level. When you exit the main doors, look right. You'll see a dark blue sedan parked in front. Hop in. My partner will take you to a safe house."

"But Padrino's man—"

"Let us worry about him. We'll make sure you both get away."

When Rosa's hands shook, Sloane had but one chance to ensure she wouldn't change her mind. Careful not to apply too much pressure and aggravate whatever injury Padrino had inflicted, she wrapped her hands around Rosa's and looked her in the eye. "Trust me. This will work. You and Antonio will be safe."

Rosa flinched when a locker door slammed but gave Sloane a firm yet shaky nod.

"We'll be set up in fifteen minutes," Sloane said. "We'll wait, but don't take too long."

Padrino was already suspicious, which meant Sloane had little time to account for his armed guards. Taking Rosa and her son to safety wouldn't be easy.

* * *

Unsure when Padrino might leave the hotel, Sloane leaned against an interior wall near the first-floor building entrance, trying to settle her nerves. She rechecked her watch. *Twenty-two minutes*. They had no time to waste, and Rosa was seven minutes overdue.

Finn rubbed Sloane's arm. "She'll come."

"I don't know, Finn. She's terrified." Sloane punched her thigh to tamp down her doubts. "If I only pushed a little harder."

"If you had, you would have lost her for sure. Be patient."

Another five minutes passed. Sloane thrust herself off the wall and paced the width of the sleek, modern building lobby. Every time an elevator door opened and Rosa didn't step out, Sloane's confidence waned. "She's not coming."

"Maybe she's having trouble getting her son ready." Finn's calm voice did little to soothe Sloane's nerves.

"Maybe—" Sloane's cell phone rang. She stopped pacing and answered it. "Sloane…got it. Thanks." She sent a short text to Eric and then slid her phone back into her pocket.

"Security said they're coming, and the goon is with her." Sloane slid a hand inside her jacket and wrapped her palm around the butt of her holstered Sig Sauer. Having her firepower within a second's reach reassured her they'd have the upper hand.

Soon, an elevator door swooshed open. Rosa stepped out, adjusted the backpack slung over her shoulder, and guided Antonio by the elbow. Her ashen face revealed her nervous state. Sloane gave Rosa a slight nod, imperceptible to anyone not looking at her, sending the message they were ready.

Rosa, Antonio, and the goon walked toward the main doors where Sloane and Finn waited. When they passed a foot beyond them, Sloane drew her weapon and held it against her outer thigh to not draw attention. Finn did the same.

This was it. The cartel paid their bodyguards well, which meant their lives were expendable. When killed doing their jobs, the cartel compensated their families. But when they failed, the cartel exacted swift punishment and their families got nothing. The goon guarding Rosa wouldn't blink twice about shooting to prevent her from being taken.

As the goon opened the glass door for Rosa and Antonio, a black Town Car pulled up two car lengths behind Eric's unmarked sedan. *Shit*. Sloane's breathing and pulse quickened. She hoped he'd spotted it too and readied his weapon.

As Rosa and Antonio passed over the threshold, Sloane stepped behind the goon and held the tip of her gun against his neck. "Police. Don't move." He remained still, but Sloane prepared for resistance and pressed harder.

Finn pushed Rosa and Antonio out the door toward the right and Eric's waiting sedan. Her head pivoted left toward the idling Town Car. "Hurry, hurry!"

At the Town Car, the front passenger door opened. A hulk in a suit as black as his hair emerged and took off toward Finn and the others. Sloane had only a moment to react. With every ounce of her strength, she slammed the barrel of her gun against the back of the goon's head. The loud crack buckled his knees, sending him to the floor. As she maneuvered her booted leg over him and darted through the door, the man from the Town Car pulled a gun from his waistband and trained it on Finn.

"Nooooo!" An image of Finn lying on the sidewalk in a pool of blood momentarily blinded Sloane. *Not her*. In a millisecond, everything of importance came into sharp focus: Finn, Rosa,

Antonio, the sedan, the Town Car, and the armed man. Her racing pulse calmed to a protracted, deafening beat. Her index finger steadied on the trigger while the rest of her fingers tightened on the pistol grip. She fired. Once. Twice. Center mass. A string of blood floated in the air. The man toppled to the sidewalk, the blood spattering beside him.

Panicked screams pierced the air, breaking Sloane's focused trance. Pedestrians stampeded like a wild herd, yelling, "Gun! Gun!" In the pandemonium, some dove to the ground for safety, while others took refuge behind cars and other objects.

Rosa screamed and crouched on the sidewalk, trying to pull Antonio with her. He remained frozen with his hands covering both ears, uttering low-pitched screams.

Finn dove for Eric's sedan and opened the rear passenger door. Rosa flew inside, but Antonio refused to move. Finn tried to push him inside, but he wouldn't budge.

Meanwhile, the driver's door on the Town Car swung open. A second man stepped out, a gun pointed toward Antonio and Finn.

Eric flew out of the driver's door, swung around, and aimed at the second man. "Police!" The man didn't yield and fired one shot—a miss. Eric got off two powerful blasts and the man dropped to the street, a crimson pool oozing from underneath his body—a sure sign he would soon be dead.

All her senses heightened, Sloane's head spun like a whirly top, searching for danger. Her eyes first searched for Finn—she was safe. No time to be thankful. A simple grab-and-go had turned into a public shootout with two men dead. They'd taken down the apparent threats, but she couldn't chance others being in the car or hotel. She approached Eric's sedan, listening and looking for anything and everything and readying to use her service weapon if another target appeared. "Get Antonio!"

Holstering his gun on the fly, Eric ran around to the passenger side and wrapped both arms around Antonio, eliciting even louder screams. Though he and Eric were similar in height, Eric struggled to lift Antonio's feet off the ground. Adrenaline eventually won the battle.

From the backseat, Rosa yelled, "Don't hurt him."

Eric dragged and threw Antonio in the backseat and then jumped in beside him. Finn flew into the front passenger seat and Sloane jumped in the driver's seat and slammed the gas pedal to the floor. The tires screeched, and the smell of burning rubber seeped into the cabin. In the rearview mirror, Sloane saw tears rolling down Rosa's face while she tried to quiet Antonio's shrieking.

Sloane's heart raced, matching her speed down Market Street as she dodged the midmorning traffic. She had to get to a protected area. She glanced over her shoulder at Eric. "I'm going to Bryant."

"Good, good. We can regroup there," he said over Antonio's screams.

"Shhhh. It's all right." Rosa positioned her face in front of her son's. She placed her hands over his, providing an extra layer to muffle his ears from the loud noises around him.

When the chaos in the car settled and Sloane's pulse slowed, she took Finn's hand. As Antonio quieted, she drew their hands to her lips. With her eyes still focused on the road, she whispered, "I could've lost you."

Finn squeezed her hand for several beats. When they glanced at each other, briefly locking eyes, she mouthed the words "I love you."

I love you, too. Sloane wished she could have mouthed the words too, but the courage to do so still hadn't come to her. She instead reluctantly put the hand down and drove as if their lives depended on it.

* * *

Twenty-three stories up, a juice glass tumbled in the air toward a wall in the luxury hotel suite. Orange liquid spun over its lip and, for a split second, floated as if suspended in midair. When the glass crashed against the large television, both shattered, launching splintered shards in every direction.

Not a minute earlier, Rosa's escort had interrupted Padrino's morning meeting. He'd told him of a woman police officer who'd hit him over the head and knocked him out. And how, when he came to, two of Padrino's men were dead on the street the officer had left, and Rosa and Antonio were gone.

Padrino turned a cold eye on the man. He twisted his mouth like lightning bolts to hold back the thunder brewing inside him. "Describe her."

The man's head hung low. No matter what he said, his fate was sealed. His hand-wringing meant he knew it. "I can't. She was behind me."

Padrino walked to the window. On the street below, police cruisers and an ambulance had arrived. His men could do nothing more. He snapped his fingers over his shoulder at his lieutenant. "Take care of him."

Padrino knew his instructions needed no explanation. The man had made his last mistake, and no one would ever find his body. The lieutenant pointed at two other men standing near the door. Like well-trained soldiers, they came up behind the man, each grabbing an arm with ruthless pressure. They dragged him, struggling, to a bedroom in the suite, his heels leaving raised trails on the carpet in their wake.

All the way the man yelled, "Padrino, no. I can find them."

Moments after one of the soldiers kicked the door shut, the goon's screams were muffled and then stopped. It was done.

Padrino turned from the window. His square jaw tensed as he turned to his lieutenant. "I know it was her. What has Gringo told you about Manhattan Sloane?"

"She's squeaky clean. Widow. Lives in Hunters Point with her daughter, sixteen. No other relatives."

"And Finn Harper?"

"Also clean. Unmarried. Lives in a condo on Market Street. Daughter of a prestigious lawyer."

Knowing that Los Ochos was preparing to strike at the slightest sign of weakness, Padrino couldn't afford not to act. Manhattan Sloane and Finn Harper had to pay the price for taking his son and now his grandson. Padrino's voice turned icy. "Eye for an eye. Take their family."

CHAPTER TEN

One by one, Antonio lined up his french fries, setting them side by side, equal distances apart, on Sloane's desk according to length, from longest to shortest. He arranged each one meticulously with an end butted against an imaginary line, the graph-like row seemingly providing him with a sense of order that countered the chaos he'd gone through a few hours earlier. Placing the last fry in its appropriate position, he began eating them, one at a time, working his way from shortest to tallest.

Sloane considered the young man. If not for him being on the spectrum, what barbaric things would Caco and his grandfather have had him doing? Would Caco have conditioned him to be a good soldier and do whatever he asked because money and power were his rewards? Would Caco have ordered him to plant the bomb that killed Avery?

A part of Sloane wanted to hate him because of Caco, but she couldn't. Antonio wasn't anything like the man who helped raise him. He was an innocent amidst the death and chaos his family created. "You're just a boy," Sloane mumbled.

Antonio chewed more of his fries. "I'm a good boy."

"I'm sure you are."

The door to the squad room swung open, and Rosa walked in, her visit to the restroom to wash her face appearing to have helped clear her head. Sloane looked to Finn, who was right on Rosa's heels. *Why can't I say I love you?* It should come easy as it did with Avery. Was she reverting to her old ways, retreating from love to protect herself from inevitable heartache? She hoped that wasn't the case, but the fact that it was a possibility raised questions. Answers, though, would have to wait until this case ended.

Rosa dabbed her puffy red eyes with a tissue. In a raspy voice, she asked Sloane, "When can I get him to a hotel?"

"My partner is working on that," Sloane said. "Maybe in a few hours. Until then, we've asked David to be here in half an hour."

"So soon?" Rosa's face turned ashen again, a sign she might be on the verge of regretting her decision.

Finn grabbed the guest chair by Eric's desk. "Here, Rosa. You should sit."

"I know this is coming fast." Sloane patted Rosa's hand, a gesture that would likely come short of easing her nerves. "But after what happened at the hotel, we need to strike now. Our bosses can keep a lid on things for only so long."

"You're sure they'll keep their word?"

Sloane's expression softened. "Do you trust me?" Rosa's nod was firm. "I trust Agent Harper with my life. She's assured me if you hold up your end, you and Antonio will go into federal witness protection."

"But what if David doesn't cooperate?"

"After what you told me, I think he will." Sloane gave Rosa's hand a gentle squeeze. "Trust that he's the good man you say he is."

Sloane looked over her shoulder toward the next set of desks. "Hey, Jim. Mind taking Antonio now?"

"Sure, Sloane," Jim said. "The kid and I will be fine."

Rosa slid her hand up and down Antonio's back before kneeling to meet his eyes. "I'll be right back. Be a good boy and go with Jim. He'll get you more food and drink if you want it."

Without an apparent worry in the world, Antonio rocked in his chair, keeping his focus on two remaining fries. "I'm a good boy."

"Yes, you are." Rosa patted his hair and then followed Sloane and Finn.

Morgan West checked her watch when Nate Prichard walked through the squad room doors with David Quintrell in tow—twelve minutes late. Though that was early if she went by Quintrell time. Prichard gave her a quick headshake, signaling that Quintrell had given no sign he knew what was in store for him.

"Agent Prichard. Mr. Quintrell." Morgan shook their hands. "Thanks for coming. You remember ADA Kyler Harris?"

"Of course," both men said and shook Kyler's hand.

"I hear you've stumbled across a big break in Los Dorados case. Let's make this quick." Quintrell ended with his expected smugness.

Sloane had prepared Morgan for his brusqueness. "He's a pompous ass through and through. Just make him feel like he's in charge," she had said.

"Yes, sir. Follow me." A smile from Morgan and returned wink from Kyler meant they were on track. Morgan waved her arm toward a corridor to the left of her office. She then gave another detective a nod, signaling him to send a prepared text message to Sloane and Eric.

Fox in the house. Sloane read the text before tucking her phone into her jacket pocket and giving Finn a nod. Everything they'd worked toward for the last few months was about to come to a head. Diego, who sold the drugs that killed Shellie Rodriguez and Michael Wong, was dead. Diego's cook, the man who manufactured the drugs, was dead. Caco, who managed the drug operation and ordered the booby trap that killed Avery, was dead. Only two known links in the chain remained—the cartel leader who financed the drug operation and Quintrell, the leak in the federal government who helped him. In minutes, she hoped to snare both.

"He's here," Sloane told Rosa. When Rosa's hand shook atop the interrogation room table, Sloane gave her one last calming pat. "You'll do fine. Just like we practiced."

Sloane stood and paced the length of the small room in her walking boot, waiting for the signal to begin.

Sloane's phone buzzed, but she didn't have to read the text informing her that everyone had assembled with Quintrell in the observation room on the other side of the two-way mirror. She tried to imagine Quintrell's reaction when he realized Rosa was on the other side of that glass seated across from her. Would he give any hint of recognition, or was he the sly fox she expected? Either way, if he was half as smart as she suspected, he had to feel a noose tightening around his neck.

She stopped pacing and slammed the folder she was holding atop the table. That part she hadn't practiced with Rosa, hoping to elicit a genuine reaction. Rosa recoiled in what Sloane could only construe as fear. "Let's go over this again."

Taking a seat next to Finn, directly across from Rosa, Sloane opened the folder and flipped through several papers fastened to the inside top edge. "You've been married to Vasco Sánchez, a.k.a. Caco, for over twenty years, and you're telling me you know nothing about his business."

Rosa shook her head. "Our marriage was one of convenience, not love. We were never close."

"But you have a son together. You must have been close at some point," Finn said.

"Caco is not his biological father."

"Well." Sloane closed the folder. "This just got interesting. Who *is* Antonio's father?"

"It doesn't matter. He was a man I dated in college. When he moved to the United States, I had no way of contacting him. Caco married me out of pity, to give my unborn child a future, not a father."

"I see." Finn leaned back in her chair. "So his birth father didn't abandon him because of his deficits?"

"No." Rosa shook her head with the vigor of truth. "He doesn't know he has a son."

Sloane read a second text from Eric: *On the hook.* She slid her phone back in her pocket. That meant Quintrell was beginning to circle the chum they'd thrown in the water, and it was time to reel him in.

From the folder, she drew out a photograph, a duplicate of the one Eric had ready in the observation room. "Who is this man?" Sloane pointed to a snapshot of El Padrino from the hospital security cameras.

"My father-in-law, Arturo Campos," Rosa said.

"But your husband had a different last name?"

"Arturo adopted him when he was twelve."

"Arturo? Is he also known as El Padrino?"

"I've heard his business associates call him that."

"Is he head of the cartel in Mazatlán?"

"As I told you, I know nothing of the business."

Sloane laid out a second picture from the hospital and pointed to it. "And this man. Who is he?"

"My brother-in-law."

"What is his name?"

"David Campos." Rosa buried her face in her hands and wept.

Sloane stood and turned toward the two-way mirror behind which she'd trapped Quintrell with nowhere to run or hide. She couldn't see him, but she could smell his fear. Her stare turned as cold as ice. "Gotcha, you son of a bitch."

Rosa leaped to her feet, her eyes pleading for the man she'd fallen in love with decades ago, not the despicable man Sloane hated. "But you promised to keep him safe."

Sloane whipped her head around, jaw clenched. She'd led Rosa to expect mercy, and she'd thought she could give it when she concocted this plan. But Quintrell was the one who'd leaked the information that led to her wife's death. Mercy was the last thing she wanted to show him now. David Quintrell, a once-trusted officer of the court, deserved retribution. "My wife is dead because of him and his family. He needs to rot."

"You promised to do the right thing. You told me to trust you." Rosa shrank back. "You're as bad as Caco and Arturo—take what you want, no matter who you hurt."

Sloane had manipulated Rosa into a corner—the stamp of good police work. On most days, this part of her job left a bad taste in her mouth, but not today. Having David's head on a platter tasted good. Mired in murderers and drug dealers every day, she walked a minefield, caught between good and evil, right and wrong, and the law and justice. She gave a mental sneer. Bad was bound to seep into her skin at some point.

Finn whispered in Sloane's ear. "Do the right thing."

Sloane closed her eyes to the path she'd turned down. She recalled her wife's words to her when she'd announced that she was going to go after Diego, the decision that had set all of this in motion. *"I know you, Manhattan Sloane. You always do the right thing."*

This wasn't the path Avery would've wanted, and if Sloane were honest with herself, it wasn't one she was proud of. She bit the inside of her cheek, the coppery taste that resulted reminding her this case already had spilled too much blood.

"All right, Rosa. I'll do my best to convince him to tell us everything he knows. If he doesn't, we may still need your help. Are you up for that?"

Rosa nodded as if David's life depended on it.

A burst of confidence shot through Sloane. Even the leaky pipes from the restroom one floor above the interrogation room were pitching in, filling the space with an odor that was literally nauseating. Quintrell's usual arrogance was muted, though not his air of self-assurance. Thus far, he hadn't said a word. He was a lawyer and prosecutor, so Sloane held little hope of tricking him into saying something he didn't intend. Perhaps, though, she could make him want to talk.

She didn't rush her next tactic. With Eric seated next to her at the metal interview table, she thumbed through case folders they'd compiled on David. Running her finger down the first page one line at a time, Sloane counted out loud. She flipped the page and continued counting. When she came to the end of the list, she closed the folder and turned to Eric. "Forty-six."

Eric shook his head. "This will be a mess."

"Forty-six drug cases that Quintrell—" Sloane glanced at David. "Correction. Forty-six drug cases that Campos prosecuted that were not related to Los Dorados or his father's cartel. These guys will enjoy having him on the cellblock."

If not for the bead of sweat rolling down a corner of David's forehead, Sloane wouldn't have guessed she'd caught his attention. He straightened his suit jacket. "Other than legally changing my name, what do you think I've done?"

Sloane slowly lifted her gaze to meet David's eyes. She had him talking, and now she had to get him talking about his father. She cocked her head, sizing him up for the kill. "I don't think anything. I know you tipped off your brother about Diego Rojas. His death is on you."

David raised a single curious eyebrow.

Eric pulled a sealed evidence bag from his coat pocket and placed it on the table. "After you left the Federal Building, we executed search warrants on your office, home, and car. We found your burner. It matches the number that called Caco's burner following the lab explosion and the day Diego was killed in lockup."

David's eyes darted back and forth, signaling his awareness that Sloane and Eric had him on the ropes.

"You're probably wondering how we knew his number when we didn't find Caco's phone after the fire." Sloane grinned, relishing her next words. "Your brother may have thought he had it all worked out—kill Diego before he could lead us to him. But Caco didn't count on Diego surviving the cartel hit long enough to tell Eric his burner number. After that, tracking down Caco's phone was child's play. And this little puppy," she tapped David's burner, "called Caco."

"You never had a head for the business, did you?" Eric snickered. "If you did, you would have chucked the phone after the fire. Then again, we've been on to you for quite a while."

"What do you want?" David's expression remained unchanged.

"Besides taking down Los Dorados and choking off the supply chain?" Sloane narrowed her eyes. "I want your father."

"He's one fish you'll never hook. His hands are always clean."

"Which is why we're willing to offer you a deal." Sloane thought she might vomit on those words, but she'd made a promise. "You give us enough for an arrest while he's still on our soil, and we'll put you in protective custody for the duration of your sentence."

"We both know he has a reach beyond any protective custody. If he wants me dead, he'll get to me."

"You're his son. Surely he wouldn't come after you."

David burst out in maniacal laughter before slamming his hands on the tabletop, causing Sloane to flinch. His eyes turned flinty, resembling Sloane's vengeful mood before the fire. "I'm his blood, but Caco was his son. If I help you, Father will get to me. If I don't, his competitors will. Either way, I'm dead."

"What about your son? Do you care what happens to him?" Sloane asked.

"He can't be my son."

"Why? Because he has autism?"

"That has never mattered to me."

"Then what is it?"

"He's too young. He couldn't be mine."

"How old do you think he is?"

"Twenty."

From the case file, Sloane pulled out a folded yellowish piece of paper. Unfolding it, she placed it in front of David. "Your father can wipe out government records but not personal copies hidden from him."

David read the information on the birth certificate. "How can this be?"

His stunned look told Sloane he was ready for her final push. "I'll let Rosa explain."

Not an hour earlier, Rosa had told Sloane it no longer mattered if the truth caught up to her. She'd spent decades fearing an ill-timed wistful gaze or a slip of the tongue whenever David visited. But today, Rosa was beyond the prying eyes and ears of the Mazatlán family compound. She was free to unearth the truth Padrino had forced her to bury.

Standing on the other side of the two-way mirror next to Eric, Finn, and the others, Sloane watched as they reunited, holding her breath. She was betting the reality in that birth certificate had had time to sink in and that David realized now that Padrino merely considered him another pawn to manipulate, not blood.

Inside the interrogation room, David's jaw clenched when he slid the certificate across the table toward Rosa. "Tell me why."

"You never came back to Mexico City after graduation and never returned my calls. What was I supposed to do?" Rosa leaned back in her chair and folded her arms in front of her chest, refusing to accept blame.

"You weren't supposed to marry Caco." He sharpened his words to a fine point, cutting to the heart of the truth.

"Your father gave me no other choice."

David straightened the flaps of his suit coat and then his back. "Tell me everything."

Grateful that Rosa's skin had toughened over the years, Sloane blew out a relieved breath. She would soon reel in everyone who had a hand in her wife's death.

Rosa stiffened. "When I found out I was pregnant, you had already disappeared. Caco was the only one in your family I knew, so I went to Mazatlán. I told him it was important, but he refused to help until he knew why. I had to tell him you were the father."

"And I'm sure he dutifully told Father."

Rosa nodded. "A week later, Arturo came to my apartment in Mexico City. He told me you had found someone else and moved away, that you were to marry the following month. I was heartbroken."

"It wasn't true."

Rosa's eyes softened. "I learned that the first time you visited the compound and you had no wife with you."

"I remember." David shook his head. "That was when I learned you had married Caco and had a son. He was what, two?"

"We told you two, but he was three."

"He was so tall for his age. I guess I didn't doubt Caco was his father."

"That's what Arturo wanted you to believe. He made it clear he wanted to be part of Antonio's life and for him to have a family legacy. That's why he arranged for me to marry your brother."

"After you learned I hadn't married, why didn't you tell me the truth then? Did you love Caco?"

"How could you ask such a thing?" Rosa wept. "No, I never loved him. I had no choice. Your father threatened to take Antonio away if I told you."

"I see my father manipulated you just as he did me. I'm sorry you were caught up in my family's mess. Had I known, I would've—"

"You would've disobeyed your father, and who knows how that would have turned out."

"I know things haven't turned out as we talked about at university, but I can make up for it right now." David stood, turned, and stared into the two-way mirror. "Sergeant Sloane, I'll take that deal."

* * *

The international drug operation involving Los Dorados in California and the cartel in Sinaloa employed every breed of criminal. From the dealer on the street to the mole in the Justice Department planted years ago, they all worked in unison to peddle their drugs. To those investigating this case, David Quintrell, a.k.a., David Campos, was worse than Diego Rojas, only the first in a long line of dominoes to fall. His betrayal cut deep, and everyone wanted a piece of him. Sloane was first in line.

While David stewed in a holding cell and Rosa in the squad room, everyone around Lieutenant West's conference table voiced their opinion on how to proceed. Competition between the overlapping government agencies made consensus seem out of reach.

"This goes beyond the jurisdiction of San Francisco." Prichard flapped his arms, seemingly aggravated with their twenty minutes of bickering.

"I'm not saying it doesn't." Kyler Harris folded her arms across her chest, a sign she'd drawn her line in the sand. "I'm saying capital murder trumps drug trafficking."

"Which is why the DEA should be in charge if we want Quintrell's full cooperation. He'll sing better in the federal system without the death penalty lingering over his head," Prichard said.

"This isn't the time for a pissing contest." Finn squeezed the bridge of her nose. If she felt half the frustration Sloane did, her temples were pounding. "You're both right. We know Quintrell has been working for his father and tipped off Caco about Diego being our confidential informant. Though we still don't know who tipped off Caco about that fake raid in Oakland. We need to find out who did and snare Padrino too."

"Finn's right." Sloane had had enough of Kyler and Prichard's tug-of-war over jurisdiction. It was time to think about practicalities. "Taking this up the chain right now isn't prudent. The important thing is to find out what Quintrell can provide. We could get both Padrino and the other leak."

"How about this?" West turned to Kyler, serving as the voice of calm. "What's your best offer for the Santos murder?"

The Santos murder. Sloane cringed. Those three words strung together stung her. Eric squeezed the top of her shoulder, prompting her to lean into his touch. If anyone knew what those words meant to her, he did. Eric had been with Sloane when she and Avery shared their first and last words, and his comforting gesture meant more than a show of sympathy. It implied he'd always have her back.

"Twenty years," Kyler said.

Only twenty? Sloane swallowed her anger. If not for Quintrell's tip about Diego, Caco wouldn't have rigged that lab to blow and Avery would still be alive. In her mind, twenty years behind bars didn't equate to Avery's life.

"Okay," West said. "I say we let Sergeant Sloane and Agent Harper present the offer with the caveat he turns over enough evidence on Padrino for an arrest. Can we agree on that?"

Prichard and Kyler nodded, placing their power struggle on hold. "Agreed," each said.

* * *

"I never liked you." Talking to Quintrell made Sloane's skin crawl more than the trashy meth-heads she and Eric endured with great frequency. Falling back into an interview room chair, she folded her arms over her chest. She reminded herself, *the enemy of my enemy*. "My wife is dead in part because of you."

"I had nothing to do with operations. That was all Caco."

"Don't bullshit me." Sloane slammed her fist on the tabletop. "You tipped him off about Diego. Because of you, he rigged the lab to blow."

When Quintrell leaned back and adjusted his suit coat, Sloane recognized his tell. His amped-up smugness meant he thought he had the upper hand, and that pissed her off.

"You're focusing on the wrong issue, Sergeant Sloane." David's face took on its trademark haughty expression. "He may have been tipped off, but you're missing the real question. Why would Caco blow up his product and equipment? I knew my brother. He would never risk losing money and never tolerate anyone under his command who did. A bullet to the head was his form of justice. You should ask whose idea was it to use an explosive. And how it got there when you had his lab under surveillance."

Sloane turned to question Finn but was met with a subtle headshake. If true, this insinuation meant the other leak had had a hand in the bomb that killed Avery. A wave of nausea hit her at the prospect. *Focus*, Sloane told herself. "Do you know who did?"

"I told you." He shook his head. "I never involved myself in daily operations."

"Then what *do* you know?" An edge of impatience crept into Finn's voice. "What *can* you give us on your father?"

"His hands are always clean, but I can give you locations of his compounds and where he meets with his lieutenants."

"That could take weeks, months, to gain actionable intel." Finn shook her head in apparent disappointment. "Our deal of twenty years is for something we can prosecute with now."

"I have nothing to offer but myself." David re-buttoned his tailored jacket.

"Are you offering to wear a wire?" Sloane's conscience was clear. She had kept her word to Rosa and hadn't asked David to put himself in harm's way.

"Yes. My father took from me. Now I will take from him."

Working with Quintrell made Sloane sick, but she'd do it if it meant that by this time tomorrow, she'd have one more man responsible for Avery's death behind bars or, better yet, in a pine box.

CHAPTER ELEVEN

"You go ahead." Finn pushed herself back from the table, rubbing the cream-colored silk shirt covering her full belly. "I couldn't eat another bite."

Reagan grinned with the eagerness of a hungry puppy and peeled off one of the last two pizza slices from the oil-stained cardboard box. "Last one's for you, Mom."

"Thanks, honey, but you can have it," Sloane said. *How you've changed.* A year ago, Reagan would've taken the last slices without hesitation. Even Avery had wondered when she would make that final turn from self-absorbed teenager to a considerate young woman. Sadly, it took Avery's death to complete the transformation.

"Thank youuuuu. I hoped you'd say that." Before Sloane could change her mind, Reagan snatched the last piece, revealing a glimpse of the child Avery had left behind.

Despite the long, emotional day and takeout pizza instead of the home-cooked meal Sloane envisioned, the "get to know you" dinner had gone better than expected. Reagan peppered

Finn with questions about family, school, work, and hobbies, while Finn did the same, minus work. The grilling revealed several tidbits about Finn, and Sloane made mental notes of her joy of hiking and baseball. She'd have to invite Finn on another family hike and take her to a Giants game after they put this case to bed.

"So, Mom told me you two liked each other in junior high." Reagan fought a mouth of half-chewed pizza with the zealousness of a dog working on peanut butter. "Were you girlfriends?"

"You wanna field this one?" Finn's cheeks blushed.

"Noooo." Sloane's playful tone admitted her curiosity. She and Finn had only brushed the surface of their childhood crushes, and she craved to hear more from Finn. "I'd rather hear your version."

"O-kay." Finn rubbed the back of her neck as if stalling for time. She turned her attention to Reagan. "No, we weren't girlfriends. When I first saw your mom in choir, I thought she was the cutest thing I'd ever seen. She always wore jeans and a matching jacket that made her look so cool. Kinda like what she has on now." Finn's gaze traveled from Sloane's head to her toes and back up again. In those two seconds, Sloane felt downright sexy.

Finn turned back toward Reagan. "I didn't understand my feelings back then. All I knew was that every time I saw her, my heart raced a little faster and I got all tongue-tied. The most I'd say to her was 'See ya.'"

"I felt the same way," Sloane said. "Since I had no gay or lesbian role models, I thought something was wrong with me." She lowered her head when she recalled the confusion, anxiety, and isolating shame of her younger days. No one had explained having feelings for another girl was natural and didn't mean she was sick. Finn's broad smile reassured Sloane they'd shared the same formative experience.

"Why would you think that?" Reagan asked.

"It was twenty-one years ago," Sloane said. "The Internet was new, and few movies or TV shows had gay characters.

Unless you were around other gays and lesbians, you thought you were alone in your feelings."

"That's sad." Reagan briefly curled her lip. "I'm glad things are different now. So, who made the first move?"

"I guess I did," Finn said. "After choir practice, I'd stall until we were the last two so I could walk out with her."

Sloane smiled so hard at the sweaty-palm memories of those days that her cheeks hurt. "I did the same thing." The pull Finn had on her back then made sense. They'd both sent signals, but neither knew how to read them.

"So that's it? That was your first move?" Reagan chuckled.

"Oh, puh-lease." Finn waved her palm to dismiss the insult. "I had more game than that. One day I worked up the courage to hold her hand on our way out. It felt amazing, but it also terrified me."

"I remember my heart beating so fast that day that I felt like throwing up." The memory that flared up was so strong that the last bits of pizza churned in Sloane's stomach.

"So what happened after that?" Reagan leaned in with piqued interest.

"I had to leave," Sloane answered. Finn's frown matched the emotions tugging at her. "That was the last time I saw her." That hour had been the best and worst one of Sloane's young life.

Reagan cocked her head and opened her mouth as if to ask a question, then her expression saddened. "Oh, I'm sorry, Mom."

The cheerful mood broken, Sloane stood to clear the table. "Thank you, honey. How about dessert?"

"I should be going." Finn offered a halfhearted response as she helped.

"Oh, come on, Finn," Reagan said. "Stay. We have Mom's favorite, Oreo Cookie ice cream."

She asked Finn to stay. Sloane had hoped Reagan and Finn would get along, but Reagan's enthusiasm meant they'd actually hit it off, making her think that moving on with Finn might be possible. With a smile, she pulled the ice cream carton from the freezer. "Please, stay."

"I guess I can stay for one scoop." Finn's grin suggested she didn't need much convincing. *Or longer,* Sloane wanted to add. "At least let me take out the trash." Finn gathered up the remaining napkins and paper plates and placed them in the kitchen trash can. Before Sloane could object, Finn had pulled out the plastic trash bag and tied it off. "Where's the bin?"

"All right, you." Sloane raised an eyebrow, hoping this meant Finn thought of herself as more than a guest. "It's outside the garage on the side of the house."

As Finn grabbed the top of the bag and headed for the front door, Reagan took out three bowls and spoons. While Sloane served up the ice cream, her mind wandered to tomorrow and the things she had to balance. She had to leverage Quintrell to snare Padrino and make it back in time for the hoop-jumping required for Reagan's adoption.

"Before I forget, Kadin set up the adoption home study for tomorrow after school. The contractor is doing us a big favor, so I'll do my best to make it home early. You can let him in so he can get started."

"This is silly." Reagan rolled her eyes. "I've lived here for a year and a half. Why does some guy have to inspect our home?"

"I know it seems over the top, but the court needs to make sure you're safe here." Sloane glanced toward the front door. "So, what do you think of Finn?"

Reagan rolled her eyes again. "She's horrible."

Sloane's jaw fell open. The only word she could get out was, "What?"

A snicker. "J-K. I like her."

Sloane debated how much to press, but they'd promised each other to be open and honest with one another. "Does that mean you'd be okay if I saw more of her?"

"I guess." Reagan's deep sigh and slouched posture weren't convincing. "But is it okay if I still miss you and Mom?"

She thinks I've forgotten you, Avery. The last few days had been crazy, and Avery hadn't crossed Sloane's mind but once or twice. She hadn't even told Reagan a story about her mom in days. *No wonder she's jumped to that conclusion.*

Sloane placed the scoop on the counter before searching Reagan's hazel eyes, which were mirror images of her mother's. They reflected the same sorrow she'd endured for months, the same sadness Finn had pulled her through. She hoped to do better and do the same for Reagan.

She pulled Reagan into an embrace. "Of course, it's okay. I miss your mother every day." Reagan's body quaked, her tears dampening Sloane's shirt. Muffled short gasps reminded Sloane that despite being able to erect a robust outer façade like her mother used to, her daughter was more fragile than she appeared. *Maybe this is too soon.*

Finn returned and cleared her throat. When Sloane lifted her head, Finn's face was etched with quiet concern. Sloane mouthed, "*We're okay.*"

"I'm gonna go," Finn whispered before fetching her purse. "I'll meet you at your office in the morning."

Sloane's eyes met Finn's again, receiving a warm, reassuring message: *You don't have to choose.* When the door closed, Reagan's weeping reached a crescendo. Sloane pulled her in tight. "We're gonna be fine."

* * *

"You're such an idiot," Finn mumbled to herself while merging onto the freeway. Heavy baseball game traffic had her car moving at a crawl, giving her ample time to mull over all things Sloane. She kicked herself for hoping the invitation for dinner would inch her closer to a relationship with Sloane. It felt like the evening had done the opposite, proving Avery's death still troubled Reagan and Finn's presence was complicating her grieving.

"I should back off." She shook her head hard, hoping to knock some common sense into herself.

When her cell phone rang through the car's Bluetooth connection, she hoped it was Sloane calling to tell her everything was better and to come back for ice cream. In that instant, she envisioned herself curled up on the couch with Sloane and

Reagan, chatting about this and laughing about that. The caller ID on her dash-mounted screen, however, crushed that fantasy. She pressed the phone button on the steering wheel.

"Hi, Daddy." Finn sighed.

"Hi, pumpkin. Is this a bad time?"

"It's been a long, hard day, that's all. What's up?"

"I guess you're too tired to meet for drinks."

"You're still in town?"

"I just finished a business dinner at the Pyramid."

"I don't think I'm up to it tonight. Would you mind a rain check?"

"Of course. Give your old man a call this weekend. I'd like to have dinner with you."

Finn continued to creep along in traffic, weighing the idea that she'd have to adapt if she had any hope of Sloane becoming more than just a friend. "Daddy?"

"Pumpkin, is everything all right?"

"No, I feel like nothing is going right."

So much had gone wrong today, most of which she couldn't share with her father. Rosa and Antonio barely escaped in that shootout, and if not for Sloane, she'd be dead. Her high from Quintrell's confession had been tempered by the suggestion that another leak may have planted the bomb. Now she feared she lost all the ground she'd made with Sloane in recent weeks.

"Anything you can talk about?" he asked.

After a long, breathy sigh, she said, "Not really, except for Sloane."

"Things aren't going well?"

"Sometimes I feel like I'm on the end of a yo-yo string. She pulls me in and then lets me go."

"She's struggling, pumpkin, and needs more time."

"I'm trying, but her stepdaughter, Reagan, is having a rough go, too."

"That's right. The adoption. How old is she?"

"Almost seventeen."

"I remember you at that age. You were moody, so I can only imagine what she's going through."

"I don't think Sloane will be ready for a relationship until Reagan is too."

The call made the commute pass faster but solved none of Finn's concerns. Soon, she lay in bed, wondering if she should resist the pull between them and concentrate on friendship for now. She tossed and turned for hours, but found no answers, only doubt. One thing was certain—she couldn't imagine a future without Sloane.

* * *

Wisps of lavender-scented dark blond hair mixed with salt air, tickling Sloane's nose. She inhaled as if this were the last time she'd savor the sweet fragrance she'd come to need like an addict needed a fix. When her breathing settled into a slow, steady cadence, she tightened her arms around Avery from behind. She dug her fingers into the warm gray wool sweater that wrapped her toned frame. Avery angled her head, and every muscle in Sloane's body relaxed.

"You're a great mother." Avery's words floated in the air like clouds.

"I learned from the best." Sloane needed to hear those words, especially from the woman whose shoes she was now filling. She turned to meet her wife's face and pressed their lips together. Oddly, they tasted like Southwestern eggroll, the same flavor they shared with their first kiss. She pulled away and sensed she'd never again know the taste of them.

"I like Finn," Avery said after turning her gaze back to the bay waters.

"Do you think it's too soon?" Sloane used her nose to coax Avery's locks back before nuzzling her neck and inhaling one last time.

"What does your heart tell you?"

"I don't know. That's why I'm asking."

"Does Reagan like her?"

"She said she does." Sloane sighed at the emotional battle Reagan was facing and hoped she didn't compound her grief. "But she misses you."

"I miss her, too."

"She thinks I've forgotten you." Sloane pulled Avery's chin toward her and stared into her hazel eyes, wet with tears. "I could never forget you."

"I know you won't." Avery's smile gave Sloane a sense she was right. "My dear Sloane, it's okay to be happy. Go to Finn. She loves you."

"It's hard letting go." Sloane felt their time ticking away and pressed her forehead against Avery's. "I'll love you forever, Avery Santos."

"I'll love you forever, Manhattan Sloane." Avery's voice grew fainter along with her body. With no desperation in their goodbye, only relief, Avery disappeared into the light.

A poke to her side nudged Sloane out of deep sleep, lifting the fog in her head. She opened her eyes and turned in the direction of the jab. In the dark, she made out Reagan, who had moved diagonally on Avery's side of the bed and was buttressing her feet against her ribs.

Hours earlier, Reagan had asked to fall asleep while watching a movie in bed with her, catching Sloane off guard. That sacred side of the bed had remained empty since the morning of the explosion. The time had come, though, to let go of the place Sloane had last held and kissed her wife.

After carefully shifting Reagan's feet toward the foot of the bed, Sloane sat sentinel, inventorying the similarities between mother and daughter. Besides having the same hair and eyes, she and Avery both had second toes longer than their big ones. *So cute.* Reagan was still a work in progress, but on most days, Sloane could see the loving soul Avery had instilled in her.

You'd be so proud of her, Avery. She's growing up to be so much like you.

She rubbed Reagan's back and whispered. "I'm proud of you, too."

Reagan stirred and mumbled, "Huh?"

"Nothing, honey. Go back to sleep."

Gentle snores signaled Sloane could safely move again. The dream of standing on the deck with Avery in her arms came back.

The kiss had felt real, sparking a sudden craving for Dylan's Southwestern eggroll. She glanced at the alarm clock across the room; the time read 4:06. Too early to get ready for work, but the dream had her too awake to go back to sleep. Maybe some tea would lull her into a restful state.

Drawing the covers back, she swung her feet to the floor. Moments later, illumination from the small red and white dots of various electronic devices in the living room guided her into the kitchen. After microwaving water in a mug, she added a small bag of chamomile, dipping it several times to diffuse the tea. She turned toward the couch, clutching her mug, then sensed a pull in another direction. She turned back, this time toward the dining room.

Sliding the glass door open and stepping onto the deck, Sloane shivered at the chilly bay breeze cutting through her. She laid her cup on a small table before opening the storage bench against the far railing and looking for the blanket she had left there several days ago. She expected to find it on top but instead found it beneath the gray wool sweater Avery always wore when the cold, damp air got to her.

More of her dream came back, and she remembered wrapping her arms around Avery and this sweater. She brought it to her nose and inhaled the strong, familiar scent of fresh lavender. But how could that be? After sitting in the storage bin for months in the salty air and collecting dust, how could it smell like Avery had worn it yesterday?

She put the sweater on, the wool fibers warming her. She latched onto both lapels and brought them to her nose, inhaling again. It was Avery's scent. Picking up the cup of tea, she leaned on the deck railing, the mug heating her fingers as she gazed at the dark bay waters. Uncharacteristically clear, the night sky revealed stars bright enough to outshine the city lights.

A sip of tea warmed her throat, and the wool tickled her arms again.

"Goodbye, Avery Santos. I'll never forget you."

With those final words, Sloane was free. Free to follow her heart. Free to love Finn the way they both deserved.

CHAPTER TWELVE

Though convinced no amount of cream and sugar could turn this brown sludge back into coffee, Sloane held her nose and tried anyway. She was running late and with her home machine acting up, Bryant's break room swill posed her only option. Desperately needing the caffeine rush, she added extra cream and whisked harder, hoping it would help. When the contents lightened to a shade Sloane thought she could stomach, she flipped the stir stick into the trash and latched onto the paper cup. She debated the merits of trading indigestion for the caffeine, but last night's broken sleep dictated her reasoning. *Better nauseous than dead tired*, she thought, especially on a day when she needed to be sharp.

She hesitated before lifting the cup to her mouth. A tug on her arm stopped her.

"You're not going to drink that, are you?" Eric wrinkled his nose. "Only Wilson drinks that machine oil, and that's because he's too damn cheap to spring for the good stuff."

"I wish I had time to stop this morning but—"

"You're not drinking that." He snatched the cup from her hand and chucked it into the round metal trash can stained from years of ill-advised taste-testers. "Besides, Finn walked by a few minutes ago, carrying two lattés. If you don't take yours, I will."

When he turned to walk out, she placed a hand on his arm. "You got a second?" Other than Finn, she trusted him the most. Even when she didn't want to hear the truth, he gave it to her unfiltered. If anyone would give it to her straight about her vision, he would.

"Sure." Eric leaned his butt against the counter, crossing his arms at his chest.

Sloane's confusion must have been plastered on her face because his eyes narrowed in quiet concern. She debated how much of her dream to reveal. Talking to Avery was one thing, but she decided to leave out the parts that felt too real. "You might think I'm crazy, but at times I hear Avery's voice."

"It's not crazy."

"But I talk to her."

"Still not crazy."

"Last night, she told me it was okay to move on."

He turned to face her, his expression soft and caring. "You're grieving. I know you loved Avery, and with Reagan, she'll always be a part of you. Having said that, anyone can see that Finn is good for you. Maybe you needed to hear it from Avery to know it was okay to love again."

Sloane averted her eyes at the memory of last night's dinner with Finn. She got the sense of family but dared not entertain the prospect before Avery came to her. Now, she hoped for the possibility.

"I can say it now." Sloane raised her eyes to meet his. "I'm in love with Finn Harper."

The right corner of Eric's mouth turned upward—his tell. He was happy for her. "Have you told her?"

"Not yet, but I plan to." Reagan had half-accepted Finn, and on her back deck Avery had too. It was time to tell Finn the truth.

"I'm happy for you." Following a smile, Eric nodded his head toward the door. "We should get to work."

She turned the corner in the squad room and spotted Finn staring out the window near her desk, sipping coffee. With each step toward her, Finn's features came better into focus, as did Sloane's confidence. Though it was too soon to entertain the thought of sharing a home and raising Reagan together with her, telling Finn she loved her was a long-overdue first step.

Taking a deep breath, she considered how best to tell her. Over dinner, perhaps. Or maybe in Finn's condo around midnight while they took in the orange glow of the Bay Bridge. Her breath hitched at the possibilities of Finn's reaction. A smile. A kiss. A gaze that said, *I've always loved you.*

When Finn turned, her scrunched-nose smile took Sloane back to junior high choir and the exhilaration of a first crush. That same smile twenty-one years ago had caught her eye and made her dizzy at the realization Finn meant it for her. She wasn't dizzy at the moment, but it felt good knowing she alone could bring out that same heart-stopping smile.

"Good morning." Finn stepped toward Sloane, offering her a cup. "I thought you might have had a rough night, so I brought you coffee."

"You're a lifesaver." Sloane glided her fingers across Finn's hand when she accepted the cup. She was eager for more, but that single touch would have to suffice until they were alone. "It was a little rough, but we got through it. Reagan fell asleep in my bed, and I learned she's a kicker."

"Ahh. When she gets a partner, she'll grow out of it."

"Partner?" Sloane almost spat her sip of coffee. "She's only sixteen."

Finn raised an eyebrow. "And how old were you when you first—?"

"Older than that." A scary image of her walking in on Reagan and her boyfriend making out or worse downstairs in her bedroom made Sloane shudder, earning a laugh from Finn. She wasn't prepared for Reagan growing up like that.

Eric approached and then glanced over his shoulder in the direction of Lieutenant West's voice. "Looks like it's showtime."

* * *

Half an hour later, Sloane was peering through a small tinted side window of the ten-year-old surveillance van. From her position on the narrow bench seat, she could see the two-guard escort team flanking Quintrell. Only an hour away from meeting with El Padrino, he was making his way through a brightly lit section of the underground SFPD garage.

"Damn, he's already dressed."

"You missed it." Eric snickered. "Jailhouse red isn't his color."

Save for the chrome-plated handcuffs he was sporting, Quintrell looked every bit the part of a US Attorney-slash-cartel son, still carrying himself with a splash of arrogance. As much as it pained her to see him dressed in his signature Brioni-tailored suit and Magnani leather wingtips, Sloane needed him to get what she wanted from El Padrino.

"He's going to annoy me all day." Sloane slung a pair of noise-canceling headphones over her neck, mumbling a variety of curse words. Cutting deals with criminals to serve the greater good rarely bothered Sloane, but this time it did. In her book, Quintrell was worse than a criminal. He had severed the thin blue line between order and lawlessness and betrayed the sacred trust he swore an oath to uphold. That, besides his role in Avery's death, she could never forgive.

"I know what you mean," Finn said from the front passenger seat.

"That makes three of us." Eric slid the van side door open, turning his attention and smile to Quintrell. "Good morning, inmate."

Sloane's sour mood sweetened a bit as Eric removed Quintrell's cuffs, Eric's greeting reminding her despite his help today, he would be behind bars for a long time. But first, they had to engineer Padrino's downfall.

The moment Quintrell stepped into the van, an equipment technician leaned from his perch in the driver's seat. "Give me your jacket." The spitting image of *Revenge of the Nerds* young Robert Carradine, thick dark-rimmed glasses and all, he started replacing the two front buttons, making sure they matched so as not to draw attention to the microphone and camera hidden in one.

Quintrell plopped down on a pulled-out jump seat. He tugged on each shirt cuff and smoothed his pressed white sleeves with a sense of reverence—as if he missed his elegant attire like most people missed their dogs. "What's the range of the transmitter?"

"Don't worry. We'll be close enough in case you try to skip." Eric's words had a distinct edge to them.

"Remember…" Sloane leaned forward from the van's small, cluttered work surface. "If we don't have a case against El Padrino, we have no reason to put Rosa and your son in witness protection."

"I doubt that." Quintrell's intimate knowledge of the inner workings of law enforcement procedures negated Sloane's greatest strength—her ability to bluff. "Nevertheless, I'll get you what you need."

"We need to tie him to—" Finn said.

"I'm a prosecutor, Agent Harper. I know exactly what you need to convict my father. He's careful, but I'll use Rosa and Antonio's disappearance as a prod to get him off balance."

"All done." The technician finished his work and pointed to the buttons on the front of the jacket. "The top one is the camera and mic." He handed Quintrell a smartphone. "This is a transmitter. Keep it in your pocket."

"Thanks, James." Eric eyed Quintrell, who was inspecting the phone. "It looks real, but it's a transmitter only. Don't get any ideas about trying to arrange for a getaway."

Quintrell harrumphed. "The thought never crossed my mind."

"Right." Eric matched his lopsided grin. "This'll be simple. Get your father talking and then come back down." His smile faded into a piercing stare. "We'll have people inside, plus eyes and ears on you the entire time. If you want, though, you could try to make a break for it and give me a reason to save the state a butt load of money."

Was Quintrell a flight risk? Hell, yes. If someone he sent to prison didn't get to him, his father's long reach would. Spending two decades in segregation, where guards presented his only human interaction and monitored his every move, posed a daunting future. And despite his willingness to pay back his father, like Eric, Sloane didn't trust him.

"Don't worry, Sergeant Decker. I have no intention of saving you the cost of my incarceration."

"Can we wrap up this testosterone party and get to work?" Eager to get this over with, Sloane hoped by the end of the day, they'd have enough evidence for an arrest. Then she could be one step closer to adopting Reagan and finally telling Finn she loved her.

Upon reaching El Padrino's hotel, Eric and Finn took their positions inside the lobby and stairwell, and Sloane ops-checked the equipment with the technician in the surveillance van parked across the street. She wasn't thrilled to be babysitting Quintrell until go-time, but Eric had made the right call. This operation was very personal to her, and if anything went wrong, calmer heads needed to be first ones on the scene. That meant she needed to cool her heels with the sly fox sitting two feet away.

"Say something pithy into your mic, like 'I love the color red.'" Sloane placed one padded speaker of her headphones over an ear.

"I never knew wit was in your wheelhouse, Sergeant."

"There's a lot you don't know about me."

"I know more than you think."

"What the hell does that mean?" Sloane's antenna went up, and she fixed him with a cold stare. Quintrell wasn't one for empty threats, and him knowing personal details set her on edge.

"Hopefully, nothing."

"The only thing you have to know about me is that I'm a damn good shot."

"Of that I have no doubt, Sergeant."

Finn had already reported she'd taken up her spot in the lobby. The radio crackled again now. "In position." Eric's voice echoed off the concrete walls of the stairwell he was in.

"Ten-four," Sloane radioed back. Everyone was in place. She focused on Quintrell. "You know, a part of me wants you to fuck this up. Prison gen pop would love you."

He slid the van door open and stepped out. Before closing it, he said with what appeared to be an absolute certainty, "I hate to disappoint you, but I have no intention of fucking this up."

"Right."

The door slammed shut.

From the window, Sloane watched as Quintrell rebuttoned his suit jacket in his usual smug fashion and crossed the street as if this day didn't differ from any other. But today couldn't be any more significant. In a few minutes, he would betray his father, a choice from which there would be no going back. At least, that was what Sloane counted on.

The technician swiveled from his perch in the driver's seat. "You don't like him very much, do you?"

"No, I don't." Sliding the headset over her ears, she took a deep breath to unwind the anger twisting inside. She pushed the button on the radio. "Fox on his way."

"Ten-four," Finn and Eric each acknowledged.

Minutes later, the radio squawked and Finn reported from her position in the lobby. "Fox heading up."

Soon, from the twenty-third-floor stairwell, Eric radioed, "Fox in the den."

In the van, Sloane received a text message from Reagan: *Thanks for excused tardy. Heading off to school.*

To which she typed a short reply: *You deserved it. See you tonight.*

* * *

Quintrell's adoration of his father from childhood innocence and respect for him from youthful ignorance had long since disappeared. Today, fear of him from adult awareness had vanished as well. The only thing that remained was the realization that his father had stolen from him what he'd always wanted—a family of his own. But he couldn't let on, at least not yet. He needed to give his father enough rope to hang himself.

Padrino's bodyguard led him into the suite and told him to wait. That meant his father might appear in minutes or hours. Acting the obedient son, Quintrell poured himself a glass of scotch from the corner wet bar and made himself comfortable in an armchair. He chose the plusher one centered in the room, the one his father likely used. This seat of power symbolized what he planned to rip away from his father today. And when his father entered the room, he wouldn't give him the satisfaction of basking in its potency.

Inspecting the glass in his hand, he asked himself if this would be his last drink for decades. He sipped and savored the smoky, smooth liquor, welcoming the warm burn as it slid down his throat.

Over the next hour, his thoughts drifted to Rosa and the life that had been stolen from him. What path would he have taken if he had known she was pregnant with his child? He doubted he would have fallen in line and assumed his new life in the United States. Beyond that, sorting through the possibilities and what-ifs seemed pointless. He focused his anger on the fact his father took away his choice, not for his own good, but to further the family business and to line his own pockets.

The hour-long wait was taking its toll on Eric's calves. His post required peering through a shatterproof window the width of a shoebox and offered nowhere to sit. At the next ten-minute radio check, Sloane cracked the silence. "How are you holding up, Eric?"

"Good for now."

"Not liking how that sounds."

"I'll be fine, Sloane."

"You're no good to us if you're aching and unfocused. Break. Finn, anything on your end?"

"Quiet as a mouse."

"How about you relieve Eric?"

"On my way."

The moment Finn came into view in the stairwell, Eric's calves screamed, "thank you." Sloane was right. Whoever stood post outside Padrino's suite needed to stay alert and limber if Quintrell made a run for it.

"In place, Sloane," Finn radioed as she peered through the glass. She glanced at Eric. "Anything?"

"Nothing." Eric bounced on his toes to relieve a mild cramp.

"The chairs downstairs should give your dogs a needed rest." Finn gave Eric a curious look.

"The feet are fine. It's the calves. Bouncing helps." With no time to waste, Eric gingerly descended the stairs, stifling a groan on the first step. He pressed his radio mic. "Sloane, I'm taking the stairs to stretch this out."

Finn snickered. "Give the old man a few extra minutes."

"Old?" Eric was already one flight down. "I'm only three years older than you two."

The radio crackled, obscuring a reply if there was one. Radio and phone reception was sketchy deep inside the stairwell and elevator.

"Father." Quintrell rose to his feet and buttoned his jacket when Padrino emerged from one of the suite's bedrooms, attired in a three-piece white suit. Ever since David was a child, the white suit meant his father was ready for business. "May I pour you a drink?" He'd lost count of how many trips he'd made to the wet bar, but his dizziness meant it was sizeable. Though the scotch didn't rival his father's Osocalis, it was top-shelf and would serve as liquid courage for his next task.

"It's a little early in the afternoon for me, but it appears not too early for you, *mijo*." Padrino scanned his son with disapproving eyes.

Disregarding the rebuke, Quintrell poured himself two more fingers of scotch. This time, he didn't pause to consider its attractive color and hidden properties; he downed it in one motion. A numbness had set in, which meant his bland morning jailhouse breakfast of scrambled eggs, cream of wheat, and toast had long ago moved on, and the alcohol in his stomach had done its job. He was ready to face the man he neither adored, respected, nor feared. "Rough day."

"I would presume not as rough a day as Antonio's." Padrino maneuvered toward the chairs. "I apologize for the wait, but I needed to make sure my men carried out my orders. What have you learned about who took him?" The wrath in Padrino's voice when he first called Quintrell after learning of their abduction had disappeared. That, Quintrell feared, meant he already had a plan in place.

"I can confirm that the federal government doesn't have them." Quintrell beat his father to the chair he'd eyed, denying him the perceived throne.

"Our rivals' hands are clean." Padrino maneuvered toward the nearby chair. "My instincts tell me it must have been Detective Sloane and Agent Harper."

"My contacts aren't talking."

"Then your contacts are unreliable." A grin of satisfaction crossed Padrino's face, "Which doesn't surprise me. Nonetheless, I took care of it."

"What have you done, Father?" He had a sinking feeling. His father was not one to slowly escalate acts of retribution; he preferred sure and swift outlaw justice. "This isn't Mexico."

"First Caco, now Antonio. Sloane and Harper will pay for taking my family."

"Your family?" Heat built in Quintrell's neck like a pot coming to a rapid boil. "Caco was not your son, but I am."

"In recent years, he was more of a son than you."

"I was living the life you chose for me—your inside man in the American government, following your orders to prosecute your competitors and draw attention away from Los Dorados. And all while you and Caco lived off the riches from your narcotics trafficking."

"And I paid you well for it. Other than the purchase of your home, your share is untouched."

That tacit confession was the golden ticket. Padrino's admission, along with Quintrell's testimony, would be enough to bring him down along with his entire operation. A bittersweet ending by anyone's measure, but Quintrell was only getting started.

"Even if I wanted to, I could never touch it without raising suspicion." Quintrell hoped his words didn't come out as slurred as he thought they had.

"If?" Padrino raised a curious brow.

"Yes, if." Quintrell had done his job, and now he was free to speak his mind. The irony tasted sweeter than he expected. Padrino had chosen his path of a federal prosecutor during which he had amassed a trail of convictions on much less evidence. Now that decision will be his undoing. "I want nothing from you. You speak about family as if it means something. I know what you did. I know Antonio is my son."

"I never trusted that *puta* since the day she showed up looking for you."

Fury brewed in the back of Quintrell's throat, but his obligation to Rosa and his son tempered it. He couldn't tip his hand yet, so he clenched his jaw to bite back the things he wanted to say. "She is no *puta*. Rosa is better than either of us, raising a son with special needs on her own."

"She was never on her own and never wanted for a roof over her head."

"You provided her with things. I would have shared the burden had I known of my responsibility. You took that away from both of us and that I can never forgive."

"I taught you too well." Another grin of satisfaction flashed over Padrino's face. Then, as quickly as it appeared, a look reserved for his adversaries took its place. "Tread lightly, *mijo*. You are right to defend your family, but you must never go toe-to-toe with me."

"You taught me family is everything. You also taught me betrayal is unforgivable." Another irony, he thought. The one thing his father never tolerated from others was now at the heart of his downfall.

He looked his father in the eye. "I may not forgive you, but I can work with you." Upon receiving Padrino's acknowledgment, he continued. "So, tell me, Father. How have you taken care of things?"

"Detective Sloane and Agent Harper took from me, so I have taken from them. If they want to see their daughter and father again, they will have to bargain with me."

"No, no, no, no, no." Sloane's heart thudded so hard it drowned out the voices coming from her headphones. She ripped them off her head as if they burned and then stabbed her hand into her pocket, fishing for her cell phone. Her hand trembled as she unlocked the screen and thumbed the phone app.

"Pick up, pick up, pick up." Her breathing labored with each agonizing unanswered ring. Reagan's voice mail picked up. "No, no, no, no, no."

She dialed the school, rushing her words. "This is Manhattan Sloane. Has my daughter Reagan Tenney checked in late for school yet?"

Following several excruciating moments on hold, the female school secretary returned. "I'm sorry, Mrs. Sloane, she still hasn't checked in."

"Damn it. This is important. If Reagan checks in, don't let her leave the office and have her call me immediately."

"Is there something wrong, Mrs. Sloane?"

"I'm not sure." Finishing the call with a vague explanation, Sloane doubled over at the thought of Reagan hurt or worse. Padrino would stop at nothing to get what he wanted. She should've seen this coming. She should've been a better mother. "What have I done?"

"James, I need to find Reagan." Sliding the door open so hard the van wobbled, she darted into the street. To her left, a yellow taxicab came to a screeching stop, missing her with a foot to spare. She pounded on the hood with one hand and held up the badge that was dangling from a chain around her neck with the other. "Police emergency."

A hefty cabbie with three-day stubble poked his head out the driver's window. "What the hell?"

"Police emergency." Her voice teetering on the edge of menacing, Sloane hadn't the time to explain the details. "Take me to Hunters Point. Or do I have to arrest you for obstructing justice?"

"Hop in, lady."

Not once in her ten years with the DEA had Finn considered that her work could endanger her father. That arrogance might have cost him his life. Bile churned as she dialed her father's cell phone with one hand and pulled at her hair with the other.

"Pick up, Daddy. Pick up."

His voice mail answered. Finn dialed his office, her hands shaking. She rushed her words. "Sharon, this is Finn. Is my father in?"

"Sorry, Miss Harper. He worked from home this morning. He called in and said he was taking the rest of the day off. Have you tried his cell?"

"I did. He's not answering. This is important, Sharon. I think something may have happened to him. If you hear from him, call me."

"You're scaring me."

"I'm scared too. Call me if you hear anything." She hung up and dialed the house phone. Before the call connected, Quintrell exited the suite and approached the elevator. "Damn it!" She pressed her mic. "Fox coming down."

No one responded. What the hell was going on? She repeated. "Sloane, Fox is coming down. Do you copy?"

Three seconds of unnerving silence. She feared the worst until the radio crackled. "This is James. Sloane took off in a cab."

"Where the hell is Decker?"

"Unknown."

"Keep trying to raise him. I'm coming down. If Fox appears, hold him in the van."

"Me? I'm only a tech."

"Yes, you. You're all I have." Frustration frosted her tone. *Don't they train these guys?* An untrained civilian was the last thing she needed. "Let him in, lock the doors, and don't say anything. I'll be down in five."

Finn sailed down the flight of stairs to the next floor. She threw the door open and sprinted to the elevator. She pressed the call button, but the nearest car was five floors away. "Damn it." The moment she pivoted to take the stairs, a car moved toward her level. She waited. Once inside the elevator, she checked her cell phone—no bars. Her next call to the house failed. "Son of a bitch."

Delayed by stops to pick up more passengers, the ride down tested Finn's nerves. Each time the car bounced to a halt on another floor felt like an eternity. Her arms and legs trembled as precious seconds ticked away; seconds that would have been better spent looking for her father.

At the lobby level, the doors slid open. Finn exited first and scanned the area, but neither Eric nor Quintrell were in sight. Finally, outside the main doors, she spotted Eric quick-walking Quintrell by the arm across the street. She let out a huge breath. They hadn't lost the fox. A few cars passed, and she followed at a jogger's pace, jumped in the van moments after them, and closed the side door.

Eric shoved Quintrell into the jump seat he occupied earlier and turned his attention to James. "Where's Sloane?"

"She said something about finding Reagan and jumped into a cab."

"She's too late, as are you, Agent Harper," Quintrell said. The anger in his voice when he confronted his father had disappeared, replaced by a calmness that suggested that nothing would change the fact his father had won.

Finn grabbed Quintrell by the lapels, the scotch on his breath assaulting her nose and turning her desperation into anger. "What did he do to my father?"

"He took him and Sergeant Sloane's daughter." Quintrell showed no sign of weakness or fear. He waited for Finn to release her grip. "They're his bargaining chip. That means he'll keep them alive as long as he thinks he can get Antonio back."

"Where would he take them?" she growled through her teeth.

"I'd only be guessing."

Her gut told her Quintrell knew more, but she didn't have time to beat the truth out of him. She turned to Eric. "I need to get to Atherton."

Eric pulled out his cell phone. "Dispatch…"

Two minutes later, Finn slid into the back of a police cruiser. When they were clear of the building, its flashing lights and blaring siren parted traffic like in a cartoon. Her heart raced as every conceivable horrible outcome rolled through her head in a fast-moving slideshow. She was afraid of what the police might discover when they did their welfare check of her father's home, but she had to go. She had to find her father and fix what she had done.

CHAPTER THIRTEEN

Hours earlier

From her back deck, Reagan focused her gaze at the deep waters of San Francisco Bay. She shivered when the moist salt air tickled her skin and left goose bumps along the length of her arms.

"Here, honey, take my sweater. It will protect you." Her mother swaddled her knitted gray wool cardigan around Reagan's shoulders before wrapping her arms around her from behind to ward off the cool bay breeze.

"Umm." Reagan sniffed one lapel as if this were the last time she'd smell her mother's fragrant lavender scent. "It smells like you."

"I love this view." Her mother's sigh signaled deep contentment.

"I hated it at first."

"And now?"

"I love it." Reagan glanced over her shoulder to show her mother her smile. "And it makes Sloane happy."

"You make her happy, and so does Finn."

Reagan sighed, a long breathy one that gave away her dilemma.

"It's okay to like her too."

Reagan's eyes moistened. "I do, but—"

"But you're afraid if you do, Sloane will forget me."

Reagan nodded. "Won't she?"

"No, silly." Her mother giggled. "She could never forget me, just like you can't. Moving on doesn't mean forgetting; it means honoring me through your happiness."

"I don't know what that means."

"You will."

"I love you, Mom." Pain didn't fill those words, only the reassurance she'd love her mother forever. She wrapped her arms over her mother's, tightening the hold they had on her.

"I love you, too." Her mother kissed her on the back of the head. "Trust Finn. She loves you as well." Her mother's voice grew fainter as did the arms that were draped around Reagan. "I have to go."

"Will I see you again?"

"You won't need to." Her mother faded into the light.

"What the–?" A piercing alarm roared like a train blasting its horn, ripping Reagan from her dream. She snapped her head toward the dresser and the offending clock before burying her head underneath a pillow. "I hate that damn thing."

When it didn't stop, she emerged from her cocoon and turned it off with the pound of a fist. Panic set in when she read the time. 8:30. She was late for school. The note lying next to the clock washed away that fright.

Reagan, You're not late. You tossed and turned most of the night, so I called the school and let them know you'll be in after ten. Don't forget about the Social Services visit today. I'll be home when I can. Love, Mom

"You're the best." A grin emerged. Parts of her dream came back to her, and the words "trust Finn" echoed in her head. While Reagan still wasn't completely sold on the idea of having Finn around, Sloane going the extra mile with the little things made her feel that things wouldn't change for the worse if she were.

A growling stomach reminded Reagan that she hadn't eaten anything since pizza last night, so she decided on breakfast first, shower second. In the kitchen, she prepared a bowl of cereal.

She was pulling out a chair to sit at the dining table when another flash from her dream drew her toward the back deck. The moment she slid the door open, the morning air and the sense that she had been out here minutes ago sent a chill down her spine.

Placing her bowl on the small table between the two chairs, she opened the deck's storage chest. Her mother's neatly folded gray wool sweater was on top where Reagan had left it two nights ago. When she put it on and smelled the lapels, the strong scent from her mother's lavender perfume that she had worn that night brought back more of her dream. She finally put it together. Her mother had given her everything she needed to thrive without her—all she needed was Sloane. If Sloane needed Finn to be happy and remain a constant in her life, Reagan would make every effort to accept her.

"Thanks for giving me Sloane, Mom. I love you."

Reagan finished her cereal and dressed for school. Grabbing her backpack and house keys, she thought twice. Instead of her usual cotton hoodie, she slipped on her mother's sweater and texted Sloane: *Thanks for excused tardy. Heading off to school.*

A minute later, Sloane replied: *You deserved it. See you tonight.*

Tucking her phone into her backpack per school rules, she headed out the door and locked it up. This time of day, minus the mad rush of pedestrians and neighbors going to school and work, her street was strangely empty. The only vehicle, in fact, was a white panel van parked near the corner.

Though the streets were otherwise vacant, she checked for traffic before crossing, a safety precaution her mother had drilled into her as a toddler. The moment she stepped off the curb, the van pulled up even with her in the crosswalk. The side door opened, and a man twice her size leaned out and grabbed her by the arms. *What the hell?* In one violent pull, he yanked her inside. *Oh, God! What's happening?* The door closed, and the van continued at a rate of speed slow enough to not attract attention.

Pounding heart. Fear. Rapid breaths. Panic. *Speed, you son of a bitch, so a cop will stop you.* Arms and legs flailing, Reagan screamed so loud the walls of the van vibrated. What horrible thing did this man have in mind for her? Rape? Torture? Sex trafficking? Murder? Her life depended on an epic struggle, of that she was sure.

"*Hazla callar!*" boomed a voice from the front of the van. *Make her shut up*.

A large man dressed in a suit straddled Reagan, taking several kicks to the gut and thigh. She pelted him with slaps and fingernails to the arms and face, drawing blood in places. She got in more than a dozen good licks in all, kicking, punching, and screaming.

"*Puta*!" The barbarian drew back his right arm and, in a single blow, plowed his fist into her cheekbone. There was a crack and pain. Everything went black.

The battle of the bulge had been taking more and more time out of Chandler's day in recent years, a war in which he often considered an unconditional surrender. Top-of-the-line, his home gym treadmill offered inclines and automated variable speeds to enhance the workout. Lately, though, he had defaulted to flat and slow. In his younger days, doing two miles in about sixteen minutes would have been a snap. Today, though, he'd be lucky to keep it under twenty. Luck evaded him.

The gym's picture-perfect view of his pool and lush, immaculate backyard did little to soften the pain of his workout. As his feet pounded the rolling deck, beads of sweat, too many to count, dripped down his brow, bringing into clarity the ache in his lungs. For the fourth time, he punched down the pace to a slow jog. *Twenty-two wasn't so bad*, he reasoned.

The second the odometer clicked to two miles, he hammered his fist on the stop button and stepped off the machine. A cotton hand towel erased the streaks of sweat from his face. "Whoever said sixty is the new forty was lying through their teeth."

His phone buzzed and vibrated, threatening to fall from its perch atop a shelf near the door leading into his exercise room. The ringtone meant someone in his office needed to reach him. To his ire, working from home didn't mean escaping the usual attention-breaking barrage of questions from his secretary and associates. Inhaling deep several times but failing to catch his breath, he swiped the phone screen, leaving a streak of sweat across the glass.

"Harper." His breathy one-word greeting confirmed he needed more time to recover.

"Sorry to bother you, Chandler," Kadin said, "but you didn't answer my text."

"Yeah." He took in one more deep breath. "Just finished my daily torture session."

"Maybe it's time to switch to walking." She chuckled.

"And admit defeat?" Still spent, he bent over, placing both palms on his knees. "I think you're right. Now, what's so important that it couldn't wait until our deposition?"

"I had to push it to Monday."

"Damn. Why?"

"The witness was in a cycling accident last night. He's fine, but the hospital admitted him for observation. If he's on pain medication, I didn't want to chance the judge tossing his testimony due to competency, so I rescheduled."

Chandler had a judge-ordered hard deadline for discovery and would never get a continuance at this late stage. "Monday is cutting it close, but good call."

"We'll have our hands full Monday night, parsing his statement." Kadin filled her words with the eagerness of a newly minted partner.

"We? You mean you and your team. I have plans to take my daughter to dinner." He cringed the moment he said that. Kadin and Finn's breakup had seemed amicable, but Kadin tended to become melancholy whenever he mentioned Finn's name.

Kadin sighed. "How is she?" Her question was laced with the recognizable sound of regret.

"I'm sorry, Kadin." Chandler's voice softened to lessen the blow. "I know this is hard on you."

"It's my fault. I pushed her away." She paused as if deliberating on her next words. "Is she happy with Sloane?"

"She is. They have a history, you know."

"I do, which is why I agreed to represent her regarding her stepdaughter." Kadin cleared her throat when her voice thickened with palpable emotion. "I just want her to be happy."

"Thank you, Kadin, for loving my daughter enough to let her go."

"Hardest thing I've ever done." A deep, breathy intake of air tugged on Chandler's sympathies. She was hurting. "Enough of this sticky emotional stuff. I'll see you in the office."

Wrapping up the call, he flung the towel around his neck and dabbed the remaining sweat off his face. Debating whether to head to the office for the rest of the day, he found the cons outweighed the pros. Ever the responsible adult, he hadn't taken a hooky day in ages, and surprising his daughter for an impromptu early dinner posed a more appealing option. Maybe a nap would hit the spot before figuring out the rest of his day, which he hoped would end with picking up Finn's favorite takeout.

In the kitchen, he located Carmen, who was washing a batch of fresh fruit she'd picked up at the market. She looked a lot like her older sister, the woman she'd replaced as cook and housekeeper. They shared the same short stature, brown skin, and thick, long black hair, but their personalities couldn't be further apart—the rebel versus the people-pleaser.

Easing up to the counter, he popped a grape in his mouth. "Morning, Carmen."

"Good morning, Mister Chandler."

"You'll never be comfortable with just Chandler, will you?"

"No, sir, Mister Chandler," Carmen said, ever the charmer.

"How are classes going?"

"Econ is kicking my butt with homework."

"Veta went through the same thing. She got through it. You will too."

"But she was a business major. Econ was her thing."

He eased an elbow on the counter while comparing the differences between the two sisters whose college education he funded as part of their salary. While Veta had a head for numbers and Carmen had one for people, both women had a drive for success. "They're preparing you for upper-division work. Just buckle down, prioritize your time, and you'll get through it."

As he popped another grape in his mouth, she asked, "Would you like me to prepare you a snack?"

"I think I need to shower first." He sniffed his damp T-shirt and confirmed his suspicion—funky. "But can you make me an early lunch? My meeting in the city was canceled."

"Sure, Mister Chandler. Any preference?"

Grabbing one last grape, he turned toward the door with an extra pep in his step. He waved a hand over his head. "Surprise me. Give me an hour. I'm taking a short nap too."

Minutes later, he toweled off, splashed on a dash of his favorite aftershave, and picked out casual khakis, a golf shirt, and tennis shoes. Going back to bed for a nap seemed a little over the top, even for a hooky day. He grabbed reading glasses and the top book from his nightstand and settled into the easy chair nestled in the corner. He plopped his feet on the ottoman and grudgingly put on his glasses. Corrective eye surgery did wonders for most daily activities. However, reading still required cheaters to preserve the progress he'd gained from the procedure.

Chandler didn't realize he'd nodded off until a loud noise roused him. Removing his glasses, which had fallen lower on the bridge of his nose, he placed the book on the neighboring end table. He opened his bedroom door and called out, "Carmen?"

When she didn't answer, he ventured out to the main part of the house. "What the…?" In the living room, a man the size of an NFL linebacker was dragging an unconscious Carmen from the front door toward a couch. Meanwhile, a second linebacker was fast-stepping toward him.

Chandler froze in his tracks, his pulse popping like pistons in his Porsche. He'd never heard of burglars wearing suits. What the hell did they want? Money? Drugs? To rape Carmen? Whatever it was, he needed to defuse the situation fast to protect her.

Chandler raised his hands in surrender. "Whatever you came for, take it. We won't put up a fight."

The second thug approached fast. In full stride, he clocked Chandler on the left cheek with the butt of his pistol, toppling him to the floor. Pain shot through his face and his vision was blurred more than before his Lasik procedure.

"We're here for you." The man flipped Chandler onto his stomach and jabbed a knee into his back, drawing a painful groan. "Put your hands behind your back, or we'll kill the girl."

Whatever these men wanted, Chandler feared they'd hurt him more if he didn't cooperate. If he did what they said, Carmen had a chance of surviving. His vision came back into focus. As he complied and placed his hands around his back, he turned his head against the hardwood floor to peer at Carmen. Her head moved a fraction, and blood was trickling from a gash on her face. *She's alive.*

The man slipped a stiff plastic strap around Chandler's hands and tightened it like a vise. Chandler tested its tightness, but its sharp edges threatened to slice his skin. He wouldn't escape his bindings without something even sharper and much effort.

The man pulled Chandler up by the arms and gave him a hefty shove toward the front door. For the first time since this started, Chandler feared for his life. His head spun as he tried to figure out what enemies he may have made over the years in his law practice. His clients were mostly athletes and artists. They didn't pose much of a threat and wouldn't have any reason to resort to assault and kidnapping. At a loss, he thought about Finn. *Could this be about her?* After all, the many dangers of her job often prompted him to try to nudge her in a different direction.

The man stuffed one of Carmen's dirty cleaning rags in Chandler's mouth before they walked out the door. The taste of lemon Pledge wasn't good. "Keep it in, or I'll come back and shoot the girl."

Whoever these guys were, he suspected they had practice at this sort of thing. If Chandler had any hope of staying alive, he decided, he had to do what they said. He gulped hard as he walked single file between the men down his driveway, where a white panel van sat idling.

Damn it. An eight-foot stone wall around the property provided for great privacy but proved lousy in the event of kidnappings. It eliminated any chance of a passing neighbor seeing strange happenings like this one.

When the side door of the van slid open, one of the men shoved Chandler into the back. He almost landed on a bound-up, unconscious girl, but managed to roll inches beside her.

What the hell's going on? Me and a teenage girl? This isn't good.

While one thug slid into the driver's seat, the other jumped in the back. The one next to Chandler held up a pill in one hand and his pistol in the other. "Your choice."

Unsure which end of the gun the man intended to use, he decided the pill would likely prove less painful. Unless it was lethal. Chandler nodded toward it, gambling they wanted to keep him alive.

"Good choice." The man removed the rag from Chandler's mouth, shoved the pill in, and watched him swallow.

Whatever it contained, it was effective. Within minutes, his surroundings turned blurry. He focused on the man's face before closing his eyes and falling into what he hoped was a deep sleep.

* * *

Sloane leaped from the backseat before the taxi came to a complete stop in front of her townhouse. She'd spent the last horrifying fifteen minutes on the phone, calling the parents of Reagan's friends. No one had seen her.

Dashing up the driveway, she fished out her house key, cursing her walking boot for slowing her down. Flinging the door open, she left the keys dangling in the lock and flew up the steps, her heart pounding double time.

"Reagan? Where are you? Reagan?" Her eyes darted into every corner, searching. Hoping the eerie silence in the house meant her daughter had fallen back asleep.

Chest heaving, she roared through the empty living room and kitchen and reached her master bedroom where she had last left her daughter. The bed was ruffled but empty. She called again toward the bathroom, "Reagan?" Still nothing. Hope began to fade.

She took the stairs leading down to Reagan's bedroom, her boot forcing an agonizingly slow one-at-a-time approach. At the bottom, she forewent the polite knock and burst through the door. The bed was empty. On the floor, atop a dirty pile, were Reagan's sleep clothes from last night. Which meant she'd changed.

Her breathing was so rapid now she was getting dizzy. Reversing course out the door, she checked Reagan's bathroom. Empty. When she returned to the bedroom, her eyes searched for the clue that could have told her Reagan hadn't left the house. She fell against the door, all hope fleeing, when she didn't find Reagan's backpack resting on the dresser. Reagan was gone.

Palms against her forehead, fingers gripping her thick hair, Sloane fought back tears. "What have I done? Think, think, think." One final idea sprang in her head. As she pulled herself up the stairs, she dialed her phone, praying the call didn't go to voice mail.

"The Tap."

"Dylan, this is Sloane. By chance is Reagan there?"

"Sorry, Sloane. The place is empty. I'm just getting ready to open."

"If she shows up, keep her there and don't let her out of your sight."

"Something is wrong. I can tell. What is it?" The last time his voice contained that level of concern, Sloane was drinking herself into a daily stupor following Avery's death. He was a true friend.

"I don't have time to explain other than I think Reagan might be in danger. Please call me if she shows up."

Ending the call and walking past the dining room, she slid the glass door open and stepped onto the deck. She dialed her phone again. "Kadin, this is Sloane. By chance, did the social worker arrive early? Would he have taken Reagan anywhere?"

"I don't think so. He said he was stopping by your place after regular work hours. Why do you ask?"

"Reagan is missing. I think someone associated with a case Finn and I are working on may have taken her."

"My God, Sloane. Are you sure?"

"I'm not sure of anything. We've been chasing a cartel kingpin. We heard him say if I want to see my daughter or Finn her father again, we'll have to bargain with him."

"Chandler's missing too?"

"I don't know. I assume so." Sloane pulled at her hair again, pacing the deck.

"I talked to him a few hours ago. Finn must be frantic." Kadin's level of concern for Finn didn't escape Sloane, but this was no time for petty jealousy.

"Look, Kadin. Can you confirm the social worker isn't with her and text me back?"

"Will do. And Sloane, if she's missing, I have to notify the court."

"Fucking great. The Santoses will have a field day with this." Sloane ran a hand down her face. The last thing she needed was to rile up homophobic former in-laws who were hell-bent on finding any excuse to get their claws into Reagan.

"I'll text you what I find out."

Pocketing her phone, Sloane stood at the railing where she'd found so much strength and serenity over the years. The slight chill in the air reminded her of the vision she had of Avery hours earlier. She rubbed her arms to warm them, but her hands couldn't break the icy feeling in her bones. She may have lost Reagan forever.

"I failed you, Avery." Sloane closed her eyes in shame, tears streaming down her cheeks. She had set this in motion the moment she talked to Rosa in her hotel room. This was all her fault, and she had no clue how to fix it.

"How do I get her back?" Sloane peered at the bay, searching for an answer. Should she wait for Padrino to initiate a trade? Under any other circumstance, she'd never consider trading one life for another, but how could she not? Reagan's life was at stake.

"Tell me what to do." Sloane desperately needed Avery's guidance, but after saying goodbye to her—in this very spot—in her dream, she'd lost the connection. She looked to the sky, frustrated that she'd let go too soon. "Damn it, Avery. Talk to me."

Sloane needed to do something…anything. She needed that connection back. She rummaged through the deck's storage chest in search of Avery's sweater, but couldn't find it. "Where the hell is it?" She distinctly remembered placing it on top of the blanket and closing the lid earlier this morning.

There was only one explanation—Reagan must have taken it. Irrational as it might be, a wave of relief coursed through Sloane. Wherever the cartel had taken Reagan, she was confident that Avery was with her.

Lights and sirens parted most of the noon traffic to Atherton, shaving at least fifteen minutes off the travel time. The twenty minutes Finn spent in the backseat, though, had passed with agonizing slowness. She had yet to hear from Eric on the welfare check he'd asked local police to conduct.

He should've called by now. With each passing minute, her frustration grew. And her fear. The worst-case scenario had her paralyzed: her father lying dead somewhere in the house. She decided not to call Eric for an update. If her father were missing or worse, she didn't want to hear the news in the backseat of a patrol car.

Minutes later, they pulled past the ungated entrance to the house. An Atherton patrol car and a fire department rescue rig were parked in the circular driveway. Finn gasped. Someone was hurt.

The split second the officer put the patrol car in park, Finn flew toward the home's open front door. Inside, paramedics had bandaged and wrapped Carmen's head and jaw and were pushing her along in a gurney. A local police officer stood watch off to the side of a couch.

Chandler's absence all but confirmed Finn's fear. Her heart beat wildly out of control, but she remained calm enough to flash her badge and credentials at the officer. "Agent Harper, DEA. This is my father's house. Did you find him?" Finn saw it in his eyes. The news wasn't good.

"The house is clear. Only the housekeeper is on the premises."

A stinging flooded her chest, forcing her to clutch it. "Did she say anything about my father?"

He shook his head. "No. She's groggy with a broken jaw, but managed to communicate that two men jumped her when she answered the door."

Finn turned on her heel and called to the paramedics before they wheeled Carmen out. "Wait!" She flashed her badge at them. "I need to talk to her."

"We need to transport her, ma'am. She needs surgery."

"This is life or death." Impatient as hell, Finn raised a hand, palm forward, to stop them. "Just give me a damn minute."

Carmen tugged on one of the paramedics' arms, pleading for them to wait. Her face swollen and bloodied, she didn't look at all like herself. Finn knew it would be too difficult for her to speak. She would have to ask leading questions.

"Carmen, was my father working from home this morning?"

She nodded.

"Did he leave on his own?"

Carmen shrugged.

"Did they take him?"

She shrugged again.

"Were there only two, Carmen?"

She nodded.

"Were they Hispanic?"

Carmen nodded.

"Were they dressed in street clothes?"

She shook her head.

"Were they in suits?"

Carmen nodded.

It added up. Padrino's men had been here, and they took her father. Dead on the floor was her worst-case scenario; kidnapping came in a close second. The cartel was ruthless. Her body went numb at the possibility her father might not make it back alive.

"Are you done?" a paramedic asked at Finn's lengthy pause.

"Sure." Finn's voice was flat. "They'll take good care of you, Carmen. You're in good hands." She patted Carmen's arm before they wheeled her out.

"Damn it!" She brushed her hair back with both hands and paced the floor. She had no idea what her next step should be. Where should she look? The only thing she could think of was to call Sloane. She dialed. After several rings, Sloane answered.

"They took her, Finn." Sloane's voice had thickened from crying. "They took her."

"They have Daddy, too." Finn swallowed hard. "We have to believe they're still alive."

"But for how long?"

"Quintrell says they're his bargaining chips. Padrino will keep them alive as long as he thinks he can deal with us." Finn reassured herself as much as Sloane.

"Then we play along." Sloane's voice cracked. "I can't lose her too."

"We'll figure this out. We have to."

"Hold on." Sloane muffled the phone for several seconds. "I gotta go, CSI is here."

"Sloane—" She heard the call click to an end, but Finn had to say the next three words nevertheless. "I love you." Finn turned when a hand fell on her shoulder.

"Finn." Kadin's voice comforted her as much as her hand. Her eyes told of shared fear.

"Kadin." Finn wrapped her arms around her tightly, the full length of their bodies pressing against one another. The familiarity soothed the anxiety that had mounted for the last hour. She buried her face into Kadin's soft jawline and let a tear fall. "I did this."

"This isn't your fault." Kadin pressed Finn's head against her shoulder. "We'll find him."

If only it were just her father. Finn blamed herself for Reagan too. She'd never forgive herself if Sloane had to suffer another unimaginable loss. Releasing her grip, she pulled back. "We have to find them both."

"I know, I talked to Sloane." Kadin kept her reassuring hands on Finn's forearms. "We'll find them."

Nothing could have prepared Sloane to have Avery's CSI team combing through their house following the kidnapping of their daughter. Everything the team did seemed surreal. None of this should be happening. Not to her. Not here.

Since nothing in the house appeared to have been disturbed, Sloane held little hope CSI would find any clues. But procedures were just that. This was the place Sloane last saw Reagan, so this was the place CSI had to start. Avery had trained them well. If there were any clues, Sloane was confident they would find them.

Sloane provided Reagan's hairbrush and toothbrush as good sources of DNA and to rule out fingerprints. Meandering through the main floor, she noted where the team had dusted for latent prints. Something gnawed at her. Not about Reagan, but about Avery.

"Hey, Todd," she said, getting the attention of Avery's second-in-command, now supervisor of the CSI Lab. "Do me a favor and dust the storage chest on the deck. It may be nothing, but Avery's sweater is missing."

"Sure thing, Sloane." His expression turned soft. "I want you to know we'll do everything possible to get her back."

"I know you will." She placed a hand on his shoulder for a moment.

"How are you holding up, Sloane?" A voice sounded behind her.

Sloane turned to the sound of her name. "I'm fine, L-T."

"You don't look fine," West said.

Sloane felt like falling apart, but she couldn't. She needed a game plan, and as distasteful as it was, the only one she could think of was to use Rosa and Antonio as bait.

"Where are we with Padrino?" Sloane asked, shaking off the waves of emotion threatening to break her.

"We got a search warrant, and we're picking him up for questioning. Prichard wanted reinforcements, so he sent two of Finn's agents to the hotel to work with Decker."

"Damn it!" Sloane clenched her jaw and placed both hands on her hips. "Quintrell hinted someone on Finn's team could be dirty. We don't know who we can trust."

The small, overworked Atherton police department finished taping off Chandler's home. It was now a crime scene. Meanwhile, the city's only detective methodically marked items that might provide clues as to who took Finn's father. He had the skills to preserve the evidence, certainly, but Finn doubted that he or his department was equipped to handle a kidnapping with international implications.

While Kadin called Chandler's law firm and confirmed Reagan wasn't with the social worker, she moved outside to wait impatiently on the front lawn for her DEA forensics team to arrive. Kadin slipped her phone in her coat pocket before turning to Finn. "The firm is in shock, but they know to keep this under wraps until he's found."

"Thank you, Kadin. I don't think I could've made that call."

Kadin gripped Finn's hand and laced their fingers together in a welcome tenderness. For the better part of two years, that hand had been as familiar to Finn as her own. Finn had held it countless times and kissed it just as many, but doing so had never moved her as much as she had been moved when Sloane had held and kissed her hand during their visit to the accident site. There had been no mistaking at that moment how much Sloane needed her in order to free her from her grief.

"I'm here for you. Anything you need." Kadin raised their clasped hands to her lips and kissed a soft patch of Finn's skin.

Finn sensed regret in Kadin's voice and eyes—but the last thing she needed at the moment was an overture to reconcile. She squeezed Kadin's hand before slipping hers away. "I appreciate that. Right now, I need to focus on how to get Reagan and Daddy back."

Minutes later, two black SUVs and a dark sedan pulled into the curved driveway. Prichard stepped out of the sedan while the forensic team unloaded equipment from the SUVs. The ball was finally rolling.

"How are you holding up, Harper?" Prichard asked.

"I'm okay." It was a lie, but she didn't have time to fall apart or cry. She straightened her back. She needed her team to come up with a game plan. "Where are Quintrell and Padrino?"

"Quintrell is in a holding cell at Bryant. I sent Shipley and Barnes to the hotel suite to search the suite with Decker and scoop up Padrino for questioning."

"You did what?" Finn stiffened at his shortsighted thinking. "You realize someone in our office may be on Los Dorados' payroll. You may have tipped him off."

"This is still a DEA case. I had to send someone. Shipley and Barnes were the only ones available." Prichard checked his watch. "They should hit his hotel suite right about now."

CHAPTER FOURTEEN

"Wait for the fucking DEA, my ass," Eric grumbled under his breath as he approached the unmarked sedan that he'd parked in front of Padrino's hotel. He didn't have a holding pattern in mind after ADA Kyler Harris worked fast to get a search warrant of Padrino's hotel suite, but here he was, holding. Joint operations like this one, fraught with delays while the brass coordinated people and resources, frustrated him more than commuter traffic.

In the meantime, though not expecting the need for overwhelming force, he prepared for it. Popping open the trunk, he donned his bulletproof vest, slipping it over his head and torso and fastening the Velcro straps on the sides. He changed out to his thigh holster to ensure quick access to his service weapon.

"This is ridiculous." Eric had run out of patience. He stepped up to the patrol officers staking out the front of the hotel and then pressed the mic on his radio to communicate with the others in the back. "If the DEA isn't here in five, we're going in."

"Ten-four," a voice crackled over the air.

The group of officers and Eric checked their firearms, leaving their thumb straps unsnapped. A minute later, a black SUV rolled up to the front of the hotel. Two Fed-looking, business-suited white males approached.

"You Decker?" one asked.

Eric nodded and rolled his eyes. "About time."

"I'm Barnes. This is Shipley. You got the warrant?"

Eric pulled a folded piece of paper from his vest and forced a grin. "Let's go."

The street cop he had monitoring the security cameras reported that no one had entered or left the suites since Quintrell left the hotel, but Eric had a bad feeling. It had taken him fifteen minutes to secure Quintrell after he met with Padrino and post surveillance at the hotel exits, and anyone could've slipped out in a blind spot.

Armed with passkeys, Eric, Barnes, and two officers took position outside Padrino's suite. Similarly, Shipley and three uniformed officers set up outside Rosa's old suite. Eric gave the nod to the group across the hall. Simultaneously, he and an officer from the other group each pounded on a door.

"San Francisco Police. Search warrant."

He hoped for a response, but his gut told him Padrino had already slipped out. When no one answered after a five-count, he and the officer at the other door used the passkeys. Each team flooded the two suites in single files, guns drawn. Finding the main room of Padrino's suite unoccupied, they broke into two groups of two, targeting the two bedrooms. Without a pause, each team entered.

From the other room, a voice boomed, "Clear."

Eric said the same after he entered the empty room. He pressed his mic to raise the other team, hoping for a long shot. "Anything?"

"Nothing. All clear."

Eric lowered his head. They were too late. Padrino could be anywhere. He dialed his cell phone.

"West."

"Hotel's a bust. Are we set for Oakland?"

"Almost. We'll have the warrant and Oakland PD in place by the time you get there."

Eric checked his watch. With the evening commuter traffic still hours away, he should make it there in twenty minutes. "Heading there now."

With the weight of all this taking its toll, his neck muscles stiffened. Reagan was missing, and Sloane depended on him to be hot on her trail. Though she didn't know it, he'd already turned her world upside down in the worst possible way, and he wasn't going to let that happen again. He'd be a better person than he had been in his youth.

Dealing with multiple jurisdictions complicated matters, and Prichard's two wildcards were slowing down his search. He'd have to adapt on the fly. Not knowing who in the DEA he could trust and without Sloane or Finn there to back him up, he was going to have only his gut to trust in enemy territory.

The fact that this was going to go down in the Lower Bottoms of Oakland added yet another layer of complication. A hotbed of drugs and violence, it was well known for a robust street communication system that warned the local gangbangers of police activity in the area. Oakland police had warned that lookouts would spot them as much as four or five blocks out. To avoid detection, the search warrant execution team was therefore staging from ten blocks away. Everyone was going to have to be fast and know their part.

Since Eric was outside his jurisdiction, Shipley and Barnes had assigned him to back them up. They would approach in a trailing vehicle and secure the front perimeter once SWAT breached the building. Eric was unaccustomed to serving as a straphanger, but having no time to worry about a bruised ego, he swallowed his pride and rolled with it.

Unlike at the hotel, the DEA and Oakland police suspected this location was a cartel stronghold and expected heavy resistance. Consequently, the twelve-man SWAT team loaded for a small war, equipping themselves with tactical battering rams, smoke grenades, bulletproof shields, automatic rifles, and semiautomatic pistols.

At the signal, the caravan of armored vehicles and dark SUVs rumbled down the streets of the Lower Bottoms, scattering drug dealers, gang members, and the streetwise. A handful jumped on their cell phones, likely warning their various bosses. The vehicles came to a halt in front of the house Sloane had followed Padrino to two days earlier.

Without a single word of instruction, the SWAT team moved in. Wearing ballistic armor, they carried assault weapons with thirty-round magazines, red-dot sights, and tactical flashlights mounted to their barrels. One carried a battering ram in his left hand.

"Now, we wait." Shipley leaned against a fender of their SUV, which was safely parked behind the armored vehicles.

Fucking coward. Eric got the impression he was more than happy to be letting someone else take point and possibly a bullet for his case. In all his years wearing a badge and all the stories his father used to tell of his days on the force, he'd never been less impressed with a fellow cop. Though, his and his dad's old partner, Peter Rook, came in a close second.

A loud rap on the front door—"Police! Search warrant!"—was followed by the obligatory five-count.

An officer swung the battering ram, splintering parts of the door and frame, then shifted to one side. Without making a noise, other officers swarmed through the open door in a single file like a fast-moving trail of ants on the hunt. Eric had seen how the well-oiled SWAT machine trained for silence to catch the bad guys off guard. He expected that team members were fanning out, some taking preassigned flanks, left or right, while others plowed forward. Gunshots in rapid succession rang in the air. Too many to count. Smoke from tear gas grenades billowed from an upstairs window.

Silence.

Eric bounced on the balls of his feet, waiting for news. Were Reagan and Chandler inside? Had they been caught in the crossfire? He'd never forgive himself if a bullet found Reagan, especially from friendly fire.

When the lead SWAT officer emerged from the front door, he raised his face shield, signaling they'd secured the scene. Eric rushed forward, his eyes questioning the team leader.

"The man and the girl aren't here." The officer slung his automatic rifle lower before wiping sweat from his forehead.

Eric nodded in a mix of relief and dread. Blood wasn't on his hands this time, but Reagan and Finn's father were still missing. "Anyone injured?"

"Not a scratch on our side, but we have five dead perps."

He shook the man's hand. "Appreciate the fine work today."

Eric walked back to Shipley and Barnes, who had stayed back, content with gnawing on toothpicks. "No hostages and no Padrino."

"It was a long shot." Barnes shrugged as if he didn't care. "There's no telling where he has them."

"Thank you, Captain Obvious." Eric sharpened his words, hoping one would pop Barnes' overinflated ego.

Shipley flew from his resting perch and squared off toe-to-toe with Eric. "You're here as a courtesy, asswipe."

"Courtesy, my ass." Eric stiffened his posture. "I'm here because no one can tell the good guys from the bad."

"What the hell does that mean?" Shipley's nostrils flared.

Eric had said too much already, and he didn't know who to trust. All he knew was Quintrell had hinted someone on the team trailing Diego Rojas was likely on the take.

"Nothing." Eric swallowed his pride and walked away. No time for pissing contests while his team needed to regroup.

* * *

Heavy eyelids kept Reagan wrapped in a dark fuzziness as she slipped back into consciousness. "*Don't lose my sweater*," flittered a woman's faint voice in her head.

A moment later, a different female voice drifted to her ear. It sang to the rhythm of a mariachi trumpet, guitar, and maybe an accordion in a language she couldn't make out. She next realized that the right side of her face was resting on something hard and cold. Something with parallel ridges and grooves about two inches wide and two inches apart. Below that, she heard cadenced rumbling and gentle vibrations that reminded her of the Tenneys. She'd often fallen asleep to that sound on trips to Lake Tahoe in the back of her grandparents' station wagon. She must be in a vehicle.

Fluttering open her eyes, she struggled to bring her surroundings into focus. Rolling her head an inch to the left brought the ceiling and white walls into view. *Shit!* That man had dragged her into a white van, and she was still in it. Her heart doubled its pace. She'd been kidnapped.

When she parted her lips, her left cheek and eye socket throbbed in dull pain. She tried to swallow, but her tongue dragged on a dry, cottony taste—he'd probably drugged her too. The attempt to move her legs proved fruitless—she was bound at the ankles. Her arms were tied behind her back as well. She yanked once to try to free herself, but something sharp cut into her wrists.

Even through the haze, she sensed remaining quiet was her safest option. With bound hands, she randomly searched the floor behind her for anything that could help release what she now assessed were sturdy plastic bindings around her wrists and ankles. Her hand bumped against something soft, something skin-like. She jerked back. That something was somebody. One of them?

Sensing no movement, she reached out in a second tentative search. She touched a hand larger than hers with rougher skin. A man's perhaps. It twitched. She pulled back again, fearing the unknown. But what if he wasn't one of them? Sloane had drilled into her over the past year to be aware of her surroundings. *You can think your way out of most dangerous situations if you pay attention.* She never thought her stepmother's pestering would come in handy.

Reagan waited until what she now deciphered as Latin pop music playing on the car radio was loud enough to mute the rustling of her movements. Craning her neck, she leaned backward to glimpse the man to her side. His back was to her, and his hands and feet were also tied with bindings. With his graying hair and casual clothes, he looked nothing like the man who had taken her. Was he another hostage or a plant? Instinct told her he was a hostage too, but she'd seen enough horror movies to suspect a trick.

Chandler's head bounced against the floor, the impact rousing him. Road reverberations and Latin music pulled him even further from the fog of whatever the thug had used to drug him. He was unsure which annoyed him more, the resulting headache or the cottonmouth. Both resembled a cheap tequila hangover. A turn of his throbbing head revealed that things hadn't changed much since he was abducted. The young woman he'd almost crushed earlier still lay bound next to him.

Returning his head to the floor, he stifled a groan. The hard ridges there made for a less than comfortable bed and an even worse headrest, especially when they seemed to be traveling at highway speed on what seemed like pretty rough road.

Better uncomfortable than dead, he rationalized.

Though he never made it past Tenderfoot in the Boy Scouts, one lesson that had stuck with him was how to navigate, either by the sun, stars, or other landmarks. Coupling that with his primary adult lesson—knowledge was power—he decided the more he knew of his circumstance, the better chance he'd have of escaping.

Chandler strained his neck and eyes toward the front of the van. Two men occupied the seats there, both focusing on the road ahead. Given the streaks of sunlight filtering through the passenger side window and the assumption they had knocked him out several hours ago, he calculated they were likely heading south.

A pungent scent of cow manure seeped into the cavity of the van and persisted for well over a minute. To his memory, large cattle ranches ran along Highway 5 and Highway 99, both of which ran north-south. The air-conditioner blast coming from the front to counter a stifling heat hinted they were in one of California's hot valleys. The noise from passing traffic sounded like one big rig after another. If so, they were probably somewhere along the two-hundred-mile stretch between Modesto and Bakersfield. Not a big help, but at least they weren't off the beaten path—one thing in his favor.

The young, blond woman he narrowly missed crushing earlier brushed against his hand, prompting him to roll toward her. She lay, facing away from him. He nudged her with his bound feet, and she responded by twisting her neck and making contact with the corner of her left eye. The muscles surrounding her eye socket twitched. Sensing fear but not panic in her, he tipped his brows up to convey a shared understanding of their predicament. He pursed his lips and offered a silent "shhh."

She cast her chin toward the front and then back at Chandler. Her timid nod reassured him that she understood the need for silence. She rolled to face him and mouthed, "Where?"

He shook his head and widened his eyes, sending the message he wasn't sure.

Rolling several degrees onto his belly, he stretched his arms to get her to focus on the plastic tie. Making a sawing motion with his fingers, he hoped she'd understand to look for something to cut it. She furrowed her brow, prompting him to point his chin toward his hands and make the sawing motion again. Her eyes widened with understanding before she mouthed a silent "oh."

Both scooted to the edges of the van's interior and slithered against their respective walls. Chandler tapped his fingers along the sliding door side, searching for anything with an edge to it, but found nothing. Reagan's eyes bulged and she stopped her slow creep along the wall. She must have snagged something that could work. Twisting her body, she swished her arms up, her face looking strained. Beads of sweat dripped onto the metal van floor as she labored to sever the band.

"Working," she mouthed before a ringing noise caused her to freeze. Her eyes grew extra round.

Chandler mouthed, "Stop."

They both rolled over. He hoped she pretended to be asleep like he did. The music faded, and the ringing stopped. Chandler strained to hear the voice from the front seat.

"…I know the address… three hours… yes, Padrino…"

Wherever the men were taking them, he gathered he and the girl would have several more hours in the van before he'd have to worry about this mysterious Padrino.

* * *

The squad room had quieted down finally from the buzz of Reagan's kidnapping. Grateful everyone was keeping their distance, Sloane huddled with Finn in the corner by her desk. In order to get through the next few minutes, she needed a gentle rub on the arm, a squeeze of a hand, or a whisper in her ear, not pep talks from well-wishers.

As Sloane hit the dial button on her phone, she reached for Finn's hand. She dreaded making this call. Janet Tenney had become a surrogate mother to her while her ankle mended following Avery's death, and she was about to break her heart. When the call connected, Sloane squeezed Finn's hand to siphon courage from it.

"Janet, it's Sloane."

"This is a pleasant surprise."

"Janet…" Sloane closed her eyes to the painful reality of her next words. "I'm afraid I have troubling news."

"What is it, Sloane?"

"Reagan is missing."

"What do you mean, missing?" Janet's voice trembled.

"An evil man connected to a case I'm working on took her, and he wants to exchange her for a vital witness."

"My God," Janet gasped. The following silence was deafening.

"I'm so sorry, Janet." Sloane's lips quivered with a mixture of guilt and regret. "This is all my fault."

"You have to find her, Sloane. You and Reagan are all Caleb and I have left."

"I'm doing everything I can." When sobs replaced Janet's silence, Sloane said, "I promise, I'll get her back." Though she had no clue where to start, she would grasp at every conceivable straw to do just that.

"We're coming down from Reno. We can be there in five or six hours."

"Dylan has a spare key to the house at the Tap. Let yourself in."

"All right, dear. We'll see you soon. Love you."

"Love you, too." When Sloane hung up, she realized that marked the first time she'd told Janet she loved her—a troubling fact. She should say such things to the people she loved at every opportunity, not only when her back was against the wall. Sloane promised herself not to make the same mistake again, especially with Finn.

Moments later, Kadin trudged over and invaded Finn and Sloane's private corner. Lines of worry framed her expression. "Sloane…" When Kadin's gaze fell on her and Finn's clasped hands, her jaw twitched. "I did what you asked and notified the Santoses' lawyer about Reagan. He's requested an emergency hearing to reconsider custody. If the judge denies my motion to postpone, you may have to appear in court tonight or tomorrow."

"You're fucking kidding, right?" The Santoses' thoughtless manipulations had made Sloane clench her jaw many times, but this one crossed the line. "Damn it, Kadin. Gloves off with them." Sloane dropped Finn's hand and pointed an index finger in Kadin's face. "I'm paying you to fight them with everything you can. I don't care how dirty it has to be."

Kadin flinched.

"Sloane." Finn's voice contained too much disapproval for Sloane's liking, making her pause. She turned when Finn placed a hand on the hollow of her back, finding a set of hazel eyes begging her to back off.

"I'm sorry, Kadin." Sloane's voice had lost its power. She regretted her outburst. "I know you're upset about Chandler."

"We're all on edge." Kadin softened her expression but stood her ground. "You concentrate on getting Reagan back, and I'll handle the judge."

"Thank you." After Kadin retreated to a polite distance, Sloane gave her a grateful nod.

Finn took Sloane into an embrace, providing the tender, reassuring touch she needed. Sloane fixed her gaze on the window near her desk and the sliver of bay water visible there for more strength. The sense of home centered her enough to allow her to focus on the next step. "We'll find them." A tingle in her spine gave Sloane the feeling her words weren't conjecture, but a foretelling of a positive outcome.

"I know we will." Finn squeezed extra tight, bunching fabric beneath her fingers and pulling it against Sloane's back.

"Sloane."

"Yeah?" Sloane turned her head in time to see Eric checking out Kadin's backside as she left. She ignored his ogling and focused on the prospect that she'd have one less thing to worry about if Kadin handled the judge.

"Everyone's here. We're moving it to the briefing room down the hall," he said.

Sloane turned her stare back to Finn before releasing her grip. "Let's go find our family."

Eric, Sloane, and Finn filed one by one toward the squad room doors. The moment Sloane rounded the corner, she stopped dead in her tracks, like she'd hit a brick wall. She couldn't believe her eyes. Days ago she'd only caught a glimpse of him and from a distance, but she recognized the man.

"What's wrong?" Finn's shaky voice told Sloane she'd sensed her growing tension.

"The guy standing next to Prichard." Sloane's stare focused on the man like lasers, a treacherous reality coming into focus. The two-for-one tailored business suit didn't mask the clean-cut look that had made him stick out like a sore thumb the first time she saw him.

"Who? Barnes?" Finn probed.

"He's yours?"

"Yeah, why?"

"Son of a bitch." Her breathing labored.

Sloane stabbed her hand beneath the flap of her jacket, her fingers wrapping around the grip of her Sig Sauer. In a single motion, her index finger slid against the trigger guard while her arm whipped the pistol toward her target.

"Hands! Show me your hands!" Sloane barreled toward Barnes, applauding herself for deciding to dump the walking boot earlier despite weakness in her foot. Both hands gripped her weapon with the crushing force of an elephant as she kept the gun pointed at his chest.

Like an extension of Sloane's right arm, Eric drew and aimed his weapon too. They were a well-tested team, and many hairy situations had forced them to back each other up in a fraction of a second. He didn't hesitate to back her play now.

All heads turned, and the room's chatter silenced. Lieutenant Morgan West, ADA Kyler Harris, Agent Shipley, and everyone else in the room parted like the Red Sea, creating a direct path between Sloane and Barnes.

Barnes froze, except for the bob of his Adam's apple.

"What the hell?" Prichard stiffened, his last word sharp.

"She said 'hands,'" Eric said.

Sloane glanced for a second at Eric, who was nodding the barrel of his gun up and down an inch. He then sidestepped to give Barnes multiple targets if he was dumb enough to try something.

"Better yet, resist," Eric said.

"Do as she said, Barnes." Finn's quick order defused the thick tension in the room. He eased up his hands like an outgunned desperado. Finn approached and removed his weapon from his shoulder holster.

"What the hell is going on, Harper?" Prichard asked.

"I have a feeling Sloane just ID'd the other leak."

"This son of a bitch was at the Lower Bottoms house when Los Dorados ambushed me." Sloane clenched her jaws with crushing force, biting the inside of her cheek. A bitter, salty taste trickled into her mouth. "I saw him come out with Padrino."

Her index finger shifted from the trigger guard. Ten pounds of pressure on the trigger would send a bullet into the chest of the man who'd likely made it possible for Caco to rig Diego's lab to explode. She raised the barrel of her gun so her aim evened with the bridge of his nose. There, between the eyes, was the sure kill shot. A firm hand pressed on her forearm, and she glanced down at the annoying distraction.

"Good job, Sloane." Eric guided her arm down until her weapon pointed at the floor. Holstering his gun, he smiled, and Sloane did the same. Giving her a wink, he turned and coldcocked Barnes square in the face with a crushing punch, cracking the cartilage in his nose. "That's for Avery."

CHAPTER FIFTEEN

You know the difference between the law and justice and that the two don't always mean the same thing.

The words Eric had said to Sloane on her first day as a detective replayed in his head like a mantra. Eleven years on the job had taught him that justice sometimes required not only bending the law but also breaking it. Today, he would do as much for Sloane.

Several feet away, Lieutenant Morgan West and Agent Nate Prichard were consulting each other in the corner of the observation room between Bryant's interrogation rooms. With time running out, each whispered back and forth, deciding on the only option left. They nodded in apparent concurrence before turning toward the others.

"Do what you have to, but don't put him in the hospital." West's support was in keeping with their shared history. They'd been in this situation before.

"Do yourself a favor and make sure it doesn't show beyond what you've already done," Prichard said before closing the door behind him and West, leaving only Eric, Sloane, and Finn to discuss how to extract information out of Barnes about Padrino.

Eric removed his jacket and draped it over the back of an observation room chair, focusing on the task ahead. He rolled up his sleeves, one at a time, evening each of the folds. What he was about to do, he'd done only twice before in his career. He reserved it as a last resort, to be used only when a ticking clock worked against him. The previous time a missing toddler's life had hung in the balance. He considered himself lucky to have returned her to her parents that same day. He considered Reagan family and would do tonight whatever it took to find her.

"I'd prefer it if you two left." Eric glanced first at Finn before settling on Sloane's somber face. This represented a chance to make a hefty down payment on a debt he could never repay, a debt he'd owed her since she was a child. He couldn't let Sloane see how far he'd go to right what he'd done, though.

"We're partners, Eric." Sloane's pursed lips and headshake communicated the conflict brewing inside her. "I should be in there with you."

"What you don't see, you can't testify to." Eric narrowed his eyes, preparing himself for the violence he would soon carry out. "I'll let you know when it's done."

"Let's go." Finn grabbed Sloane's hand. "I need a cup of coffee."

Once the door closed behind Sloane and Finn, Eric stared through the two-way mirror at Barnes, alone in the small interrogation room with his left hand chained to the table. Minutes earlier, after Barnes had said the magic word, "lawyer," Eric decided the situation called for drastic measures. He was confident he could get Barnes to talk. The only thing he didn't know was if the information he provided would lead them to Reagan and Chandler before it was too late.

He opened the door leading to the interrogation room. The sewer smell there had reached an all-time high, turning Barnes an amusing shade of green.

"Where's my lawyer so I can get out of this shithole?" Barnes' nose turned up, seeking less putrid air perhaps.

"I'm afraid he's not coming."

Eric's pulse remained steady when he pulled out a second pair of handcuffs and latched one cuff to Barnes' right wrist. He then unlocked the cuff connected to the table crossbar, knelt behind Barnes' chair, and linked the dangling end of each handcuff underneath the seat of the chair. Barnes was now chained to the chair with his wrists tight against the sides of the seat. Helpless. The look Barnes threw Eric signaled he was sure this wouldn't be a by-the-book interrogation.

Eric jerked the chair, teetering Barnes on its back legs and scraping it across the tiled floor. The jarring noise resembled a train braking to a halt, forecasting the rest of the questioning would be equally jolting. When he thudded Barnes against the wall, he'd set the stage to maximize pain.

"Where did Padrino take them?"

"I want my damn lawyer."

Breaking him wouldn't be easy, Eric knew. His first blow needed to set the tone and leave no doubt.

Balling his right hand, he dipped his shoulder and hurled his fist into Barnes' gut with his full weight, bouncing his head off the wall. Barnes released a guttural moan and drooled spit onto his pants. An abdomen punch, while uncomfortable, rarely yielded lasting pain, but Eric needed to show how this interrogation would proceed.

"Where are they?"

Barnes gasped for air, spat on the floor, and took several haggard breaths. "You're fucking nuts."

One punch seldom sent the message that this wouldn't end until Eric had gotten what he wanted. He shifted to his left and wielded a sharp blow to Barnes' right side—a direct shot to the liver that would hurt for days. Barnes grimaced as he coughed and spat more, gasping again for air.

"You will tell me everything you know about Los Dorados and Padrino." Eric fixed a sleeve that had unfurled one roll. "The only question is: Will I have to rupture your spleen before you do?"

Punch after punch, Eric worked up a good sweat. As expected, Barnes lasted longer than others before him. He faced a lifetime behind bars, and as a cop turned bad, he'd be a target for either a shank or spending years as someone's prison bitch. Holding out for a deal posed his best option, but Eric broke him and learned everything he knew without one.

"You better be telling me the truth." Eric rolled his sleeves down, signaling the beating had ended. "Or you'll share the same fate as Diego Rojas—shanked in a jailhouse brawl."

Eric had played it smart as Prichard suggested and gave Barnes only body shots that didn't leave a mark. Internal injuries were another matter. Barnes limped out under the escort of a uniformed officer, his elbows tucked tight against his sides to soothe the pain. The official report would read he sustained injuries from unspecified prisoners while in the holding cell.

Sloane waited with Finn at her desk, sipping stale coffee and exchanging the fewest of words. A distant thought took her from that crowded, cluttered squad room to wherever Los Dorados held Reagan. Was she still alive? Was she hurt? Were Padrino's thugs doing unthinkable things to her?

When Eric stepped through the door, her gaze zeroed on him. He gestured toward Lieutenant West's office and walked inside, sparking a glimmer of hope inside Sloane. She and Finn followed and closed the door behind them.

Eric pinched his lips together, telegraphing his disappointment. "He doesn't know where they are."

Finn dipped her head to the devastating news. Sloane did the same. Barnes had represented their best hope for the element of surprise. Now it seemed Padrino held all the cards.

"What *did* he tell you?" Prichard asked.

"He's been on Padrino's payroll. He tipped Caco off about the fake raid the night of the wildfire."

"That one is on me." Prichard rubbed the back of his neck. "I called his team from the café that day to see if they knew anything about the raid."

Eric turned to Finn. "He also fed Padrino information about Diego when you first flipped him. Padrino ordered him to take care of it." He redirected his attention to Sloane. "Barnes was the one who planted the bomb at the lab."

Finn gasped at the realization choking the room.

"He also fed Padrino's man information about Sloane's and Finn's personal lives. That's how he knew to go after Reagan and Chandler." Eric gritted his teeth.

Sloane doubled over at that punch in the gut, palms on her knees. One of the supposed good guys—Finn's man—had killed her wife, and now her daughter might die because of him. She'd guessed perhaps that whoever turned dirty may have turned a blind eye to what happened as a result, but she never suspected this. The bitterness of the truth paralyzed her.

"I'm so sorry, Sloane," Finn said. Sloane raised her stare. The lines on Finn's face revealed her overwhelming regret. "This is my fault. He was my responsibility."

"He was on the take long before you came along." Eric shot daggers at Prichard. "If anyone is to blame—"

"No one is to blame but Barnes." West rocked both hands up and down a few inches to calm the room. "Let's focus on the case."

"Fine." Eric took in a deep breath. "Icing on the cake as far as Barnes goes is that he also ratted out Quintrell. Padrino knows he wore a wire."

"That's just great." Prichard threw his arms in the air. "What about the cell he used to contact Padrino?"

Eric shook his head. "A burner that he threw off the bridge. Even that call was to Padrino's lieutenant, whose phone is likely at the bottom of the bay too."

"We're back to square one." Finn shook her head in defeat. "Do we wait for Padrino to contact us?"

"No." Sloane righted herself with a deep intake of air and gave Eric a thankful nod. "Cases never solve themselves." He had taught her cases only got solved through hard police work, a philosophy that earned them the highest closure rate in the division. She wasn't about to give up now. "We bring in Rosa and Quintrell."

* * *

Sloane glanced up from her desk chair when the door of the squad room opened to reveal her last hope, flanked by two armed uniformed officers. Quintrell's arrogance had long disappeared along with his expensive tailored suit and leather wingtips. In their place—jailhouse reds, black flip-flops, and a hefty dose of humility. If not for the nightmare of the last six hours, Sloane would have taken great joy in his plight.

To Sloane's left, Rosa raised an index finger, asking David to wait one minute after the guards had unchained him. Rosa turned to Antonio, who sat inches away, again meticulously ordering each french fry against an imaginary line atop Eric's desk.

"Be a good boy and stay with the officer." Rosa caressed his arm, preparing him for another absence from her. "I'll be right back."

"I'm a good boy." Antonio kept his focus on the almost-finished line of fries.

Sloane's heart went out to this young man. To his mother, Antonio represented the reason she woke up every day. To Padrino, he was something to control and possess. Trading this good boy for Reagan's life meant condemning him without his mother as a buffer. How far was Sloane willing to go?

When Rosa turned toward David, he stretched his arms out and then folded her hands in his. "Are they treating you well?" he asked. "Do you need anything?"

"We're fine." Rosa offered a weak grin, but the way she looked at him despite everything she'd withstood—the lies and time lost—it was obvious she still loved him. "We have everything we need."

Sloane cleared the lump in her throat. "We should get started."

She directed them to Lieutenant West's office, where the usual players gathered. West, Kyler, Sloane, Finn, Quintrell, and Rosa sat at the conference table, while Eric and Prichard stood several feet away.

"We brought you two here because Padrino has kidnapped Sergeant Sloane's stepdaughter and Agent Harper's father," West said.

Rosa gasped and covered her mouth with a hand.

"He slipped away. He's not at the hotel nor the Oakland location we knew about," Prichard said.

"I see." Quintrell nodded. "And you expect my help."

Sloane did need his help, so she calmly rose to her feet and placed both palms on the table. "I expect you to help me get my daughter back, just like I did with your son." She refused to break her stare until he responded.

"Has he made contact yet?" Quintrell continued to lock eyes with her.

"No."

"Interesting."

"What the hell does that mean?" Sloane squeezed her lips, mustering what little patience she had left.

"I know my father." Quintrell leaned back in his chair, a sign of growing confidence and, to Sloane's ire, arrogance. "If this were a simple exchange, he would strike while the iron was hot."

"And because he hasn't?" Sloane returned to her seat but leaned forward, fighting to keep in check her extreme dislike for this man.

"It means this is personal, and he's carefully planning the exchange so no one but he will walk away with what they want."

"So he's using our family as bait, not a bargaining chip."

"He blames you for killing his favorite son. Now you have his only grandchild. This is about evening the score, and in his world, he settles scores with a bullet to the head."

"So he won't let our family walk away alive?"

"Doubtful."

Sloane sank in her chair and turned toward Finn. She recognized the emotion in her eyes because it matched the fear overtaking her. This nightmare had her feeling like a caged animal, and her daughter would die unless she figured a way out.

Finn folded both hands around Sloane's. "We'll solve this."

"Where would he take them?" Eric had rested a hip against West's desk. Uncharacteristically, he tucked his right hand in his pocket, likely to hide the bruises Sloane saw emerging on his knuckles.

Quintrell twisted his head toward him. "I only know the cities of his compounds, not exact locations."

"Where?" Finn's tone sharpened with her scowl.

"Santa Rosa, but that burned to the ground. Oakland, which you raided. Then there's Los Angeles, Fresno, and Las Vegas."

"Fresno?" Rosa turned her head.

"Yes, why?" Quintrell asked.

"We flew into Fresno from Mazatlán."

"Did you go anywhere in town?" Eric asked.

"Yes, but he had me and Antonio wait in the car."

"Do you remember exactly where?" Eric asked.

"It was a potato farm outside of town." Rosa patted her lips with an index finger. "I think I can show you if you have a map."

Sloane closed her eyes and tightened her hand around Finn's, receiving an eager squeeze in return. Thanks to Rosa, they might have another lead. Which offered hope. At this point, she was willing to latch on to anything.

"This is good, really good." Finn's eyes brightened. "Our Fresno field team can execute a search warrant within an hour."

"Let's think this through, Finn." Eric turned to Quintrell. "This place could be a fortress, right?"

"Our Modesto office has five available teams." Prichard rubbed his fingers as if calculating something in his head. "That would make a dozen agents. I can have them in place in less than two hours."

"That should be enough." Quintrell nodded. "The only downside is that my father has had a six-hour head start. Anywhere he has them, they'll be barricaded and likely booby-trapped."

"Fresno PD has a bomb squad." West picked up the handset on her desk phone. "I can coordinate."

"If Fresno PD will be with you, we can get a county search warrant. I'll alert the Fresno DA, and she'll have it waiting." Kyler pulled out her mobile and scrolled through her contact list.

Sloane turned her gaze on Rosa. "This could be the break we need. I can't thank you enough."

Minutes later, at West's desk computer, Eric showed Rosa maps of Fresno, and she marked the roads she remembered taking with Padrino. An Internet search of farms in the area narrowed down the possibilities. Eric brought up Internet satellite photos. "Is this it, Rosa?"

She studied the narrow two-lane roads, rows of green planted fields, and a cluster of buildings nestled in the center. "I'm not sure." She cocked her head back and forth. "Can you zoom in closer?"

Eric clicked the troublesome, sticky computer mouse, pounding it several times on the desktop. "Damn it."

Rosa laid a soft hand on his. "It's okay, Eric. Let me." She grabbed the mouse and blew several sharp breaths into its wheel housing. "I've learned not to ask for things and make do with what Arturo gives me. Sometimes these things need gentle encouragement."

Tapping it a few times, she clicked to zoom the photo on the screen. Her eyes squinted as they followed the road up to a building. "Yes, this is it. I remember the red building and the large white tank."

A toothy smile formed on Eric's face. He followed it up with a big, sloppy kiss on her cheek. "Rosa, you're beautiful."

Eric jotted down the address and name of the farm before turning to Sloane a few feet away. He gave her the same grin and raised his hand with the piece of paper in it. "Got it."

She stared at Finn, who had escaped to the distraction of West's window, the spot where she first laid eyes on her childhood crush seven months ago. Thinking back to that day, Sloane felt her arms chill to emerging goose bumps. That was the day she, Finn, and Padrino were put on a collision course. Now that had come to a head.

Her eyes welled in relief when Finn's eyes finally met hers. If they were lucky, Reagan and Chandler were in Fresno. And if they were even luckier, Prichard's teams would catch Padrino's men by surprise, and Reagan and Chandler would sleep in their beds tonight. The only catch—they needed to hurry. She didn't want to think about what might happen if they were too late.

The more time Los Dorados had to fortify, the riskier a rescue attempt would become.

A flurry of phone calls ensued, with everyone working like parts of a well-oiled machine. Kyler added the critical last piece of information to Fresno's search warrant request—the address. Prichard sent his DEA teams photos to give them the lay of the land, and West confirmed the bomb squad was gearing up.

Finn walked up to Sloane and squeezed her hand. "Let's go watch them get our family back."

* * *

Finn swiped her access card over the electronic reader to gain entrance to the DEA technical operations center. The secure door clicked and buzzed and she pushed it open with a thrust of a palm. She walked through first. "We need the room." Her curt order didn't contain her usual courtesy.

The three technicians logged off their computers, gathered their belongings, and scurried out, leaving the chilly room to everyone vested in the rescue attempt. While Prichard took what appeared to be the command chair in the center of the upper level, West and Kyler paired off in chairs on the lower level two steps down. Eric paced behind them.

Sloane stuck by Finn's side in the middle of the room, where her nimble fingers were gliding over a workstation keyboard at a blistering, mesmerizing pace. Seeing Finn's confidence and expertise with the equipment impressed Sloane and gave her hope. If Finn was this focused under pressure, she couldn't help but have a good feeling about the teams Finn had trained and dispatched to save Reagan.

Moments later, static snow replaced the charts and surveillance videos on three of the giant screens mounted on the far wall. Identifying tag words appeared in the upper left corner of each screen: FR Tac 1, MD Tac 2, and MD Tac 3.

Up to this point, Sloane had been focused on the next step and how to pull it off. Now, with nothing more to do, nothing more to plan, she had to wait to find out if their family was alive. Doing nothing was excruciating. A hunger pang that verged on nausea reminded her that she hadn't eaten all day either. She rubbed her abdomen and grimaced.

"Are you all right?" Finn asked.

"I'm starving."

"Me too. Hold on." Finn pressed the microphone at the control console. "Modesto Tac Two, this is SF Two. What's your ETA to the rally point?"

The radio sparked static. A second later, a voice replied, "We're twenty out."

"Copy. Advise when you're five out."

"Roger. Modesto Tac Two out."

"SF Two out." Finn gestured toward the door. "We have about half an hour before they'll be ready to breach. I keep a bunch of snacks in my office."

"I knew I liked you for a reason." Sloane forced a smile.

Minutes later, while Finn rummaged through a bottom desk drawer, Sloane scanned her office. She'd visited it once before but was too upset following the ambush to really take it in. The furniture was made of real wood, not metal with scuffed pressed-wood accents like the other field agents. That meant Finn was an executive. The walls were void of the typical "I love me" trappings, certificates, diplomas, and awards displayed to impress visitors. Obviously Finn didn't think she had to put her accomplishments on display. Her work spoke for itself.

"Let's see." Finn still had her head bent over the bottom drawer. "I have almonds, pistachios, beef jerky, dried apricots, popcorn, and dark chocolate bars. Pick your poison."

"How about smorgasbord?"

"A woman after my own heart."

I am after your heart, and it's time you know. The stress of the last few hours melting slightly.

Finn unfolded two paper napkins atop her desk and placed small helpings of each snack on them. She also retrieved a bottle of water from her drawer. "Sorry, only one bottle. We'll have to share."

"I can live with that." Sloane sat in the guest chair, placed perpendicular to Finn's desk, and picked at her food. "You were impressive in that ops center."

"It's pretty cool, isn't it?" Finn dug into the popcorn.

"It is." Oddly, the idle chat, a moment of normalcy amidst the chaos, provided a sense of comfort. Sloane pointed to a framed picture atop the wood credenza behind Finn's shoulder. "Is that you with the president?"

Finn shrugged after glancing at the frame, the only visible display of her accomplishments. "Yeah. I worked a case that ended up breaking up a large Mexicali cartel ring running into Yuma. That got me a meet-and-greet with POTUS and put me on the fast track." She spread out her arms as if surveying her kingdom. "Now, I have an incredible view of the city."

Sloane took a swig from the bottle before offering it to Finn. She pushed up from the chair to get a better view from the window. Finn joined her.

"You're right, this is amazing. But I think I like the view from your condo better. It's cozier than this." Sloane stared at the early evening cityscape, fixing her gaze on the city lights that were coming to life in the waning sunlight. The reminder of the city she called home brought on a familiar sense of calm.

"Me, too, but I think the view from your townhouse tops the one from my place. It's so peaceful on your deck."

"I know what you mean." That deck had been the source of many serene moments over the years. Too many to count. The most vivid was the one she had last night. When she had said her final goodbye to Avery. Sloane had the sudden sense their goodbye was timed for a reason. "I hope to share that with you one day."

Sloane turned to face Finn, who turned too, the quiet pulling them closer. For a moment, Sloane tucked away her worry and took Finn into her arms. "I love you, Finn Harper." She whispered into her ear while clutching the cloth of Finn's suit jacket until her fingertips numbed. "I've always loved you."

"I've always loved you, too." Finn sank into Sloane's embrace, tugging on Sloane's jacket.

Sloane had finally done it. Had said the words she'd known were true since the night of the wildfire. Words that acknowledged that she'd loved Finn since the day she held her hand walking out of choir. She had expected the words to eat away at the remaining memory of Avery and the love they once shared, but they hadn't. She was at peace with the truth. And somehow she knew Avery was too.

She loosened her grip to kiss Finn on the lips softly. Once, twice, three times. "It's good to say it," she said, pulling back enough to look into her eyes.

"It's good to hear it."

Sloane drew her hands to Finn's cheeks. She pressed their lips together again, but this kiss went deeper and had enough heat to melt sand into liquid, the force of it bouncing Finn against the glass. Her lips seared Finn's apart, and when she sent her tongue searching, a spasm clenched her inner walls.

Sloane was unsure if the deep, guttural moan was hers alone, but it made her want to touch more of Finn. This was not the time, though. Her lips found Finn's silky neck and drank her in like a fine wine. When this was over, when they had their family back, Sloane promised herself to finally surrender her body to the woman she'd already surrendered her heart to.

"Ahem. Sorry to interrupt." Eric's voice cut through the heat that had built between them.

Sloane stilled, relieved he had poor timing. She wasn't prepared to take this further, but she was unsure if she could have stopped on her own. She turned her head a few degrees but not enough to give away the conflict brewing inside her. "Yeah?"

"They're five minutes out," he said.

"We'll be right there."

Eric left without a word.

Sloane explored Finn's deep hazel eyes, the ones she'd chased all her life. She saw in them the same emotions growing within herself—love and desire, tempered by worry. "I'm ready for us but—"

"But first we have to get our family back."

The three ops center wall monitors came to life with high-definition live video feeds from the vest cameras of the team leaders, signifying their people had arrived at the rally point. Finn had assigned Fresno Tac 1 to take command and brief the other teams on the tactical plan. This was their turf, and she had confidence that Gomez, the lead field agent, would handle the operation with finesse.

Soon the feeds showed a dozen agents piling into three SUVs and then taking off in a high-speed caravan. One feed showed the SUV dashboard, another the bumper of the lead vehicle, and the other oncoming traffic. The Fresno bomb squad tactical vehicle was likely taking up the rear.

Within minutes, they would arrive at the farm's perimeter. Finn's pulse quickened in anticipation. Resting her elbows on the cold, smooth console, she glanced at Sloane next to her. Sloane's pale face and shaky hands signaled she was as nervous as she was.

Lives she couldn't bear losing hung on the precision of the teams she'd trained over the past year. Had she done enough? In her head she considered each team member, focusing on their strengths and weaknesses. Andrews was their best marksman, but his wife had a baby last month, and he might not be on a full night's rest. Dickey, former military and calm under pressure, was new and untested in a close-quarters firefight.

All twelve were well trained for raids, but this was a hostage rescue. She hoped Johnston and Gould would be the ones to breach the room where Los Dorados held her and Sloane's loved ones. Those two had the best reaction time on the DEA's version of Hogan's Alley, each with a perfect score and not a single good guy hit. Finn could do nothing more than hope she'd done enough to prepare her agents for this daring operation.

"They have the element of surprise going for them." Finn darted her gaze between the monitors. "These are some of my best agents. They'll do it right."

"I hope so." Sloane sounded uncertain. Finn knew placing trust in people she didn't know didn't come easy to Sloane, and with Reagan's life hanging in the balance, her doubt was likely ten times worse.

On one screen in the fading sunset, the pavement disappeared following a turn, replaced by dirt and gravel. One monitor showed a clear road ahead with planted fields on the left and right. The other two showed SUVs ahead with dust clouds rising on either side. Finn adjusted a few controls on her computer monitor and brought up the audio feed from Fresno Tac 1, the lead vehicle. The wheels crunched over the gravel in a rhythm reminiscent of a native drum calling warriors to battle. A red building came into view, the one Rosa had recognized, as did an old farm pickup truck. A beat-up sedan was parked to its side, suggesting that people might be inside.

Radio crackle. "We have two vehicles. Safeties off." That marked the last voice communication the teams would use until they breached the building. The sound of tires skidding on gravel grew loud. Then movement on all three screens came to an abrupt stop.

Before Finn could clutch Sloane's hand, she felt gripping pressure on her own, increasing with each passing second. Sloane's fingers throbbed in a rapid beat against Finn's palm. Hers did the same, matching her quick, shallow breaths. Whatever happened next was out of her hands…and Sloane's.

One video feed showed eight men and three women falling into position. Each was dressed for war in green tactical uniforms, bulletproof vests with gear pouches, helmets, and dark goggles. Each carried an AR-15 automatic rifle and a thigh-holstered sidearm. Three had battering rams slung over their shoulders. They fanned out in three sets of four in complete silence, one vest camera with each team. In synchronized, choreographed movements, each maneuvered to their assigned entry point on one of the three doors. Though it was not on screen, Finn knew the bomb squad had remained behind to secure the perimeter until called. She hoped they wouldn't need their expertise.

The radio cracked twice, the signal the first team was in place. Another double crack and another. All three groups were ready to breach. The next sound, a triple crack of the mic, would come from the operational commander, signaling "go" in their earpieces.

Crack. Crack. Crack.

Tactical battering rams splintered all three doors open. The teams entered and fanned out according to their assignment, depending on the layout. The high-definition video feeds blurred with the fast pace of the teams but showed an empty machine room, an empty hallway, and a break room filled with a half-dozen men.

"Federal agents!" a good guy's voice yelled.

Three men dressed in farm wear dove for cover while the others seated next to them reached for their waistbands. Agents fired, some shots hitting their targets. Oncoming gunfire forced the agents to take up defensive positions.

"Tac Three taking fire!"

The motion from the other feeds sped faster with walls, doors, and flashes of overhead lights passing in a blur. Tac One entered the break room through a secondary door, the bad guys in their line of vision with Tac Three yards beyond. They were in a crossfire, and every shot required accuracy. A single errant volley could find a friendly.

More shots. A bullet winged a female agent in the arm, but she got off one more shot.

Silence.

The monitors showed six bloodstained bad guys lifeless on the floor.

"Clear the rest of the building," the op commander ordered off-screen.

One by one, images of rooms and hallways flashed on the screens. Sloane squeezed Finn's hand like a vise. Both their breaths became audible in a synchronized beat like soldiers on a double-time march. Every muscle in Finn's body tightened, threatening to snap at the slightest addition of pressure.

"Tac Two clear."

"Tac Three clear."

"SF Two, this is Tac One. They're not here."

Finn collapsed in her chair as did Sloane. They'd wasted hours and were now out of leads. She dropped Sloane's hand when the hammer of reality hit her over the head—Padrino still controlled whether Reagan and Chandler lived or died.

CHAPTER SIXTEEN

A foreboding stillness choked the crowded elevator on the way up to the Bryant station squad room. The devastating disappointment of wasting time chasing ghosts had Sloane kicking herself for getting her hopes up. She knew better. Now she faced the crushing reality that kidnappings rarely ended well.

Her eyes focused on her feet, she was momentarily surprised by the sight of matching sneakers. She couldn't remember the last time her ankle had throbbed since she had dumped the walking boot. *Funny how the mind can only concentrate on one pain at a time*, she thought.

The elevator door swished open. Everyone disembarked but Sloane. Thoughts of her ankle and all the pain she'd endured the last few months swirled like a tornado. She glanced up, her eyes tracking Finn as she turned toward the squad room.

Eric held the door open before it closed. "Sloane, you coming?"

The sympathetic voice drew her attention and gaze. "We have to give him something more painful to think about."

"Who?"

"Padrino."

"What are you talking about?"

"Padrino took something valuable from us because we took something valuable from him. We have to convince him there's more at stake than making us pay."

"How do we do that?"

"Quintrell."

"I don't trust him."

"Neither do I, but he knows his father. If anyone knows his weak spot, it's Quintrell."

Sloane had one arrow left in her quiver, and she planned to use it to strike at Padrino's heart. She took off at a brisk pace toward the squad room, but Eric placed a hand on her shoulder to slow her.

"Wait a sec." He scanned the hallway as if making sure they were out of earshot of anyone else. "Back in Finn's office, I gather you told her."

"I did." All her adult life she had reserved the words "I love you," saying them only when she felt it in every fiber of her body. She had felt that with Avery, and now she did with Finn. Under any other circumstance, she'd grin from ear to ear, but tonight she didn't have time to savor the feeling nor to show Finn they weren't empty words.

"And?"

"We didn't get much past that point." Sloane inspected the tops of her sneakers again. "Maybe when all of this is over, I can do it right."

"I'm glad you have each other right now."

"That makes two of us."

As Sloane passed through the doors of the squad room, a narcotics detective caught her attention. He handed her a cardboard messenger envelope. "This came for you while you were at the Federal Building."

The hairs on her arms tingled and she came to an abrupt halt. This had to be from Padrino. She pulled the perforated tab to open the envelope, reached inside, and removed the contents—a single piece of paper and a flip phone. Turning over the paper and reading the first line, she gasped.

"This is it." Sloane's voice boomed loud enough to silence the room.

Finn jumped from her seat near Eric's desk and rushed over. As Eric looked over Sloane's shoulder to read the note, West, Kyler, and Prichard emerged from West's office. Sloane's heart pounded harder as her eyes passed over the first few words on the page again. Air stuck in her lungs when she deciphered Padrino's demands.

"What does it say?" Finn crowded her, demanding a response.

"He says you took from me. Now I've taken from you, Detective Sloane and Agent Harper. I propose an exchange: my son and grandson for your daughter and father. Call by seven p.m."

Sloane glanced at the clock on the wall, and an overwhelming sense of dread hit her like a tidal wave. She turned her wide-eyed gaze to Finn, her heart palpitating. The clock read 7:02. "We're late."

The muscles on both sides of Finn's jaw twitched with what must have been an equal sense of dread. "Call."

Everyone circled Sloane as she flipped the phone open and brought it to life. Pressing a button and arrowing down to the only saved number, she hit send. It rang once, twice, three, and four times. She snapped her eyes shut, squeezing hard at the fear gripping her. Was she too late? A click. The ringing stopped. Sloane waited a moment for someone on the other end to say something, but no one did. Cautious, she said, "Hello?"

Deep breathing came through the speaker, a wave of seething anger seeping through the line. A cold, male voice broke the silence. "You're late. Do you want your daughter to live?"

"I do." *No excuses, no weakness. Show only strength*, she told herself. "What do you want from us?"

"I want my family back. It's that simple. Then I will leave your country." Padrino's calm inflection and cadence were appropriate for conducting a business deal, not negotiating for the lives of innocent victims.

"How do you propose the exchange?"

"In one hour at a place of my choosing."

An hour meant Reagan and Chandler were close or already dead. Either way, she couldn't let Padrino have the upper hand on all the terms. Her instinct told her that if they were alive, he didn't intend to let them go. Nor would he walk away without exacting revenge. She needed to peck away at the unknown factors. To do that, she needed to stall. "Then we have a problem."

"What kind of problem?"

"Rosa and Antonio are already out of state in witness protection. It will take time to get them here."

"How much time?"

"We could get them here by morning."

Several silent beats passed.

"You have seven hours. If you don't call by then, the girl and man will die."

The call clicked and ended. His last words gave her hope Reagan and Chandler were alive. Sloane slipped the phone from her ear and turned to Finn. "It sounds like they're alive. I bought us seven hours. Until two o'clock."

Finn released a long, relieved breath. "Gives us time to come up with something."

West extended her hand palm up to Sloane. "I'll see if our tech guys can get anything off the phone. Maybe trace the call."

"I doubt you'll get anything." Sloane handed West the phone and pointed at it. "I have to call him back on that. Make sure they don't screw it up." Phone in hand, West trotted out the door. Turning her attention to Eric, Sloane filled her voice with a glint of confidence. "We need to get Quintrell and Rosa back here."

"I'll call holding." Eric strode to his desk.

Sloane had a detective stir Rosa from the breakroom and escort her back to the squad room. Minutes later, interrupting the traditional Thursday evening jailhouse meal of Salisbury steak and creamed corn, guards gathered up Quintrell and ushered him in from his cell. Sloane snickered mentally when he shuffled through the doors in his flip-flops. Seeing him in jailhouse reds had become a guilty pleasure.

Rosa's smile outshone the overhead fluorescents when her gaze turned to him. With everything Sloane had gone through since reconnecting with Finn, she understood that kind of enduring love, and her sympathies grew for Rosa. Once she entered witness protection, even if Quintrell made it out of prison alive, she'd never again see the man she loved. Was it fair? No, but a new name and a new life presented the only way to protect her and Antonio from Padrino's long reach.

In a take two, all the players reassembled in West's office.

"They weren't at the potato farm," Prichard announced.

"I'm so sorry." Rosa's soft eyes did more than acknowledge Sloane and Finn's pain. The pooling moisture there said she felt it. Sloane nodded her thanks.

"It was a long shot." Quintrell's unfazed response pissed off Sloane. Hell, everything that man said and did grated on her nerves.

"Padrino made contact," West said. "He wants to exchange you and Antonio for Reagan and Chandler in six and a half hours."

"Me?" Quintrell's eyebrows inched up. "So he knows I betrayed him. How did he find out?"

"The dirty DEA agent told him you wore a wire at the hotel," Eric said.

"That explains the move to isolation." Quintrell hunched in his chair. "I suppose I should thank you."

"We need your help." Sloane kept her tone calm. Until she'd exhausted every option, used every trick in the book, she refused to panic or, worse, give up. "Padrino has to have a weakness. Something we can use as leverage."

"Father cares about three things: loyalty, money, and family in that order, which is why I'm dead to him now. Any leverage I might have had is gone." Quintrell rubbed his chin. "Maybe… but I'd have to get her here."

"Who is her?" Sloane asked, grasping at the only straw visible.

"My sister."

"What are you proposing?" Sloane asked.

"Money he can replace, but family he cannot. Mother is dead. Caco is too. I'm as good as. Melina is the only family he has left." He straightened in his chair, a hint of his habitual smugness returning. The way he tugged at his baggy sweatshirt, Sloane reasoned he thought he was onto the solution. "She is your leverage."

"Does she work for your father?" Finn asked.

"No. She never had the stomach for it, and, Father did not hold her to the same standard since she's a woman. She does love the riches the family business brings, though. Her only failing in his eyes was never providing him with more grandchildren."

"We can use this." Sloane's mind raced to devise a solution before Padrino could control the outcome. "But can you get her here without alerting your father?"

"Yes."

Minutes later, Sloane and Finn gathered near the lieutenant's corner window, too anxious to remain seated. They were out of options and time if this failed. Sloane ran through the likely scenarios of a hostage exchange wherein Padrino held all the cards. None of them ended well.

Close enough to Finn to feel the heat from her body, she clasped her hand. "This has to work. It just has to."

"I can't think about the alternative. Daddy's been my only constant. He has to come home."

"He will. And so will Reagan."

Sloane glanced at Quintrell sitting at the conference table in his jailhouse reds, one leg crossed comfortably over the other. He looked too relaxed for a man about to try to entice his sister across the border in a high stakes bluff. Either he was a real bastard, or Melina was. Whichever, the Campos family was responsible for all of this, and they deserved whatever happened next.

West handed Quintrell one of the flip phones unearthed from the warrant search of his home. "You better sell it, or the deal is off."

Quintrell shifted his glance to Sloane and Finn. "I want him as much as you do." He dialed and then put the phone to his ear. "It's good to hear your voice, *flaca*. Have you put any meat on your bones yet?… Christmas would be nice… Maybe we can eat Crackerjacks for five hours at my home like we did last year… That would be nice. We'll make plans…See you then." He flipped the phone shut and handed it back to West. "It's done."

"That's it? Crackerjacks?" West asked.

"Yes. It's the family signal that our safety and all methods of communication have been compromised."

"And you told her to meet you at your home in five hours." The code wasn't hard for Sloane to crack. She and Eric had similar designated duress words for dangerous situations that had come in handy once or twice.

"You're not as thick-headed as you appear, Sergeant Sloane."

"You, though, are as big of an asshole as *you* appear." A crude retort, but it felt good and earned a chuckle from Eric from the other side of the table.

This plan had to work. Sloane hoped once Padrino realized his entire family hung in the balance, he'd let Reagan and Chandler go, and she and Finn would walk away alive.

CHAPTER SEVENTEEN

Sunlight had all but disappeared, making the van's windowless back compartment even darker. Chandler thought that following the phone call that they'd turned around and headed north—a change of plans directed by that Padrino guy, he surmised. After a while, the van settled into a slower pace, occasionally stopping and moving again. They'd found heavy traffic, which meant they were back in a populated area. At one point, the driver lowered his window, and after some fumbling, rolled it up again. The change in road vibration and rumbling from the wheels led Chandler to believe they'd passed through a tollbooth, but to which bridge, he wasn't sure.

Chandler and the girl had yet to exchange a spoken word. Her arms and shoulders were rocking all the while as she worked on fraying her plastic hand bindings. He hoped she'd made some progress, giving her a chance of escaping the brutal thugs in the front seat.

He tried wetting his lips, but his mouth had dried too much to work up enough saliva. Awake now for hours, he was thirsty, hungry, and needed to pee. Add to that his cramping arms and legs and the prospect of his kidnappers treating him humanely was more than uncertain. He'd have to make the best of the environment.

Chandler gauged the girl's emotional and physical state. Despite appearing as uncomfortable as he felt, she didn't seem panicked. If they needed to make a break for it, he surmised she wouldn't slow them down.

The road noise changed again after a turn, the sound now reminiscent of driving on gravel. This wasn't good. Gravel meant they'd turned off the beaten path and away from people. A charry smell seeped inside. A campfire? A burn pile, maybe? Whatever their location, minutes had passed since he last heard other traffic.

The brakes squeaked, and then the van came to a creeping stop. *Uh-oh*, he thought. Things would soon change. Reagan's eyes widened, and her chest rose and fell at a faster rate. Chandler gave her a reassuring nod, and she calmed a bit.

Chandler rolled over to face the side door. If trouble was on its way, he wanted to see it coming. Both front doors opened, and the men exited, slamming the doors shut behind them. A moment later, the side door slid open, and the burning smell flowed in, more robust than before, seeming to come from every direction.

The sun had set long ago, and the only illumination came from the moon and the headlights bouncing off a structure. Through the faint light, Chandler made out the man who pistol-whipped him. He had drawn from his front pocket a metal item about the length of a cell phone but much narrower. When he pressed a button on it, a shiny four-inch stiletto blade sprung out and snapped into position. He waved the switchblade around in a slow figure-eight motion as if deciding which hostage to filet first.

Chandler glanced back, sensing movement behind him. The girl slithered along the floor until her back hit the side of the van. She remained quiet, but her body quivered in the dark. He turned his stare back to the danger, remaining still in the dim light but meeting the man's glare with one of his own. Was he afraid? Hell yes, but he wasn't about to give the thug the satisfaction of knowing it.

When the driver appeared, the first man pointed the tip of the blade at Chandler. "You, sit up."

Chandler bent his knees toward his chest, flung his feet over the van step-up at the opening, and strained his abdomen muscles to upright himself. He silently thanked himself for staying in good enough shape to maneuver from a prone position like that. Those lazy treadmill jogs had paid off. The only problem: the pressure in his bladder reminded him he had to pee.

"Now you," the man said, pointing the blade at the girl. Chandler turned his head over his shoulder and followed the direction of the knife with his gaze. When the girl hesitated, the man grew impatient and waved the knife around again. "Now!"

Chandler offered a soft nod. "It will be all right. Do as he said."

Still appearing unsure, the girl scooted across the van floor, inching her way to the edge of the opening. She got herself upright and maneuvered until she was even with Chandler.

The man with the knife closed in on her, eyeing her like a piece of fresh meat. He ran the blade's tip over the cotton of the T-shirt covering her breasts, causing her body to shake like the frightened puppy he once brought home to Finn.

God no, not the girl, Chandler thought. It took every ounce of restraint not to take the bait and tackle the barbarian.

The man then ran the blade down her abdomen and over her jeans to the top of her thigh. When tears streaked the side of her face, he shifted downward and snipped the restraint on her ankles, freeing them.

A whimper escaped.

Was he done yet?

The man sidestepped in front of Chandler, giving him a stern look. "You try anything, and I'll slice the girl's throat." Chandler offered a cautious nod. Then the man cut his ankle restraints. "Stand up."

The men pulled and pushed Chandler and the girl thirty feet toward a small building with a double garage door lining its front. They guided them through a smaller side door with a boarded-up glass window, into a space where the smell of fertilizer and smoke mixed in stale air. The thugs pushed them further into the dark garage. Chandler and Reagan turned toward the door.

"Water," Chandler blurted before they stepped out. This might be their only chance for it. "It's been hours. Please, we need something to drink."

The driver pointed toward the other man, who retraced his steps out the side door and disappeared around the corner, returning moments later only to throw a half-full plastic water bottle to the floor. Without a word, the men left, closing the door after themselves. The click of a deadbolt sounded, leaving Chandler and the girl standing in the musty dark as prisoners, their hands still secured behind their backs.

"Did they hurt you?" Chandler whispered. He had noticed earlier in the day a large welt around her left eye and cheek.

"I'm fine. I tried fighting him off." She stretched her jaw before settling her gaze on his face. "Looks like you did too."

"I'm no such hero." Chandler slackened his sore jaw and moved it from side to side to test its range of motion. It hurt like a toothache. Nothing felt broken, but he'd have one hell of a shiner. "He sent me a loud and clear message."

"Why are they doing this?" Her voice ended on a high pitch. Her head swiveled to survey her surroundings.

"I'm not sure, but I think it has something to do with my daughter." Chandler scanned the corners of the garage, making out only a wood workbench along the far wall.

"What would your daughter have to do with these guys kidnapping us?"

"She's a DEA agent, and these guys seem like the type she would investigate."

"Is her name Finn?"

"Yes, it is. How do you know her?"

"She's been working with my stepmom."

"Would that be Sloane?"

"Yeah. You know her?"

"I met her the night of the fire at the hospital." Chandler recalled the relief he felt that night, knowing Finn was safe after outrunning the wildfire. The reality of their situation sunk in. It appeared he and this girl now had to outmaneuver the drug lord his daughter and Sloane were after.

"So you think this has to do with the case they've been working on?"

"It would explain why they targeted us."

"I heard Mom and Finn talking." Her voice cracked. "They think these are the guys who killed my mom."

"Finn told me about your loss. I'm very sorry. My name is Chandler."

"Thank you. I'm Reagan." Her voice cracked again, emerging this time through trembling lips. It was the recognizable sharp ache of losing a loved one, an emotion Chandler knew all too well. "I have a bad feeling about all of this, Chandler. We need to get out of here."

"I haven't heard the van engine, so I'm guessing they're still out there. Even if we broke through the door, they'd see us, and we wouldn't get too far with these straps." Chandler raised his bound hands behind his back a few inches.

"I think I may have weakened mine on that sharp edge in the van. Let's see if we can find something to cut through it."

"Good idea."

They divided up the space with Chandler taking the side with the workbench and Reagan taking the other. Faint slivers of moonlight filtered through the gaps in the wood covering the broken door window, giving him occasional glimpses of the surface. It was dusty, but only in parts. He presumed someone had recently cleared away its contents. Hastily, he hoped.

"Find anything?" His voice remained low in case the two thugs were close enough to hear.

"Only some big flat bags." Reagan kept her voice low too.

"That must be the fertilizer I smell."

Chandler raked an arm against the edge of the workbench. At home, he'd hammer nails there to hang things like goggles and particle masks. He hoped whoever used this garage had done the same. He reached the end of the long edge and continued his exploration along a short side. About a foot in, he felt something metallic sticking out. Bingo! A nailhead.

"I got something," he whispered.

Reagan joined him. "What did you find?"

"A nail." Chandler moved out of the way to show her. "We could use it to whittle away at these straps like you did in the van."

"I should go first since I already have a head start."

"Another good idea."

Reagan maneuvered her bound hands over the nail, its height forcing her to reach up inelegantly. She positioned her hands even with the nail and placed its head against the frayed plastic of the strap. After several minutes, as sweat dripped down her cheek, she paused. "I have to pee."

"Me too." The awkwardness of the situation soaked in. With hands tied behind their backs, he and Reagan would need out of their restraints. The thought of another knuckle sandwich from those thugs didn't sit well, but if anyone was to run the risk, it would be him. "Let me talk to the guards."

Chandler approached the door and yelled through the boarded-up window. "Hey you! Unless you want a real mess on your hands, you're gonna have to let us pee."

Moments later, the door flew open. The one with the switchblade stomped in, looking more menacing than before. He pointed the blade at the girl and waved her forward. "Her first." Reagan timidly advanced. She trembled when he dragged the blade down her front again. The ruffian turned her around, drew her bound hands toward the moonlight, and focused on them. Chandler gulped. How far had Reagan gotten at fraying her binding? Was her progress apparent? He hated to think she'd pay the price for his escape idea.

"You try anything, and you both die." The thug yanked her hands and cut the strap.

Chandler's tense muscles relaxed. She was safe for now.

Their captor allowed them one at a time to relieve themselves in a dark corner and bound them again. He then left them alone in the dark.

Reagan stomped a foot. "Damn it. All that work wasted." She marched toward the workbench with a strong gait.

So much like Finn, Chandler thought. Hardhead and intractable.

Chandler dragged his tongue along the roof of his mouth. They needed to quench their thirst while they had the chance. Plus, she needed a minute to cool off. "Wanna try the water first?"

"I *am* hella thirsty." She licked her dry lips.

Reagan crouched near the bottle and picked it up with the mouth facing upward. Chandler moved in and unscrewed the cap. He rolled his fingers around the bottle and took it from her. "You go first. I'll tip it, and you can maneuver under it to take a few sips."

"Got it."

Once kneeling, she placed her mouth over the top of the bottle. Chandler tipped it enough for her to drink. She took three good sips before releasing her grip, which was his cue to turn the bottle upright. They repeated the steps for him to drink.

"We make a good team," he said after they nimbly put the cap back on to preserve the remaining water. "Now, let's get to work again on getting these straps off."

CHAPTER EIGHTEEN

Despite the shelter provided by the building's overhang, biting wind and the spray of drizzle forced Eric's hands into his coat pockets for warmth. The high-pitched hum coming from dozens of revving and idling jet engines, though muffled by spongy earplugs, made it impossible to decipher a spoken word. He stood silently next to Sloane, Finn, and the customs agent, an ex-Marine who still sported a high-and-tight and two matching guns for biceps.

Over four hours had passed since Quintrell had directed Melina to come to San Francisco, and minutes earlier, Customs had signaled that her private jet was on approach. Much was at stake. They couldn't chance anyone recognizing Sloane and Finn. If Melina was traveling with Padrino's men that meant Eric had to board the plane. Once he separated Melina from her muscle, they'd be in the clear.

He glanced at Sloane, noting her persistent fidgeting. She'd become so much like him; waiting on the sidelines wasn't her forte. The fact some of his other, better traits had rubbed off on her made the debt he owed her a little less burdensome but fell very short of wiping the slate clean.

A sleek Gulfstream coasted to a stop, lining up its wheels with the painted apron markings. When the engine whined down, the narrow door opened from the top and unfolded into a ramp that reached the tarmac. The customs agent stepped toward the plane with Eric following. That was Sloane and Finn's cue to go inside.

What happened in the next few moments rested on the element of deception. The customs process had to appear normal until the agent and Eric separated Melina from the eyes and ears of Padrino's guards. The pilot-in-command, a former Mexican Army pilot according to the flight manifest records, also posed a danger and might be armed. If anything went wrong, Eric would provide extra firepower.

Following airport customs procedures for private VIP international arrivals, the customs agent boarded the plane. Eric, dressed in a customs Windbreaker, accompanied him. The pilot shook the agent's hand and turned over the flight's paperwork. It included four immigration forms and passports, some likely fake: one each for him, his co-pilot, Melina, and another male passenger, possibly Melina's cartel escort.

After eyeing the passengers, Eric glanced at his phone and the photo Rosa had sent him. The short woman buttoning up a cream-colored wool coat had the same facial features and long, brown wavy hair as the one in the picture. He nodded at the customs agent, confirming Melina's identity. Now he just needed to usher her off the plane and separate her from her large, dark, suit-wearing bodyguard without revealing why or who he was.

The agent scrutinized the immigration forms for several minutes and checked his government tablet. He turned to the guard. "Mister Cortez, we have a problem here. Your name matches that of someone on the international terrorist list. We have to hold you until we verify your identity with the Mexican government." He turned to Melina and handed her a passport. "Miss Campos, you're cleared. You may proceed with Agent Decker."

"She needs to wait with me." Cortez narrowed his eyes.

"Suits me." The agent shrugged. "This could take hours."

"I don't have hours," Melina said, her tone rushed. "I need to leave now."

"Then follow me, Miss Campos." Eric placed a hand on her elbow. "I'll escort you through Customs."

Cortez grabbed Melina's other arm, stopping her from deplaning. Eric shot him a cold stare. "Do we have a problem here? Maybe you *are* the Cortez we've been looking for."

"No problem. I'm leaving." Melina threw off Cortez's grip and turned toward him. "I'll take the Town Car. You can taxi over."

With Customs set to tie up Cortez until morning, Eric accompanied her off the plane, stepping onto the tarmac through the wind and the drizzle. As Sloane spotted them through the window of the private aircraft lounge, every muscle in her body appeared to relax. Whether or not Melina cooperated, the leverage they needed on Padrino had arrived.

Seconds later, Eric and Melina entered through the door. This time of night, other than the lone attendant, the sleekly furnished room was unoccupied. Melina placed her leather travel bag on a chair near Sloane, and then shook the rain from her long hair and wool coat.

"Melina Campos?" Sloane asked.

"Yes?" The bags under her eyes and smudged eye makeup told of hours of travel and worry.

"Police." Sloane flashed her badge. "You need to come with us."

"What have I done?" Melina's posture turned defensive, a reaction they expected.

"We need to ask you some questions." Sloane extended her arm toward the exit. "Now, please come with us."

"I'm not going anywhere until you tell me what's going on."

A lifetime of living in the cartel's shadow had molded Melina to be skeptical at every turn, so Sloane placed a reassuring hand on her shoulder. "We have your brother, David. He told me you'd understand the word 'crackerjack.'" Melina flinched at the family code word but refused to budge. “You either come willingly, or we drag you in. Now hand me your cell phone.”

Melina’s eyes widened at Sloane’s threat. She still appeared unsure but retrieved a phone from her coat pocket and handed it to Sloane.

* * *

It was now well past midnight, and the squad room had all but emptied. The only light there was coming from Lieutenant West’s office. Sloane flipped on the overheads, lighting the way for Finn, Eric, and Melina. A mix of aromas tickled her nose—oregano for sure and perhaps cheese and pepperoni. Someone had ordered pizza. She turned to a confused but patient Melina. “Come with me.”

While Eric went straight to his desk, Sloane entered the office with Melina, Finn trailing behind. Morgan West was sitting behind her desk, working on a slice of pepperoni pizza.

“We got her, L-T.” Sloane nodded to Kyler and Agent Prichard, who were seated on the far side of the conference table. Finn directed Melina to sit at the table next to her. “Eric’s calling the jail. Where’s our other guest?”

“In the overnight room.” West took a seat at Melina’s side before Sloane left.

The overnight room, located a few rooms down the hallway, came in handy on nights like tonight when a case ran long and at odds with Sloane’s sleep schedule. It wasn’t much, not furnished with much beyond two old army cots. It was now providing a decent resting place for Rosa and Antonio.

Sloane glanced at the cot where Antonio slept. Even asleep, despite his age and fully grown body, he had the innocence of a child. She dreaded the thought of sending him to Padrino and a lifetime of manipulation without his mother. Following a regret-filled sigh, she knelt in front of the other cot and gave Rosa a gentle tug on the arm.

“Rosa.” Sloane waited for her eyes to flutter open before placing an index finger over her lips. “Shhhh. Melina is here.”

Rosa glanced at her sleeping son and nodded. Folding the blanket back, she tiptoed out with Sloane and returned to the squad room. Her gaze, and then Sloane's, settled on the glass doors leading to the hallway when it swung open. Quintrell stepped through, wearing his jailhouse reds. Eric had a firm hand on his elbow as he pushed him through the door. Quintrell's expression instantly softened into a warm smile when he locked gazes with Rosa. And when Sloane glanced at Rosa, her sorrowful eyes and the sense of longing there reminded Sloane again that she loved him. What a shame. Rosa was wasting a love like that on a man who must now pay for his crimes.

"Whatever happens, you and Antonio will be safe." Quintrell raised his cuffed hands from the front of his belly to graze Rosa's cheek. "I'll see to it."

Whatever David Quintrell had become, whatever his father had turned him into, it was apparent he loved the woman Padrino had forced him to abandon. This tender scene, however, came short of making Sloane feel sorry for the bastard who helped her wife's killers. Before Rosa could respond through tear-filled eyes, Eric tugged on David's arm, directing him toward Morgan West's office. "Time is running out."

Rosa stepped past the threshold after Sloane.

"Rosa!" Melina approached her with open arms, giving her sister-in-law a warm embrace. "What are you doing here? Where is David?"

"I'm right here, Melina." David Quintrell appeared next in the doorway.

"David!" Melina rushed over, her hug lasting through several of Rosa's tears. She pulled back, inspecting his restraints. "What is this?"

"Let's sit down," Eric said. Once they were settled around West's conference table, Eric removed the handcuffs, prompting Quintrell to rub his wrists.

"Will someone please tell me what's going on?" Melina's stare bounced from person to person in the room.

"The police discovered who I am and that I was helping Caco before he died," Quintrell said, exhaling a deep breath.

"So now you're helping them?" Melina recoiled.

"I'm helping them because our father is an evil man. He robbed me of the opportunity to be a father to my son."

"What are you talking about? What son?"

"Tell her, Rosa." David glanced at the woman he earlier pledged to protect.

Rosa averted her eyes. "Antonio is David's son, not Caco's. Arturo threatened to take him from me if I told the truth."

"And Caco knew this?" Melina recoiled again at Rosa's nod. "But why?"

"To keep me in line." The muscles in Quintrell's jaw twitched. "So I wouldn't deviate from the plan of becoming his inside man in the American government. Rosa wants a way out, and these officers have offered it to her. Now, with Caco dead, Father has kidnapped her daughter and her father." Quintrell glanced first at Sloane, and then Finn. "In a mad attempt to get Antonio and me back."

Melina buried her face in her hands. "Dios mio."

"My daughter's only sixteen for God's sake." Desperation filled Sloane's voice.

"Children have always been off-limits." Quintrell shook his head. "He's crossed his own line. He's gone mad and won't stop until he gets what he wants."

"My father has done nothing to deserve this." Finn's voice contained as much desperation as Sloane's. They both were at the end of their rope. "Will you help us?"

"If he's gone mad, how can I help?" With everyone bombarding her with information, Melina's expression grew more tense than it had earlier at the word "crackerjack."

"You and I both know he has no intention of letting their family go even if he gets us back." Quintrell wrapped his hands around Melina's upper arms. "You're the only child he has left. You can talk to him. If he knows he'll lose you too, maybe he'll think twice before double-crossing them during the exchange."

"What do you mean, the only child he has left?" Melina's eyes begged David for an explanation.

"He knows I betrayed him, and you know how much he values loyalty," Quintrell said. "I'm no longer a son to him."

Melina threw off her brother's grip. "You may have betrayed him because of what he did to Rosa and Antonio, but I won't."

Sloane dipped her head. After everything they'd done to get her here, they'd lost her. In all probability, they never would have had her cooperation.

Shaking his head, Quintrell turned toward Sloane and Finn. "You can still use her."

"I know Father hurt you, but he's still your blood." Melina's face flushed as her voice rose an octave. "I don't understand how you can help them."

"They've given me my son and have ensured he'll be safe and out of the reach of the man who stole him from me. I owe them this much." Quintrell turned to Sloane and Finn. "You need only show proof you have her and tell him if you and yours don't walk away alive, she'll rot in prison or worse."

Quintrell proposed a good old-fashion bluff—a tactic Sloane had used almost every day for the last two and a half years as a detective. She didn't need Melina's cooperation. She only needed her to stand still long enough for a few pictures. Those would serve as her proof.

Sloane turned to Eric. "Take her down to booking and get a few good photos. Be sure they show today's date."

Eric nodded his understanding and grabbed Melina by the arm. She threw off his grip. "I'm not going anywhere with you."

"I'll arrest you for assaulting a police officer if I have to." Eric wrapped his fingers around her arm, tightly this time. "After we get a few convincing pictures, you can cool your heels."

Quintrell didn't surprise Sloane with his suggestion of pitting his sister against his father. However, his failure to object to Eric's manhandling of Melina did. Quintrell almost fooled her by the show he put on with Rosa. He may have a soft spot for her and Antonio, but that was as far as his good nature went. The apple didn't fall far from the tree.

Eric pulled Melina out the door.

Sloane stewed for a bit, checking the clock on the wall. It was now five before one o'clock. She had one hour before Padrino's deadline, but they still had to discuss the hostage exchange with Quintrell and Rosa. Handing over Quintrell didn't bother

her, but she couldn't stomach anything more. There had to be another way. Even if they planned to shoot their way out, she couldn't fathom putting Antonio in harm's way. Sloane excused herself from the group and pulled Finn toward the quiet of the empty squad room for a private discussion.

"I can't do it, Finn. I can't put Antonio at risk." Sloane had learned one thing facing down Caco—some lines should never be crossed. This was one of them. She couldn't be like Padrino and endanger a child.

"I can't either." Finn let out a huge breath. "The thought of ripping him away from his mother is heartbreaking."

"And what if something goes wrong?" Sloane released a deep, weighted sigh. "There's no telling how he might react. He could put all of us at risk."

"Then what do we do?" Finn brushed back strands of hair that had long ago lost their wavy curl. "Padrino is expecting both him and Quintrell."

So many things could go wrong, any of which could cost them Reagan and Chandler. Ideally, whatever plan they devised needed to consider contingencies, minimize risk, and be flexible. Padrino calling the shots with time and location made that nearly impossible. The element of surprise represented the only thing in their favor.

"Our only option is to use a decoy." Sloane swallowed her fears. "And we shoot our way out."

"You're right." Finn nodded.

Though Sloane returned a slow nod, she feared she might lose everything in this daring operation. Her call to Janet came to mind and the guilt she felt for not telling her how she loved her sooner. She wasn't going to make that same mistake right now. She took Finn by the hand, but before she led her back to West's office where they would devise their final plan, she drew their hands and bodies close. "I knew I loved you since the day you held my hand after choir."

"I did too." The smile on Finn's lips confirmed what Sloane already knew—they were meant to be together.

"Following the accident, I tried everything I could to reach you, but I didn't know how." The sense of loneliness and desperation she had experienced while she adjusted to her new circumstance as an orphan crept into her mind.

"I tried too, but the school would only tell me you'd gone to live with family."

"I was here the entire time, dreaming of you. Every woman I got close to, I chased the memory of you. Even Avery." Sloane averted her eyes. Though unashamed by this admission, the knowledge she might not have loved her wife for just herself still had a bite to it.

"I did the same thing for years with Isabell and Kadin." Finn pulled their hands to her bosom. "I didn't know it then, but I was always looking for you."

At the comforting thought it wasn't a coincidence she and Kadin shared many of the same features, Sloane let a faint grin grow on her lips. "And now we've found each other again."

"Yes, we have." Finn pressed their foreheads together.

Sloane closed her eyes. Were it not for the lives hanging in the balance, she would have sensed her life was falling into place. Her grief had faded, love had emerged from the ashes, and she had Finn in her arms.

"Ahem." A loud, familiar clearing of the throat from across the room broke the tranquil moment.

Sloane flicked her eyes open and turned toward the sound. "Where's Melina?"

"She was a little scrappy." Eric drew closer. He twitched his mouth up into a lopsided grin, rubbing the reddening side of his jaw. "So I told booking to keep her in a holding cell on assault charges until we get back."

Sloane snickered. Eric had never failed to bait a perp when the situation called for it, and this one did. A holding cell eliminated the opportunity for Melina to alert Padrino.

"I have the photos." Eric waved his cell phone at her before forwarding the pictures via text message.

After the ding, Sloane thumbed her iPhone to life. Her mouth fell open, too late to stifle a laugh with her hand. "These are perfect." The running mascara and tousled hair made for an authentic booking photo. They made Melina appear like every other woman she'd booked after a drunken barroom brawl.

"Are we ready to make the call?" Eric asked.

"We need to talk first." Sloane glanced at Finn to make sure they were firm in their agreement. "Finn and I won't give up Antonio. Besides being wrong, it's too risky."

"I have a problem with it too," he said.

"We want to use a decoy to buy us time during the exchange," Sloane said.

"That could work." Eric ran a hand across the back of his neck as if running through solutions in his head.

"We don't have much time, though." Fear cut through Finn's voice.

"Antonio and I are about the same height. He's leaner than I am, but I think I could pass for him in the dark if I dress in his clothes and maybe wear a hat." Eric rubbed the day-old stubble along his cheeks. "I'd have to shave off this five o'clock shadow first."

"I'd feel a lot better with you there." For a moment, Sloane rested a hand on his shoulder. Except for Three Owls Vineyard and the Lower Bottoms ambush, Eric had been by her side for every dangerous situation she was in for the last two-plus years. If a firefight ensued, she wanted him there to back her up.

"You don't think I'd willingly let my partner go off into harm's way without me?" Eric cocked up one eyebrow, a not-so-subtle reminder she'd left him in the dust to confront Caco without him.

Sloane lowered her chin, regretting she'd let him down. "I'm sorry, partner." She raised her head to acknowledge her misstep. "It won't happen again."

"All right then, let's go work this out with Quintrell." He gestured toward West's open office door.

* * *

Sloane debated what the tears in Rosa's eyes meant. Was she relieved Antonio would be safe? Terrified David would never come back? In any case, Sloane had to respect Quintrell for agreeing to come along with no strings attached. "I'm dead either way. My father will get me one way or another. This way I have a chance to right things."

The department techs had returned the burner phone Padrino had sent her, having failed to get anything useful from it. Sloane texted Melina's booking photo to it and checked the clock—two a.m. on the dot. She looked Finn in the eyes. "Ready?"

Finn nodded.

Sloane dialed.

On the third ring, someone answered. "Do you have him?"

"Yes, Antonio is here." Sloane's voice thickened, straining to tamp down the emotion begging to be let out. "This is cruel, separating a mother from her son."

"Rosa is welcome to come along."

"We both know that will never happen," Sloane said. "You should know I've leveled the playing field."

"I doubt that."

Sloane sent Melina's pictures to Padrino's number and waited for a response. Dead silence told her she'd gotten his attention. "You'll never see Melina again if we don't walk away alive."

"I see I've underestimated you, Sergeant Sloane. That won't happen again. We'll make the exchange at three thirty at the place where you left my son to die. You and Agent Harper are to bring only David and Antonio. No guns."

The call went dead before she could negotiate any more time or a change of location. Sloane calculated in her head: this early in the morning the drive to the vineyard would take a little over an hour, but with lights and siren, they could probably shave off some time. That only left a few minutes to gear up. She closed the phone and turned to Finn. "We're going back to Three Owls."

Not taking any chances, Sloane retrieved her bulletproof vest and SFPD Windbreaker from her locker. Next to her, West pulled out the same.

"Take mine." West handed the items to Finn. "You'll need them."

"Thanks." Finn's natural smile had left her, as had Sloane's. Their focus was solely on the risky task ahead.

Mirroring Sloane, Finn removed her blazer and slipped the heavy vest over her head and shoulders, covering her vital organs, front and back. Finn pulled the Velcro straps tight against her torso on each side to ensure the vest wouldn't shift when she needed the protection the most.

"No guns, my ass." Sloane slammed shut her locker door. Despite Padrino's order to lose their guns, she wanted her trusty backup, a compact Barretta Nano. She changed out its ankle holster for a Velcro one that attached to the front of her vest.

"I know you Feds aren't allowed to carry backups." West reached into her locker. "So, I want you to have my little black dress." She handed Finn a small Smith & Wesson MP Bodyguard .380 pistol, also encased in a Velcro holster that could attach to her vest. "It's not regulation, but it's my favorite."

Who knew? Sloane raised a single eyebrow along with a sly grin. The MP had earned its nickname for its concealability even when wearing a little black dress. She didn't think West was the type, but she'd love to see her in a daring cocktail dress.

She and Finn stuffed their primary weapons into their Windbreaker pockets, and then met Eric in the squad room. He had changed into Antonio's clothes. The pants were a little tight, so he had left them unbuttoned and used his belt to hold them up. With the young man's shirt and jacket on, no one should be able to tell the difference. To top it off, he dug out of his locker a well-worn San Francisco Giants ball cap. It would serve to hide his hair and face. For added insurance, Rosa gave him some pointers on how to mimic Antonio's posture, walk, and mannerisms.

"Where's your vest?" Sloane asked, noting that the cloth beneath his unzipped jacket appeared too smooth.

"Antonio always wears his jacket fully zipped. It wouldn't fit with these clothes." Eric didn't have much of a gut, but he had a broad chest from hours of weight lifting.

"I have a bad feeling about this," Sloane said. Every raid or tactical operation she and Eric had been on, they had on their vests, and every time they had walked away unscathed. Changing things up now gave her a bad vibe.

Eric patted his right coat pocket before zipping the front. "It'll be fine. I have my primary."

Quintrell remained in his jailhouse reds, but Eric had removed his handcuffs and let him throw on a light jacket and sneakers that he had found loose in the locker room. Sergeant Wilson would have to learn the lesson the hard way. It was called a locker for a reason—you were supposed to lock it.

West handed small two-way radios with earpieces and lapel mics to Sloane, Finn, and Eric. "Nate and I will stay back on the main road, but we'll remain in radio contact."

Sloane glanced at the clock again. It was time. "We need to go."

Everyone turned to walk out, but Rosa called out. "David." She rushed forward and draped her arms around his shoulders.

Quintrell wrapped his arms around her back, squeezing his eyes shut. "I never stopped loving you." He loosened his hold and pressed his lips against hers. The kiss had passion, but to the onlookers like Sloane, it also had a sense of finality. Prying her arms from around his neck, he said, "Take care of our son."

Tears rolled down her cheeks, and as the group retreated through the doors, Rosa yelled, "I love you, David."

CHAPTER NINETEEN

Thick tension filled Sloane's crowded undercover sedan, only its wailing siren piercing the dead silence among the four passengers. In the last forty minutes, Sloane had glanced at Finn in the passenger seat only once or twice, trying to keep her mind on the mission and eye on the road as she roared through the predawn traffic. Minutes away from Three Owls, an uneasiness gripped her. It was more than the fear of losing Reagan. She had a sense that no matter what happened next, her life would never be the same.

The last time she and Finn had driven the road leading from Santa Rosa, fire had been engulfing the surrounding hills. A heaviness weighed on her as she passed the first remnants of the wildfire's destructive force, made visible by a handful of undamaged city streetlights. The fire had reduced once-bustling neighborhood businesses to charred frames and piles of twisted black metal and lumpy ash. They'd escaped that night with their lives and with Sloane still abiding by her oath. If not for Finn and the memory of Avery, Sloane would have crossed the line from cop to killer. She shook her head hard to clear out the cobwebs of that horrible ordeal.

"You okay?" Finn laid a gentle hand on Sloane's arm.

"Yeah, I'm fine." She turned off the siren and checked her rearview mirror. West and Prichard had kept up, trailing in another unmarked sedan. "It's this place."

"It's getting to me too. If it weren't for those two in the back, I'd suggest singing." Finn offered what looked like a forced grin, something Sloane couldn't bring herself to do.

"Maybe later."

Singing had helped diffuse the tension while they narrowly outran the wildfire ten days ago, but now was not the time. Sloane checked her rearview again, this time eyeing Eric and Quintrell. Eric had on his serious, yet relaxed game face, the one she'd seen dozens of times before. She didn't have to ask. He was ready for this to start. Quintrell, on the other hand, had a distant look about him. Was it regret or fear of death? Either way, Sloane could tell he didn't want to be there. She shared that feeling. She couldn't shake the sense of foreboding that had sunk into her pores.

Sloane tapped her brakes three times, the signal she was about to make the final turn before they separated from West and Prichard. "Radios."

Two clicks, each followed by a short squelch, meant Eric and Finn had turned on their hidden radios. Sloane did the same.

"L-T, you there?" Sloane said through the mic.

"Gotcha loud and clear, Sloane," West replied over the radio. "Decker?"

"Right here, L-T, feeling like I gotta lose a few pounds."

Sloane glanced in the mirror and caught Eric rolling his shoulders to release the pinch of Antonio's snug-fitting shirt and jacket. In a futile effort to ease her stress, she forced a chuckle.

"Harper?" West said.

"Loud and clear."

"We're taking up position. Good luck." That meant they were laying back off the main road. If all went according to plan, they wouldn't be needed until Reagan and Chandler were safe in Sloane's and Finn's arms.

Sloane continued down the paved access road to Three Owls Vineyard. The digital clock on her dashboard showed they had about eight minutes before the deadline. What would the minutes following that bring? Would things turn out for the best like the last time she and Finn were here? The back of her neck tingled at the thought of the alternative.

Sloane gulped when the faint moonlight and her headlights illuminated the remains of the main house: three brick fireplaces and chimneys, mangled household appliances, and a scattering of cinderblocks among a field of scorched, tangled debris.

Her headlights swung toward the driveway. The two SUVs that had sat there the night of the fire had since been removed, though outlines where they ignited remained on the asphalt. She pulled up short of that spot, the place where she and Finn had left the two guards and abandoned them to certain death. Those men undoubtedly would've slaughtered them if given a chance, but Sloane had left them helpless and that left an irrevocable bitterness in her mouth.

Throwing the gear shifter into park, she gripped the steering wheel tightly, twisting her fingers around the vinyl wrap. What was coming next troubled Sloane. In her parents' car and the drug lab explosion she'd experienced brief brushes with her mortality. In the pool days ago, she'd come closest to death. There in the water, she had had hours to consider her demise. Only being with Finn had gotten her through it.

"I'm glad you're with me," Sloane said, staring into the darkness.

"Me too," Finn said.

"Game time." Sloane doused the headlights before staring in the rearview. Eric and Quintrell both acknowledged with a nod. "Hey, Finn, open the glove compartment and grab the flashlight," Sloane said. Finn fished out a metal mini-Maglite.

Sloane and Finn opened their doors, slid out of the sedan, and moved to the back doors. They'd have to open them to release their passengers, the rear door interior handles having been disabled for transport. The odor of weeks-old burned waste lay heavy in every direction, reminding Sloane of the hours she'd spent in the pool. She opened the door for Eric, and Finn opened the other for Quintrell.

Eric went into character, assuming a slumped posture and slapping a hand against his thigh with a thumb and two fingers pressed together. Quintrell circled the trunk to Eric's side and took him by the arm.

"This way." Finn waved her arm toward the rubble. She took point with the flashlight, illuminating a path toward what used to be the back of the house.

The four waded through the debris field in a single file with Sloane in the rear. Stretching their legs over piles of soft ash, sidestepping twisted metal, and crunching through sections of singed drywall, they reached what once was the terrace. Yards beyond it lay the pool.

Sloane caught up, and for the first time, glimpsed what she had feared would be her and Finn's watery grave. She came to an abrupt halt. An unnerving silence had replaced the crackling wind-whipped flames that taunted them when they were last there. Dim moonlight showed that the water had turned murky, made worse by floating rubbish. For hours, she and Finn clung to life there under their soaked jackets, convinced it would be their tomb. She rubbed her hands together, remembering the searing heat that nearly boiled her skin away. If not for her and Finn's two coats, she doubted they'd have much skin left from the neck up.

"Where do you think Padrino wants to make the exchange?" Finn asked.

The sound of Finn's voice pulled Sloane from her real-life nightmare. She shook her head and forced her mind to focus on the present. "Where we left Caco for dead."

"The pathway." Finn's words were accompanied by a breathy exhale.

Sloane nodded slowly, deliberately. The pathway, where she had beaten the flames and stopped the cycle of death, sent chills down her spine. There she had defeated her greatest fear, and there tonight, she would have to defeat her greatest foe.

Finn pointed the flashlight's beam toward the pool's edge, marking their course. Eric stayed in character, taking Antonio's trademark long strides. Quintrell followed, and as scripted, pulled Eric back every few steps to match his own pace. Sloane fell in line, bringing up the rear.

They rounded the corner of the pool and stopped at the spot where Caco had pushed Sloane into the water and nearly drowned her. She now realized his ploy had actually saved her and Finn. If they had followed him down the path, they would have met the fate he did.

Dreading what came next, Sloane reached forward and grabbed Finn's hand. Finn squeezed without looking back and turned toward the pathway trailhead.

"I have a bad feeling," Finn said.

"Me too." Sloane peered at the treetops. The night of the fire, flames had engulfed them, lighting the way for her and Finn to navigate their way to safety. On this predawn morning, the trees resembled rows of skeletons, propped up in the dark as a reminder the fire had taken its death toll.

Sloane gave Finn's hand an extra squeeze before letting go. "I'll take point."

Her breathing speeded up as she grabbed the flashlight and slow-marched toward the spot where they had discovered Caco's charred body. She glanced over her shoulder to make sure that Quintrell and Eric, his hat pulled down low, mimicking Antonio's gait, were following with Finn in the rear.

At a slight twist in the trail, having reached what she assumed was the meeting place, Sloane stopped and Finn joined her. When she took in a deep breath, a strong odor tickled her nose. Something in the pit of her stomach warned her they'd entered a trap. "You smell that?"

"Gasoline." Finn lowered her voice to a whisper. "I smelled it all along the trail."

The strong presence of gasoline meant one thing: Padrino wanted them to burn. Her breathing became shallow and ragged. *Why is it always fire?* First, her parents and later, the police officer who rescued her from their accident. Then Avery.

She thought she'd beat fire and death when she and Finn survived the wildfire, but her gut told her Padrino intended for her and Finn to meet the same fate as Caco. *Keep it together*, she scolded herself.

Cracking noise from further down the path snapped her to attention. Another crack and another. Someone was approaching in the dark. Her every muscle tightened, sending a jolt up the back of her neck. She felt like prey.

Shadowy figures appeared several yards down the trail. Two of them. They grew in size as they floated closer. Sloane pointed the flashlight beam at the shapes, prompting them to stop. The light revealed two dark-haired, brown-skinned men in suits. One yelled something in Spanish and raised an arm over his eyes as a shield. The other reached beneath the flap of his blazer. Sloane assumed he'd reached for a gun.

"Whoa! Whoa!" She lowered the beam to their feet. "Settle down."

The men yelled more Spanish words in the shadows, but she refused to escalate. In case this went sideways, she darted her eyes to the left and right, looking for an avenue of escape. On each side, the once lush landscaping that edged the pathway had burned away, replaced by blackened spines and branches and muddy puddles from the recent rain.

Finn stepped up even with her, and as expected, several feet away. They had chosen different paths in law enforcement, Sloane with the SFPD and Finn with the DEA, but their tactical training had been the same. Never bunch up. Always make an adversary have to choose between multiple targets.

The men quieted and parted when a voice from behind sounded, "Enough."

The dull orange glow of a lit cigar signaled the approach of a tall, gray-haired man in a white suit. His rounded belly and close-shaven gray beard were unmistakable.

"Where is my daughter, Padrino?" Sloane steadied her voice. Jaw set, she waited for his response.

"She's here, as is Agent Harper's father." His calm and measured tone again reminded Sloane of a businessman conducting a trade. He stepped closer, remaining about twenty yards back, and took a drag from his cigar, sending a curling ribbon of smoke upward.

"Let's get to it." Sloane's fast clip signaled her impatience.

"Guns first, ladies."

"You said no guns."

"Don't insult me." Padrino's posture stiffened.

Sloane eyed the goons flanking Padrino. "Them too."

"Now that wouldn't be sporting."

"Remember. We have Melina." Sloane met his chilly stare with one of her own. "You have just as much family to lose as we do." Padrino nodded at his men, proving Sloane had her edge.

At the same time, the two men reached beneath their blazers. They threw their guns into the mud and burned-out brush on either side of the path. Sloane and Finn reached into their coat pockets and did the same. The men likely had backup weapons, even as Sloane and Finn did, but this show of apparent good faith would at least slow them down when Eric's cover was blown.

"Now, my son and grandson." Padrino took a second drag from his cigar.

Sloane waved up Quintrell and Eric, dousing the flashlight to better mask Eric's appearance. When they were almost even with Sloane and Finn, Sloane glanced back.

In character, Eric slouched and took full strides. Then Quintrell jerked him to a stop. Eric kept his head down and hands in his jacket pockets. As Rosa had instructed, he bounced on his feet, alternating between his heels and toes.

"Father." Quintrell's monotone voice and stout posture projected a sturdy wall of defiance.

"David." Padrino's tone was frigid. Quintrell was right. He'd be dead before sunrise once in his father's custody.

"I hate to break up this charming family reunion, but show us Reagan and Chandler." Sloane's impatience reached a crescendo, heat flushing her body.

"Very well." Padrino snapped his fingers over his shoulder. Moments later, more shadowy figures appeared behind him. She counted four.

"Thank God." Sloane's heart pounded wildly out of control when Reagan's outline came into view in the slivers of moonlight. Chandler appeared beside her. "Honey, are you all right?"

"Mom?" Reagan's voice shrilled in the near darkness.

Sloane tried to make eye contact to assure Reagan they were there to rescue her, but it was too dark.

At Sloane's right, Finn cocked her head, also trying to make out the figures. "Daddy?" her voice was shaky.

"I'm all right, pumpkin," Chandler reassured. "I knew you'd come for us."

"Let's do this." Sloane stowed the flashlight in her coat pocket before inching down the zipper on the front of her Windbreaker inches past the grip of her Barretta Nano. The fabric still hid the gun she'd strategically placed atop the left breast of her bulletproof vest.

Sloane watched out of the corner of her eye, as Finn also lowered the zipper of her Windbreaker. The next few seconds would determine whether they all lived or died.

Sloane's heart rate slowed, and the surrounding sounds muted into muffled silence. As the threats facing them came into sharp focus, every motion happened at a fraction of its average speed. She lifted her arm over her shoulder and waved up Eric and Quintrell.

When the men pushed Reagan and Chandler even with Padrino, Quintrell pulled Eric forward, just as he would've done with Antonio. Sloane barely registered the fact Quintrell and Eric had walked between her and Finn and past them. Her focus lasered on the two men on her side of the pathway, one a good five paces further back than the other. She trusted Finn was doing the same with the two men nearest her side.

"You may go." Padrino flicked the ashes from the tip of his cigar.

Reagan and Chandler slowly came forward, their hands bound behind their backs. They matched Quintrell and Eric step for step.

Padrino extended both arms and smiled, exposing his white teeth in the moonlight. He beckoned his grandson to race forward. "Antonio, come." The motion and inflection were practiced, like he'd been doing it for years. When Eric slowed, though, his lips pursed as if something was amiss. "Antonio?"

Eric, now well past Sloane, stopped. Another step and Padrino would make him out for sure. Reagan stepped closer. She lunged at Eric, draping her arms around his neck. "Eric."

"Shit," Sloane mumbled and reached for her backup gun, sliding her palm over the grip and yanking hard.

"Kill them!" Padrino ordered, stepping back toward the darkness.

Eric spun and pushed Reagan back toward Sloane, snapping her wrist binding loose. She stumbled and fell on her knees into a small slick of gasoline. Chandler dashed toward Finn, his wrist binding breaking apart as well.

Sloane got off the first double-tap, while Finn got off the second. Both managed to avoid their loved ones. Dark liquid sprayed in the air as the two men in front fell to the ground before getting off a shot.

By the time Eric spun back around, the two men behind Padrino had drawn their weapons and pushed forward. Both fired in mid-stride, striking Finn high on the vest and Eric in the chest, forcing both to the ground, one in a spray of blood. Eric rolled, coughing up dark gore.

"Nooooo!" Sloane double-tapped her trigger, striking a third man. With both Eric and Finn down, hers was the only good guy weapon remaining. She couldn't rely on Quintrell to help. She dove to the ground into a puddle of gasoline, tucking and rolling to avoid gunfire from the fourth man.

A shot from behind her rang out, and the man fell to the ground. Quintrell approached fast from behind, weapon in hand. Had he picked up Eric's gun? Sloane didn't have time to figure it out, but given he'd just saved her ruled him out as an immediate threat. Quintrell had the barrel of his trained on Padrino, who had retreated down the path.

"Father, stop!" Quintrell called out.

Sloane turned on the ground. She had the perfect view as Padrino stopped, pulled something from a waist holster, and turned. Moonlight sparkled off the barrel of a small-caliber chrome-plated revolver. He fired at the same time Quintrell did. Both bullets found their targets, each of whom toppled to the ground amid fallen branches and mud.

Padrino rolled on his side, a spot near his chest darkening his white suit. He stretched out his arm and flicked his lit cigar in the air. Bits of smoldering ash broke off as it tumbled end over end in slow motion and landed in a pool of liquid. The gasoline there ignited, sending tendrils of fire racing down the path in Sloane's direction.

"You won't win this time." Sloane cursed the flames. They were her enemy, but like last time, she knew she could beat them. Pushing herself off the ground, she stumbled toward Reagan. "Fire!"

She holstered her gun on the fly. When she lifted Reagan by her arms, she winced; her tender ankle had been strained again when she dove to the ground. She turned her head to the left. Chandler was tending to Finn, who was sitting up and struggling to get to her feet. She seemed groggy but not injured.

"We need to help Eric!"

Chandler rushed over. As the fire drew closer in three roaring lines, Finn followed, clutching the spot where the bullet had struck her armored vest. Sloane had seen this before—she'd be bruised for weeks.

"We have to save him!" Sloane was frantic. Eric had pulled her from the explosion, and now she had to do the same for him.

Chandler pulled Eric's arm up and slung it over his shoulder. Eric coughed up red spit and groaned in agony. He was losing blood fast. Finn grabbed the other arm, and they dragged him along the path with Sloane and Reagan in the lead.

"Sloane, flames!" Finn yelled in a panic.

Sloane glanced over her shoulder to see that one line of fire had sped faster than the others and passed Finn, the bluish flames barely missing her leg. Finn steered Chandler and Eric off the path into burned-out muddy brush, sidestepping the flames.

The burnt brush was too thick and thorny where she and Reagan were to offer an escape from the fire. Sloane refocused on the path ahead. The trailhead came into sight at last, with the safety of the pool decking yards beyond. She glanced back again. The flames, about two feet high and inches away from Reagan, lapped at their feet just as they had the night of the wildfire. Only this time, they were gaining ground. Knowing that both of them were gas-soaked, she tugged Reagan's arm, trying to pull her out of the path of the blaze, but she was too late. Reagan's sweater caught fire.

"Nooooo!" She cursed the fire again. "You won't win."

Every muscle in her body tightened. They needed only a dozen more feet to escape this killing field. The pungent scent of burned hair seared Sloane's nose as flames bubbled up on Reagan's garment.

"God, no," Finn yelled.

Stopping to remove the sweater would let the fire win. A hair-raising scream from Reagan made Sloane fear the worst, but she refused to look back. Ignoring the pain in her ankle, she stretched her stride to the fullest, pulling Reagan with her and driving toward the cement pool decking. With every ounce of strength she had, when she reached it, she whipped her arm forward and flung Reagan in the air.

Time crawled, her heart slowing to a funeral's pace. Each moment Reagan spent in the air meant another percent of her skin could be blistered beyond saving. This might be Sloane's last chance to see her alive.

She focused on the teen's body, gripped by a frightening déjà vu. Her mid-length dark blond hair was floating weightlessly in the air, just as Sloane's mother's hair had done in the family car before her death.

Reagan's body twisted in the air, the motion bringing the bottom of the sweater into view. Sloane expected to see a horrid blaze there, but saw just a faint ashy orange glow instead. Only a small portion of the sweater had been eaten away. How? Why?

Splash!

Reagan's fine strands sank beneath the surface of the water, freeing Sloane to take a breath. She wasn't too late. She had kept the promise she made to Avery the day they married. "*...and* *keep you and Reagan safe in my arms."* Half of it anyway. Her only regret was not keeping Avery safe.

Reagan's head bobbed up, arms flailing much as Sloane's had done weeks earlier. She gasped for air. She wasn't the best swimmer, but Avery had made sure she knew the basics. When Reagan sank again, Sloane dove in, forgetting about the heavy bulletproof vest she was wearing. Struggling to breathe, she wrapped an arm around Reagan's waist and started kicking. Within seconds, she had them both in the shallow end.

"Are you hurt?"

"No." Reagan cried, whipping her head from side to side, spraying water in every direction.

"Thank God." Sloane guided her to the edge of the pool. "Stay in the water. You'll be safe here. I have to find Finn and Eric."

"Don't leave me, Mom." Reagan gripped Sloane's jacket, her lips trembling as much as her hands.

"I have to, honey. Eric's shot." She pried Reagan's fingers loose and gave them a reassuring squeeze before crawling out of the pool. "Stay low. Conceal yourself as much as possible. I'll be right back."

Returning to the pathway, which was ablaze, she drew in a rattled breath. Where were they? Where was Finn? She couldn't bear losing another woman she loved. Her wet clothes clinging to her skin like plastic wrap, Sloane moved toward the trailhead, but the flames had grown too intense. Then, to the right through the skeleton trees, she spotted movement. "Finn?"

From the shadows emerged a figure. Unsure if they were good guys or bad, she drew her gun. She wasn't sure the primer on the bullets would fire so soon after being submerged, but the threat of gunfire seemed better than none.

"Sloane!" Finn called out, stepping from the dark alone. Sloane expected the others to be on Finn's heels, but no one came. Finn closed the distance and wrapped her arms around Sloane's neck, sweat smudging her cheeks.

"Where's—" From the corner of her eye, Sloane saw Chandler and Quintrell appear, each with one of Eric's arms slung over a shoulder. Eric's legs weren't moving. She felt queasy as she loosened her embrace of Finn and holstered her gun. "Is he alive?"

"Yes, but it doesn't look good." Finn rubbed mud and sweat from her face with the sleeve of her jacket. "What about Reagan?"

"She's unhurt, I think." Sloane took in a rattled breath before focusing on Eric's limp body. A dark stain covered the front of Antonio's jacket. He'd lost so much blood. Too much. When Eric lifted his head, wincing in pain, she released another deep, shaky breath.

As soon as they cleared the muddy area, Sloane removed her damp jacket. "Put him on the ground." She unzipped Eric's coat and located the bullet wound. It was to the left of his sternum, deadly close to his heart. She pressed her balled-up jacket against the oozing opening. "Stay with me, Eric." She turned her stare to Finn, her words coming out pained. "Did you call it in?"

Finn nodded. "West has multiple ambulances en route."

Sloane whipped her head around, looking for Reagan. She had crawled out of the pool and stood next to Chandler. Both were looking on with blank expressions.

"He's so pale." Still applying pressure to his wound, Sloane glanced up again, her vision blurred from her tears. "Where's the fucking ambulance?"

Finn pressed two fingers against the ear containing her radio earpiece. "West says they're five minutes out. She and Prichard will lead them in."

Sloane drew in more rattled breaths as her partner coughed up dark blood on her arm. "Stay with me, Eric."

He clutched her forearm and gripped hard—as if her arm would be the last thing he'd ever hold. "All my fault."

"This isn't your fault. Your vest wouldn't fit under these stupid clothes." She forced a laugh, but it fooled no one, especially herself.

Eric strained to lift his head an inch off the cement decking. "The accident. It was my fault. I was young, driving too fast."

"You're not making sense." Sloane flinched, moving her head back a fraction. "What accident?"

"I'm so sorry." He coughed up more blood, his eyes looking distant. As if he saw the end coming. "I was the other driver." His head fell back. His eyes closed.

Sloane only half-processed what he said. She barely heard the sirens of the ambulances pulling up to the front of the burned-out shell of the main house. "Don't you dare die on me."

The rise and fall of his chest had all but stopped. Eric had slipped away. She removed one hand from her makeshift compress and swiped it against his cheek to rouse him, but he didn't respond. He lay there, still, pale, and cold. *This can't be happening*.

"Damn it, Eric." Tears streamed down her face. "Don't you die."

A paramedic tapped Sloane on the shoulder as another deposited a gurney and loads of equipment on the ground. "You've done well. Let us take over."

The medics worked at lightning speed to assess and prep Eric, attaching cuffs and monitors. "No pulse," one said. The other slapped on defibrillator pads, one below Eric's right clavicle, another over his left ribs. "Clear."

Eric's torso arched off the cement, but nothing about his color or breathing changed. Life had drained out of him. Powerless to help the man that had saved her more times than she could remember, Sloane could only watch in horror, realizing she and Reagan were about to lose the man they considered family.

The device charged again. "Clear." Eric's body arched a second time before the digital line on the monitor screen spiked. A single beep.

"I got something. He's weak and thready. We need to transport now."

Sloane had seen her share of gunshot wounds during her career. Chest wounds like Eric's rarely ended well. While his chances were slim, she held on to the fact that he was a fighter. Pulling Reagan with her, Sloane raced after the medics as they rushed Eric into the ambulance waiting in the circular driveway. "We're coming with you."

"We don't have room for both of you." A paramedic raised a single hand, palm forward while standing inside the open doors.

"Mom?" Reagan's voice revealed her panic.

What Reagan had undergone in the last sixteen hours was still a mystery to Sloane. Had they hurt her? Was she raped? She couldn't think of leaving Reagan at a time like this. "Which hospital?"

"Valley."

"We'll follow." She had no choice but to trust this wouldn't be the last time she'd see Eric alive. She locked eyes with the paramedic before he slammed the back doors shut. "He's a cop, a damn good cop. You take care of him, you hear me?"

She vaguely remembered Eric saying similar words when the paramedics rushed her off following the drug lab explosion and Avery's death. They were partners in every sense of the word, but…

Dread seeped into her like water into a sinking ship. Her mind rewound his last words to her. Eric said he was the other driver, but from what? Her parents' accident? Was that the confession he wanted to make before he died? She had a sinking feeling that once she figured it out, even if he survived, nothing between them would be the same.

West laid a comforting hand on her shoulder. "He's a fighter, Sloane. He'll make it."

Prichard, Quintrell, Finn, and Chandler joined them, steps behind West. When the siren's wail faded down the access road, Finn turned to Quintrell.

"Why did you help us instead of making a run for it?" Finn asked.

"I owe Sergeant Decker my life." Quintrell threw his jacket off. Wincing, he pulled Eric's bulletproof vest from his torso and flung it to the ground. He rubbed his ribs where Padrino's small bullet had struck him.

"You!" Sloane bolted toward Quintrell and slugged him in the jaw. She wound up for a second strike, but Finn clutched her arm.

"Finn! He's the reason Eric may die. He should've been wearing that vest."

"Padrino is to blame, not him." Finn's voice remained calm but firm. "Eric knew the risk of coming here without a vest, yet he did it. After Eric and I were shot, Quintrell took out Padrino and another guard. He's the reason the rest of us are alive."

"There's no time for this," West said. "Finn, take your father, Sloane, and Reagan to the hospital. Nate and I will catch up after we deal with Quintrell and the local police."

"She's right." Finn's face twisted in pain as she held out a hand, palm up. "Give me your keys."

"You're hurt, I'll drive." Sloane fished her keys from her coat pocket, but Finn snatched them from her hand.

"Like hell you will. It's only a bruise." Finn turned on her heel toward the undercover sedan. "Get in the damn car."

Chandler raised an eyebrow with a slight grin. "I've seen her like this before. We better do as she says." Without another word, he and Reagan slid into the backseat of the car.

"Fine," Sloane said to the space Finn had left behind. She then plopped into the passenger seat. Once on the main road, she glanced at Finn. "I'm sorry."

"We're all on edge." Finn released her right hand from the steering wheel and extended it over the center console, palm up.

Sloane clutched it. She had never before had Finn's temper directed at her, but she knew she deserved it. Finn had shown her determination, feistiness, and unwillingness to back down when she knew she was right—precisely like Avery. Or was Avery exactly like Finn? Either way, having Finn by her side was a comfort.

"Eric is strong. He'll pull through." Finn drew their hands to her lips.

"I hope so."

CHAPTER TWENTY

The mighty swoosh echoing off the cold tile walls sounded more like a submarine blowing its ballast tanks than a single toilet flush. Sloane speculated that the extra force was probably needed to wash away untold numbers of bacteria, a thought that bolstered her long-standing dislike for hospitals. She stepped up to the sink and peered into the spotless bathroom mirror. The unflattering fluorescent lights highlighted every smudge, dark circle, and hair out of place. She felt the way her nearly dried clothes looked—like shit.

She pulled the soap dispenser lever, the antiseptic scent of the soap reminding her why she hated emergency rooms. Every hospital was the same—sterile smells, bare floors, overly cooled air, and depressing alerts announcing incoming traumas. Everyone there who wasn't a patient or worker had the same blank stares while they waited for news of their loved ones. Tired of hospitals and even more tired of this case, Sloane hoped the fiery culmination at Three Owls marked the end of Padrino, Los Dorados, and Kiss, the drug that had killed one of

Reagan's best friends. And, more importantly, her seven-month-long nightmare.

Sloane held her hands under a stream of lukewarm water, recalling the lives cut short in her dogged pursuit of justice. Shellie Rodriguez and Michael Wong—kids looking for a weekend high who ended up in the morgue. Then Diego's cook—the first life Sloane ever took. That moment's kill-or-be-killed scenario made that fact easier to swallow, but only a little. Then her beloved Avery. In the written report, she was listed as collateral damage, killed while performing her job. In reality, she became the driving force behind the trail of death that followed. Diego, Caco, Padrino, the men in the wildfire, the men guarding Rosa, the men at the Lower Bottoms house, the men at the potato farm, and the kidnappers all were dead. Twenty-eight lives lost, and countless lives impacted.

A knock on the door pulled Sloane from her morbid trance. "Are you done in there?" a muffled voice called from the other side of the door.

Sloane took a deep breath to focus her wandering mind. "Just finishing up." She snatched a few paper towels from the dispenser, dried her hands, and opened the door.

Waiting on the other side was a thirty-something, paunchy woman smartly dressed as if she were on her way to work, her dark hair matching her ebony skin. Her hands rested atop the shoulders of a young girl no older than eight whose skin matched hers. The girl, dressed in leggings and a pink zip-up hoodie, fidgeted, bouncing on the bottoms of her sneakers.

"Sorry." In her squishy shoes, Sloane sidestepped what she assumed were mother and daughter. "All yours."

The woman's eyes narrowed in concern. "Are you all right, miss?"

"It's the waiting." Sloane forced a smile.

"Looks like you've had a rougher night than just waiting."

"I have, but I'm hoping the worst is over."

"If you need a little peace and quiet, the north wing has a serenity garden. It's beautiful this time of morning."

"Sounds like you know your way around this place."

"We're old pros here." The woman squeezed the girl's shoulders. A half grin appeared, the type that implied their expertise was born out of an unwelcome burden. "Her younger brother is a frequent flyer—a cancer patient."

"I'm so sorry."

"Mom." The young girl tugged at her mother's sleeve.

"All right, Elizabeth." The woman offered Sloane a sheepish smile. "A mother's duty never ends."

"Of course." Sloane imagined Reagan at that girl's age and how Avery must've had her hands full as a single parent. She respected that kind of dedication. Reagan was almost seventeen now and for the most part, self-sufficient, though her plea a week ago proved she still needed a full-time mother who didn't face danger every day. Maybe it *was* time for a career change.

Sloane turned to leave, but the mother placed a soft hand on her shoulder. "I hope everything works out."

"Thank you." Sloane sighed, her shoulders drooping at her welcome concern. "Same with your son."

The door closed behind the woman and girl, and Sloane retraced her route back to the examination area. The moment she slid the curtain open, Reagan jumped from her seat.

"Want your chair back, Mom?"

"Keep it." Despite her exhaustion, Sloane waved her off. After what Reagan had gone through, her first concern was for her comfort. "The doctor said you should rest for a few days."

"I'm fine. It's just a few bruises."

"And a mild concussion. Sit. I'm good standing." Sloane pointed at the chair. A great weight had lifted when the doctor confirmed that the blow to the head was the worst of Reagan's injuries. Besides the initial knockout punch, the thug hadn't laid a hand on her. The full trauma of her ordeal had yet to hit her, of course.

"Nonsense." Chandler rose to his feet from the other chair. "A lady should sit, especially the one who rescued us."

"Uh-uh." While appreciating his chivalry, Sloane wagged her finger at him. "You're supposed to be resting too. Sit."

Finn slid her legs to the far edge of the gurney she was lying on, back propped to a sixty-degree angle. She patted a patch of thin mattress. "There's room for both of us."

As small as it was, sharing a bed with Finn while sitting close enough to feel her warmth sounded perfect to Sloane. She shimmied in next to Finn's legs. "Still no word on your X-rays?"

"Not yet, but I don't think anything is broken." Finn sat up straighter and rotated her shoulder in a circular motion.

"Looks like the pain meds have kicked in." Sloane focused on the emerging bruise peeking out from her loose collar. "I'm glad we're getting you checked out. You could barely lift your arm to get the bulletproof vest off in the parking lot."

"I'm glad too, pumpkin. My heart almost stopped when I saw you fall to the ground." Chandler cleared a swell of emotion from his throat. Sloane now understood fully a parent's devastation of witnessing their child in peril. Only hours earlier, she feared Reagan, a daughter she'd come to love more than she thought possible, would burn to death. She was sure this ordeal was something neither of them would soon get over.

Sloane ran a finger along the hospital gown above Finn's right breast, where West's bulletproof vest had stopped the bullet. Moving it a fraction, she saw where the force of the armor plate had burst blood vessels and left a bloody red circle about the size of a silver dollar. She'd have to give West the hug of her life for saving Finn's life. "I don't know what I'd do if I lost you."

Sloane turned toward Reagan, grateful she hadn't failed her…or Avery. She extended her other hand. "Or you. I almost lost hope of getting you back alive."

"I was so scared." Reagan's voice cracked when she gripped Sloane's hand, the first display of raw emotion since emerging from the pool. "I thought they were going to kill me, but Chandler kept me from losing it."

"We helped each other." Chandler's eyes misted over when he clutched Reagan's other hand. "Then again, I knew Finn would come for us."

"Thank you for taking care of my daughter." Something in Sloane broke. She'd come close to losing everyone she loved again, but luck was on her side this time. The only uncertainty remaining was Eric. Word on his surgery was still hours away. With one hand holding Reagan's, the other Finn's, she couldn't hold back the tears rolling down her cheeks. "I love you both."

Finn reached out to hold her father's hand, completing the circle. At that moment, a family was born. Horror had drawn them together, but their love for each other would connect them forever.

A familiar young redhead in blue scrubs, a stethoscope draped over her neck, entered, pulling the privacy curtain closed behind her. Everyone gave the other's hand an extra squeeze before letting go.

"Good news, Agent Harper. No broken bones. Not even a fracture. You're one lucky lady." Doctor Sarah Freeman shifted her eyes toward Reagan. "As are you. You're lucky you were wearing wool, or you would've had some awful burns."

"So the sweater protected her?" Sloane asked.

"I'd say so." Doctor Freeman nodded. "Wool is one of the slowest burning fabrics."

Sloane turned to Reagan, believing the unbelievable. Despite what common sense would dictate, she knew it was true. "Your mom protected you."

"I felt her there." Reagan offered a confirming and reassuring nod. Avery may be gone, but Sloane was sure the strong connection between her and Reagan remained. Sloane and Reagan had turned the final corner—they'd be all right.

"Does that mean we can get out of here?" Finn asked.

"Absolutely." The doctor gave Finn a gentle pat on the arm. "You'll be mighty sore for the first week, so I'll write you a scrip for the pain."

"Thank you, Sarah." Sloane glanced over her shoulder at the doctor, who had helped her repeatedly. "This is such a relief."

"I'm glad to be the bearer of good news this time," Sarah said to Sloane. "Did you take care of the bad guys?"

Finn narrowed one eye, staring at the redhead with curiosity.

"We did." Sloane gave her a grateful wink before turning to Finn. "Sarah deserves a medal. She helped me avoid detection when Padrino was here. Because of her, we blew the case wide open." Sloane's grin faded in an instant. "Now we're waiting for news on my partner. He took one in the chest."

"He must be the gunshot wound that came in not long before you," Sarah noted. "When I get a break, I'll check on him and let you know how it's going."

"That would be a great help, Sarah."

"Will you be in the ER waiting room?"

"Either there, or someone mentioned the serenity garden."

"That's a much better place to wait it out." Sarah opened a cabinet above the small sink the doctors used to wash their hands and removed two light blankets. "Here, in case it's chilly. I'll look for you there."

Sarah excused herself.

Sloane's thoughts drifted to Reagan, who appeared beyond exhausted. She needed to get her home for some long, overdue rest. "Let's get you dressed, Finn, so we can get these two home."

"Sounds like our cue. We'll meet you out in the waiting room." Reagan popped up from her chair. "Let's go, Gramps."

"Who you calling Gramps?" Chandler frowned playfully, earning chuckles from all three. He drew the curtain, leaving Sloane and Finn alone.

Sloane grabbed the string tie of the large plastic bag containing Finn's shoes, clothing, and other belongings and placed each item on a chair. Finn slid her bottom down the top of the gurney, flung her legs over the end, and struggled to untie the hospital gown with her left hand.

Sloane maneuvered behind her. "Let me."

With her thumb and forefinger, Sloane released the three ties in the back, revealing smooth, porcelain skin. Though the bullet struck Finn in the chest, a reddish discoloration was already appearing on her back, testament to the amount of force behind that bullet. Sloane circled it with a finger and then ran the finger down a thewy flare. Weeks earlier, when Finn was wearing her workout clothes, Sloane had caught a brief glimpse of these well-defined flank muscles. Tracing them now, she appreciated the muscle's sexy definition and the random appearance of small, dark freckles. Then she remembered the moment Finn was hit. Like Chandler, her heart had stopped, fearing the bullet had somehow found its way between the minute seams between the vest's armor plates.

"I'm so thankful you wore that vest."

Finn took in a deep breath when Sloane pressed her lips on top of the injured shoulder. Holding up the front of her oversized cotton gown, Finn twisted at the waist to peer into Sloane's eyes. "I'm so relieved Daddy and Reagan made it out alive." Her words were clear, but Sloane recognized an opioid-induced lilt in them and in the sway of her head.

Sloane kissed Finn lightly on the lips, as if she would break if she pushed harder. Finn deepened the kiss, wrapping one hand and then the other around the back of Sloane's head and letting the gown drop to her narrow waist. Only a few layers of clothing now separated Sloane from Finn's bare breasts. Her head swirled, envisioning Finn's half-naked body pressed against hers. The temptation to caress her was strong, but a hospital examination room with only a flimsy curtain for privacy was not where she wanted to make love to Finn for the first time.

She forced their lips apart and leaned back. Despite the strong urge to do otherwise, she kept her eyes on Finn's. "As much as I'd love to continue this, we need to get you dressed."

The sun had risen over the horizon an hour ago. This time of the morning, without a natural disaster looming, there were only a handful of people in the emergency room waiting area when Sloane walked in, holding Finn's hand. Three muted, wall-mounted televisions scrolled the news in closed-caption to sparsely populated rows of hard plastic chairs. Off in one corner, away from the outside chill that flowed in whenever the automatic doors swooshed open, Reagan and Chandler sat with the Tenneys, wearing fresh clothes Reagan's grandparents apparently had brought with them.

Sloane pulled Finn to a stop shy of the open doors leading from the hallway. "Good, they're here."

"Janet and Caleb must have been worried sick."

"They were, which is why I asked them to come. We don't know how long it will be until Eric is out of surgery, and Reagan needs her rest." Sloane took a deep breath, preparing herself for the worst. "If he doesn't make it, I'd rather tell her at home."

"Daddy should rest too."

"You should go with them." Sloane rubbed Finn's arms to make up for her less than convincing plea. "The Tenneys can drive you and Chandler home."

"Not a chance." Finn raised a single defiant eyebrow. "I'm waiting this out with you."

Shot hours earlier and numbed on painkillers following an emotionally and physically exhausting day, Finn remained yet at Sloane's side. Somehow "thank you" didn't seem enough. She said it anyway, hoping her eyes and smile said much more.

"There's nowhere else I'd rather be." Finn squeezed Sloane's hand, confirming what Sloane already knew. They'd become each other's rock, and until they knew Eric was out of the woods, they would remain by the other's side.

After several warm, teary greetings, Janet handed Sloane a small travel bag. "I brought you ladies some toiletries and a change of clothes."

"You're a lifesaver, Janet. My clothes may have dried, but the shoes are still sloshy."

"Clean clothes do feel great." Chandler fiddled with Caleb's borrowed sweatpants and Windbreaker.

When Reagan's face contorted to stifle a yawn, Caleb threw an arm around his granddaughter's shoulder. "It's time to get you home, young lady."

Sloane kneeled in front of Reagan. "I don't want to leave until I know something about Eric, so the Tenneys will take you and Chandler home."

Reagan turned her gaze to Finn. "Are you staying with Mom?"

"Yes, I'm staying."

"Good." Reagan pressed a hand against her chest as if Finn had taken an overwhelming worry from her. "She shouldn't be alone right now."

"Your mom would be so proud." Sloane smiled at Reagan's final turn from adolescence into adulthood. Weeks ago, Sloane would've mourned the fact Avery wasn't there to see it, but after the events of the last few days, she believed Avery already had.

* * *

Lush foliage in various shades of green lined the walkways of the serenity garden, centering Sloane somewhat as she meandered down the path. Some of the plants were dark as the skin of an avocado, others as light as a thirsty, yellowing lawn in the heat of summer. Some shrubs were tall as trees, others shorter, like dandelions. The mix of bushy, leafy, and airy greenery combined to form a tranquil outdoor escape from the harsh reality that lay inside—the fact that Eric might not survive.

At the end of the trail an inviting bench perched under a spacious pergola that was nestled beside a manmade waterfall and pond. This was the perfect spot to wait for what might be devastating news.

"Sit with me, Finn."

Wooden trelliswork diffused the direct sunlight enough to hold in the morning chill. Sloane covered her and Finn's legs with one of the blankets Sarah had loaned them, the cotton providing a thin layer of comfort. Finn wrapped the other blanket around their shoulders.

"This is cozy." Finn scooted close until their bodies touched from arms to their feet.

"It is." Several peaceful minutes later, Sloane's mind rewound the moments after Eric was shot, processing what he had said when he saw death coming. "Something is bothering me, Finn."

"What is it?"

"Eric said it was all his fault. That he was young and driving too fast."

"It bothered me too. What do you think he meant?"

A knot formed in Sloane's belly as she came to an unsettling conclusion. "I think he was talking about my parents' accident."

Finn shifted to face Sloane. "How can that be?"

"He talked about growing up in Pinole, not far from us." Sloane did the math in her head. "He would've been about sixteen at the time of the accident."

"But why wouldn't he have said anything before?"

"I don't know. Guilt, maybe." Sloane wracked her brain to come up with any hints she may have missed over the last two and a half years as his partner. Nothing screamed "I killed your parents."

She shook her head. "All I know is that this changes everything."

Soon, a figure appeared on the walkway, red hair and blue scrubs recognizable from a considerable distance.

"Hey, Sloane. Finn. I checked on your partner," Sarah said.

Sloane rose to her feet, hoping the long look on Sarah's face was a product of a long overnight shift and not from being the bearer of bad news. "How is he?"

"The surgery went well. The bullet missed anything vital, and they repaired the tissue damage." Sarah rubbed the back of her neck. "He lost a lot of blood, so the next few hours are critical. If he makes it past that, the prognosis is good."

Sloane's preoccupation with the high cost of this case and resulting silence prompted Finn to stand and respond on her behalf. "Thank you, Sarah. When can we see him?"

"We'll have him in ICU in about half an hour, but even if he pulls through, he won't be responsive for days." Sarah glanced at Sloane, her eyes narrowing in clear concern. Addressing Finn, she asked, "Is she all right?"

No. She wasn't all right. Sloane had stared into the distance. Closing this case had come at too high a price. Avery had died. Reagan was kidnapped. Finn was shot. Eric might not make it. And she might have just learned that the mentor she'd admired for two and a half years, the man she considered a brother, was the reason she was orphaned. Even though it put a major dent in a drug-running operation, keeping Kiss out of the hands of kids like Shellie, no case was worth all of this.

"We've had a tough few days, but she'll be fine." Finn shook Sarah's hand before thanking her again and saying goodbye.

"Sloane?" Finn wrapped a hand around Sloane's.

No job was worth this amount of confusion and heartache, Sloane concluded. Only Finn's gentle, warm touch made sense. This case had turned her life upside down, but at every turn, Finn had been there to right her.

"I can't do this anymore, and I especially can't do it with Eric."

CHAPTER TWENTY-ONE

The elevator door swooshed opened but not soon enough. Barry Manilow had wormed his way into Sloane's head and had her loosely planning a trip to the Copacabana.

"They've got to change that music."

"It's on the same level as waterboarding, isn't it?" One side of Finn's mouth twitched up as she exited to the thirtieth-floor hallway. "Come on, you."

Sloane laced their fingers before being led toward Finn's condo. Catnapping in a hospital chair for the last twelve hours had done little to lessen her exhaustion. Fatigue was slowing her pace, but she was determined to see Finn safely home.

Her mind drifted to the call she made before leaving the hospital. Janet had picked up her house phone, and after asking about Reagan, she said, "*The poor thing was so exhausted, she went right to sleep after dinner.*" Following more reassurances that Reagan was otherwise okay for the moment, Janet added, "*Take all the time you need and take care of Finn. She's been through an ordeal as well. We'll be fine until you get home.*"

At the door, Finn fished out her keys and paused, her gaze fixed on the knob. "I'm dead tired," she said, "but I don't want to say goodbye."

"Me neither."

They'd spent more than forty-eight hours together, tearing down one stumbling block after another in the effort to get their family members back. The ordeal was finally over and Eric was showing positive signs of recovery, but going their separate ways wouldn't do.

"How about I whip us up something simple?" Finn said.

"Only if you let me help."

"Deal."

Sloane felt the first unforced smile in days creep onto her lips when they walked through the door. It felt good. Finn tossed her keys into the handmade cobalt blue bowl sitting atop the wooden entry table. She removed the zip-up hoodie Janet had brought and hung it on a wall hook a foot past the table. Sloane did the same with her light jacket.

As tempting as it was, taking in the evening amber glow of the Bay Bridge from Finn's dining room window would have to wait. Bypassing the sleek, not-a-thing-out-of-place living room, they made quick work in the small but efficient modern kitchen.

Finn pulled eggs, milk, chopped green onion, and shredded cheese from the fridge. While she assembled the ingredients on the counter, she glanced over her shoulder. "I have fresh berries if you want to pull some out. Oh, and how about some toast?"

"Sounds great." Sloane scanned the countertop for any sign of bread, unsure where Finn kept things.

Finn tipped her chin toward the cabinet at her left. "I have a loaf in the pantry. Bowls are to my right."

"On it."

She and Finn exchanged glances while preparing and plating the food. It was not unlike what she and Avery used to do, Sloane thought. She expected the memory to have a sharp edge, but it didn't. It reminded her of happy times instead and provided a glimpse into the future. She welcomed the special feeling and could see herself and Finn doing this every morning before heading off to work.

At the table, when their plates were empty, Sloane turned her attention to the bay and the heavy commuter traffic on the bridge, which glowed in the waning sunlight. "The bay always calms me."

"Feels like home, doesn't it?"

Finn's wistful tone made Sloane shift her gaze to meet hers. A reality finally became clear. Finn was home. "Yes, it does."

"Have you thought more about what you're going to do about Eric once he recuperates?" Finn asked.

"I don't want to think about that tonight." Sloane squeezed Finn's hand. "I want to focus on you."

"Same here, but I would love a shower first." Finn flipped her napkin on the plate, pushed her chair back, and grabbed the empty plates. "How about you?"

"Washing away the last few days would be nice." Sloane picked up their drink glasses and followed Finn into the kitchen.

"The guest bath is stocked. How about I meet you out here in fifteen minutes?"

"Sounds like a plan."

Soon hot water was cascading over Sloane's drained body. She let the warmth penetrate shoulder and back muscles that ached from sleeping upright in a hospital chair. Putting those hours out of her mind, she focused on the quiet minutes she had shared in Finn's office. Was it last night or the night before when she told Finn she loved her? The days ran together, but she remembered the heavy weight that had lifted when she said it.

While she was drying off, her wedding ring caught on the bath sheet's plush cotton fibers. She moved to push it back on, then stopped and removed the plain gold band. She turned it at an angle to read the inscription. "Forever."

Short and straightforward. Avery had suggested they engrave that one word on each of their rings to capture how they loved each other. Even now, after death, the message rang true. Sloane still loved her, of that she was sure. She had been a fool for avoiding love all those years. If Avery taught her one thing, it was that life without love was no life at all. Now, she had love with Finn.

When she finished dressing, she tucked her wedding ring in her front pants pocket, whispering, "Goodbye, Avery."

Refreshed by the shower, Sloane returned to the living room. When she didn't find Finn in the kitchen tending to the rest of the dishes or in the living room splayed out on the couch, she thought perhaps she'd finished too fast, but when she checked her watch she saw she was right on time.

She poured a glass of mint water from the refrigerator and returned to the panoramic dining room window. The eclectic buildings, dark water, magnificent bridges, and rolling hills on the horizon painted a beautiful picture, one that never failed to conjure up the feeling of home.

Sloane grew concerned after several minutes passed and Finn still hadn't reappeared. Had she fallen asleep? Did she slip in the shower? She tiptoed to the master bedroom door to find out. She knocked. "Finn, are you all right?"

"Having a little trouble getting dressed." The door between them muffled Finn's voice. "Would you mind lending me a hand?"

"Sure." Sloane eased the door open, unsure what she'd find. Was Finn naked or partially clothed? Both prospects had her mouth watering; neither would disappoint her.

When she stepped inside, both Finn and the exquisite unobstructed view of the bay from the windows took her breath away. The ninety-degree spectacular corner view of the water would have to wait, though. Finn was sitting atop a cushioned bench at the foot of the bed, naked from the waist up, her porcelain white back to Sloane. The discoloration on her shoulder had turned from red to a mix of blue and purple.

"So beautiful."

Finn turned a fraction toward Sloane's voice, the warm glow of a floor lamp outlining the curve of a breast. Each muscle on her right side flexed, delineating one lean mass from the other. Days earlier, when Sloane had explored patches of the soft skin beneath her shirt, those muscles had sparked fantasies. Seeing them now, along with the shadow of her breast, caused Sloane's breath to hitch.

Finn lifted her good hand, clutching a white lace bra. "Undressing was a lot easier than the reverse."

The movement broke Sloane's trance, prompting her to step forward. "It's been hours since your last pain pill."

"I took one before I hopped in the shower." Finn twisted back toward the windows, slipping a bra strap over her tender arm first. "I didn't realize how sore I was until the water hit me."

"Does it hurt much?" Sloane traced the small spot on her shoulder blade again.

"Only when I raise it too high." Before scooting to one side of the bench to make room for Sloane, Finn slipped on the second strap and adjusted the cups over each breast. She craned her head over a shoulder in slow motion, letting one cup droop when she patted the tufted cushion. "Mind hooking it?" Her voice had dropped to a seductive tone, revealing the question was somewhat halfhearted.

"Actually, I *do* mind." Sloane sat beside Finn. Her practical, rational side told her to help Finn dress and say goodbye so they could each return to their loved ones and get a good night's sleep. But nothing about her growing desire seemed practical or rational. Lingering fear that she was being disloyal to Avery was gone, and the only thing Sloane had in her heart was love for the woman sitting inches away.

This moment had been building since the day they'd outrun death at Three Owls. But not since the first time she and Avery made love had Sloane been so unsure about how to start. Hesitantly, she placed her fingers at the base of Finn's neck and trailed them outward along the top of each shoulder, ending at the triceps. When Finn shivered beneath her fingertips, Sloane sensed she'd rather dispose of the bra than put it on.

She ignored the dangling bra clasps and traced with her lips where her fingers had just been, across one shoulder and then the other. By the time she returned to Finn's neck and her semi-dry hair, those light brushings had turned into wet licks. When Finn swallowed a moan, Sloane paused. How far should she take this with her injury? "I don't want to hurt you."

Finn turned to meet Sloane's eyes. They contained the same desire Sloane refused to fight any longer. "You won't hurt me."

Sloane inched her head closer to Finn's until their breaths mingled, setting off the first spark. Practicality and rationality were no longer options. Heat rose in her chest, escaping in increasingly steamy exhales until she leaned in for that first fiery kiss. Every nerve ending came alive when their moist lips pressed against one another. But when she opened her mouth to dart her tongue into Finn's, Finn pulled back with a sudden force.

"Did I hurt you?" Sloane's voice ended in a panicked uptick.

In slow motion, Finn shook her head from side to side. A measured smile built on her lips. She stood and turned, facing Sloane with her arms folded across her breasts to keep the bra in place. Taking a step back, she lightened her grip and dipped one shoulder at a time, letting each strap droop low on her forearms.

Sloane gulped past the lump in her throat when Finn lowered her arms and let the bra drop to the floor. Their earlier encounters had failed to prepare her for this moment. Before she could take a breath, Finn lowered her lounge pants and bikini briefs to her ankles and stepped out of them. Every inch of Finn, from sculpted muscles to curved hips and rounded breasts, seduced her.

Finn stepped forward, bent at the waist, and gave Sloane a single luscious kiss. "Why are you still dressed?"

Getting her mouth to form words at this point was an impossible, if not unnecessary, task. Sloane could barely think about breathing, let alone stripping off her clothes. She let Finn pull her up until bare breasts grazed her top as they'd done in the emergency room. Every doubt and reason to pull back disappeared. Shallow breaths took over, and every muscle tingled with anticipation. When Finn reached over to lower the zipper on her jeans, all coherent thought escaped her.

"You'll have to do the shirt yourself."

Somehow Sloane processed the word "shirt." She eased it over her head and discarded the garment in the air, not caring where it landed. Finn inched forward, pressing their bellies together, skin to skin. Sloane melted into the sensation, every piece of her screamed for contact.

Finn's head lifted toward the ceiling, inviting Sloane to take her. Unable to resist, she dragged her lips across Finn's smooth, alluring neck, igniting a burn everywhere clothing touched her skin. Screw slow and sexy. She needed to strip. Now!

With little effort, Sloane discarded her shoes, socks, and sports bra, but her jeans proved difficult. They slipped over her slender hips well enough, but their narrow legs bunched at her ankles. Lifting a foot, she shook it with all her might—and promptly lost her balance, falling on her butt with a thud and knocking over and breaking the floor lamp. If not for their previous encounters and knowing Finn loved her, embarrassment could've ruined the moment. The pratfall only made her more determined. This was not the time for apologies. She thrust her feet in the air. "You do it, damn it."

Finn stifled most of her laugh, but a toothy grin gave away her amusement as she ripped the jeans from Sloane's legs. Dressed now only in her underwear, Sloane made a mental note to scold Janet later for her choice of clothing. Tight jeans and boy shorts? Really?

Sloane bounced up from the floor and drew Finn in with one arm, bringing their hips together. "You think that's funny, do you?"

"Absolutely."

Sloane snaked her other arm around her back, drawing them even closer together and transforming Finn's sly grin into a lusty one. When their bare breasts pressed together for the first time, the sensation was explosive. *Concentrate*, Sloane scolded herself.

"Now, where were we?" Sloane resumed nuzzling that long neck with wet sucks and licks up to an ear, losing herself in Finn's muttering. She focused long enough to nudge Finn backward until the backs of her thighs hit the edge of the mattress. "Lie down. I don't want to put any pressure on your shoulder."

While Finn positioned herself flat on the bed, Sloane removed her boy shorts, discarding them wherever they happened to land. Faint city light streamed through the panoramic window, illuminating Finn's searching eyes and heaving breasts that begged Sloane to move faster. But fast wouldn't do. The day at the accident site had set her and Finn on this course, and rushing was the last thing she wanted. This moment called for savoring Finn's intoxicating body like an eighteen-year-old scotch. *What do I touch first? A breast? Her center?*

Climbing onto the bed at its foot, she knelt between Finn's outspread legs. Starting at her calves, Sloane dragged her hands up Finn's silky skin. Nothing had ever felt so delicate. When her fingertips passed Finn's knees, Finn's abdomen muscles rolled in anticipation, waking Sloane's center with a roar.

"Please," Finn's husky voice begged. She bucked her hips inches off the mattress and offered her core, inviting Sloane's touch.

"All in good time."

Finn's suggestion wasn't one Sloane was ready to take her up on. No, she wanted to bring her to a slow boil. Bending her arms at the elbow on either side of Finn's head to avoid placing weight on the injury, she brought together their hips, centers, and bellies, skin to skin, heat radiating between them. Staggered by the sensation of their naked bodies pressed together, Sloane paused. She'd never felt more alive, not even with Avery.

"Every inch of you is sexy." An understatement but Sloane needed to give voice to it. She knew she'd hit the right tone when Finn's eyes glassed over with more desire.

Without warning, Finn arched up and captured Sloane's lips, sending her tongue searching through her mouth. She signaled her mounting impatience, digging her fingers into the long muscles of Sloane's back and stoking Sloane's fires.

Weeks of fantasizing had Sloane primed to touch and taste Finn for the first time. She'd dreamed of taking her from every direction, every position, but Finn's injury obliged her to tame the fantasy. Sloane broke the kiss and worked her lips down to Finn's breasts, taking one into her mouth. The taste of citrus swirled on her tongue, reminding her of the scent that had riveted her so when they were teenagers. She pulled her mouth away long enough to say, "Oranges never tasted so good."

Switching between breasts, she savored each one until Finn's rocking motion sparked her own. *Slow is good*, she scolded herself for the second time. She tightened her pelvis and leg muscles to force her thighs to stop. Finn, however, continued. Her rocking turned into mounting thrusts. Throaty moans signaled a frenzy of need —Sloane's cue to move on.

She shifted up to peer into Finn's hungry eyes, the reflection of love and lust she saw there urging her on. She slid a hand down Finn's belly, past her navel, into soft short hairs. She dialed up Finn's desperation, leaving quaking muscles and goose bumps in her wake. A rush of warm blood had readied her folds. They pulsated with a need for release against Sloane's hand and fueled a need to fill her.

"What do you want?" Sloane rasped.

"Inside," Finn croaked in between hot, ragged breaths.

Sloane entered with two fingers. Fleshy, warm, and moist. She didn't expect how much she'd missed intimacy. It was like returning home after a winter alone in the wilderness. She was riveted by the contortions of Finn's facial muscles, her flushed skin, and the jaws that snatched for air between sensations. The sight, she was sure, was enough to make her ignore her own growing need and satisfy Finn all night long.

Finn's breathing was struggling to keep up with each stroke. Climax was on the horizon, but first, Sloane wanted—no, needed—to discover if Finn's nectar tasted as sweet as she envisioned. She cut her tempo in half, causing Finn to groan in frustration and increase her bucking to compensate.

"Patience," Sloane whispered into her ear, urging Finn to slow. She kissed her on the lips, her tongue going deep and adding a good swirl as a preview of what was in store. On her way past her belly, she stopped to give each breast one last kiss.

Sloane scooted further down and encouraged Finn to open her legs wider. She took a deep breath, the first intake of musky scent, arousal mixed with citrus, sending tingles through her. Leaning in, she sampled Finn's unique flavor. The tangy and sweet taste, more enticing than she'd imagined, reminded her of a favorite dish she couldn't devour quickly enough. She forced herself to go slow, savor the alternating flavors, and consider her next step. Did Finn prefer to be sucked, like she did? Or did she like to be rubbed? Either would give Finn a needed release, but only one would give her complete satisfaction.

She ran a fingertip across her clit, settling into gentle circles. Finn's whimper and subtle body movements signaled a craving for something more intimate. Sloane shifted and latched her mouth on it, earning a piercing groan. She'd pinpointed Finn's desire. Without releasing her lips, she plunged two fingers inside and resumed their internal kneading in a slow, steady pace, one she could enjoy as much as Finn. Within moments, Sloane took her over the edge. Each contraction reassured her she'd given Finn the ultimate pleasure.

Soon Finn flopped her good arm over her face, panting. "That was so worth the wait."

Sloane was sure now. Every earlier near-encounter with Finn was premature and would've ended in disaster. Waiting was the best decision she'd ever made. She threw an arm and a leg over Finn and rested her head atop a breast, tipsy over the sated smile she'd put on Finn's face. "That was even better than the fantasy."

"Much." Finn guided Sloane's chin up with a hand and kissed her.

"You should sleep." Sloane pulled up the blanket to cover their tired bodies.

"No, you don't." Finn adopted a challenging yet seductive tone and threw back the covers. "You deserve a proper orgasm."

"But…your shoulder?"

"Oh, come on." Finn's wry expression set a playful tone. "You'll have to turn in your lesbian card if you can't figure this out."

"I think I just proved I know what I'm doing." Sloane gave a hip thrust for good measure before softening her expression. "But I don't want to put you in any more pain."

"Trust me. The Norco is doing its job." Finn slid out from under Sloane and propped herself up in a seated position, resting against the headboard with her legs outstretched but pressed together. "Besides, I have a few fantasies of my own." She curled an index finger several times toward Sloane, giving her a sexy, come-hither look.

No one had touched Sloane since Avery, not even herself. That urge had disappeared until her and Finn's steamy encounter in the interview observation room days ago. Now it had returned in spades, making Sloane eager to straddle that inviting body. With her legs bent at the knees and spread wide, she inched forward over Finn's upper thighs. When Finn's hands skimmed the hot skin of her waist and sides, each surrounding muscle twitched in succession. She'd all but forgotten what it felt like to be touched this way and welcomed every exhilarating moment.

Finn cupped both breasts and squeezed their soft flesh with splayed fingers, sending tingling waves up and down Sloane's spine. Finn fixed her eyes on them. "They're perfect."

Sloane's fit body had drawn in countless women over the years, but only the fascination of two of them meant anything to her—first Avery and now Finn. She'd never wanted a woman's touch as much as she wanted Finn's now. She couldn't wait for her to decide which breast to ravish first and offered her right. Finn's warm, soft, licking strokes fired a jolt to Sloane's swollen core, waking it from its seven-month dormancy.

"I need you inside." Sloane was ready for Finn to fill her. She had been ever since saying goodbye to Avery on their misty back deck. That morning had marked the end of her grief, but not the end of her appreciation of the intimacy they had enjoyed. The sharing of bodies always met her physical needs, but once she embraced love, sex became more intimate. She'd surrendered herself to Avery, and now, she was surrendering to Finn.

Two fingers slid inside, and she rocked against Finn's hand. Her walls were tight, having not been filled in more than half a year, but… "More. I want more."

Finn released the breast from her mouth. "I don't think I can."

That pulled Sloane out of her head, forcing her to halt and open her eyes. "Do you need to stop?"

"Not on your life." Finn sat up straighter and eased her other hand between Sloane's legs. "I just needed to shift to give you double the pleasure."

"You sure?"

Sloane got her answer when Finn dipped her other hand in. The added sensation tipped the balance, setting off an avalanche. Sloane was no longer in command of her body. Finn had complete control. Sloane's breaths shortened, forcing her lungs to cry for more air. A tremor in her foot spread to her thigh at lightning speed. Release was nearing. In the next instant, she tumbled over the edge. Every muscle in her weakened, but she was careful to fall to Finn's side. Unable to do much more than roll over, she reveled in the pulsating euphoria.

"Alexa, close drapes." Finn slid down flat, resting her head on the pillows and bringing the covers with her. Under the blanket, their bodies entwined.

With only the warm glow of the city lights penetrating the sheer drapes for illumination, Sloane closed her eyes and rested her head on Finn's breast. She listened to her strong, rhythmic heartbeat. This had been the first heart to capture her own, and it was the one that now turned her months of misery into joy. Its beat soothed her into a peaceful state, something that had been absent for months. As her mind cleared, setting the stage for a long, overdue tranquil sleep, she had a sense that lying in Finn's arms was where she was supposed to be.

"Love you always," Sloane whispered before nodding off.

"Always," Finn whispered back.

CHAPTER TWENTY-TWO

Eric surveyed the tubes and wires of every type that were running to and from his battered body. When he'd returned to consciousness two days ago he'd learned that doctors had kept him on heavy sedation for five days, waiting for his vital signs to improve. The numbers on the nearby monitors and scribblings on a wall-mounted whiteboard told him the recovery had been long and slow.

A morphine fog had made yesterday a blur. Today, the opiates had been reduced, and he awoke whenever the technicians and nurses came to draw samples, check his blood pressure, or change bandages and IVs.

He looked up as five-foot-nothing Nurse Castro, a cute, forty-something brunette in blue scrubs, carried in a food tray. She placed it off to the side atop the rolling bed table. "Ready to try a little food today?" Her cheery question brightened the dreary room and his mood. She didn't wait for an answer before pressing the up button on the bedrail to bring Eric to a seated position.

"Do I have a choice?" Eric croaked at half his regular pace, trying to smile.

"Not if you want to get better." Nurse Castro adjusted the height of the tray table to roll over Eric's legs and removed the chrome lids covering the food. "We'll start you off with a little warm broth, and if you can hold that down, we'll try oatmeal."

"Sounds yummy." Food still had little appeal, but he needed something to concentrate on other than the hole in his chest. He started to lean forward, wincing when the tube inserted near his gunshot wound pinched. "I hate this damn thing."

"Drainage is way down"—she fiddled with the line—"so I'm guessing we'll take this out after the doctor makes her rounds."

"Good. It's disgusting."

She laughed, offering him a spoon. "Want to give it a whirl yourself?"

"Sure."

Grasping the spoon gave Eric a hell of a surprise. Even with his good arm, it felt like he was lifting a hundred-pound barbell. For the first time since waking, he realized how weak he'd become. He dipped the spoon into the broth bowl and raised it toward his mouth, shaking and spilling most of the liquid in the process. He clenched his jaw. "Damn it."

"You're doing fine, Sergeant Decker." The nurse gently wiped the drops from his hand with a paper napkin. "You've been through a lot and haven't used your arm in a week, so it'll take a little patience until you get your strength back. Let's try it again."

It took some doing, but eventually Eric served himself several spoonfuls of both broth and oatmeal. When a wave of nausea roiled his stomach, he dropped the spoon on the tray. "I've had enough for now."

A familiar voice called his name from the doorway. "You're looking great, Decker."

"Hey, L-T." Morgan West looked nice in her navy-blue pinstripe suit, but she wasn't the person he'd been hoping to see.

Though the details of what happened after he was shot remained vague, bits and pieces had been coming back. Last night he remembered having told Sloane something about her parents' accident, and that terrified him. The fact his boss was the first to visit and not Sloane had his spidey senses up.

"It's good to see you sitting up." West stepped closer when Nurse Castro waved her in.

Eric checked the doorway behind her. "Is Sloane with you?"

"No, she's not coming." West frowned, telegraphing Sloane's absence was by choice.

"Oh." His heart shrunk. He *had* said too much that night.

"I'll come back," Nurse Castro said. "Keep working on that oatmeal."

West sat in the guest chair near the head of the bed and remained quiet until Nurse Castro left the room. "You gave us quite a scare." She smiled, the kind of smile that said she had worried more than she cared to let on. "You should know that everyone made it out alive except the bad guys. You guys got them all, including Padrino."

"That's wonderful, but how are Reagan and Chandler?"

"Just a few bumps and bruises."

"And Reagan. Did they…" Afraid of the answer, he was unable to say the rest.

West shook her head. "No, they didn't rape her."

"Thank goodness." He expected the news to make him feel better, but his body felt heavier. He didn't expect reliving that night would be so draining. A twinge shot through his back. He searched for the down button on the bed rail and reclined halfway. "How about Finn?"

"She took a round in the vest and is badly bruised, but she's fine."

"That's good. It would devastate Sloane if anything happened to her." The thought of Sloane losing more than she already had made Eric uneasy, prompting him to shift on the thin mattress to find a more comfortable position. "And Quintrell?"

"Took a plea. Kyler had him shipped to Atwater Supermax in case anyone in Padrino's organization is inclined to come after him."

"Good." Except for the bullet that had to be taken out of his upper chest, the results couldn't have been better. Well, almost. The only question left revolved around his partner, but he feared he already knew the answer. "L-T, about Sloane…"

"All she told me was that she couldn't be your partner anymore." West pulled an envelope from her blazer breast pocket and handed it to Eric. "She asked me to give you this. Care to explain what's going on?"

"I'm sorry, L-T, but that's between Sloane and me." Eric closed his eyes, ashamed of the actions of his sixteen-year-old self, the root of their rift. "I hate to cut this short, but I'm pretty tired."

"Sure." She rose from the chair and placed a comforting hand on the part of the blanket covering his leg. "You get some rest, and I'll check on you tomorrow."

Eric opened his eyes and focused on her. "I appreciate the visit. It means a lot."

"Hey, no chasing the nurses." West patted his leg one more time and then left him to his conscience.

Eric tapped the envelope on the table, mulling over its life-altering significance. If their partnership had ended, did this mark the end of their friendship as well? For twenty-one years, Sloane had been the reason behind everything he did, and spending the last few as her partner had given it all meaning. He didn't want that to end.

Placing the envelope on the tabletop, he eyed the sealed flap. How to open it became a challenge. Breaking the seal would be tricky with the use of only one weak arm. He thought about tearing it open with his teeth, but he didn't want to chance ripping the letter. He wedged the envelope under the oatmeal bowl and then hooked his pinky beneath a small section where the glue hadn't fully adhered, but it slipped out.

"Why are you always so anal about your mail?" He imagined Sloane standing there, laughing at his predicament.

Eric tried leaning forward to use his chin to hold it in place, but a sharp pain at his incision stopped him. He had no other choice. He pressed the nurse's call button. Minutes later, Nurse Castro strolled in, sunny as ever. "How's that oatmeal coming?"

"I'm not hungry, but I was hoping you could open this letter for me."

"Sure thing." Nurse Castro slid her slender finger under the flap, and in a few short swipes, had it open. "Want me to pull out the letter?"

"That would be great." Eric unfolded the handwritten, single-page letter, but had difficulty focusing on the words. "Wow, I think I need glasses."

"The medication makes it hard to focus. Would you like me to read it to you?"

Eric tilted his head from side to side, uneasy about his options. He wanted to know what Sloane had to say, but he was never one to air his dirty laundry. "It's kind of personal."

"You're my patient, Sergeant. Consider this room Las Vegas. Anything said here, or read here, stays here."

His first unforced grin felt refreshing. Eric handed her the letter. "Vegas it is."

Nurse Castro slipped on her reading glasses that were dangling from a cord draped around her neck. She gave him a reassuring nod before clearing her throat.

"Eric. You've been much more than a partner, you've been my mentor, friend, and family, which makes this even harder. You taught me partners have to have an unspoken trust in one another, and above all, have each other's back. You've broken that trust. From day one, you hid the truth from me, and that hurts me more than you can imagine. It makes me wonder if you're just that good at deception, or if I'm just that bad at judging character. Either way, I will always doubt you. I wish I didn't have to say this, but I can no longer be your partner or friend. Sloane."

Without another word, Nurse Castro folded the letter and slid it onto the bed table. She gave his arm a warm caress and closed the door on her way out. That was it. He had fucked up, and there was no going back. All those years spent keeping tabs on her. All those months working by her side to make sure she fulfilled her dreams were now wasted. His days of trying to redeem himself were over.

CHAPTER TWENTY-THREE

The gaggle from the courthouse wandered into The Tap. Caleb and Chandler's laughter combined with Janet's cackle to create a ruckus.

"Please, Daddy, not another story." Finn rolled her eyes as he launched into another embarrassing account of her childhood while holding the door open for her and Sloane.

"Don't listen to her," Sloane said over her shoulder. "I like hearing about her shenanigans."

"Me too," Kadin said with a giggle. "Smoking in the girls' bathroom? Who knew you were the little rebel?"

Kadin's familiar shoulder nudge and the one Finn returned raised Sloane's antenna. *Can't see the forest for the trees*, she thought. Finn could crack an international drug ring with the scantest of leads, but she couldn't see that her ex was making a play for her. Sloane would be keeping her eye on Kadin Hall. The one positive facet of that eye-catching exchange was seeing that Finn's shoulder had fully healed since the showdown two months ago.

"Looks like you've been outvoted, pumpkin." Chandler laughed as the door closed behind him, cutting off the bright late afternoon sun. He rubbed his belly with both hands. "Where are those famous burgers?"

Sloane had never accused the burgers at The Tap of being gourmet, but they were pretty damn tasty. Dylan flame-grilled the beef patty and topped it with cheddar cheese, raw white onions, pickles, and a tangy sauce. It was perfection on a toasted buttery bun—Reagan's favorite and a fitting treat for her and Sloane's special day.

Most of the group headed toward the tables Dylan had shoved together for their celebration. Reagan, however, dashed to where the scruffy salt-and-peppered-haired bartender was now gathering up menus. She launched herself almost on top of the bar, her palms on its surface, her black heels six inches off the floor, catching his attention with her eager smile.

"Is he here yet?" Reagan called out, loud enough for Sloane to hear.

He gestured over his shoulder with his chin. "Over there."

Sloane shook her head with a delighted grin. Her gaze followed Reagan as she plopped back down to the floor and slinked between the half-filled tables toward the corner of the room. *My girl's smitten all right.* Reagan tiptoed behind the server, who was clearing dishes from a table, and tapped him on the shoulder. "Hey."

Damp dishtowel in hand, Emeryn turned, the toothiest of grins plastered on his face. He swiped back his shaggy, light brown hair and pushed his glasses up higher on the bridge of his nose. "How did it go?"

"It was perfect," Reagan said. Sloane imagined her smile was as toothy as his. "I'm now officially Reagan Tenney-Sloane."

The pride in Reagan's voice drew an even fuller grin from Sloane. Reagan was her daughter now, legally and in all other ways, and the Santoses would have to wait until Reagan decided she was good and ready to see them again.

"That's great." Emeryn edged forward until they were inches apart, his grin morphing into a poster for teenage lust.

He whispered something Sloane couldn't hear, but when Reagan tilted her head lower, she gathered it made her blush. *Definitely smitten*.

Emeryn peeked over Reagan's shoulder toward Sloane and then gave her a quick kiss on the lips. The chatter in The Tap grew, making it hard for Sloane to decipher the rest of their conversation.

"Emeryn!" a loud voice called from the kitchen.

He flipped the dishtowel over his shoulder and stacked the last dirty glass in the busboy tub and returned to the kitchen and his duties. Reagan joined her family at the table, where everyone had already dipped into the fries Dylan had dropped off.

"Where did you disappear to, young lady?" Janet raised an eyebrow.

"Emeryn is busing tables today," Sloane said without looking up, dipping a french fry into a glob of ketchup and popping it into her mouth.

Reagan sat next to Sloane, her cheeks rosy. "Can I go out with him tonight?"

"It's a school night." Sloane tried to sound firm, but Reagan's frown melted her tough façade like butter on a hot stove. Today of all days, she couldn't disappoint her. "All right, but be home by curfew."

"Thank you, Mom." Reagan bounced in her chair and kissed Sloane on the cheek.

The label "Mom" took on a special meaning for Sloane today—because she had kept her promise to Avery. Reagan was legally hers—the prerequisite for the two of them moving on as a family. No one else had a claim to her, and no one could interfere in how Sloane raised her.

Finn whispered into Sloane's ear, "Softie."

"I can't help it." Sloane turned and pecked Finn on the lips. "I can't believe she's really mine."

"She's been yours for a while now." Finn brushed back a strand of hair covering Sloane's eye before caressing her jawline. "It's about time the law recognized it."

Moments later, Sloane looked across the table. Kadin had paused her conversation with Chandler and fixed her stare on

Finn. Her sad eyes confirmed Sloane's earlier suspicion that she still had a thing for Finn. *Face it, Kadin, Finn will always be the one that got away.*

Sloane lifted a spoon and clanked it against her water glass. Once she had caught everyone's attention, she returned it to the tabletop and scanned the faces staring at her with anticipation. She paused at the changing landscape of her family. Before Avery, she had defined family by blood, first with her parents and then with her grandmother. But today, looking at the faces of the people she loved, she realized family was a choice.

Janet and Caleb, who loved her like a daughter at a time when they had no connection with her other than a dead daughter-in-law, had showed her love had no boundaries. Reagan, the reflection of the woman who taught Sloane how to love, had proved love might come slowly, but it could be unconditional. Chandler, Reagan's protector and shining example to Finn, had showed her that love could be unexpected. Finn, her dear, sweet Finn, had taught her that love, above all, was enduring and that the barriers she placed in front of herself, out of fear or doubt or pain, had power over her only if she let them. And Avery, the beloved face missing from the table, had taught her that love was limitless, able to overcome obstacles greater than time and distance, able to reach beyond the physical.

Sloane cleared her throat, pushing away the thought of Eric's absence. "I'd like to thank everyone for being here today to witness Reagan and me become mother and daughter in the eyes of the law. Each of you in some measure helped to make it happen, so thank you for your love and support."

"Here, here." Chandler raised his glass, and everyone followed suit.

"Since this is a day of celebration, Finn and I have an announcement." Sloane turned toward Finn. "You should tell them."

Kadin squirmed in her chair while the others leaned in with eagerness.

"Sure, babe." Finn gave Sloane a wink. "After much discussion, Sloane and I have each decided to resign our positions."

Chandler and Reagan turned toward each other with matching grins and wide eyes. A second later, they gave each other a high-five.

"We're starting a private investigation firm, The Sloane-Harper Group," Finn said.

"I still think we should go with The Harper-Sloane Group." That was an argument Sloane still hoped to win.

"Hot damn." Chandler hooted and raised his fists over his head like he'd scored a touchdown. "Finally."

"I'm so glad, you guys." Reagan's eyes sparkled with what Sloane could only define as profound relief.

The table quieted suddenly, all eyes directed at something behind Sloane and Finn. Sloane turned her head, feeling her heartfelt smile fade. "Eric."

His usually erect posture and burly physique had disappeared since Sloane last saw him in the intensive care unit. They'd been replaced by a hunched, slimmer frame, the consequence of two months in the hospital and rehab. Dark circles and lines covered his once vibrant, chiseled face. Sloane's throat thickened. This wasn't the man who had taken her under his wing and taught her everything he knew, nor the man who she had trusted with her life. That man no longer existed.

Eric favored his cane until he stopped close to Reagan and placed a half-filled cloth shopping bag on the floor. "I heard today was the big day. I wanted to congratulate you two."

"You look so much better." Reagan popped up from her chair and gave him a tender hug. "Here, take my seat."

Better? What did he look like before? Sloane's heart broke at the thought of Reagan seeing him looking even worse while she had done nothing to help him through the toughest time of his life.

Eric briefly locked gazes with Sloane, the pain in his eyes signaling he knew he wasn't welcomed. "I can't stay, sweetheart." He pulled a small red gift box with a white bow from the shopping bag. "But I brought you a little something."

"Thank you, Eric." Reagan opened the lid and held up a sterling silver necklace with a ruby pendant. "It's beautiful."

"It's your birthstone." Eric straightened the best he could. "I thought today was like being born into a new family."

"It's perfect. I love it." Reagan hugged him again.

Family. Despite everything, Sloane and Eric were on the same wavelength—a fact that tugged at Sloane but fell short of weakening her resolve. The trust they once shared had disappeared. She still couldn't bring herself to be his partner or friend.

"This is for you." Eric handed the shopping bag and its remaining contents to Sloane. "Open it later."

"Thank you, Eric," Sloane said as a lump formed in her throat. He turned and limped out on his cane without saying another word. Sloane lowered her gaze, her lower lip quivering. An ache radiated in her gut. She'd lost her best friend and a part of her family forever.

* * *

The cool, moist breeze, twinkling lights dotting the distant hills, and navigation lights cutting across the dark bay waters presented a familiar view from Sloane's back deck. They gave her the extra sense of comfort she needed after coming face-to-face with Eric. Keeping her gaze straight ahead and leaning her forearms on the railing, she gripped her water glass extra tightly when the sliding door opened behind her. The skin beneath her jacket tingled, anticipating Finn's light kiss or warm embrace. Not disappointed, she leaned first into her lips and then her arms.

"Ready to open Eric's gift?" Finn asked, resting her chin on Sloane's shoulder.

"He looked horrible, Finn."

"I won't lie. His injuries were severe, but he should have recovered a lot faster than he has."

"I can't imagine what he's been through."

"Can't you?" Finn tightened her embrace. "He was almost killed and he lost a woman he loved on the same night. Guilt is eating him alive. It's exactly what you went through."

"I did this to him." Sloane's lips trembled at the depth of his pain. Though the rift between them seemed too wide to repair, they remained so much alike.

"He did this to himself, and he knows it. He'll work his way back. Just like you did."

Would he? Sloane suppressed the overpowering guilt she felt. She had worked her way back because she had Finn. And Eric had no one. Part of her still wanted to be the shoulder he needed to lean on. She blew out a long breath to remind herself that he was no longer her concern. "Let's do this."

Moving inside to the couch, Sloane folded a single leg under her bottom. Finn did the same after handing her Eric's shopping bag. Sloane pulled a book out of it, a type of album or scrapbook, and opened it to the first page. Taped to it was a yellowing clipping with a black-and-white picture of a traffic accident after police and fire trucks had arrived.

Sloane slapped a hand over her mouth. She had never seen the newspaper account of her parents' accident, and reading it gave her a chill. She ran her fingertips across the text as if reading from a sacred scroll. Many of the details seemed correct—the date and time, the location, and road conditions—but the article got the most important part wrong.

"This isn't right. They didn't die on impact." Sloane wished her parents had. Maybe she wouldn't have feared death all those years.

"Have you seen this before?" Finn asked.

"No." Sloane shook her head, surprised that recalling the accident now didn't come with the normal numbness of guilt. This time she felt angry. "It says I was the only survivor and that police had no reason to suspect any other vehicles were involved. Why didn't Eric report it?"

"If the police didn't suspect another car, there must not have been debris in the road or skid marks from the opposite direction," Finn said. "He might not have even realized you went off the road until much later."

"It doesn't change a thing. This proves that he knew what he'd done and that he didn't tell anyone. Didn't tell *me*."

Sloane turned to the next page, which contained a folded internal SFPD flyer soliciting rookie cops as volunteers to operate the department's booth at the local college job fair. Sloane squinted and checked the year.

"I was there. This is where I met Eric for the first time. He gave me such an impassioned pitch. Made me think working for SFPD was the best job in the world."

"So he convinced you to become a police officer?"

"Oh, no. I knew I wanted to be a cop at thirteen after Bernie died." Sloane smiled when Finn laid a comforting hand on her shoulder. "Eric just convinced me where."

"Bernie was the officer who saved you after the accident, right?" Finn asked.

"Yes, he was. Bernie was a hero. He saved me. And he died trying to save someone else while he was helping me find you." The memory of his death still stung because if not for her, he'd still be alive.

Finn kissed the top of Sloane's shoulder. The gentle touch told Sloane she understood the lingering pain. Only Sloane's nana knew what that kind man genuinely had meant to her and how his death so close to that of her parents had convinced her she was a death magnet. Thankfully, that was a fear Sloane had put behind her—because of the woman sitting beside her.

Sloane flipped through the next half-dozen pages, all containing a newspaper clipping or SFPD newsletter article featuring something Sloane had done as a uniformed officer. A heaviness settled in her chest. "He followed my entire career."

"It sounds like he kept an eye on you until you two partnered up."

"He asked for me, you know."

Sloane's mind drifted back to her first day as a detective, when she and Eric caught a new case. It all made sense now. That's when, even before he saw her in action, he'd told her, "*You know the difference between the law and justice and that the two don't always mean the same thing.*" That kind of knowledge couldn't have come from a personnel file. He must have talked to her previous partners.

"Are you going to talk to him about this?" Finn asked.

"Maybe someday. When I'm not so angry. He's the reason my parents were killed, and he kept that from me for years." Sloane placed the scrapbook on the coffee table and fell back into Finn's arms. "Thank you for taking Reagan to see him. I hate the idea of her being collateral damage."

"No need to thank me. I love her like she's my own." Finn twitched and tensed up. As if she thought she'd said something wrong or too soon.

Sloane lifted her head to face Finn, smiling so hard it hurt. "Really?"

"Yes, really."

Sloane pressed their lips together in a kiss that promised a lifetime together. When she pulled back and peered into Finn's hazel eyes, the eyes she'd chased all her life, she read the message that had been there since they were thirteen. It was the same message she'd seen the night of the perilous wildfire when they crawled from the flames and ashes, one that marked the depth of their connection. The message was that Finn was hers.

"Move in with us."

Bella Books, Inc.

Women.. Books. Even Better Together.

P.O. Box 10543
Tallahassee, FL 32302

Phone: 800-729-4992
www.bellabooks.com